Author: Teddy Baire
https://www.teddybaire.com/
Cover Designer: Ri Juna
@milkiynoway
ISBN: 978-1-955410-11-3

I0717206

READER BEWARE

This novel MAY CONTAIN depictions of sex, racism,
fun with toy hammers, hugs, kisses, multiple phobias, and
other questionable acts.

CHAPTER 1

Sami had taken a seat at her desk. She was in an office area where an assortment of her co-workers were either working or chatting amongst themselves about whatever the current events of the day might be. The sound of staplers, paper copiers, and clicking keyboards provided the daily rhythm of her life.

The daily discomfort came from the cold air on the back of her neck from the vent directly above her. But she'd tolerated it because her desk was nearest the elevator, which allowed her to leave faster than everyone else. The television on the wall was turned to some random station speaking on an issue that no one in the office would care about the moment the day ended, and outside that floor's window was what most would have said was the beautiful skyline above and a marvelous metropolis below.

But Sami paid no mind to her surroundings, as her

attention was fixed on her phone. Because there, written across the screen, her mind was fixated on four little words.

I'm sorry. It's over.

She spoke the words aloud as she stared at the screen, but they were spoken so low that they might as well have been silent. Her words left her mouth, flowing over dry lips as she sat there with a growing tightness in her chest. Trying to prevent the moisture of emotion from overcoming her eyes, a blink, then another blink to bring the world back into focus. She glanced over to the right, past her phone to a website where across the screen read, 'Losing the Spark? Here's How to Find Love and Enjoyment in Your Relationship Again.'

More muffled words drifted over her ears from nearby co-workers, but she wasn't really interested. That was, until a pair of hands floated in front of her face. They pulled themselves apart only to then bring themselves back together with a loud "CLAP!" sound that woke Sami from her daze.

"Sami! Earth to Sami. Are you in there?" asked the woman, who was now standing in front of her.

"Huh! What?" asked Sami, dropping her phone after being brought back to reality. The sound of a squeaky chair reminding her where she was as she shifted about nervously.

"Wow, you're jittery," said a blonde-haired woman, who placed her shoulder over the top column of Sami's desk. "What's got you all stiff, looking like you've seen a ghost?"

"It's nothing, Becca," said Sami, reaching down and turning off her phone. "Just a bad morning. You know; where nothing seems to go right."

"Dammit!" screamed a girl from across the room.

Sami peaked over her desk to see it was a tall blonde woman who was kneeling, attempting to gather a stack of fallen paper that was spread out on the floor.

"Well, you could always have the week that 'Mrs. Bad

Luck' over there's been having, losing your boyfriend and a potential job in the same week?"

"Wait, what do you mean? Jewel lost her job?" asked Sami.

"Okay, well, she didn't lose her job technically. She thought she was going to get another job, but it went to another girl on the twenty-second floor who may or may not, might have been caught with a certain head of management's dick in her mouth. Just a rumor, of course." Becca waved her hand over at the tall woman. "Jewel, come here a sec."

"Hey, what are you doing? Don't just---" Sami feeling a bit of embarrassment for the woman, shuffled around in her squeaky chair, trying to grab onto her arm.

But Becca just playfully flailed her arm away. "Hey Jewel, what you got planned for tonight?"

"What?" asked Jewel, looking at the two women suspiciously. "Why?"

"Oh, nothing, me and Sami here were going to go out tonight and celebrate her break-up?"

"What?" asked Sami, looking confused.

"You think I don't know that look on your face from a moment ago?" said Becca. "You had that same look when Peter dumped you and when you caught Greg sleeping with another woman at your apartment." She then turned back to Jewel. "So, you in?"

"What... I mean, I'm not sure, I'd have to..."

"Really, Jewel?" asked Becca, shaking her head. "Everyone here knows you broke up with your man. You've been moping around the office for days. So put aside that pride of yours and bring that hot body out for a night on the town with us. It'd be good for you to get some fresh air. You might even get lucky. Then maybe everyone wouldn't keep calling you 'Bad Luck Jewel.'"

Jewel looked around, seeing if anyone heard her. "Stop that. Not everyone knows everything like you do, Becca.

Some people mind their own business. And besides, you're the one who started that nickname."

"Well, given your history, I'd say it's well deserved. Wouldn't you?" asked Becca with nod to the muddled-up papers in Jewels hands. "But enough of that, you in or what?"

Jewel's eyes swapped back from Becca to Sami before looking down at the floor, before muttering in a low voice. "Fine, what time."

"Good," said Becca, with a smile on her face as she patted the top of Sami's desk. "We'll meet out around nine for drinks at Greenock's, downtown. It'll be fun."

"Wait, I haven't even agreed to going yet," said Sami in protest.

"Yes, you have. You just don't want to admit it. How you gonna give people romance advice when you're not out there trying to experience romance?" Becca clapped her hands together. "So that's what we're going to do. Don't be late, okay?" And with those words, she left Sami and Jewel both with confused expressions on their faces as she headed out of the office and around the glass wall toward the elevators.

"Okay, so that happened," said Jewel, turning back towards Sami. "Does everyone here really know about my breakup?"

"Yeah, kinda. But it's fine. It's not like we all haven't been there before."

"Well, what about you? I thought things were going well with your guy. What happened?"

Feeling a bit embarrassed, Sami just shook her head, "Well, you know, thing just—"

"Hey Sami," a man shouted from across the room. "Addison wants to see you."

Grasping the opportunity to avoid the current topic of discussion. "Sorry, time to go," said Sami, standing up from her desk, the sound of one final squeak sending her off, a sense of relief filling her chest. "Looks like I'm needed. We can talk about this later." *Hopefully, never.* "On my way," she

4

happily yelled before quickly stepping out from behind her desk and making her way into the aisle towards her boss's office.

Really, their entire working environment was just a completely open area with computer desks on either side of the walls and an island in the center where the modern machinery sat. Printers, cappuccino machines, pens, and sticky notes were spread out for them to use. Addison's office sat at the end, next to a window overlooking the city. But since her walls were completely glass, it didn't really stop anyone from looking inside. Sami could see that she was talking on the phone with someone.

It wasn't long before Sami was knocking on the sliding glass door as the woman sitting at a desk waved her in.

"Close the door behind you," said Addison.

"Yes, Ma`am," said Sami, closing the door as she stepped inside and stood in front of her desk, sitting down when her boss gestured for her to do so.

"Yes, dear," said Addison on the phone, "And be sure to bring my baby with you when you come. She seems to enjoy talking to the security guard for some reason." She shook her head. "Of course, I'm not using the security guard as a babysitter. He's doing that of his own volition." She laughed. "But for the first night, we can leave her with the babysitter." With a bite of her tongue, a smile came across her lips. "Then we can get some time alone, and I can wear that outfit you like. The one with—" The mischievous look on her face faded as her eyes lowered over the phone. "Ohhhhhh,.. your parents are coming with you this time. How Great! Please, you know how I feel about your parents, but don't worry, I've played nice before, haven't I?"

I guess that's her husband. Sami couldn't help but notice the change in tone as she brought up her mother-in-law.

"Well, your mother shouldn't have insulted my cooking. At that point, I feel she deserved to have it thrown in her face." Addison rolled her eyes while shaking her head. "Yes,

yes, I love you too. Kiss the baby for me." She hung the phone up and smiled over at Sami. "Sorry about all that."

"No, it's no problem. I didn't know you had a child."

"Really? I guess I never mentioned her before. Well, I do, and hopefully she'll be the only one I have. I love my daughter, but I've never felt the motherly type."

"Really. Why not?"

"When you have a kid, you constantly wonder if you're just repeating the same mistakes your parents made with you," said Addison, shaking her head. "Sure, you might say that you don't want to repeat their mistakes, but a lot of those mistakes are the reason most of us are who we are."

"Well, I can promise you that my parents weren't perfect. But they tried. Where I grew up, a lot of parents barely even did that."

"I grew up in a similar situation," said Addison. "So, I sometimes let myself make those little mistakes that I think are still the best thing for her."

"Where's she now?"

"Usually my husband keeps her, but he has her visiting her grandparents for the month since school is out."

"I take it you don't find it easy getting along with your mother-in-law?"

"Huh? That? The woman is an excellent grandmother, she loves her grandbaby to death. She just doesn't approve of the mother that birthed her. So, I make sure to be on my worst behavior when she comes into town." Addison then stood and walked around her desk, sitting on edge and staring down at Sami. "But enough of that. Do you like your job here, Sami?"

"What? Of course, I do. Wait! Am... am I being fired?"

"No, of course not. Quite the opposite, actually. I'm going to be stepping away from the company for a while and am looking for someone to take my place. I'm thinking of putting the company through a bit of a rebranding, so I'm looking for a few young girls to audition for the job of...

well, of my job."

"You're quitting?"

"I wouldn't call it quitting, per se. I have several other companies to take care of and to be quite honest, doing it while also running this one has become a pain in my ass. So, I'm looking to pass on this burden to someone else so I can focus on my other endeavors."

"Well, I'm flattered. But if I may ask... why me?"

"Because you are the head of our little website's romance section and most of our little subscribers only pay their monthly fees so that they can read about your weekly outgoings. And seeing as I have decided to rebrand this particular company under a romance and fashion design. I figure why not."

"Oh."

"Plus, it may be a bit of a cool look for my brand, having a non-white head up one of my companies."

"Wait. What? So, you're only offering me the job because I'm black?"

"No, I'm considering you for the job because you're a hard worker and have a current alignment for what I wish the company to be. And you just happening to be black is more of an 'icing on the cake' type of thing."

"I... I don't know what to say to that." *Should I feel offended? Isn't this what people sue over? Wait, can I sue someone for offering me a promotion?*

"But don't worry, that darkness covering your body will only get you so far. "

Darkness covering my... who talks like this?

She raised a finger, swirling it around in the air in front of her. "Now don't devalue yourself thinking you're just getting this opportunity because of a bit of pigment." She nodded her head and raised a brow toward an Asian woman at one of the desks outside her office. "If that was the case, I'd hire poor Lan Ling for the job, but that girl looks like she can barely tie her own shoe, let alone tie a man around her finger." She smiled and waved at the girl, who looked confused for a moment before slowly raising her hand, and forced a smile back at her. "Poor thing, I'm not even sure she knows what seduction is; probably thinks it's something to pick up with those little chopsticks she's always using."

Okay, that was definitely racist, right? Or at least prejudice. "Wait! But isn't Lan Ling married?"

"Arranged marriage, my dear. Marriage and knowledge of romance are hardly the same thing. How many passionless couples have you seen in your lifetime?"

I don't want to admit she's right, thought Sami, trying to keep a straight face as she listened to her boss.

"Besides, the only reason she works here is because I know her husband's brother. We went to school with him, actually. I did him a favor and hired her here. Anyway, enough about that," she said, turning back to Sami. "If you want the job, I'm going to need you to give the world spicier advice. We aren't trying to do the same cookie cutter stuff. No, you must shock and awe them with the stories of a woman who knows the secrets that men always keep to themselves."

Sami nodded her head. "I think I can do that." *I have no idea what she's talking about. What secrets? It's not like men live in a cave. Most pay for a date and try to fuck you the same night. Actually no, most don't even pay for the date anymore. What am I supposed to write about? Ghosting? I don't think sitting in a bar alone waiting for a guy who fell asleep playing video games will be what people want to read about.*

"Good," said Addison, lifting herself from her desk then performing a clap of her hand. "You have two days to submit another article on how you as a woman are tackling love int this city. Then I will make my decision."

"Two days?" asked Sami, the disbelief clan in her voice.

"Of course. Seduction happens to be an art, and time is its enemy. There's you and nine other women trying for this job, so I'm expecting you to kick ass." She gestured her hand
8

toward the door. "So go on, get out of here and get it done."

"Ah, okay," said Sami, standing up a little confused before heading for the door. Closing it behind her, she headed back through the office. She caught a few stares as she moved forward, but she knew it was nothing more than the eyes of those looking for more office gossip. As she turned the corner of her desk, her foot caught on something that went "Argh!" almost causing her to fall over.

"That hurt," said the voice of a man beneath her.

"Dammit," said Sami, rubbing her hand on her knee, which also grazed the side of the wall. "What in the—" she looked down, spotting dark skin, dark hair, and the wide shoulders of a man in a blue jumpsuit looking up at her. "Patrick, what are you doing down there?"

"I was fixing your chair," said Patrick, rolling over and rubbing on his ankle. "Argh. you stepped on me with those sharp ass shoes on yours."

"You should have put a sign up or something."

"Sorry, but we don't have any working with chair signs. Can you at least start wearing something softer around the office if you're going to start stepping on people? Also, I can see up your skirt. You have nice legs."

"Do you want me to kick you again?"

"No. I prefer not to be assaulted at work."

"And I'd prefer for you not to look up my skirt."

"It's not like I can help it. I mean, I'm down here and you're up there. White panties are cute though."

"For the love of..." said Sami as she reached over him, grabbing her phone and purse. "Did you at least fix it? All that squeaking is a pain in the butt to listen to all day."

"Not yet, but I'll get it done," said Patrick, rolling onto his side and wiggling the seat to show it still squeaked. "And I'm going to complain the whole time I'm doing it."

"Fine, go ahead. I won't be here. I have to head home for the day."

"What's wrong?" said Jewel, coming back over to her

desk with Lan Ling.

"Did you get fired?" asked Lan Ling with a smile on her face. "If so, can I have your desk?"

"What, no?"

"Lan Ling, how can you ask that?" responded Jewel, placing a hand over her face in embarrassment.

"I'm sorry. It's just that I'm over there by myself and when the sun comes down, it's always in my face and it's annoying."

"Wait, if you're fired. Then why am I fixing your chair?" asked Patrick before attempting to get up. "Screw this. I'm going to lunch."

"Oh, no, you're not," said Sami, pushing him back down to the floor before he could stand. "I've been trying to get you up here for two weeks to fix this chair, and you're not leaving until you do."

"It's a lot of floors in this building. Squeaky chairs aren't on the top of the list of problems that I need to fix. I have other jobs that need to be done."

"I don't think I've ever actually seen you fix anything," said Jewel, pointing over the island table in the center of the room. "One of our printers is still broken, and it's been that way for a month already."

"I don't remember seeing a work order for a printer. It must've gotten lost in the mail," said Patrick, shaking his head as if certain.

"How do you lose an email?" asked Sami.

"File got corrupted, probably."

Sami shook her head. "I don't have time for this. You both make sure he fixes my chair. I need to go home and do my hair before tonight."

"Alright," said Jewel.

"Bye-bye," said Lan Ling.

"Great, see you tonight, Jewel," said Sami as she grabbed her keys and headed out of the office and over to the elevator. *What the hell am I gonna do?* She pressed the button to go down. *But really? She wants me to run the company? Okay, whatever new company that she's making up. But romance and fashion. Can I really do this? Fuck that, it's money, and I'll fake it till I make it. I mean, I'm cute.* She looked at herself, reflected on the elevator door. *But more than that, I can be sexy, right?* The door opened and Sami saw a man in a suit as it opened.

"Well, if it isn't little Sami," said the man with a smile. "Going down?"

"Yes, in fact, I am," she said before stepping into the elevator, seeing that the first floor had already been pressed.

"How goes things, little Sami?"

"Jamal, you know, you don't have to call me that anymore. You're not my babysitter anymore," she said as the elevator closed and they descended.

"True, but you're still shorter than me."

"Everyone's shorter than you. You're over six feet."

"Six foot three, actually. And you'll just have to live with it. Remember how hard you had to work for me to stop pinching your face?"

"Yeah, kicking you in the knees every time you did it," said Sami before turning to him and folding her arms. "Hey, did you really get caught getting a blowjob in your office?"

"What? No, of course not," he said, looking away from her. Sami's angry moan growing louder in the small space. "Look, I said I didn't, okay? I was in the file room reaching for something on the top shelf and she was next to me, reaching for something on the bottom shelf. Someone walked in and it looked like something that wasn't true."

"Really? That's the story you're going with."

"It's true. I would never do anything at work. And besides, if anything did happen. She was the one trying to corner me."

"She... cornered you?"

"It's true. Stop looking at me like that. It's making me uncomfortable. I feel like your beady eyes can stare into my soul."

"I do not have beady eyes."

"Oh, they're certainly beady."

"Whatever. Just watch yourself. I swear it's like you're dancing on the edge of a sexual harassment charge. And I don't feel like going down to the police station to get you again."

"Okay, first, it was one time, and it was after we won the championship, plus we were in college, and I was really drunk. And second, I'm done with all that. I met this girl a few nights ago and I think it's really going to work this time."

"Define work?"

"Now you're just being mean," said Jamal, as the door opened, and they stepped out into the lobby area of the building and headed for the exit. "I'm serious this time."

"You were serious the last time, and the time before that, and the time before then. If I remember correctly, you were trying to impress a girl down at the aquarium and almost died. Now you know damn well a black man has no business swimming with dolphins."

"How was I supposed to know how vicious they could be? Those little snoots can knock a man unconscious."

Sami couldn't help herself as she hunched over with laughter, barely able to manage extending an arm to wave down a cab. "God, you're an idiot," she said as a cab pulled up and Jamal opened the door for her. "Whatever. I wish you the best. See you next time and don't show up at my apartment drunk and depressed this time."

"Always gotta rub that in my face."

"I wouldn't have to if you'd stop doing it."

"Bye, little Sami," he said as he closed the door to the taxi, and it took off.

Back in the office, Jewel had watched as Sami got on the

elevator before turning back around to Lan Ling. "Hey, do you two think dating is easy now?"

"Probably not," said Lan Ling, that's why Sami's articles and blogs are so popular.

"Why," said Patrick. "You still reeling after breaking up with your boyfriend and losing out on that job?"

"What?" said Jewel, looking around to see if anyone else had heard. "How do you know that?"

"The delivery guy told me in the elevator on my way up here. But cheer up, girl, you're pretty, you'll find somebody."

"The delivery man? Really?"

"Yeah. Daniel brings the third-floor hot wings at least three times a week. That brother knows everything about the companies he delivers to. He even knows a lot about Lan Ling and how she collects exotic pets and how you got that snake tattoo."

"What?" said Lan Ling, her eyes wide and her lips smushed together.

"You collect exotic pets?" asked Jewel. "Wait! You have a snake tattoo?"

"What? No! Okay, maybe, but so what? I got it for my husband."

"Your husband... wanted you to get a snake tattoo? Where is it? Wait, is that why you wouldn't go to the beach with us that time?"

"It's on my leg. It was supposed to be a surprise since he likes snakes." She waved her hand dismissively. "But forget about me. Let's talk about something else."

"Well," said Patrick, standing up with a grunt. "You girls can enjoy yourselves. I, on the other hand, have to get back to work. Tell Sami she owes me one. She should take me out on a date or bring me one of those cupcakes that they bring in from the fifth floor every morning." He waved bye to them. "And good luck getting yourself that new man, Jewel. He's out there... somewhere."

"Okay, now I know he's just being an ass on purpose,"

said Jewel as she watched Patrick walk away.

"Maybe, but..." Lan Ling paused as her phone rang and she glanced at the screen. "Sorry, it's my husband. Good luck on getting a man." And she ran off to take the phone call.

"I'm not..." she sighed. "I'm not looking for a man." Annoyed, Jewel walked back across the room and over to her desk, then began looking over the papers that he had printed out. Amongst them were pictures of plants as she took a marker and checked off on the ones she liked. It's not like I need a man. *Yeah, I didn't need him, anyway. I don't even need that other job.*

She then logged into her computer, clicked over to her workspace inside the company and at the top of her area were the words, 'Five Tips for keeping your plants healthy.' She sat there for the next hour but wasn't able to type anything new. Instead, her mind wandered as she stared at the blank screen. *Don't think about it. Come on, focus. Don't think... don't think, ahhh! Fuck it.*

On her screen, she brought up the messenger and scrolled down to find the name 'Gavin Holmes.'

Hey Gavin. Can I come see you? she typed into the messenger.

Sure, what up? You know where I am.

Thanks, on my way.

She looked around the office one last time before heading towards the elevator and stepping inside, pressing the button for the second floor. After stopping, she exited and stepped into a room where the sound of humming filled the air. Ahead of her sat rows and rows of computer equipment.

She strolled through the aisles of humming machinery until she saw a glass office with a man sitting behind a computer. A knock on the glass caused the man to look up at her and wave her in.

"Hey, I'm surprised you came for a visit," said the man

as he leaned back in his chair.

"Hey, Gavin," said Jewel, stepping inside the room as she quickly closed the door behind her, silencing the sound of the humming from outside. "I really don't see how you work down here. It was almost as if she could feel the vibrations through the glass."

"You get used to it after a while."

"I hope you don't mind me coming down here."

"Of course, not," said Gavin while performing a stretch in his chair, before rubbing his shoulders. "What can I do for you?"

"I was just curious if you knew—"

"About your breakup and you losing that job you wanted. Yeah, but it's cool. You'll get it next time."

"No, not— wait. Who told you?"

"The cleaning guy. We chat sometimes after he's done mopping the floor in here. Apparently, the delivery guy told him."

"Really, the cleaning... No! No..." she took a breath. "No, you know what. Never mind. Can you help me and tell me who got the most attention last month on sales and subscribers?"

"So, you wanna see how you stack up against the rest of the people up there on the sexy floor?"

"Yes, and don't call it that."

"Yeah, no problem, gimme a sec," said Gavin as he began clicking around on his computer. Several web pages changed until finally stopping on a list of names. "Okay, there we go. You have one-hundred and twenty subscribers to your personal company page. And according to the out reading you are the tenth most read writer in the magazine."

"Tenth? But there are only eleven of us," said Jewel as she began to rub her arms trying to keep warm. The room was a little to cold for her liking.

"Sorry," I don't have a jacket to offer you."

"It's fine. But tell me; who's below me?"

"Ahh, Amy is."

"Amy? But she's been out the last four months since she had a baby."

"She still has more subscribers than you, though?"

"Great, so you mean a woman who hasn't worked in over a quarter of a year is bringing in more revenue than I am?"

"Pretty much, yeah? But technically, you're more popular than she is."

Jewel sighed before lifted her head and sighing. "That's because she's been gone for four months, Gavin."

"Hey, I was just trying to cheer you up."

"Fuck, then it's no wonder I didn't get that job. Wait, then who's first in the company?"

He scrolled up on the mouse. "Let's see, it looks like Sami is."

Jewel sighed again, "Of course she is."

"Don't feel down, people eat that romance stuff up. I bet if you started posting about your breakup, I bet you'd get a ton of views."

"Great, except that I'm not a romance columnist. I write about plant life and what set of flower arrangements are safe to put outside during the cold seasons."

"Just saying, it might be time to go in a different direction."

"Thanks for the advice," said Jewel while patting Gavin on the shoulder. "But I don't think I cut out for that."

"No problem. Anything else you need?"

"No, that's it. I just learned that I'm absolutely worthless to the company I work for. So, I think that's enough information for the day. I should just go home and sleep on that."

"Come on, don't be like that. Tell you what, why don't you come over tonight and hang with me, Jasmine, and the kids?"

"Yes, a Friday night with my sister and my brother-in-law. No thanks."

"Suit yourself, but if I remember correctly, you're the

one who had the most fun last time."

"Yeah, well, not tonight. I have plans to meet with Becca and Sami, so I really should be going."

"Well, have fun at your girls' night. But stop by the house sometime soon. The kids love you and they want to see their auntie," said Gavin as he pressed the button to open the door.

"I'll do that," said Jewel with a smile as she left the office.

CHAPTER 2

The air of the city was cool as its nightgo'ers waited at top of streetlights for their chance to cross. Flashing signs and pavement went on for over a dozen city blocks; it's people in a merging of fine dining clothing and the casualness of their dress attire. A night out with friends, densely filled groups populated the downtown nightlife. Amongst the many cabs that filled the stop and go traffic was one in which Jewel sat. The fake leather seats and a talk show host over the radio were things she was familiar with.

The yellow cab came to a halt at the entrance of one of the now closed evening shops, where she saw Becca and Sami waiting on her as people passed by behind them. The door opened and outside stepped Jewel into a city of concrete and colorful lighting that seemed to spread its way for miles down a street of parallel lines and blacktop roads as vehicles of all shapes moved back and forth; their red taillight seeming blurry in the night. Her feet hit the pavement as she handed the cabby a twenty-dollar bill, not worrying about the change as she stepped onto the curb to join her friends that waited on her.

"Girl, what took you so long?" said Becca, before looking down.

"And what's with those shoes? Where are your heels?"

"I'm taller than both of you and most men." said Jewel, a feeling a bit disheartened, but still with a smile. "I don't get to wear heels."

"You *get* to do whatever you want. That's why we're here."

With a bit of laughter in their voices, they walked together down the street, their outfits just as colorful as the signs above the multiple clubs and nighttime restaurants that they passed. Sami wore a two-piece black blouse and skirt with strappy red heels to match her purse. Becca wore a short coat where beneath it sat a halter top and a long skirt with a slit up the side to show just enough leg that it would ride up her thighs when she sat down. And then there was Jewel, who wore a sleeveless gray and black pants suit, with low wedge sandals, blonde to match her hair and purse.

"I like your outfit, Jewel," said Becca, continuing to look her friend over. "But why the pants? Girl, you got those long legs, so you might as well show them off."

"Are you going to criticize my outfit all night?"

"If I didn't," said Becca, with a smirk across her lips. "Then where would all my fun come from?"

"I thought the reason we were out was to have fun," said Sami, shaking her head.

"We are. But who says that's the only fun I'm allowed to have?"

Jewel proudly placed a hand on her chest, patting herself softly. "My arms are out, and I've been told that I have very sexy arms."

"I really don't think it's your arms that men are going to be looking at."

"Don't worry about me. You girls worry about yourselves."

"So what club are we going to?"

"Club?" asked Becca? "No, it's only eight. We have plenty of time for that. I've got something better for us to do before we go to the club. Think of it as a bit of a time waster." She then reached into her pocket and pulled out three golden tickets.

"What are those? Tickets? Is there a concert nearby?" asked Sami, looking around.

"No. These are tickets to the restaurant St. Helon's, just over there," said Becca, pointing down and across the street?"

"Why do we need tickets to a restaurant?" asked Jewel, catching the glimmer of light reflecting off the golden tickets. "Don't we just need reservations?"

"We need tickets, because we are doing group dating tonight with men who are looking for a fun and intelligent woman such as ourselves."

"What?" asked Sami, her voice a little louder with surprise. "You have us doing speed dating?"

"Don't worry, it's just a way to waste time. I told you; the club comes later."

"Oh no, I'm out," said Jewel, attempting to turn around. "I don't even want to think about—"

"Oh, no you don't," said Becca, grabbing her by the arm. "We are going to have a girls' night out and do plenty of fun things together. So come on, this will be a story to tell, rather than just going home and watering your plants."

Jewel slowly turned back around, looking across the street at the restaurant where she could now make out the figures of men shuffling about through the windows. She frowned as her eyes lowered. "I'd rather water my plants."

"Just quit that. You both owe me for having to put up with you and your breakups. Now it's my time to have some fun and I'm going to do it with my friends, who are both acting like children."

"Fine," said Sami, looking ahead to the restaurant. "Let's just get this over with, so we can then go out and enjoy ourselves."

Jewel sighed and allowed herself to be pulled back as they all made their way across the street and headed towards St. Helon's. They reached the entrance, where a man stood in a tuxedo next to a carousel door.

"Hello, are you three ladies here for tonight's event?"

"Yes, we are," said Becca, showing the man her three tickets.

"I see, well show me your wrists please."

They did as asked and the man slid on each of their wrists a single golden bracelet with a diamond in the center. On one side of the bracelet, Jewel couldn't see it was engraved with the number five.

"Wow. Do we get to keep these?" asked Sami.

"Yes," said the man. "Each one is valued at around three hundred dollars, but it makes sense with the cost of each of these tickets being a thousand. Please enjoy your night." He stepped to the side and allowed the ladies access.

"You paid three thousand dollars for these tickets? How much money are you making?" asked Sami.

"Of course not. I just happened to get these tickets from a friend who found herself making other plans. And it'd be a shame to miss out on a group of successful men wandering the city looking for love. And I just figured that at least one or two of them might get lonely in their penthouses."

"You're trying to set us up with rich men?" asked Jewel with a smirk on her face as they entered the main hall of the building.

"You? Who cares about you? I need you girls to be here and support me and my search for a rich man. After that, I don't care what you do. Oh, look at that one." She said as she pointed over to a man with dark hair and a bit of gray in his goatee as he sat at the bar. "I wonder what he's looking for tonight."

Inside, the building was a grand setting with golden lights that hung from its ceiling in little cubes that shone off a glossy wooden floor. Off white chairs, set under mahogany tables where number cards were placed above. The room was littered with attractive men in expensive looking suits and well-trimmed facial hair that completed the smiles the girls received as they made their way through the lounge area.

"Don't these men seem a little older?"

"Money doesn't have an age," said Becca with a smile and a wave over to the guy at the bar. "And besides, we're all in our late twenties. What's wrong with dating a man ten, fifteen years older? Especially the ones who are looking for someone to take care of."

"Wait?" said Jewel, looking down at her friend with a finger between her lips. "Did you really take us to a sugar-baby meet and greet?"

"You make it sound so dirty."

"Really, Becca?" said Sami, placing a hand over her face as she began to rub at her eyes.

"Don't worry. You're here now. We might as well enjoy it," said Becca, as she took both girls by the hand and led them deeper into the building. "Come on, let's take a seat until they're ready for us."

"I'm the one who's not ready for this," said Jewel, as she rested next to them on a plush brown lounge seat. "How could you think bringing us here would be okay? Sami, talk to her."

"What? Sorry, I wasn't paying attention," said Sami, who was now waving over at one of the nearby men.

"Sami, now I know you can't really be thinking about doing this?"

"Jewel," said Sami, shaking her head. "It's Becca's crazy idea, and we're already here now. It's not like we're going to just run out of the restaurant. So, we might as well make the best of it. It's just meeting a few guys and talking, and I think it'll be good for us to have some fun for once."

"I can't believe you're okay with this."

"Okay," came a woman's voice, sounding over the calm atmosphere of the room. "Please come and gather around. We will begin shortly."

"Well," said Becca, as she patted herself and Sami on the leg. "Us girls are going out there to enjoy ourselves and live our lives. But if you wish to go back home and water your plants, then we won't stop you. Come on Sami."

As her friends stood, Jewel sat there for a moment. *It's not like that's all that I do.* With a bit of regret beginning to grow inside of her, she watched as her friends stepped together towards the gathering. *Fine. I just know this isn't going to work.* She stood up and walked her way over, standing beside them.

"I knew you'd come," whispered Becca, a subtle smirk across her lips.

"It's not like you gave me much of a choice."

Reaching down, Becca took Jewel by the hand. "Come on. Don't be like that. Even if you don't find anyone, you'd have talked to some cute guys and now you have a story to tell."

The woman who seemed to be organizing the event raised her hand. "Now that everyone's here, we have an equal number of men and women. And to make things less awkward. Men on your watches, you will see a number and women on your bracelets, you will also see a number. Please go over to the corresponding table that matches your number. There, you will chat for ten minutes before the men will switch to their right until they complete a full circle. Now, if at any point a couple finds a connection, they are free to leave and head out together."

With a nod of their heads came the silent agreement from the crowd to follow the order as they dispersed, heading towards where their bracelets and watches would guide them.

Jewel looked down at her wrist. When she'd confirmed that she had remembered correctly, she headed to table. As she reached for her chair, a man appeared on the other side of the table, reaching for his; their eyes meeting over the large golden number five.

"Hello, I'm David," said an attractive dark blonde-haired man as he sat down at the table with her.

"I'm Jewel."

"Jewel," that's an interesting name. "Are you sisters named Diamond and Pearl?"

A blink of the eye was the only sign of discomfort she would display as she tilted her head, and a pleasant smile came across her lips. *Oh lord, make it end now.* "No, one of my sisters is named after a jewel, though. What about you? What do you do?"

"I'm the CFO of the Hurr candy business."

"CFO?" *Wait, David? Isn't that...* "You said your name was David. Are you David Hurr? The son of Jason Hurr the candy maker?"

"Yes," he said as he reached over, placing his hands on her. "And I do enjoy sweet things. Just like my father."

Okay.... that's kinda creepy. Jewel slowly pulled her hand away from him, hiding it underneath the table on her lap where he couldn't see that she began trying to rub off the creepy feeling. "Tell me, why is the heir of a candy empire here tonight with us regular folk?"

"My friend brought me. I wanted to have some fun. See what everyone down here does. I'm usually trapped in the office or in meetings. Do you have cats?'

"What?"

"Cats. I was asking if you had them."

"No, why do you not like cats, or—"

"No, you just seemed like a cat lady."

"What? I mean, I like cats. But how do I seem like a cat lady?"

"Your hair. It reminds me of a lot of the cat ladies I saw

as a child."

Where is this conversation going?"

"Black cats, white cats, brown homicidal cats."

"Homicidal cats?"

"Yeah, the brown ones are the ones who bite their owners the most. When I was young, my nanny had these two brown cats that would just terrorize us. I think they ended up killing her, because when I was ten, my father hired a new nanny and said Mary had gone off to a better place."

I have no idea how we ended up talking about cats. "Really? I didn't know that," said Jewel as she looked over to Becca and Sami who both seemed to be enjoying themselves. *Of course, they're having fun. How much time is left? Can this please be over?*

"Damn, seems like our time is up," said David, after a few more rounds of random questions and the sound of a ringing bell from the organizer signaled for them to swap.

"Really, that's a shame," she said as she pointed over to the next table. "I hope you enjoy yourself tonight." She then took a sigh of relief as she waited for the next date to take his seat. *I can't believe I let Becca talk me into this. I swear I'm never—*

"Hey there," said a man who appeared and took the seat in front of her. "That look on your face says that you've just been through hell."

"You have no idea?" said Jewel, shaking her head. This new man had a nice enough smile. He was dark-skinned, with short curly hair. She had dated some black men in college before, but just like all her other relationships, they never lasted long.

The man laughed. "Oh, I think I have some idea." He looked over toward the previous man. "Seeing as that fool is my boss, and I'm the one who convinced him to come out tonight."

Jewel just stared at him for a moment. "You mean to tell

me you're the reason I had to go through that tonight?"

"No, I mean to tell you that I'm the reason all the girls here will have to go through that tonight. And I made sure that I would be placed right behind him. That way, I wouldn't seem so bad by comparison."

Jewel couldn't help but laugh. "Are you actually admitting that the only way for you to get a date is to subject the woman to torture beforehand?"

"Well... when you say it like that, it kinda makes me look like a bad guy." He rubbed his chin in contemplation. "How about we say that tonight I am just giving the ladies tonight a bit of perspective as to the type of men that are out there for them?"

Jewel rested her arm on the table as if annoyed, but had to admit that he was somewhat interesting. "I'll be sure to tell the rest of the girls at the end of the night who they should thank for inflicting him upon them."

"Well..." he leaned in with a smile. "Hopefully, I won't make it to the end of the night."

"Really? You think someone's going to leave here with you tonight?"

"That is the plan. But I'll admit not all plans go the way that I expect."

Well, he is confident, and he doesn't look bad. I like his humor. "Okay, Mr. 'Man with the plan,' what do you expect to happen?"

"Well, after I got here. I swapped bracelets with one of the gentlemen here, so that I could end up beside The Candy Man and then..."

"The Candy Man? Is that what you call him? I thought he was your friend."

"Only after being friends can you refer to the head of a billion-dollar corporation as 'The Candy Man,' and not be escorted out of the building." With a smirk, he pointed his finger over at his friend. "And after his undeniable charm had worn down the woman in front of me. Then I would swoop in with a breath of fresh air with a wonderful smile and pleasant conversation."

"Trust me, he's not wearing us down with his charm."

"Charm, complete awkwardness, or his intense fear of cats, either works for my needs," he said as he bit his lip, never losing his smile. "So, tell me. How am I doing?"

"Honestly. Not bad. You do seem a little overconfident, though. Might want to tone it down just a little."

"The confidence is mostly there as an attention grabber. But I'm still not too sure of my chances," he turned his head, glancing down a few seats away. "You see that woman down there? The ones with the twists in her hair. I noticed her when she walked into the gathering a moment ago. I'm interested in getting to know her a bit more."

Jewel coughed, placing her hands over her mouth as she instinctively turned her head to where the man was looking, and spotted Sami a few chairs down. *Are you serious? Could you not have said that from the beginning?*

"Are you okay?"

"I'm... fine. I'm fine. I just... no, you know what, it's nothing."

"Oh, I'm stupid. I apologize. I'm really only interested in dating black girls," he jokingly placed a fist to his chest before raising it beside his head. "Black Power and all that."

"Huh, nooooooo, no. I understand. We all like what we like. I wish you would have said something sooner, but you know what? I'm okay with it."

"I mean no offense. If I were to date a white girl. You'd definitely be my type. I like the power outfit with a vest exposing the arms. You got that warrior woman thing going on."

"I knew it," she said, raising a finger in triumph before pointing it at him. "See, I told my coworkers that some men like arms."

"Most definitely. But what about you?"

"What do you mean?"

"I mean, what type of men do you like? Big, tall, hairy, muscular, a lumberjack, a fireman. I mean, since we're just talking here and probably never gonna see each other again. We might as well share a few fun stories, right?"

"Taller than me."

"Taller than you, or taller than you in heels?"

"Okay, taller than me in heels. How'd you know that?"

"My mother is six-one, and my father is six-six. She specifically told me that she went out with him at the start because she wanted to wear heels."

"Well, I don't see any six-six men in here."

He looked around the room. "Okay, you got me there. But they're all sitting down, so I'm not sure. In fact, I think—"

The woman organizing the event once again shook the little bell in her hand and the men started to shuffle to their next prospective dates.

"Looks like my time is up. Time for me to follow the candy man. I hope you find your six-foot six warrior."

"Thanks," said Jewel, extending her hand. "And I wish you luck over there."

And with that, he left for the other table.

A few seconds later, another man sat down at the table and extended his hand to her. He introduced himself as Mark and Jewel introduced herself with a shake of the hand.

"Jewel, huh? That's an interesting name. Are your parents in the gem business?"

"No, they just liked the name, apparently." Everyone mentioned my name. *I guess it's a nice icebreaker to have. Well, that previous guy didn't mention my name. But that was only because he's interested in Sami.* Jewel squinted her eyes and turned her head. *Wait. What was his name again? Did he tell me? Did I tell him mine?* Her mind came back to reality to see the moving lips on the man in front of her. *Damn, I should probably be paying attention.*

"And that's why the housing market is in such bad shape."

28

"Oh, okay. Yeah, ahhh, that makes sense," she said, having no idea what was going on.

"So, do you live in a house or apartment?"

"Me? I have a small apartment. I can't really afford to live on the outskirts of town. I don't even have a car."

"Well, if you're ever interested in buying a home. Give me a call," he said as he pulled out a business card from his coat pocket and handed it to her. "Or, if you are just looking for some company one night."

"Oh, ahh. No thanks," said Jewel, raising her hands, not wanting to take the card. "I don't think I'm going to be looking for anything soon. I really do have—" Suddenly she heard a chair screeching across the floor and turned to see Becca getting up from the table and stepping over and taking the arm of the Candyman, David.

"I think we're done here. We're going to go out for some candy?" said Becca as she stepped forward, locking with the Candy Man.

"Enjoy your night," said the hostess.

While Jewel was shocked, she couldn't help but see the shock on the face of the man she had just previously talked to as his so-called friend and Becca went walking past him and out of the door. *I'm glad I'm not the only one surprised by this.* He then looked back over at her, with a face that seemed to ask, "What do I do now?" To which Jewel couldn't hide the grin on her face as she shrugged her shoulder back at her.

With one less couple, the group dating continued with the next few men that sat at her table being nice, but non-piqued her interest particularly.

Finally, there were only three men left in the rotation that Jewel hadn't seen; another blonde man in front of her and a dark-haired man after him and finally a bald man who sat down at the end talking to another lady.

Thank goodness. It's almost over. Dammit, Becca, you're the one who invited us out and you're the first one to up and leave.

She looked far down from her and saw the man whose name she hadn't gotten was now one row of chairs away from Sami. *Good luck Sami.*

"Excuse me, I need to take this call," said the dark-haired man one row down from her as he got up from the table, placed his phone to his ear and headed out the door, which seemed to make his date somewhat relieved that he had left.

I guess that means I'm probably not in for an entertaining time.

"How many speed dates have you been on?" asked her current speed date companion.

"Me?" asked Jewel, once again coming back to her reality. "This is actually my first time speed dating. I've done groups before, you know, with friends from work, but that's it."

"This is only my second time," he said. "The first time one of my dates ended up making balloon animals at the table."

"Balloon animals? Really? What did you do?"

"What could I do? I let her teach me how to make balloon animals for ten minutes." He shook his head. "She actually wore a military uniform to the date and there was no way I was going to say no to someone who thinks it's okay to bring balloon animals on a date and who may or may not have been carrying a gun. I was only a few seconds away from replying to everything in Yes Ma`am and No Ma`am."

Jewel laughed. "What happened to her? Do you know?"

"Oh yeah. I set her up with my brother. Don't ask, he has this weird fetish. I don't want to try and explain it. Let's just say they both have a passion for blowing things?"

Jewel's eyes went wide with the revelation. *I don't know whether he's serious or making a joke. I guess I should just finish this night out. It's not this guy's fault. He's cute. I'm just not into these kinds of things. Maybe I should—*

Once again, the bell of the hostess rang, signaling that it was time to swap.

"It was night meeting you, Miss Jewel," he said, extending his hand to her. "I hope that you enjoy your night."

"You too." She shook his hand. "Enjoy your night."

As the man moved to the next table, she realized that the man who had left with his phone hadn't returned yet, thus leaving her sitting down at the table alone as everyone was chatting with their partners.

It's not like I haven't been here before. Alone again. I guess this is my life. But it could always be worse. She took a sip of her wine and tilted her head back, closing her eyes, and savoring the taste. *So, what now? Should I just leave?* She peaked an eye over at Mr. No Name, who was now over by Sami and they seemed to be enjoying themselves as they were smiling and laughing at their table. *And the tall girl is left alone again. Fine. If my date who left isn't coming back, then there's no need for me to stay here any—*

"Hey, what's up?" came a deep voice. "You're my date, right?" he asked as he sat down. Jewel didn't pay the man much mind at the moment as her thoughts were still elsewhere, emphasized by how she continued to sip at her wine. He looked around with a smile. "I see all the other ladies have dates, so I'm hoping I'm right."

"Huh? Yes, sorry, I was daydreaming." She turned back to face her date. "My name Jew—" Her words paused as she stared at the man. She wasn't sure but thought that perhaps this wasn't the same man from before. *Am I losing my mind? Didn't the guy from before have darker hair?* The man in front of her was a well-built man, which she could tell by how he filled out his suit. But he also has a low brownish-blonde hair cut.

"Jew? That's a weird name. But I guess I know a few people named Christian, so who am I to judge?" ?" he smiled but Jewel was still studying him.

Didn't he have darker hair? And I don't remember him being this well-built. Maybe I'm jus... "What? No, I meant... Jewel. My name is Jewel."

"Huh, okay, that makes sense," he placed both hands on the table, staring her in the eyes. "Hello Jewel, my name's Nathan. So, tell me about yourself. Why are you here?"

Why am I here? Isn't that obvious? "Ahh, you know. Like everyone else. We're all here looking for love in the city."

He looked around the table at all the people. "Yeah, I bet it's hard finding someone you can trust. Do you think this works? This whole speed dating thing?"

I feel like I'm being questioned by the police. "For some, it does. What about you? What brought you here?"

"Truthfully, I just wanted to escape for a moment. This seemed like a good way to pass the time."

"Oh!" said Jewel, "So you're not really looking for anything, but still… spending all this money just to waste time." *Is this really what rich people do with their money? Well, whatever, if he's not looking for anything. At least that takes the pressure off.* She relaxed and began rubbing the side of her neck. "Where are you from? You don't sound like you're from the city."

"No. I'm from the country. I'm only visiting the city on business."

"I see. I guess I can understand why you're not really looking for anything then."

Then once again, the sound of screeching chairs interrupted her conversation as she looked over and saw Sami getting up from her table with Mr. No Name.

"We'll be leaving now," said Mr. No Name, as he and Sami got up to leave the restaurant. Sami turned to Jewel and smiled back at her, waving bye as she took Mr. No Name by the arm and headed out of the restaurant.

Great! Now I really am the only one left. And she's probably going to just write about it tomorrow and I'll be back writing about my plants.

"What's wrong?" asked Nathan.

"What?"

"I asked what's wrong. When those people got up to

leave; your face, it looked angry for a moment. Do you know those two?"

"What? How could... it's nothing. She's a coworker, that's all."

"It doesn't seem like nothing. Seems like you're angry about something, or at least aggravated."

"Well, you know," said Jewel, feeling a bit of anger bubbling up inside of her. "Maybe it's the guy in front of me asking all these weird questions. You think he might be making me angry?"

"Nah, you're not mad at me. I'm just some guy. After tonight, you never have to see me again. So, if something's got you angry. What are you going to do about it?'

"What are you, a therapist?"

"At times, when I need to be. So, tell me, are you just going to sit there and be mad or are you going to do something to make yourself feel better?"

"Okay, this is weird. I'm leaving?"

"You're running away?"

"From you, yes I am," snapped back Jewel as she tucked her purse under her arm.

"No, from your life," said Nathan in the same calm voice.

"And what do you know about me?"

"Ma`am," said the hostess in a calm voice. As she nodded to the rest of the room. "There are other people here."

Jewel looked around the room, seeing the faces staring back at her, and sighed before dropping her head looking down at the floor.

Nathan turned in his chair to face her and gave a smile that, even in the heat of the moment, she found welcoming.

"You want to talk about it, or are you gonna just go home?"

Jewel glanced down at him as he sat stern in his chair waiting for a response. Then, feeling the tension slowly leave from her shoulders, she shook her head and sighed. "You're not going to charge me, are you?"

"First night's free," said Nathan as he stood up from the table and extended his arm to her. "Let's go for a walk, little lady."

Jewel laughed before looking at him. "Little lady? I don't think—" Her words froze in her mouth as she realized she had to look up to him. "Oh."

He took her arm and then led her out of the restaurant and out into the street. "Okay, so what do you want to talk about?" he asked as they left the building with the cool night air now nipping at her arms in a way that it hadn't before.

"I... I don't know," said Jewel, as she began rubbing her shoulders a bit. "I didn't think that far ahead before I came out here."

"I see," said Nathan as he removed his coat and then stood behind her, wrapping it around her shoulders as he patted her on the back. "Then let's talk about why you got upset when that woman and man left the bar earlier. I'm sure that will lead us in the right direction."

"Has anyone ever told you that you're like, really forward?" she asked as her fingers gripped the fabric of the coat, pulling it in closer. His warmth and the scent of his cologne were lightly drifting around her now.

"I get that sometimes."

Having found a restaurant nearby, Sami and her dating companion for the evening were now sipping glasses of champagne as they sat at a table.

"So, Andrew, how did you end up working for a candy company?" asked Sami."

"I went to college with the grandson of the company. We hit it off in class. He had questions; I had answers. I was a broke college kid, and he had all the money in the world to pay for those answers."

"You sold him the answers to tests?"

"Of course not. I assisted a college companion in rigorous trials of higher academics. The money was just an expected bonus for necessities. You know, things like a car... or an apartment."

"That sounds like exactly what I just said. You just used prettier words."

"Prettier words for a prettier person."

Sami gave a slight laugh as she rolled her tongue around her cheek. "Okay, okay, that's good. You're a quick thinker. I see why you were selling answers."

"Thank you. I hope you're enjoying yourself tonight."

"I am. Which is surprising since I didn't think I would." She sipped a bit of her wine. "But tell me, it seems kinda lucky for you to become best friends with a multi-millionaire."

"Honestly, that was all his doing. I thought he'd just buy the answers for one test and go back to the world of rich people. But he kept following me around campus. I used to play football, and the idiot wanted me to teach him how to play so he could join the football team."

"Really? I didn't get a good look at him when he left with my friend. Was he any good?"

"God no. He was terrible," said Andrew, waving hand dismissively. "They destroyed him."

"But you still became friends?"

"I respect the fact that he tried. He would show up for practice every day for months and get his ass beat every single day. It got so bad the coach just had to sit him down and tell him how bad he was."

"Oh," said Sami with a laugh. "I'm sure that wasn't good."

"No, but after that day, I stopped taking his money. I kinda respected him going out there like that."

"And you both lived happily ever after?"

"Something like that," he said, taking a sip of his own wine. "Okay, so what about you? You said that you work for a website?"

"Yes, but it's more than that. We promote the latest

fashions and have videos that complement our articles and show off the designs that we try to promote. We also have things like romance columns, and what places to visit in the city. And rich people pay to be featured on the site and magazine."

"Okay then, tell me. How did you wind up working there?"

Sami smiled as she took another sip from her class. "I know it may sound weird to say this, but my babysitter got me a job there."

"Your babysitter? You have a child?"

"No, it's a long story."

"It sounds like it. But it's still early in the night. I think we have enough time for a few more stories."

"Then I guess—"

"I see it didn't take you long to get over me," came a woman's voice as she entered the restaurant and walked over to their table.

"Are you serious?" asked Andrew, standing to meet the woman as she approached. "Why are you here? Are you seriously doing this right now?"

"Am I seriously doing what? You breakup with me and a few minutes later, you're out with someone else."

"Sami, I'm sorry about this," he said before looking up at the woman. "Macy, we broke up over a month ago. Why are you out here?"

"I'm sorry, Miss... what's your name?"

"Ahh... Sami. I'm sorry, but should I leave?'

"No. You both enjoy your date. Just know that this man is a cheater."

"I did not cheat. We broke up. We agreed to see other people."

"No, you wanted to see other people?"

"That's because we didn't work out. And that's primarily because of things like you're doing right now. Look where we are and look how your..." his eyes glanced over to a lone man looking at their table with the unmistakable face of embarrassment and loss. "Wait, are you here with another man? And you still come over here to call me out? Go back to your date? Don't leave him hanging back there?"

"I will go back," she leaned over, placing both hands on the table. "This isn't over." She turned around, knocking over Sami's wine glass, spilling it on her outfit."

"I know you just did not..." said Sami, hopping in her seat as she raised her hands, the drink spilling across her lap, before dripping to the floor.

"Oh, I'm sorry," she said, shaking her head, a small smirk across her lips. "You should probably go home and clean that up."

"Are you serious? What are you, a child?" said Andrew, standing up from the table and pointing toward the door. "Go home now. Take your date and—" His words froze as he looked toward the door. Sami saw it, too. The man who was there before was now gone. "Your so-called date's gone, and I can't blame him. You are just unreasonable. I'm sorry, Sami. We can leave, and I'll pay for you to have a ride home. You shouldn't have to deal with this."

Sami just looked down at her dress with a smile on her face while shaking her head. "You know what? I always said that I would never fight over no man." She reached over and took Andrew's half-drunken glass of wine from his side of the table. "But I damn sure am going to fight and defend myself." She stood up, raising her arm as fast as she could, sending the wine splashing into the woman's face.

Macy screamed as she reached out for Sami, grabbing at her hair. But Sami moved as the woman bumped against the table and, in turn, Sami grabbed her by the hair and pulled her back hard. But as she pulled, the woman's hair came off her head and Sami found herself stumbling back towards another set of patrons. She bumped against their table, her hand and the woman's wig splashing into another customer's soup.

"You bitch!" yelled the woman.

And before Sami could regain her footing, the woman came charging at her and tackled her as they both went flying over the couple's table next to them, falling to the floor along with the couple's food.

Both women ended up wrestling each other on the floor until her date and a restaurant employee pulled them off each other.

"I am sorry, Ma`am. I saw everything, but I am going to have to ask you to leave. We cannot have things like this happening in our establishment."

"Yes, you're right," said Sami, releasing herself from her date. "I'm leaving. I don't need this." Her body heated, she walked back to her table, grabbing her purse, and headed out of the restaurant, the lower half of her outfit soaked to the through to her thighs. Her temper high and having taken as much as she could for the night, she walked through the restaurant and out of the building back into the night and tried waving down a taxi.

"Wait, wait." said Andrew, coming out after her. "I'm so sorry about that. Please believe me when I say I had no idea that she would be there tonight."

"Well, it doesn't matter, does it.? She did, and it happened. This night is over. Goodbye."

"At least let me take you out again."

"Really? Why? You have another girlfriend you want me to beat up?"

"Well, if you're offering, there was this girl in high school," said Andrew before looking in her face and probably seeing the obvious sign that she wasn't having it. "Okay, probably not the best time for a joke. But I promise to take you somewhere nice and where I don't have any ex-girlfriends."

Sami looked at his smiling face and felt her heart give just enough for her to take a deep breath, trying her best to calm down. "Fine! But it better be a good date."

"I promise it will be. I can call you in a few days to set things up?"

"Fine," she said as the cabby pulled up. "Can I go home now? I just want to forget about this night."

"Great," he said as she stepped forward, opening the cab door for her. "I'll see you then and I promise it'll just be me this time. No crazy ex's." He closed the door and gave the cabby forty dollars and stepped back as the car took off down the street.

"Where ya headed, Miss?"

"Take me to seventh and ninth, please."

"Yes, Ma`am."

Down the sidewalk of the nighttime cityscape, Jewel and Nathan walked a few blocks; past the bright red glow of stop signs as the purr of impatient vehicles waited for their signal.

"So, you're upset that you didn't get a job that even you think you didn't deserve?" asked Nathan, as they continued through the illuminated concrete surroundings on their way through the hotel district. The bright lights of custom establishment titles reflecting off the small puddles near the side of the road. "And you're scared that you're not as outgoing as your friends."

"Yeah, for the most part, that's it."

"Well, you're out right now, walking through the street with a guy you just met. If you're trying to change, I'd think you're off to a good start."

"I'm happy you think so," said Jewel, still clutching the side of his jacket around her. "Thank you for listening to me complain. I know this isn't exactly how a first date should go, but it's better than sitting home alone."

"Is that so?" asked Nathan as he stopped and turned to her; his soft green eyes looking into hers as he slid a hand inside of his coat, slowly running it up her arms, letting them rest on her shoulder as he stepped closer to her, leaning in.

Wait! Is he going to kiss me now? Isn't that too forward? Quickly, she began to feel hot, her heart beating a bit faster as she held her breath. *Well, this man has been forward all night. I guess I shouldn't be surprised. But a kiss... a kiss is fine. It's just a kiss. It's not like I don't like him.*

Suddenly Jewel found herself being pushed into an alley, Nathan's hand over her mouth as he held her, her back pressed up against a wall. Her eyes wide, she tried to scream, but his hand covered her mouth so completely that all she could do was manage a few muffled moans between his fingers.

What's happening? Her heart now racing in her chest, suddenly the small feelings she had developed for him quickly turned into fear as her chest heaved and her breaths came shorter. She tried to move, but he was pressed against her so tightly that she found him suffocating. He leaned his head closer to hers as she grimaced and closed her eyes. *Oh god, help. Jewel... Becca. Somebo—*

"Quiet, we're being followed?"

Her eyes opened wide as she stared at his face and saw that he wasn't looking at her, but instead was looking outside of the alley. *Followed? What? Why would...* Outside of her own panic, she began to hear the footsteps of someone coming closer.

What the fuck is happening? Is he one of those crazy people? She could feel his elbow brush against her breasts as he released one of her arms, reaching past her into his coat that she still wore. She looked down and saw him pull out a gun from the inside of his coat. *Oh god, he has a gun. He is fucking crazy. Just let me make it through tonight. I promise I won't go on anymore dates with overly aggressive men. Even the tall ones. Just let me—* Her eyes froze on two men in suits who had appeared from around the corner as he removed his hands from her lips. One of the men was large with black hair in a ponytail and the other was medium-sized with short hair and a scar that ran up his lips.

"Can I help you two gentlemen?" said Nathan, a seemingly innocent smile across his face. "If you don't mind, I'm having a moment with my wife."

"That's a lie. We know that's not your wife," said the man, one hand behind his back. "We saw you enter that restaurant and then walk out with that woman."

"Mistress then? Either way, I would appreciate a little privacy."

"Either way. You will be coming with us. We have some questions for you."

"And if I say no?"

Jewel felt her stomach sink as she saw the man speaking ahead of them expose a gun from behind him. The barrel sticking out just beyond his fingers.

"Not an option, sir. You and the lady will be joining us tonight."

Jewel felt the back of his knuckles press against her stomach and he raised the gun inside of his coat.

"That's a shame," said Nathan as Jewel felt the impact of the gun going off through his hand as two sharp sounds came and both men went tumbling down to the ground. "Let's go," he said, taking her by the arm, heading down through the outside of the alley. "There's probably more of them."

"Oh god, oh god, what's going on?" she asked, looking back to see the men down on the ground writhing in pain as she was taken away. "You shot them."

"Either I shoot them, or they shoot us. They probably have on vests anyway, and I don't. So, better them than us."

"Are you serious? I can't—"

He raised the butt of his gun, bringing it down hard on the window of a black car that was parked as they emerged from the other side of the alley, shattering the window. He then knocked free any remaining glass before reaching inside and unlocking the door. Quickly, he entered the vehicle, sliding himself over into the driver's seat.

"Come on, get in."

"What? You can't be serious. There's no way I'm—"

He reached his hand out to her, the seriousness in his eyes conveying the urgency of the moment that she was in. "There are men coming down that alley with guns. They saw you. Their friends are on the ground, probably bleeding. Do you want them to find you?"

Her hands shaking, the pounding in her chest feeling unrelenting, she couldn't think straight. Turning back to peer down the alley, it looked eerie. The darkness inside seemed to play with her mind as the fear grew inside of her. Without thinking, her body seemed to move on its own as she leaned down, falling into the seat. She felt compelled for any type of security, and Nathan's words are what she clung to.

Inside, she saw he had ripped off a piece of the car under the wheel and was fiddling with wires. The next thing she knew, the engine started and at the same time the back window of the car exploded, causing her to raise her hands over her head for protection as Nathan pressed the gas and sped off down the street.

She felt a few shards of the broken glass come forward, bouncing off on her shoulders and hair. She let out a scream as she leaned forward, her head close to her knees as the roar of the engine thrummed in her ears.

"Why is this happening? I shouldn't be here?" screamed Jewel as the screeching of tires and the car's momentum disorientated her.

"Stay down. They're following us."

"What?" she turned her head to him in confusion, before slowly raising back up only to sit in disbelief as she saw a car speeding its way toward them. "What are we going to do?"

"My gun. I dropped it between my legs on the floor.

Grab it for me."

"What?"

"My gun. Between my legs, grab it," he repeated, his tone now more aggressive.

"Okay... okay," she said, the panic clear on her lips as she quickly laid over his leg. But there was nothing to see, only darkness with a few glimmers from the streetlights, which zoomed by too fast for her to focus on. Frantically, she just ran her hand across the open space beneath her. "I don't see it."

"It's down there," he said as he turned the corner, the tires screeching louder as the force pinned her against his lap. She could feel the weight on his arms pressed against his back as he steered the vehicle. "Hurry, grab it before they catch up."

She screamed in frustration. "Fine" as she reached in again, trying to be more aware of anything that felt odd in the blackness. A peddle, the back on his shoe, the edge of a mat. "Dammit, where is it?"

"It's probably under the seat. Pull you hand back and—"

And then her finger grazed against the hard feeling of something cold and metallic. Without questioning it, she grabbed it, wrapping her fingers around the nozzle. "Got it!"

"Good, give it to me," he said as he reached one hand down, his arm sliding against her face. His skin against her cheek, the smell of a light cologne drifting over her nose.

Feeling for his fingers, she placed the gun in his hand, struggling in his lap to get back up as the car shook. "Dammit, why did you bring me into this?"

"Sorry, but I needed a cover. I didn't..." He fired the gun three more times as she heard the roar from the other car as it came closer. "I didn't know they were so close that they'd seen me enter the restaurant."

"Sorry. You can't just say sorry when—" She heard the thunk sounds as a few bullets hit the side of their car. The fear mounting, she closed her eyes, gritting her teeth as the heat from him and the heat from the car hung over her body as she clung to his thigh. "Just get me out of here."

"I'm... trying!" He growled, his elbow pressing hard against her back as he pinned her down, trying to shield her as best as he could while not losing control of the car.

Another turn, more screeching tires, another round of shots, one of the hot shell casings fell off her back and hit her finger, before rolling around on the floor. Then there was a sudden jerk of the car which gave her the momentum she needed in the franticness for her to sit back up in her seat. Her breath hurried as she tried to calm herself down while looking around. The city was a blur. She had no idea where she was. Everything flew by so fast and was only getting faster. But as she turned to face him, she saw the other thing beside him that seemed clear. The people who were keeping up next to them in the opposite car. But the moment was short-lived. Their faces were there one second and gone another as the next sound she heard was that of a car colliding. The metal and glass breaking sound that felt terrifying and other worldly.

Through the hole in the back window, she saw the car launch and spin in the air before crashing back down in a mass of sparks and crushed metal, tumbling over and over again as pieces of the vehicle began to litter the street.

"Oh god, oh god. Are they dead?"

"Probably," he said as she took another turn. "Are you okay? Were you hit?"

"What?" asked Jewel before she began patting her own body down. "I don't think so. I... I think I'm okay."

"Good. We're going to have to get rid of this car. I'm pretty sure the police were called, and if not, they will be. Do you know any place nearby?"

"Ah!" She looked around the street. "Slow down, I can't tell." Her eyes darted back and forth as she desperately tried to figure out where she was, searching for anything familiar, and then something caught her eye. "Up there, by the big waffle sign. My friend, she… she lives there."

"Okay," he said as she pulled the car up, reaching into his pocket and handing her a card. "Take this. My number is on the back. Call if you think anyone is following you in the next couple of days."

"What?" asked Jewel as she began looking around, the adrenaline and paranoia still having a hold on her. "People are going to follow me?"

"No, I don't think they will. They don't know who you are. But this is just to make sure. If nothing happens, then don't call."

Her heart still racing in her chest, she took the card from him and opened the door, once again looking around to see if there was anyone else."

"It's safe for now. Go inside, and I'll go dump the car."

"You're not coming back?' asked Jewel. Even though he had got her into the mess, she found herself clinging to the security he seemed to carry with him."

"I'll be watching," he said, his voice even deeper, but just as confident as before. Although he looked more rugged, a few buttons of his shirt had come undone and she could see his chest as it heaved under his shirt.

Jewel swallowed, believing his words, and got out of the car, closing the door. Then, with a nod of his head and not another word, she watched as the car then took off. Only then, when it began driving away, did she notice the bullet holes in the back side of the vehicle.

Feeling planted in the spot where she stood, she watched as the car headed off down the street, turning at the next exit and disappearing behind a corner. Now, in the quiet of the night, she once again clutched her hands at her side only to realize she was then still wearing his coat, the only security left for her in the cold. Her hands gripped tightly onto the cloth as she turned around, looking up at the apartment complex in front of her.

Its yellowish apartment lights piercing out of its

windows, faintly casting its glow down onto the street below. With a body that still trembled, she shakily placed one foot in front of the other and opened the door leading inside.

The air was as calm as she remembered. Stale air from the lack of ventilation, and a floor rug that looked to badly be in need of cleaning. She shook her head, but she placed her hands on the railing of the steps. *I hope she's home.* Just as the thought crossed her mind, a car arrived outside. A sudden jolt of fear shot down her back as she heard its breaks squawking as it came to a halt.

With a growing fear inside of her, she turned around to see Sami getting out of a taxi and then heading quickly inside the building. The relief Jewel felt made her feel for a moment lightheaded as she saw her friend coming through the door.

Stepping inside as she began fumbling around in her purse, Jewel couldn't help but wrap her arm around her.

"What!" Yelped Sami, surprised by the moment. "What the—"

"I'm so glad to see you," said Jewel, embracing her friend as tightly as she could.

"Huh? Jewel? Is that… what are you doing at my place?"

"It's… it's been a long night," said Jewel, the relief in her voice escaping with every breath. But that relief was soon interrupted, because as she pressed her face against Sami's, she felt something sticky. Slowly she pulled herself away and saw several strings of a clear liquid dripping from their faces. "What… what's this?" asked Jewel, as she rubbed the side of her face with the sleeve of Nathan's jacket.

"That…" said Sami with a saddened expression and a shake of her head. "Is the result of a terrible night out. I probably should have just listened to you and gone back home." She rubbed the side of her face, trying to remove more of the stickiness from her hair. "What are you doing here?"

"Can... can I stay with you tonight?"

"Ahhh! Sure, I guess. Is everything alright?"

"Honestly... I don't know."

"Okay," said Sami, unable to hide the worry on her face. "Let's get up to my apartment. We can talk there."

Their footsteps almost in unison, they ascended the stairs together. On the second floor, they entered the apartment hall, headed towards the corner. Small lights against a gray-painted wall greeted them at the entrance, the symmetry of the aligning apartment doors causing Jewel to try and remember the last time she'd come to Sami's place.

Which one was it again? She asked herself. But the question became irrelevant the moment they turned the corner. As there, sitting beneath one of the doors, was a man slouched over, his back against the entrance.

"Wait, isn't that your door?" asked Jewel, her finger pointed towards the man. "Someone's there."

"What?" asked Sami, turning her attention away from Jewel and looking ahead, before giving a sigh. "That's not someone. That's an idiot who never learns his lesson," she said as she stepped out into the hallway and walked her way down the hall to her door, where she stood over the man who sat blocking her path. He was asleep, so she nudged him with her foot to rouse him. "Wake up. You got dumped again?"

"What?" said Jamal, half waking from his sleepy slump with his eyes hazy with alcohol. "No, it's her fault. She... she had a husband."

"Oh! You were on the other side this time? Serves you right."

"So... mean," he said, trying to lift his hands to her, but gave up halfway, letting it drop to the floor.

Sami shook her head at him. "Just a mess." She turned back to Jewel, who was peeking around the corner cautiously. "Come on. Since you're here, help me. I can't just leave him out here."

Jewel slowly came down the hall, her eyes close enough to recognize the man's face. "Is that Jamal?"

"Yeah, that's him, or what's left of him." She slid her key into the door, opening it and letting him fall backwards on the inside floor. Stepping over him, Jewel followed behind her. "Okay, grab his arm and we'll drag his sorry ass over to the couch."

Feeling a bit unsure, Jewel did as she was asked and they both drug Jamal across the floor of the room, struggling to lift him up and lay him out across the sofa.

"Woo... That's better," said Sami as she walked back and closed the door. "I swear, I'm the one who should be getting paid for being a babysitter now. So, you want to tell me why you're at my apartment?" She gave Jewel a look over. "You're wearing some guy's coat. Did your date go bad, too?"

"What? Oh? Well, I... I didn't know where else to go," said Jewel, taking a seat on the other sofa across from the passed-out Jamal. *What am I supposed to tell her? That I was just shot at? Do I call the police? What am I supposed to do?*

She walked over to the fridge and grabbed a bottle of water before coming back and handing one to Jewel. "Either way, I doubt that your date was as bad as mine."

"Thank you," said Jewel as she took the water, nodding over to the other sofa. "Has he done this before?"

"Jamal? Yeah, almost every time he has a bad or semi-bad breakup. I've kinda just gotten used to it at this point."

"So, he comes here crying every time he has a breakup?"

"I don't know about that. I haven't seen him cry since we were in school, and he got in trouble for fighting the school bully. More like he just passes out and when I wake up in the morning, he makes me pancakes."

"Pancakes?"

She waved her hand. "It's a long story."

"But come on, spill it. Becca is probably off somewhere dancing with whoever she went out with. So, what about you? What happened on your date?"

Jewel thought for a moment before staring back at Sami. "Okay, you're not going to believe it, but..." Her mind drifted away for a moment as she stared at the side of Sami's head, her eyes squinting as she tried making out what she was seeing. "Is... is that spaghetti?"

"What?" asked Sami.

"There... in your hair. I think..."

Sami's face looked confused for a moment as she raised a hand to her hand, rummaging into her hair, her mouth and eyes slowly going wide as pulled free a long stringed noodle along with a sticky substance glazing over her fingers. She let out something between a moan and a scream before hopping off the couch. "I forgot... my hair. I just had my hair done. Oh, no, no, no."

Hopping off the couch, she ran to the bathroom and in less than a minute came the cursing words, followed by the sound of the shower running.

Jewel then took another sip of her water and looked back over at Jamal, who then proceeded to fall back down on the floor with a loud thud that didn't even wake him up.

Jewel just shook her head. *I don't know what life is anymore.*

CHAPTER 3

Jewel awoke to the muffled sounds and vibration of the phone beneath her pillow. The waking moans that came along with any other morning rustled in her throat as she stretched her legs and arms forward. Through squinted eyes, she caught a glimpse of the sun through the window and rolled over to avoid the light. There, she saw Sami's sleeping face next to hers. Staring at her for a moment, she blinked several times as the memories of the night before came reluctantly back into her mind. Bad dates, car chases, and falling asleep in her friend's clothes after showering at her place.

Sitting up, she began looking over the room, then looking down at herself. One of Sami's oversized shirts, her own clothing resting folded on top of a chair near the wall.

There was something else in the air. A delicious smell of something warm and sweet. As if pulled by the aroma, she slid herself out of bed, taking another look at Sami before slowly making her way barefooted over the cold floor towards the living room area. Stepped past the wall that separated the bedroom and the kitchen, she peeked her head around the corner to see Jamal. With the kitchen counter littered with grocery bags, he stood over the oven as a plate of pancakes rested on the countertop behind him.

"Oh, hey," said Jamal, spotting her. "I saw you both in there, so I'm making enough for three." He slid the spatula under the pancake, bringing it over to the countertop, stacking it with the others. "Go on, those are yours. Eat up before they get cold."

A little suspicious but also with an empty stomach, she stepped away from the corner, out in the living area and sat down at the kitchen counter as Jamal slid over the syrup. "Thank you?'

"Sorry, I showed up here like I did. If I had known you two were together. I would've... well, I didn't know?'

"What?" She looked back at the corner of the room before shaking her head, realizing his meaning. "No. We're not like that. We both went out on dates, and I just ended up here, is all."

"Oh yeah. She did say she was going out yesterday after she, ahh—"

"I should have stayed my ass at home," said Sami as she came around the corner scratching her head. "And you need to stop just appearing at my door every time you get dumped."

"Now is that anyway for you to talk to the guy making you pancakes in the morning? I even got up early to get everything and... what happened to your hair? I thought you said you were off to get it done yesterday."

"Shut up," said Sami with a frown as she walked over to the windowsill, picking up a scrunchie and tying her hair into an afro ponytail and coming over to them.

"Wait," said Jewel. "You have a key to her apartment.

Then why were you sleeping on the floor when we got here?"

"I didn't want to walk in and see something I wasn't supposed to see. You know, lady stuff."

"Didn't I tell you to be quiet?" said Sami, turning to Jewel. "He has a key because, remember when I had my dog? Well, when Addison would send me out of town. I'd used to ask Jamal to come and walk him and water my plants." As she took a plate of pancakes, she turned back to Jamal. "How is buddy doing now, anyway?"

"My mom probably has him running around the yard with the rest of the dogs. I still don't understand why you got a dog when you know you're too busy to take care of one."

"Well, at the time, I wasn't. Now, I am."

"Anyway," he said, making the last pancake, then pointing to Jewel. "I'll leave you here with Miss Indecision. As much as I enjoy seeing the bare legs of two half-naked women, unlike you ladies, I should probably be getting to work."

"You're not going to shower?" asked Jewel.

"I keep an extra suit at the office for days like this. I'll clean myself up there." He then grabbed his coat off a chair and then headed for the door. "Take care ladies. Love you Little Sami."

"Get out. And stop calling me that."

And with a quickness, he left the apartment, shutting the door behind him.

"Hey," said Jewel, turning toward Sami. "Did you two ever hook up?"

"Once, we tried dating. Didn't really work out, though. Then there was a lonely new year's night when we both were too broke, drunk, and lonely to know any better."

"Then what happened?"

"We both admitted it was a mistake. Then I said he was a whore, and we agreed it would just be a one-time thing."

"But he still has a key to your apartment," said Jewel, and a suggestive smirk across her lips.

"Nothing's going on between the two of us now. It was once and we don't even bring it up anymore."

"Okay, if you say so," she finished the last bite of her pancakes. "He does make good pancakes, though." She stood, sliding the stool back under the counter. "Anyway, I should get going. I still have plants to write about." She then walked back over into the room and slid back on her pants.

"You know, you never did tell me exactly why you ended up at my place last night."

"No," said Jewel. "And hopefully, I'll forget all about it by tomorrow." *It feels like a dream, anyway. How am I going to talk about almost getting shot at and ending up in a car chase?* "Thanks for letting me stay over. I'll pay you back."

"Girl, you're fine. Don't worry about it."

"See ya," she said as she left the apartment and headed downstairs.

Jewel took a cab across town to her home, where she'd bathe again before changing clothes. Try as much as she could, she couldn't shake the memories of the night before. *I'm glad I stayed with Sami. I probably would have been up all night.* She thought to herself as she finished her morning routine. Having had breakfast at Sami's, she grabbed a pail of water and slowly began making her way around the apartment, feeding her plants.

The apartment was littered with different types of vegetation that were housed in little pale pots that sat on shelves. Each section had plants that responded to various situations. "Here, you go babies," said Jewel as she dipped her pail, letting the cool water dropout onto the pot-housed soil.

The act of feeding her plants finished calming any nervous feelings that were left over from the night before. The way the water slid off the green leaves was as calming a sight as she had ever seen.

"I just need a few more plants and then it'll be perfect," she said to herself as she turned around after finishing and looked over her well-watered apartment. "Okay, now I can go to work."

After finishing getting dressed, Jewel headed back downstairs, once again hailing a cabby. The ride wasn't long. The cab driver was silent as he let the radio play on the way there. Soon the cab stopped, and Jewel exited out, stepping on the concrete walkway before staring up at her building. There weren't many people outside except for the few who had stepped out for a smoke.

Jewel stepped out onto the concrete sidewalk and stared at her work building. Outside, there were the regular passers-by and a small group of those who had already stepped outside for a smoke, or were having a quick smoke before heading in for the day. It was strange to her how they seemed to know each other's routines. People from different levels, different departments, even different companies altogether, came together for a smoke; one in the morning and then one at midday.

Although feeling calm earlier, the thought of her job made her neck stiffen as a nervous tingle came down her spine. Gripping her purse, she walked forward, trying her best not to dwell on it as she walked past the smoking crew, the hit of burning tobacco washing over her nose as she passed them.

Inside, she nodded to the security guard as she had done many times before and headed over to the elevator. She pressed the button but heard the ding as the doors opened up for her and out came a little girl, almost bumping into her.

"Oh," said the little girl, stopping herself before running into Jewel. "Sorry."

"It's fine," said Jewel, as she stepped to the side to let the girl pass.

"Hey Cory, I'm back," said the little girl, and she went off toward the security guard, who gave her a hug as she ran up to him.

The simple affection between the two caused a smile to appear on Jewel's face. *I guess his name's Cory. I never knew that.*

Stepping inside of the elevator, Jewel pressed the button to her floor. But she soon noticed that the floor inside was a little wet. Patting her foot to the floor, she felt the small puddle beneath her. *Did that girl drop water in here?* She frowned, but thought nothing of it after that as the elevator doors began to close.

But before it could seal itself, a wayward hand split between them, forcing the doors to open back up again as Patrick appeared through its reopening slit, the sound of his tools jingling on his belt as he stepped inside.

"Sorry," he said, pressing the button for the top floor.

"You're in a rush," said Jewel, noticing that his blue jumpsuit was halfway on, not having slid his other arm in.

"Yeah, they called me, saying that the plumbing on the top floor isn't working." He sighed. "Or to be more correct, that it was overflowing. Took me thirty minutes to get here?"

"I guess that's why the floor's wet in here," said Jewel as she nodded to her feet and before patting the mound of water with her heel. "Wait, will that affect the elevator?"

"Let's hope not."

"Hope? Aren't you supposed to know? You're the maintenance guy."

"No, I'm the guy who's walking into a big pile of shit. I won't be the maintenance guy until I reach the top floor and see what I need to do."

"Okay, but thirty minutes to get here? Were you on your lunch break? Aren't there any other maintenance people who could do it?"

"Well, there's this new guy. But he's the one who called me when he fucked it up."

After such a revelation, Jewel was grateful when the elevator reached her floor. With hurried vigor, she stepped out before turning back to Patrick. "I really have no idea how this building works?"

"You know the funny thing," said Patrick. "Neither do I."

Jewel shook her head in dismay as the elevator closed. "God help us all." Then, turning back, she headed into her office area where the rest of her co-workers were shuffling about handling their tasks.

"Hey Jewel," said Lan Ling, standing in front of the copier as it hummed while shooting out several sheets of paper. "I knew you'd be the one to show up."

"What do you mean?" asked Jewel, walking over, setting her purse down on her desk. "Everyone else is…" She looked around again. "Where's Addison?"

"She didn't come in today. Neither did Becca and Sami called in saying that she was going to stay home today. So, she emailed her article already. But we all made bets, saying that you'd still probably show up for work."

"Great. Good for you." *I'm the only one who showed up? I'm the only who one doesn't have a life, apparently.,*

"So come on, tell me. You're the only one who came in after your girls' night out. Tell me what happened."

"Nothing happened. We all went out and Becca apparently went home with a grandson of the Hurr Candy empire."

"What? You went out with millionaires?"

"No, she went out with 'a' millionaire. I went on a normal date." *It was normal for the first few minutes at least.* "And then I slept over at Sami's place after we were done."

"That's not exciting. All you did was eat and go back home and go to sleep. You need to live more."

"Well, I'm sorry that I'm not as exciting as—" her attention migrated over to the TV. There was a newsreel where she saw an overturned car surrounded by police tape as a news caster stood with a microphone. Being drawn towards the television, Jewel lost track of the conversation.

"That's right, amazingly no one died in this wreckage you see behind me., although one person is in critical condition, I'm told. We've received reports that another two men were seen limping away from the vehicle, but no one was able to get a clear view of them," said the newscaster. "But at this time, it's unclear where they are. But judging from the amount of bullet holes in the vehicle and the reports of loud engine noises right before the crash. We are assuming that they may have been some sort of gang warfare. But the police have yet to give us a report on just who the person inside was."

"Oh, that's near where Sami lives, I think," said Lan Ling. Stepping in beside Jewel to gaze up at the TV. "Did you see that when you left?"

"No," said Jewel, unable to take her eyes off the screen. "I... I live in the opposite direction, so... I wouldn't have caught it."

"I guess that explains why she didn't come to work today then. Traffic is probably bad on her side of town."

The camera panned over to an ambulance, and suddenly Jewel felt a sinking feeling in her stomach. *Gang warfare? They didn't seem like a gang. They had on suits. But they said no one died. But two people were shot. What happened to the two men that followed us near the alley?*

"That's weird," said Lan Ling. "Things like that are happening a lot more often in the city these days, I guess. I heard about a month ago someone big and important was taken in for ransom."

"Yeah!" said Jewel, swallowing nervously. "I'm... I'm going to go and finish my story." Leaving a confused-looking Lan Ling, she then turned, heading back to her desk. *I guess I can't pretend it was a dream now. But it's fine. I'm here now. I'm safe.* She sat down at her desk, where her papers from the previous day lay scattered about her desk. Logging on, she was greeted to her work tab, where she had already typed the first few words of her article. Taking a deep breath, she tried to clear her mind, lowering her fingers over the keyboard.

She typed: 'The Philodendron White Princess is a rare plant that any serious collector might want to at least consider having in their collection. Its leaves are able to transform into... into...' *into... What am I going to do? I've been shot at. Lost out on a job, and probably going to lose my job because not enough people read my work. Is this the life I always dreamed of, sexless with a lot of plants?*

Placing her elbows on the table, she rested her face between her hands. *What a mess. I don't even feel like writing now. But I need to send them something, even if they reject it. I need to...* With the birth of a new idea, her eyes opened, staring at the screen through the spaces between her fingers. Then slowly she lowered one hand and pressed and held the 'delete' button until the words all vanished, leaving her with a black screen casting its light back out at her.

And with fingers that slid over the keys almost instinctively, she typed the title: 'Plant lady's night out.'

Sami sat at home sipping tea and looking over her computer. "Well, if people enjoy a good bit of drama. I guess they're going to like reading about fighting inside of a nice restaurant and snatching the weave off a woman's head." *Let's see what Addison thinks of this.* She laughed. *It's not exactly romantic, but why not? If there's other people vying for the job. Or God forbid Becca and her Billionaire Candyland experiment. I really don't see how I can keep up no matter what I do.*

She leaned her head back, looking up at the ceiling. "I have really no idea what I'm doing anymore." Glancing to the side, she could see the still dirty dishes left over from the pancakes earlier that morning. "I guess I should do the dishes then."

Straightening her posture, she sat up on the Sofa, then stood up and walked over to handle the dishes. Grabbing the milk carton on the way to place back in the fridge, she noticed it was empty.

"If you were going to buy food. You could have just bought more than the basics." She shook her head. "Okay, I guess it's time to buy groceries then," she said as she looked over at the dirty dishes. "I'll put that off until I get back."

Getting dressed, she then headed out of the door, making her way downstairs and headed into the city. She looked around for a cab. *I guess they cleaned up that mess down the street now.* She saw one off in the distance. She raised her hands, only to look around and then lower it. *The store's not that far away and it's pretty nice out. It won't do me any harm to go for a walk.* So, with that thought, she went on her way. Her part of the city was as noisy as ever. Cars beeping their horns, the chatter of people getting off from the subway. To her, it all had a peaceful hum .

It wasn't long before she arrived at the store, the cold air of their so-called convenience hitting her in the face as she entered and went browsing through the aisles. She circled the store floor, grabbing the milk and tossing it into her basket before taking a turn into the snack section.

Her favorite chips were missing. Usually stuffed in the middle row between the sour cream and the nachos would be her barbecue flavored chips. But they were gone. Looking around, she soon spotted them now on the opposite aisle, now sitting peacefully on the top shelf, out of her reach. She sighed before walking up the shelf and lifting herself up on her toes, trying to reach them. She frowned and grunted as her fingers still were a few inches away from them until she saw another hand reach up and pluck them from their perch.

"Hey Momma. You want me to get that for you?" said a dark-skinned man looking down at her.

Sami lowered herself back down, "Yes, thank you. This store doesn't appreciate small people."

"What's your name?" asked the man, a smirk on his lips as he looked her up and down.

Sami's lip twitched as she noticed that he still had the bag of chips that was out of her reach. "My name is Sami. Now can I have that bag of chips, please?"

"Sami, that's a cute name. Well, Sami, can I ask if you have a man?"

She gave the man a quick look over. He wasn't unattractive. His low hair cut fit his face, strong jawline, and through the small opening of his shirt she could see a neck tattoo of some sort. *He looks good. Probably would look good in a suit. College Sami would probably go out with him.* "You can, and yes, I do. Are you really going to hold my food hostage while you try to get my number?"

"That depends. Will it work?"

"No, I'm not the type to cheat on my man." *How long is this going to take?*

He bit his lip for a moment, smiling down at her. "Okay, you win," he said as he brought down the bag of barbecue chips, handing it to her.

"Thank you," she said, staring up into his face for a moment. *Well, if I went out with him, I could write about it.* She sucked on the inside of her cheek. *But he seems to be like a player, and I don't feel like having another crazy ex-girlfriend coming after me.* She raised a finger, the smile still on her face as she pointed a finger at him. *Maybe if it was another day, but right now I really don't feel like dealing with men I don't know.* "Thank you. Bye bye." She then placed her chips in her bag, then proceeded to turn around and walk away.

"Hey. Now come one, Momma, don't be like that," said the man as he followed behind her. "Aren't you going to ask my name?"

"Sorry, but I don't need your name since the only men's names I need are my boyfriend's and my father's. And you're

60

not them."

"Hey, maybe I can be more than them. You never know, right?"

This one is persistent. Kinda like a puppy. Sami shook her head as she turned the corner, smiling as she spotted a familiar face standing in front of one of the kiosks. "And besides, my boyfriend is waiting for me?"

"Ha, you're playing. Come on, give a brother a chance. You might like it. I'm a good man."

"Patrick," she called out in the store as she reached into the basket, raising the chips the man had gotten for her. "You want something else?"

Patrick looked over at her and smiled before waving his hand, looking a bit confused.

The man beside her slowed himself, letting her make her way over to Patrick as he turned down another aisle.

"What's up," said Patrick. "You said you wanted something?"

"No? I just saw you and decided to come over and talk. What are you doing on this side of town?"

"Oh, the top floor at work flooded for a bit. So, I have the water off. I have to run to the hardware store to get some new pipe and fixtures and I figured I'd stop here and pick up a few things I've been missing out on at home. Actually, I didn't see you at your desk today. Took the day off?"

"Yeah. The morning traffic was jammed, and I didn't really feel like going in today, anyway. So, I just emailed my article in."

"Must be nice to just sit at home all day and get paid for it," he said, shaking his head. "And then you abuse me with fixing chairs you don't even come to work to sit in."

"Oh, shut up," she said as she linked her arm in his and escorted him around the store.

"Now, what are we doing?"

"We are going shopping, and you are going to pick everything that I need off the top shelves today."

"This feels like an abduction. This is why you need a man."

"Good, because that's exactly what it is. Now grab those rolls of tissue paper for me."

With a frown spread across his lips, he reached up, grabbing the item. "You're going to make me carry this home for you, aren't you?"

"See, you're already catching on."

The two went about their time around the store, with Sami only catching a glimpse of the man from before only once and assumed he left. Then out of the store she had Patrick escort her home, holding her groceries.

A little while later, they exited the store headed back towards her apartment.

"Hey, did you ever fix my chair?"

"I did. Just had to put some grease on one of the screws." He looked up at her apartment windows as they reached the entrance. "Wait, you're not trying to lure me inside to fix some in there again, are you?"

"What? No, of course not. And that was only one time. I needed to call someone; the power went out."

"You do know apartment complexes are supposed to have their own handymen?"

"But you came faster than they did. And besides, when you got the lights back on. I made you lunch, didn't I?"

"I guess that's true."

"Stop being negative and accept my thanks," said Sami as they reached the steps of her apartment.

"Alright. I accept," said Patrick, handing Sami the grocery bags. "I'll go now. I still got a few more errands to run before I head back."

"Thanks Patrick. I'll bring you some lunch tomorrow."

He stopped and turned around to her. "How about I take you out to get something to eat?"

"What? You mean like on a date?"

"Not 'like', I mean on an actual date. That is, if you don't mind me picking things off the top shelf for you a little while longer."

Is he really asking me out? She looked him over again. *I guess he is cute in his own way.* She looked down at her groceries. *It would be something else to write about.* "Fine," she said, looking back at him. "But just one date. And that's only if that chair isn't squeaking when I come in tomorrow."

"You make it sound like you don't trust me."

"It's hard to trust a man who was down on the floor looking up my skirt just a day ago."

He raised a hand to speak, but then a grin came over his face. "Fair enough. I'll ask for permission next time."

"Next time?"

"I'll call you," he said, heading down the street, not giving her a proper chance to respond.

Sami took her groceries up the stairs to the second floor. *Jackass, Maybe I should have asked him to carry these up the steps as well.* She sat the bags down and began fumbling around in her purse for her keys. Finding them, she pulled them out, about to slide it into the lock. But the sounds of her phone rang startling her, causing her to drop the keys to the floor.

"Dammit," she said, digging back in her purse. "Really, even on my day off." Frowning as she pulled out her phone and seeing it was from Becca. Sliding her finger over the screen and she placed it to her ear.

"Hello?"

"Hey Sami. What's up?"

"Nothing much," she said as she dropped to her knees, picking up her keys before opening her door and dragging in her groceries. "Just getting back home and being annoyed by a phone call on my day off."

"Good, you're back home then. I called at work, and you weren't there, so I came by to get you?"

"What?" she asked as she finished sliding in her groceries, closing the door, placing her back against it. "What are you talking about? Where are you?"

"I'm outside waiting for you. Look out your window."

Suddenly, from outside, she heard a horn blow. "You've got to be kidding me." She walked over to the window, looking down to see Becca waving at her as she and a well-dressed driver stood on the street corner.

"Hurry up, bring your ass down here," said Becca, waving at her.

"Do I want to ask how you got that car?"

"You can ask when you bring your ass down here. Now hurry up."

Sami looked down at them for a moment and then looked around her apartment, and then at the groceries still sitting down by the door. *Screw it. It's not like I had anything planned. I might as well enjoy myself.* "Fine, I'll be down in a moment."

She changed her shoes and quickly put the milk into the refrigerator and headed out the door, down the stairs, where she saw her friend still waiting for her.

"Girl, you better not take me off to some crazy place. I still haven't had the chance to fix my hair yet."

"You're fine. Now hop in. My friend said he can take his spot on his trip since he had other business to attend to." They both got into the car as the driver closed the door, before taking his place in the front seat and they set off down the street.

"I guess you really hit it off with the Candyman," last night.

"First, his name is David. And second, we spent the entire night talking about our families and things we want to do. He's actually really sweet."

"Really?" asked Sami, a sly smile across her lips. "Is that all you really did was talk?" asked Sami as she looked around the car. It was a luxury vehicle, she was sure. It had a lush interior and fancy etched seats from some maker that she didn't recognize.

"Yes, that's it. We have a second date planned tomorrow. We were going to try today, but things happened, and he got caught up in a meeting. I've decided to spend this date we had planned with you."

"Wait? So where are we going?"

"It's a surprise," said Becca as she leaned back in the seat. "So, tell me. How did things go for you after I left? Did you and Jewel just go back home and sleep?"

"I wish that was all I did? But tell me something. Did you know that Addison is planning to leave the company?"

"Yeah. And she wants to hand it off to someone at the company. No idea who, though. If it were a guy, I'd say it'd be whoever he was sleeping with. But since it's her, and she's married. I honestly don't have a clue who it is."

"So... you're not trying for the job?"

"Me? God no. What makes you think I want it? Sounds like too much of a hassle, if you ask me. The next thing you know, I'll turn into Addison and start calling people by the wrong name and start cursing out children in the streets."

"Cursing children, really?"

"Okay, I don't have any proof of that, but it's not hard to imagine her doing that."

Sami laughed, shaking her head. "Well, hopefully, I won't be that bad. She said she might want me to take it over?"

"What? Seriously? Well, damn, that's a step up for you, isn't it? I hope you get it," said Becca as they went along their way through the city, with Sami telling Becca about her meetup while grocery shopping.

"Were here," said their driver as the ladies got out of the vehicle. Outside, Sami stood before an exceedingly tall building, one of the largest in the city. Along the side of the building was a golden awning between flags that Sami was sure represented the different nations.

"Greetings," said a gentleman in a suit as he approached them. "I was told you would be arriving soon. This way, please."

"You know who we are?" asked Sami.

"No, but I recognize the driver and the car. I was told there would be two of you arriving."

"Don't worry, Sami," said Becca as the door opened for them and they followed him inside. "This is how the upper-upper crazy people live. You must pretend to be like them. Straighten your back, narrow your eyes, and purse your lips as if you've been sucking on something sour your whole life."

Sami laughed at the joke and Becca's imitation of her words before looking around the opening hall of the building. "I don't think that's an accurate image of how real people are."

"Rich people aren't real people. I thought you knew that," said Becca, turning to her with her lips still pursed.

"So that Candy man of yours isn't real either?"

"Oh, he's real. Or at least his money," She winked at Sami before placing a finger to her lips. "Him... well, I still have to finger if the other part of him is real."

"Stop looking at me like that," said Sami, trying to hold in another bout of giggles.

"You mean stop looking at you like I'm about to be super wealthy and not have to worry about anything anymore? It's called the good life. Isn't that why we're all working? Isn't that why you're trying to get Addison's job? You better get used to this look."

"I'm not after her job. I'm looking at a position that will become open soon."

"Yeah, a position that she currently has her ass sitting in. You know, it's not a crime to just admit you want something. Even if it is money."

The inside of the building was elegant, with several golden chandeliers hanging over their heads. A very ornate carpet that spread throughout the entire floor. The Pillars of the building seemed to have been carved out of marble in the shape of people lifting each other up to the ceiling. After taking a moment to stare at the decor of the building, she proceeded to the elevator. A bright light fixed in the center of the ceiling cast down the letters of the word "Apex" in large, elongated shadows on the floor ahead of them.

Is that the name of the hotel brand? Thought Sami as she and Becca were escorted through the main hall over and into the elevator, where their escort pressed the button for the top floor. *I guess places like this cater to people who can spend thousands of dollars a night on a room.* She turned to Becca. "Where are we headed, anyway? You're not taking me to some weird rich people's party, are you?" asked Sami, looking over her own casual attire and patting her stilled fluffed hair in its afro ponytail. "I don't want to suddenly find myself surrounded by men trying to get into my pants."

"If that's the case. Then why even step outside? We're both young and attractive women. Any man would count themselves lucky to find themselves waking up beside us. Isn't that right, Mr. Escort?"

"Yes, Ma`am," said their escort in a tone showing that he was hardly paying them much attention.

"See, he agrees."

"I think he gets paid to agree," said Sami as the elevator door opened to a massive open area room with expensive looking furniture all about. "Okay, I'll admit that this room is impressive." From her view she could see the room lead out on to the rooftop of the building. While not the tallest build, she could see the vast blue sky ahead of her.

"This way please," said the escort as they headed forward to a set of glass doors.

"Exactly," said Becca as she stepped in front of Sami and gestured to a helicopter that sat on a landing deck. "And where we are going is on a trip around the city. Have you ever been in a helicopter before?"

"No. And you've got to be kidding. And what if I were to say that I'm afraid of heights?"

"Then I'd ask you to get over it fast, because I'm even more afraid, but I'm not turning down this opportunity to see the city. Now come on. I'm gonna need someone's hand to squeeze when I'm up there."

Sami shook her head but smiled as the doors opened and they were struck by a gust of air. As they got closer, their escorts held the doors open for them.

"Have fun," said the escort as they stepped outside into the open air. Instantly, she felt the breeze come flowing over her close and through her hair. Together, they stepped across the rooftop over to the helicopter as they slid the door open for them.

After stepping up inside and being instructed to put on their seat belts and ear muffs the girls then closed the door. The helicopter was loud at first, but after closing doors; the blades spun faster, creating a sort of humming sound in the cabin. And with a slight jerk of the vehicle, it lifted them into the air, swaying clumsily in the air for a bit before taking off.

I hope this is safe. This better be safe.

Having never been in a helicopter before, she couldn't help but stare at the ground below as they hovered above the side of the building. The view felt different from staring out of the window of her office. The way the tiny cars moved throughout the streets reminded her of a sort of puzzle where things needed to be placed together. Large buildings towered over the city streets, but from the sky, they seemed as if they were hand grown from the concrete walkways beneath them.

The view of the city and its scale was amazing to her. Marvelous architecture of all different shapes and sizes seeming as if they were all trying to pierce the sky with varying degrees of success.

"See, this is way better than sitting at home doing nothing, isn't it?" said Becca, a little loudly so Sami could hear her over the sound of the helicopter.

"Okay. I admit, it's fun. Are you happy now?"

"Yes."

Over the entire city, they flew, with Sami never taking her eyes off the window panel. Her eyes were fixated on the scenery until she noticed they were getting lower as they neared the waterfront. The dark river that ran across the edge of the city. Outside she could see several boats in the harbor.

"Are we not going back over to the building?"

"Why?" asked Becca, the grin across her lips present in the window's reflection. She placed a finger over Sami's shoulder, pointing down to the waters below. "Take a look down there. Someone's coming to pick us up."

Following her direction, Sami's eyes gazed down more towards the water where a few small ships were sailing about, but there between them all was a larger ship with the word 'HURR' written across its sides.

"No way," said Sami, looking back at Becca.

"We're living a different life today," said Becca, as she put on a pompous voice. "Let us live like those of the highest of high society."

With a slow swoop, the helicopter pilot came in low, the blades above causing a mist of form below them as they came around to landing the helipad at the back of the ship. Two men came up the ramp to greet them, opening the door as they landed. Sami felt the cool breeze coming off the water as it flowed over her as she stepped out with Becca. The smell of salt water stung her nose a bit as they let the men escort them down into the back of the ship. There they saw that an elegant white table along with two chairs had been prepared for them.

One of the men threw up two fingers, waving at the pilot as the helicopter raised back up, taking off into the sky, leaving them on the yacht. "Please, this way, ladies."

"Your meal will be delivered shortly," said their escort as he left, walking down into the lower decks of the ship.

"I think this might be a little too much," said Sami, looking over the water as other smaller ships floated off in every direction. "And this was supposed to be your date? Are you sure you didn't sleep with him last night?"

Becca laughed, "No, I did not. He just happens to be one of the really nice millionaires."

"And he just happened to be slumming it at a speed dating night out."

"Oh, yee of little faith. Anyway, tell me. What are you going to do about that job that Addison offered you?"

"What do you mean, what am I gonna do? It's not like I can make her pick me."

"Can't you?" said Becca with a smile.

"I don't like the way you're looking at me right now."

"Oh, come on. If you want some spice, you know what you have to do. Get out there and don't just let it be when I drag your ass out. Just because you got dumped doesn't mean—"

"I didn't get dumped."

"Uh-huh, and what else do you call it when someone breaks up with you?"

"I have your meal, ladies, and I've brought a bottle of wine," said the man from before as he came back from down below. Behind him stepped two other men, both holding trays. Setting the trays in front of the women, they removed to top lids as an aroma of freshly cooked meat and savory dressing to wash over their noses. "What we have for you ladies today is a Japanese Kobe beef alongside white truffles, and Kalamata olives. The sauce used is a mixture or blue cheese and peppercorn. The wine is imported from Italy and vintaged twenty years."

I know all that is fancy stuff, but I really don't think I'll appreciate most of it. Food is just food, isn't it? Sami looked down at her plate as the smell, along with the appearance of the food, made Sami's mouth water as she reached to her side, grabbing a knife and fork. *But it does look nice and I am hungry.*

The man then set their wine glasses and began to pour.

Giving into her desire, she plugged the fork into the meat, watching as the juices poured out of it as it was impaled. The steam that arose from inside as she cut a piece away with her knife drifted faintly upward, warming over her fingertips. She swallowed her saliva in anticipation before even putting the piece to her lips. And then, taking in a final warm breath, she took the piece into her mouth; the juices sliding down the sides of her tongue as she moaned with the pleasure of the taste.

"You know what," said Becca. "You're right, Sami. You don't need a man or that job." She took a sip of the wine before tilting her glass at Sami. "You might be okay with letting opportunities like this slip through your fingers. But I think I'll enjoy being the girlfriend of the heir to a candy empire."

CHAPTER 4

The next morning, Sami met up with Becca and Jewel in the lobby of their building.

"Good morning, everyone," said Becca, as they all headed for the elevator. "Jewel, I wish you could have come with us yesterday."

"Not thanks. After my last night out. I think I'll be good for a while."

"It wasn't that bad this time," said Sami with a laugh, as she looked over at the security guard. He nodded to them as they entered the building and then went back to reading his newspaper. Beside him was a board game, but the pieces had yet to be placed on it. *I guess he's waiting for that little girl to show up again.*

They entered the elevator and noticed that the button for the top floor had been taped over. "I wonder what they're doing up there," said Jewel, before pressing the button for their floor.

"What do you mean?" asked Becca."

"Apparently yesterday, the top floor flooded. Patrick had to fix it."

"Oh. I saw Patrick yesterday," said Sami. "That must have been what he was talking about. He said he was out running errands after something happened at work."

Soon stopping at their floor, the elevator halted before opening its doors with them all exiting into the workspace. They all paused for a moment as they noticed that their office area was somewhat busier than usual. People stood around the copying machine, checking papers, and gossiping with one another as others made quick trips from their desk, back and forth to the gossiping group.

"And what's going on here?" asked Becca, leading the group in as they walked over. But when the girls entered the room and were noticed, the gossiping island of people quickly dispersed, all headed back to their desks, giving glances towards them as they did so.

"Wait," said Becca. "Was I the only one who caught that?"

"No," said Sami. "You think one of us is in trouble for something? I mean, I skipped work, but I still turned in my article."

"There you two are," said Lan Ling, emerging from the back of the group and walking up to them. "Addison has been waiting for you two to arrive all morning. I think those people are there for you."

"People?" asked Jewel, as she looked ahead and saw that two women were sitting down in front of Addison. "Who are they?"

"I don't know. But Addison had them come in this morning. They've been in there since we all came in."

"Wait," said Becca. "Addison was here early? That's never a good sign."

"Hold on? Which two of us does Addison want to see?"

asked Jewel. "I came to work. I shouldn't be in any trouble."

"She wants to see you and Sami, of course. No one cares about you, Becca."

"You know," said Becca, wagging a finger at Lan Ling. "I want to be mad at you. But I'm just happy I'm not in trouble for once. So, I'm going to let that go." She then waved her hand and began walking over to her work area. "Good luck to you, too."

"Do you know what she wants?" asked Sami, frowning at Becca as she walked away.

"No, but if you get fired. Can I have your desk, then?" asked Lan Ling, a hopeful smile across her lips.

"Really, Lan Ling. Really?"

"What. I need to ask before anyone else gets it."

"Then why don't you ever ask for Jewel's desk?"

"Jewel works in the corner. It looks depressing over there."

"It is not depressing where I work," responded Jewel, before looking back at her own desk. "Is it?"

"Anyway," said Sami, "Let's go and see what she wants. I doubt she's going to fire both of us."

A look of uncertainty across both the women's faces, they walked through the office as each of their coworkers gave them stares of pity in their passing. *Why are they all looking at us like that? Did we really do something to upset Addison? Did I lose subscribers because of my new article?* She bit down softly on the side of her lip. *Damn, I should have checked my numbers before I came to work today.*

Reaching the outside glass of the walled off room, they watched as Addison paced back and forth, her lips moving as she talked to the two women in front of her.

"She doesn't look too happy," said Jewel.

"I don't know if that's a good or a bad thing. It's usually when she's happy that it means that we're either in trouble or she is going to load us down with work," said Sami as they reached the door.

Addison raised a hand to halt them, then changed to a finger, signaling for them to give her a minute. They couldn't hear what Addition was discussing with the two women, but it seemed serious as her facial expression never changed from a solemn brows-furrowed appearance.

Maybe those are our replacements, thought Sami.

After some time, Addison gave a nod and the two women inside stood up to leave, exiting the glass room and allowing Sami and Jewel to enter.

"Take a seat, girls," said Addison, gesturing to the two chairs the women before were just in. "And close the door behind you."

Doing as instructed, both girls took their seats while Addison stood, leaning against her desk, looking them over.

"Recently, both you girls submitted your articles, and they both went out today," said Addison as she reached over and held up a copy of the magazine. "Have either of you looked at it?"

"No, we just arrived at—" said Jewel for a moment until realization went in. "Wait! You actually published it. I thought you were going to reject it like all the others."

"Well, you see, that's the issue. One of our designer guys saw your articles and decided to make up a little graphic. Have a look for yourselves." She handed Jewel the magazine.

"What? What do you mean?" asked Jewel, as she took the magazine and turned the first few pages. "It's not here. I don't understand. Did you just remove my section?"

"Keep going," said Addison, waving a hand for her to continue through the magazine.

Jewel continued through the folds, the anxiety building as her fingers crumpled the edges of the paper until her eyes were assaulted by large images of a black sheep and a white sheep surrounded by colorful hearts.

It looked like something from the young heartthrob magazines she'd had as a teenager. The ones that had the inside scoop of whatever boy band she liked at that time of her life. Colorful outlines made to catch the attention of the reader's eye encircled the page in the form of pink and red hearts scattered throughout the article. Some were even transparent behind the words.

But the most ghastly part of it all was the title promptly on display at the top, written as 'The Love War.'. Below it sat the two black and white sheep looking angrily at each other in their cartoony way. Black beady eyes staring at each other and below them were two columns where on the black sheep side she saw her own article. Minus a few key pieces and change locations. There was her night out, written in word format. The men getting shot, her in a car chase and fearing for her life, all of it there to be read.

"Oh, my god. That's my article," said Sami, peeking over the side of her chair at the page and pointing at the white sheep as Jewel's hands began to shake. "Why is it here, instead of my normal romance section?"

"I believe I told you we were making changes to how we output to our customers. Well, when the boys saw both your articles, well they couldn't help but whip this up." She shook her head. "I had final approval, of course."

"But," said Sami, placing a finger on the page. "It makes it look like we're competing with each other."

"That because, as of this moment, you are," said Addison, as she grabbed the remote and turned on the TV. "Look, this was an hour ago. I had my friend over at channel five make a little advertisement."

As the TV flipped on, the black screen quickly transformed into color as they saw the "Pause" icon fade away. There before them were two newscasters sitting down at their desks as Addison pressed play on the remote.

"Greeting ladies and Gentlemen," said the woman on the TV. "Today's top story this morning has been the insane interest in an apparent competition of love between two mystery women, one named Black Sheep and the other named White Sheep."

76

"Yes, but obviously one is lying, right?" asked the other male newscaster. "I mean come on. Going on a date with a mysterious man and getting shot at by mobsters with guns and chased through the city. It sounds a bit far-fetched to me."

"Well, I don't know. I'm a woman in this city and I can tell you some of the dating nightmares I've had. But either way, this friendly competition is already taking the hearts of not just the city, but apparently the whole country by storm and it's already the number one most trending top on the Bird Box this morning."

"This is impossible," said Sami in disbelief. "We only submitted last night. There's no way it's gotten this big this fast."

"Well..." said Addison with a grin. "I had a bit of a hand in that. The online version released several hours ago and I'm paying to have several stations cover it. Not to mention I paid several celebrities to tweet about it." She nodded to the TV with a smile. "And it seems like my investment is paying off. God bless social media and the millions looking for the next big train wreck to fight over."

Sami shook her head. "There's no way this is real."

Addison turned off the TV. "Oh, it's very real. Traffic to our website has risen over fifty thousand percent. Check it yourselves when you go back to your desks. Apparently, our servers have been crashing all morning. People are logging in trying to find clues as to who you two are. Just an hour ago, I got a call from some movie studio offering to buy the rights to the story of you two and how this goes."

"Movie Studio?" repeated Jewel, her face twisting with confusion as she glanced between the television screen with the paused laughing faces of the broadcasters and the magazine in her hand.

"I don't understand," said Sami. "What do you want us to do? Even if it is popular. We've already been on those dates. It's not like you expect..." Sami began shaking her head.

"No, no, no, you can't expect us to really start competing against each other in dating."

"That's exactly what I expect," said Addison, raising a finger. "I told you before that if you wanted that job. Then you would have to be bold. And this is exactly what I'm talking about."

"Wait! What job?" asked Jewel.

"Oh, that's right. You didn't know, but I guess since you're involved in this, I might as well offer it to you, too." She lifted her arm, waving it around the office. "I'm going to be giving up this company soon, so I can focus on my other interests. But rather than shelf the company and firing everyone, I've decided to just pick someone to replace me. Sami here was one of the people I thought would make a good fit for the job. But I remember hearing from my hairstylist that you were passed up for another job. So, you might be interested in it as well."

"Really, you're going to allow me to run the whole company," said Jewel, unable to mask her interest. "Wait..." Jewel appeared confused. "Why would your hair stylist know of me being passed up for a job?"

"Oh, apparently, she heard it from some food delivery man," said Addison, looking over at Jewel with a raised brow. "Imagine my surprise when one of my own employees is out there job hunting and after I gave you this job out of the kindness of my heart."

Jewel swallowed, looking nervous. "Ah, well... It's not that I'm not grateful—"

"Don't bother," said Addison, waving it off with a smile. "I would have done the same thing. I promise you I didn't get everything I have just by sitting around being complacent." She stepped forward, taking the magazine back from Jewel. "But back on topic. Both you girls seem capable enough. But the real question is, are you willing to keep this going in order to get it?"

Jewel bit her lip as she looked up at the article Addison

was holding up and then over to Addison's big comfy-looking leather chair being her large desk. "And I only have to go on dates, then? That's it?"

"Jewel," said Sami. "Are you really thinking about doing this?"

"I mean... you're going out for the job too, right?"

"That's it," said Addison, closing the magazine and slapping it down on her desk. "But really Jewel. I mean, being chased through the city. Where did you ever come up with such a thing?"

"It's not... I mean, I just kinda exaggerated the date night that I had with Sami and Becca."

"A little creative freedom. I suppose our readers won't mind such a thing."

"Wait," said Jewel. "What about the other people you had set up for the job? What happens to them?"

"Oh, I just spent most of the morning telling them they're out of the running." She pointed towards the TV. "I mean, look at that. You girls have both outpaced everything that they turned in. I had just thought of selling the company when it was valuable enough. But this... this is far more than I expected to happen."

"I don't even have the number of the guy I went out with. You can't expect us to keep up relationships for a story," said Sami.

"I honestly don't care who you date. Go out there and experiment. Get involved with other girls, or threesomes if you like. Right now, you have the world's attention and I want you both to hold on to it as long as you can." She patted her hands on the desk. "Okay, so cards on the table. Are you girls in, or am I going to need to find someone else to work these articles?"

"I'm in," said Jewel, with no hesitation.

"Wait. What about our regular articles? What are we supposed to do about those?"

"Oh, don't worry about that," said Addison, opening the

magazine and showing her own page to her, which was now far in the back.

"What? But I didn't write that?"

"Of course, we hired someone else to take over your regular work. We even have an agricultural special from Michigan writing Jewel's piece. They will be writing everything under your name for the duration of the competition. I think it's best to keep the black sheep white sheep thing anonymous as long as we can. It adds to the interest from the public." She folded her arms over her chest, looking at the women intently. "Okay, so give me your answer. I have another call in like, five minutes."

Sami looked over at Jewel for a moment before sighing. "Fine, I'll do it. I mean, it's not like I can afford to pass it up."

"Good, then the next update will need to be ready in a week's time."

"A week? But the magazine only releases once a month."

"It does, but the website updates all the time. We gotta strike while it's hot. We will keep updating the site and at the end of the month, we'll include a summary of the highs and the lows of finding love in the city at the end of the month." She gestured toward the door. "Now go on. Get out, my meeting is coming up."

A look of shock across their faces. Both girls turned to look at each other, before slowly rising from their seats and heading for the door. Jewel, apparently forgetting the door was closed, bumped against the glass before opening it for them to leave.

"What should we do now?" whispered Jewel, while rubbing at her nose.

"Why are you whispering?"

"Didn't Addison say she wanted to keep it anonymous?"

"You think she meant around the office?"

"You want to go back and ask her?"

Sami took a quick glance back at the office. "The last thing I want to do is go back in there. I swear that woman lives in her own little world."

"Aren't we both trying to live in that world now?"

Sami frowned. "I guess you have a point there. Fine, then let's promise that we'll compete fairly."

"What does fair mean?"

Sami frowned. "Ah, no lying guess."

"Okay. I can do that. What else?"

"I guess we can promise not to read each other's articles. That way, we won't get jealous if we don't really know what the other is doing."

"That makes sense," said Jewel, as she finished rubbing her nose. "So, ah…" she extended her hand to Sami. "May the best woman win, I guess."

Sami smiled back and shook her hand, a smirk across her lips. "May the best woman win."

"I don't like that look on your face," said Jewel. "You know, just because you have more dates than I do doesn't mean I can't get myself a man."

"I never said you couldn't," said Sami, her smile still on her face.

"Oh, I'll show you. I can be a… what's the word?"

"What word?"

"You know. When a woman seduces a man."

"Seductress?"

"Yeah. I can be that, too."

"I'm not a seductress."

"Well, too bad, because that just means you're just going to make things easy for me."

Sami just shook her head. "Okay, Miss. Seductress. We can talk about the rest later. People are starting to look at us."

Jewel took a look around the office, catching glimpses from their other co-workers. "Well, talk later."

"Fine with me," said Sami as they both headed back to their workstations.

Sami walked back over to her desk, sitting down in

her chair. With a sigh, she placed her hands over her face, leaning on her elbows. *What should I do? That's a stupid question. I know what I should do. I should take the job. But what the hell is happening? It's not like I have had that much of a love life. I didn't even give that guy my number. What am I supposed to do now?* She removed her hands from her face and leaned back in the chair. Instantly, she noticed something different about it as she bounced herself on its cushion. *Humm, it's not squeaking anymore. I guess he fixed it after all.*

She began thinking back to the day before in the shopping mart, where she stood in line with him. *I guess we could go out on a date or two. It's not like it would hurt anything.* She took another look around the office before noticing Jewel sitting down at her desk, typing away at her screen. She then reached into her purse and pulled out her phone. Scrolling down through the list of names, she stopped on Patrick's and typed out a message.

"Are you busy right now?"

Jewel sat at her desk, her eyes immediately focusing on her screen. Upon opening her page, she couldn't help but stare as her own article sat prominently on their website. Clicking on it, she saw that where she would receive maybe two or three comments a day, now there were over a thousand. Some directed at her, asking for more dating information. But others were people arguing with each other over if the date was real and if it was; should she continue dating Nathan? And on the side was a live chat, where she could see people talking in real time.

Jewel could only sit there in amazement as she scrolled through the comments; thousands of people wanting an update on what happened after that night.

What should I do? Should I talk back to them? Am I allowed to? I mean... Sami's the one who gives love advice. Thinking of Sami, she peeked over, looking across the aisle at Sami, seeing the top of her head moved back and forth. *I wonder what she's thinking about now. Maybe she's used to this.*

Feeling a bit of jealousy, she looked back down at her screen. *I can do this. I mean, how hard could it be? All I have to do is answer questions. Nothing hard about that.*

Her fingers hovered over the keyboard for a long moment before finally typing out the words in the live chat: *Ah... hello.*

Before she even had time to regret typing anything, a slew of words flooded the comments section. So many that she couldn't keep track of them all as the cycle went on. Her eyes only glimpsed a few things. The most surprising thing was that some people were calling her Black Queen instead of black sheep. And then suddenly the chat turned into an argument about what race she was.

With smushed lips and wide eyes, she quickly exited the web page and leaned back away from the computer. *Okay, no. I think I'll stay away from that. If I told them that I was white, I feel like I'd cause more problems that I can handle right now.*

She closed her eyes, trying to let it all sink in. *This can't be real. Maybe accepting this was a bad idea.* She shook her head. *No. I really have a chance to manage a whole company. I can't not do this.*

But still... there were so many people. Wait, in order to chat, I remember you needed to be a subscriber. Her eyes opened at the realization as she stared back at the website's home page on the screen. *That means that all those people... they paid? How... how much money is that? How many subscribers do I have now?*

She scrolled her mouse over the screen and clicked on her brother-in-law's name. *Maybe I should just go down there and ask him.* Her phone rang, startling her and causing her to send her mousing falling to the floor.

"Dammit," she said, before reaching into her purse and looking over to her phone and seeing an unknown number. She frowned at it suspiciously, but decided to pick it up and accept the call.

"Writing an article about what happened that night wasn't a good idea," came the familiar voice of Nathan over the phone.

Her chest tightened as her body grew stiff after hearing his voice. "How... how did you get my number?" she asked as she began looking over the room to see if anyone had caught her outburst. Seeing that she had not garnered anyone's attention, she lowered her head and spoke softly into the phone. "What do you want?"

"I've been watching you to make sure that the men from that night never found you."

"You could have said something or shown up."

"Have you noticed anyone following you?"

"No," she said with a sharpness to her tongue. "Except the person on the phone. Why would they follow me? I had nothing to do with whatever that was. And I didn't know that they were going to use the article."

"I'm pretty sure they don't care. They'd use you to get to me?"

"What have you gotten me into?"

"I remember getting you out of it. But I believe that article may draw you back in. It would be best if you distance yourself from that company for a while."

"I can't do that. I need that article."

"Is that article worth having the men from before coming after you?"

"Can't we call the police or something?"

"You've welcome to try. What would you even tell them? You met a man you don't know, and were chased by men you don't know, and they've gone to places you don't know."

"Okay, I get your point," said Jewel, rubbing the back of her neck in frustration. "Then you tell me what I should do, since you know everything. And I'm not giving up my job."

"That's fine, but you need to be careful. Someone might end up piecing together the article you wrote and come looking for you. If I can find you, then they can."

"You haven't found me. You just have my number."

"You're sitting at your desk wearing a blue dress with your hair tied behind your head in a bun. You look good, by the way. Not too flashy, but cute."

Surprised and confused, she began looking around the office again. Nothing looked out of order as everyone went about their day working as usual, and it didn't seem as if anyone was paying any more attention to her than normal. "How do you know that? Where are you?"

"Watching you to make sure you're safe. But don't worry. You won't ever see me again. I'll watch for a while and when I'm sure you don't have a tail, I'll disappear."

"What? What do you—" and before she could finish her sentence the call ended, leaving her blinking her eyes in bewilderment as she stared down at her phone. *Just who does he think he is? Some kind of secret agent or something?* With a little bit of fury rising inside of her, she recalled the number on her screen only to receive the answering machine of what she thought to be the voice of a child.

"Hello," said the child. "We're on vacation and our mailbox is full. Don't call us, we'll call you." And then the phone hung up again?

What the hell was that? She stared back down at her phone again. She could see her own upset face in its reflection. *No, don't think about it. Don't think about the fact that I'm being stalked by some military secret agent fool who's got me involved in God knows what. This... this must be a joke or something, right?* Taking a second to collect her thoughts, she pressed to save the number on her phone and titled it, 'Crazy Stalker Idiot.'

She then closed her phone, placing it back in her purse, before turning to look out at her coworkers again. *Does he know someone who works here? I mean, Becca knows a lot of weird people and she did invite me on that stupid blind date. But there's no way she set that up. I mean that car crashed. I know it did, and I heard the bullets.* She then looked out through the window over the city. *Was he watching me from out there somewhere?*

"What wrong Jewel," said Lan Ling, approaching her desk.

"Huh? What... what do you mean?"

"I don't... you just look tired. Every time you get tired, you get those rolls on your forehead like you've been thinking too much."

"Oh, ahhh what?" said Jewel, before looking at herself in the reflection of her phone again. *Rolls in my forehead? What does that even mean?* Dismissing the thoughts, she turned back to Lan- Ling. "Maybe you're right. I've got a lot to think about today."

"It's fine. Hey, I saw Addison talking to you and Sami in her office. She asked you both about that article, right? Do you know who wrote it?"

"What?"

"You know, the article about the black sheep and white sheep. We've all spent most of the morning trying to figure out who it is. I mean, we assume it was the ladies she had in there earlier. We've never seen them before. But you know, I thought Sami handled all that romance stuff. And did you see, they pushed her article all the way to the back of the magazine."

"Hey, what's wrong with being in the back of the magazine?"

"Oh, sorry. I wasn't trying to say anything bad about your article always being back there. It's just that, well... you know... it's Sami."

She decided not to take offense to Lan Ling's words as the poor girl shifted nervously, trying to talk her way out of her previous statement. Instead, Jewel's mind started to wonder back on her own situation. So, I guess that's what she meant by asking everyone in the office the question. No one knows who it is. But wait, Becca went out with us that night. She'll know it's us the moment she reads the article, right? I should really talk to Sami about... She looked over and saw that Sami was no longer at her desk. Where'd she go? She was just there, wasn't she?

Jewel then stood up from her seat. "I'm sorry, Lan Ling, but I need to go."

"What, you too? That's what Sami said? Are you two sure you're not in trouble? Is this about your meeting with Addison?'

"What? No, of course not. Ah... hey, did Sami say where she was going?"

"No, she was just texting on her phone, and suddenly got up and left. I had just asked that before she took off."

"I see, but don't worry, I'll be in tomorrow. I just have a few things that I need to take care of before the day's over."

"What? But it's still morning."

"Yeah, sorry," said Jewel, taking a few of her notes and placing them into her bag. "I think that it'll take all day." And with a wave, she headed for the elevator.

Stepping inside, in between the cold walls of the elevator, she pressed the button for the bottom floor. And soon to match the sinking feeling in her stomach, the elevator lurched before it began its descent.

Am I really doing this? Yes, I'm doing this. But competing against my friend for the same job. That can't be good for our relationship. Maybe I should talk to her about it. She began rubbing her wrists anxiously. *What am I even thinking about? I should be focusing on the stalker man, or my fake love life.* Before she could gather her thoughts completely, the elevator opened and, still focusing on her own thoughts, she stepped out, almost bumping into someone on the way.

"Woah, there," said the voice of a man. "Hey there, I didn't think I'd run into you again."

"What? I'm sorry I…" she said, looking at him and remembering him as the man from their night out that she had actually found interesting. But he was interested in Sami. *I guess that makes sense. She is the relationship guru.* She gave him a quick look over. He wore a nice-looking suit, buttoned up in the front. "I… ahhh…."

"I believe I was one of your unfortunate dates after the candy man."

"That's right. You were… his… bodyguard, right? Your name was?"

"Andrew, and I guess that's a way to see it. Oh," he said as he stepped to the side of her and stuck his hand in the elevator door to catch it before it closed. "But mostly I'm just working for him, doing odd jobs."

"Oh. You were interested in my friend Sami, right? Did you two hit it off that night?"

"I wouldn't exactly say we hit it off." He began rubbing the back of his head with his other hand as he gave a half-hearted smile, while sucking in air through his teeth. He looked, his voice sounding a little unsure. "But she did end up doing her own fair share of hitting. I'm actually on my way up to see her."

"Sorry, you've already missed her. She left for the day."

"Well," he said, letting go of the door and stepping back, allowing it to close. "I guess I'll try again another day. I wanted to surprise her."

"I can call her if you like. She's probably not that far from here."

"It's fine. I'll just stop by at a later time. No need to keep the driver waiting," he said as they both began walking out of the building. "So, what about you? Did you end up meeting Mr. Right that night?"

Jewel laughed, "Not even close. I'm not sure many people had as bad a night as I did?"

"Really? I'm sure I'd give you a… Whoa," said Andrew, stepping out of the way for a man holding two plants in his hands.

"Sorry," said the man with the plants. "I didn't see you—"

"Pedro," said Jewel, looking at the man. "What are you doing here? Wait, are those mine?"

The man shifted, one of his eyes peering out from between the large leaves of the plant. "Perfect. Hey Jewel, just the person I was looking for." He lowered the plants to the ground before reaching to his side and pulling out an electronic pad for her to sign.

"Really? You're dropping it off here?"

"We came to your home twice. But you weren't there. You wrote this place down as your second delivery. I was gonna have the security call you when I got inside."

"What am I supposed to do? I can't take these up and leave them in the office," said Jewel as she reluctantly signed the pad and handed it back to him.

"Put them in the back of a cab?"

"Really? You think two three-foot philodendrons will fit in the back of a cab and not instantly get crushed?"

"No, I think my delivery is done. And now I have to move on to my next stop," said Pedro, before taking off back down to the street where his delivery truck was waiting. "See ya next time, Jewel."

"You usually order Pink Princesses like this?" asked Andrew as reached down, rubbing his finger against one of the leaves.

"It's part of the job, and it's kinda my hobby. I've been trying to get a Desert Rose to match them, but they're hard to..." A confused look came over Jewel's face as she stared back at him. "You know what type of philodendrons these are?"

"Yeah, both my parents were florists, so it'd be weird if I didn't know at least a little about plants. Speaking of which, being out in the cold like this isn't good for these guys. They should be inside, probably in a warmer climate, maybe something like seventy-five to eighty degrees."

Jewel just stared at him for a moment as he ran his fingers over the leaf of the plant. *Of course, we'd have something in common.*

He looked down at the plants and twisted his lips, making a face. "Let me give you a ride home. It'll be easier."

"What? No, it's fine I don't—"

"Are you sure? I mee?"

"That's right. You did say you had a driver," said Jewel before looking down to the corner and spotting a man standing beside a large car. "Ah... why do you have a driver?"

"Well one, is my boss is paying him to drive me around. So, it would be kinda rude of me to not use him, and two... apparently it comes in handy when you meet someone who has two overgrown philodendron plants that she may or may not need to transport across town."

Jewel's lips twisted with eyes narrowing at the sarcastic remarks as she looked him over, then down to the large spacious-looking car waiting and then to the overgrown plants that easily came up to her thighs. Then finally, giving into her circumstances, she knelt, picking up one of the plants. "You win, grab that one."

Joining her, they both walked down to the sidewalk, plants in hand as the driver held the door open for them. "Go to Six Twenty-Five Flannigan street, please," said Jewel as they entered the car with their forestry cargo.

"Yes Ma`am," said the driver as he closed the door, then took his seat at the front of the vehicle.

"Thank you for the ride, by the way," said Jewel, moving one of the large leaves over the plant to see Andrew. "I want to make sure I don't forget to say it. I know you came by to see Sami, so you really didn't have to."

He smiled back at her. "It's great to be appreciated. Don't worry about it."

"Well," said Jewel, the plant shifting in her lap as tried to reach into her purse. "At least let me give you her number. I'm sure..."

"Thank you, but let's wait till we've reached your place first."

"Okay. I just wanted to make sure I didn't forget," said Jewel, regripping the plant's base. "And thanks again. I can hold both of them, if …"

"No. It's fine. Really," said Andrew with a laugh as the leaves shuffled in front of his face. "I told you I've always had an interest in plants. The only reason I didn't join the family business was because my friend offered me a better job and it's not like being a florist often leads to riches."

"So, is that what you're trying to be, rich?"

"Not so much, rich. But I am looking to try to become stable. And working for the candy man does have its benefits." He tilted the plant in his lap towards the driver. "As you can see."

"Okay, if you're a flower guy. Do you keep any flowers at home?"

"Yeah, probably more than you. My parents keep sending me little gift seeds all the time. I have vase sets of String of Dolphins. I've just started a collection of Blue Lilies, but I'm having trouble finding the right temperature to keep them in. It's a quiet hobby to relax when I get home from a hard day's work."

"More than me? You think so?" said Jewel, trying to maneuver the plant so that she could see him. "I'm not so sure about that."

"What about you? What made you so interested in plants?"

"You mean, besides it being my job?" said Jewel with a smirk that she wasn't exactly sure he could see behind her mask of leaves. "When I was in college, we kinda had to join a club, and it turns out that they just so happened to have a club for gardening."

"Really, given your height, I'm surprised they didn't try to get you to join a sports club like volleyball."

"Oh, they did. I just ran away from them. I'm not exactly

the most athletic person."

"And you ran to the gardening club?"

"It was that or the cooking club. And I wasn't super excited about being stuck in a kitchen for two to three hours a day after classes."

"A fair point," said Andrew as the car slowed to a stop at their destination.

There was nothing too fancy about Jewel's building. A mid-city apartment complex like all the rest, stone and marble walls on the outside, with those sliding doors that opened when you approached.

"Should I just drop this here or in the elevator?" asked Andrew, looking around the neighborhood.

"Really?" asked Jewel, playfully sounding affronted. "Aren't you going to do the gentlemanly thing and carry them up to my apartment?"

"I... I don't' mind," said Andrew, looking a little unsure as his eyes shifted back towards the car. "I just thought that well... well..."

"Don't worry, I wouldn't normally invite someone up to my apartment. But I really don't feel like lugging both of them to my door. And besides, there's something I want to show you."

"I'll wait here, sir," said the driver. "There doesn't seem to be too much traffic, so I won't be in the way."

"Thanks. I won't be long."

Entering the building, both Jewel and Andrew headed over to the elevator, where Jewel adjusted the plant in her arm as she elbowed the button for the sixteenth floor.

"Good aim."

Jewel laughed. "I've been here a while. I'm used to hauling things upstairs."

"So, I see."

"Tell me. What's it like having a driver take you everywhere you want to go?"

"I'm not going to lie and say he's not useful. It's like

having two of me. I can send him throughout the town to handle a few issues while I work. I guess it's like having a secretary with a driver's license."

"He's a very attentive driver?" said Jewel as the elevator lurched and began its climb upward.

"A good driver is worth their weight in gold. Especially the ones who already know where you're going before you have to say it."

"Really? Is he like that with you?"

"For the most part, yeah. He's even come home with me to meet my parents on several occasions."

"That's a wonderful relationship," said Jewel as the elevator stopped and she exited out onto her floor. "It's this way." They both turned and headed down the hallway until finally stopping in front of a door. Lowering her plant to the floor, she slid her key. "Come on in," she said, stepping to the side, so he could pass."

"Okay," he said, stepping inside. "What did you want to—"

His words caught in his mouth as the visage of the room left him staring in silence for a few moments.

"Are you sure you have more plants than me?" said Jewel, stepping in beside him and bringing in her plant. She turned to him with a satisfied look clear across her face as she turned to face him while walking backwards. Across her lips was a smug smile, but she didn't care, as she was proud of her work in her home garden.

"How..." He swallowed, trying to get the words out. "How long did this take?" he asked, looking over the room. Throughout the room were dozens of plants separated into different sections. Some hung from the ceiling out of special displays that house them, their vines hanging down like curtains almost touching the floor.

"It probably took longer than you think. But it's worth it."

Spread through the room were rows of cascading

shelves. Atop each row sat small porcelain pots that housed different plant life. "Did you do all this?" he asked, setting down the philodendron and stepping over to one of the other plants, rubbing its leaf gently between his fingers.

"I did, But I'll admit it took some time," said Jewel, coming over. "That one is a Sweet Serenity Azalea and—"

"Yes, an Azalea," he said, pointing to the one beside it. "And that's a Peperomia, and that's a Yellow Trumpet. The national flower of Nigeria."

"Wow, you really do know your plants," said Jewel, genuinely impressed by his knowledge of her plant life. "I don't really get many people over who know or care about plants as much as I do."

"I'm the same, it's not like most of the people I know are interested in the difference between Green Ears and Pinks Ears, so for the most part I tend not to bring it up unless—," Andrew squinted his eyes in confusion. "Is... is that a hammock?"

"Yes, I like to do my reading there."

"Wow," he said, standing back to his full height and gazing around the room. "You've really built your own little paradise here." He took a deep breath. "Even the air smells cleaner." He laughed. "You've made your own Garden of Eden."

"It's not much but—" said Jewel, standing back up and realizing how close she was to him. He was only an inch or two taller than her. But here, now, inside of her apartment, she began to feel a bit more self-conscious as looked slightly up into his eyes.

As if catching the feel of her looking at her. He turned and suddenly found himself looking back at her. The way he stared back down at her, looking into her eyes, began to make her take in a breath.

"Jewel? Did you hear me?"

"What? I'm sorry I was thinking... I was thinking about the flowers. What did you say?"

94

"I asked how you kept the plants alive. I mean, the Blanket Flower up there requires a warmer climate."

"Huh? Oh! The shelves, they're actually heated. Well, the top ones are. They heat the soil inside so and, in the wintertime, I place a glass case on top of them to trap the heat inside. The plants themselves never really feel it."

"This really is impressive. How did you learn to do all this?"

"Mostly by just watching videos on the internet. I killed a lot of plants before I got everything right."

Andrew laughed while walking around the room. "You really have put a lot of work into it. You've done a great job. Do you bring a lot of people up here just to show this off?" he asked, waving his hand around the room. "It's not often I get to step into a rainforest in the middle of the city."

"No, I don't really get much company. But if you want, you can stop by, and we can talk about plants. *Shit! Why did I say that? I'm not supposed to be flirting with him. Dammit Jewel, he came to see Sami. Are you the type of woman to try to take your friend's man?* She looked up again and saw his smiling face. *Well, they're not dating yet. He said he doesn't even have her number. Maybe she doesn't even like him.* "I mean, if you want. It's not like I have anyone else I can talk to like this," she said, wondering if the blush on her face was showing.

"I'd like that," he said, smiling back at her before looking over the room again. "I don't think this is a place I can stand just having to see once. But I mean... I know you were at the group date night. But are you sure there are no ex-boyfriends or occasional lover who might drop by when—"

"No, I'm single," she said faster and perhaps more anxiously than intended. "Really, you can stop by whenever."

"Okay. Well, if the invitation stands, can I have your number? I'd hate to drop by unannounced. I think I've learned my lesson about not asking people for their number before disappearing from their life."

Jewel rolled her eyes before walking over to the table. "I'm not disappearing." Then, reaching into her purse, she grabbed her phone so they both could exchange numbers. She then found herself feeling just a little bit jealous as she also gave him Sami's number. As they continued to converse, she found herself enjoying his company more than she'd expected. Speaking with him didn't feel awkward and the more they talked, the more comfortable around him she felt.

"I... should probably go now," said Andrew as his phone began to vibrate.

"Oh... yeah," said Jewel, regaining track on time and escorting him to the door.

He stepped outside, where he turned to face her again. "Thanks, I guess I'll see you around."

"Yeah. I think so. Oh, and thanks... for you know... helping me get those plants up here."

"Don't worry. Honestly, now, I'm kinda looking forward to seeing you again... I mean, seeing what you do with them."

Jewel felt her lips curl with the hit of a smile as she rubbed her tongue over the side of her teeth. "I'll try to think of something interesting," she said before closing the door. Once closed, she turned around, leaning her back against the frame, unable to wipe the now full smile off her face. Feeling a slight tickle in her chest, the ping of something exciting fueling the past moment, she took in a sigh of relief that was accompanied by the sound of his just so soft footsteps as they made their way down the hall outside.

I like him. I really think I like him. And he said he looked forward to seeing me again. He acted like it was a mistake, but I'm not sure it was. He thinks he's being cute. Okay, well... maybe he is cute.

She took in another breath to calm herself as she looked around the room and noticed her laptop sitting on the countertop. *This is the type of thing I'm supposed to write about, right?* She exhaled and bit down softly on her lip as she stared at it off screen before stepping over and turning it on. "Okay, I'm doing this. Oh, I'm really doing this."

CHAPTER 5

The moon was high in the sky. Sami sat at a table across from Patrick in an old diner near the outskirts of the city. Through the window, beyond her own reflection, she could see a dirt parking lot and more than a few old pickup trucks. Underneath the dim lights outside, men in denim outfits and baseball caps stood conversation out in the night air. The roar of quite a few motorcycles as they arrived seemed to vibrate the glass as a short-order cook slapped a bell, signaling another order was ready for pickup.

"I gotta admit, I didn't expect you to bring me here?" said Sami, as the smell of eggs and cooking meat drifted past her nose.

"I like to get out of the city sometimes and Willock back there makes the best egg and cheese sandwich in the city. I wanted you to try it."

"Egg and cheese sandwich? You brought me out here to

have an egg and cheese sandwich near the middle of the night? I admit, it's not how I imagined a first date would go."

"Well, I also have some other business to handle. But the food really is good. But why did you accept my offer, anyway? I mean, I never thought you'd take me seriously."

"So, you weren't really trying to take me out?"

"I never said that. I just... you know... never figured you'd go for it. You're kinda more of a princess type."

"Princess type? Am I not supposed to take offense to that?" said Sami as the plate of food was placed down before her and Patrick was served what looked like chopped meat and eggs. Although she wasn't sure what type of meat it was.

"Be offended later. Try it out and tell me what you think."

Sami frowned, but the scent of the food before her and the sight of the melting cheese on top were very convincing. Taking her knife, she cut into the bread and watched as the steamy cheese went spilling out over the plate. Whether it was because she hadn't eaten since early that day or because the meal really was enticing her, she couldn't tell. But after another cut with the knife, creating a little bread and cheese triangle, she stabbed the top of the golden-brown loaf, bringing it up to her mouth. With just the first bite, a rush of taste flowed into her. Instinctively, she moaned, closing her eyes, savoring the moment.

"Oh well, look, the princess likes it."

"Shoot up," said Sami with her mouth full. "I mean, shut up. Let me enjoy this."

Patrick couldn't help himself but to laugh as he stared at her with her mouth full and cheeks stuffed with food. "Just that face alone makes it worth it, bringing you out here."

"Why... why is it so good?" said Sami before stuffing her mouth with another piece.

"I honestly don't know," said Patrick, nodding to the kitchen. "He's been cooking like this since I used to hang out here in high school before my father would get home from work. He just always made the best food as long as I remember?"

"You used to—"

"Oh, he's here?" said Patrick, cutting her off and standing up from the table. "I'll be right back. I gotta go handle something. Enjoy the rest of your food."

Licking the golden sweetness from the side of her mouth, she watched Patrick leave the table and walk down the diner aisle. The sound of a jingle coming from the bell above the door as he swung the door open. She frowned a bit at his leaving, but turned back around, taking another bite of her eggs and cheese.

Feeling somewhat self-conscious about being left alone in a place she'd never visited before, she looked around. Everyone seemed to be normal working-class people she would see on the outskirts of the city. Baseball caps adorned most of the men's heads as the aroma of several cups of coffee managed to fill the cafe. Everything was as normal as it could be. Several patrons sat eating their food while a random sports announcer on a wall mounted TV narrated a game no one was paying any interest in.

Suddenly there was the sound of a small jingle and Sami's purse began to make a humming noise. Sami reached into her purse and pulled out her phone. Across the screen, she saw she had a text from an unknown number.

Sorry about our date night and my ex-girlfriend. I met your friend Jewel, and she gave me your number.

"What the..." Sami shook her head. "How did he meet Jewel?" She texted back: *It's fine. How are you doing?*

I'm great now, since I know I have the right number. I was afraid she had given me the number to a random guy named Bubba or something.

Sami smiled at the message. *Sorry. I'm not a guy named Bubba.*

Don't worry about it. I can't see myself kissing Bubba. But I suppose you'll do.

Sami shook her head, the smile still on her lips. "God,

this man's arrogant." Then across her phone came a picture of a heavy-bellied man with an orange beard in a trucker hat. "What the?"

FYI: This is my friend Bubba. If you know any ladies who like truckers. He's out here looking for love and asked that I set him up. And you know, since you said you help people with relationship problems.

Fully into the conversation, Sami placed her hands on her head as she stared down at her phone. She couldn't help but laugh a little as she texted back. *I'll see what I can do.*

Good. Then would it be okay to also plan another date with you? That way we can discuss Bubba's situation?

Wait. Did you really make all that up just to ask me out on another date?

What? Of course. Bubba is a real friend of mine, and I'm using his loneliness as an excuse to further my own love life.

You're a terrible friend.

But a great lover.

Sami bit her lip as she looked up at the ceiling and rolled her eyes. "This fool of a man."

After a moment, she heard the ding of a bell.

"Alright, grab that," said the waitress. "It's for table six."

The woman's words snapping Sami out of her own mind.

Her interest quickly fixated back on Patrick as she saw him outside of the window walking over to a truck where two men stood. The darkness outside masked a lot, so she couldn't make him out well, but with the gestures of his hands and the nods from the other man, she assumed it to be just another friendly conversation. That was until she saw Patrick reaching inside of his coat and pulling out some type of brown envelope, handing it to one of the men. He opened it, nodded his head to the other man, who then proceeded to give Patrick something that she couldn't see, before he stuffed it inside of his jacket.

And with another nod and perhaps some words, she watched as he turned around and headed back towards the diner. Sami then turned back to her phone and began texting: *I'm out with friends. Enjoy your night. Text me again sometime and we'll get together to talk about Bubba's problems.* She then stuffed her phone back into her purse.

Just as it announced his leaving, the jingle of the bell on the door announced his re-arrival into the diner as Patrick returned to Sami, taking his seat, before sipping from his cup.

"Okay, sorry about that. I have to meet up with a friend I asked to meet me out here," he said with his usual smile. Then came the Sami phone Jingle along with a buzzing of her phone vibrating again.

"Is that your phone?"

"Yeah, but it's just a message. Probably from work. I'll check it later."

"Okay," said Patrick, pointing towards her plate. "But, now that I'm back, you can thank me and tell me how good the food is."

"Fine, I'll admit that they are good," she said as her eyes glanced back outside the window for a moment. "But who did you talk to? You said it was a friend. Was it someone from work? Do you guys come here just for the eggs and cheese?"

"Something like that," he said as he stood from the table and reached his hand out to her. "Come here. I want to show you something."

"What, now? I still haven't finished my meal."

"I'll bring you back next time. Now come on. I promise it'll be worth it."

She raised a brow at him before taking another bite. Then, lifting from her seat and taking his hand, he led her back towards the kitchen.

"Matty, I'm heading upstairs."

"Alright sugar," said the waitress.

Upstairs? I didn't see any stairs, and this place did look like it had a second floor. The two went through the kitchen where two cooks were making their meals and not paying them any mind. *Did I not see a—.* Her thoughts paused, and she frowned as they stopped at an older metal ladder, its red paint from years ago chipping so much that she could see the rust beneath.

"Okay, up we go," he said as he took a good grip on the ladder, shaking it to see its stability. It shook more than she thought any ladder should, its metal clanking against the nuts and bolts that half haphazardly help it together.

"Up we go?" asked Sami, the disbelief clear in her voice. "You can't be serious."

He smiled at her before climbing a few steps of the ladder and then looking back down at her. "What, you don't trust me?"

"I trust you. I just don't trust that ladder."

"Don't worry, I've been climbing this thing all my life," he said after lifting the lid to the roof and making his way back down to stand before her. "It's as solid as I am."

Sami looked at the worn-out ladder, then back at him and his stupid smiling face before closing her eyes, shaking her head, and letting out a sigh. "If I fall, you better catch me."

"Always."

Placing a hesitant hand on the ladder, she stood in front of it. And with a deep breath in, she placed one foot forward and began making her way upward, one clanky shaky step at a time. Halfway up, she looked back down at him. He was still wearing that stupid smile.

Narrowing her eyes, she frowned. "Are you staring at my butt?"

"Always," he said again, with no hesitation.

She shook her head and continued up through the ceiling until she was up on the roof. From there she heard the ladder shaking and a few seconds later Patrick popped his head out to join her out in the cool night air.

"Why did you bring me up here?" asked Sami, as she

watched him come up.

"Turn around and look."

Sami turned around and saw the city from its outskirts. "It's pretty. But it's still not much to look at."

"Really? I thought you'd have more of a surprised reaction."

"Well, I mean, it's nice and all," she spotted two seats ahead near the edge of the roof overlooking the city. "You put those there for us? Did you mean bring me up here all along?"

"Nah, well actually, yes. To the second part, not the first. I mean, I didn't put those chairs there. Those chairs are always there. But I did have to ask Matty to not allow anyone up here so that I could use it for myself."

Sami smiled as she walked over, taking a seat in one of the chairs. "Well, come on. We can talk while we sit down, and I can look over the pretty lights of the city."

"So, you do admit it's pretty," he said, taking his seat beside her. "I thought you said you weren't impressed."

"I'm not. But that doesn't mean that I don't appreciate it. And that doesn't stop it from being pretty to look at either."

"That's funny. I was thinking the same thing about you."

"Really?" asked Sami, giving him a raised brow and a smirk. "That's the line you're going to go with?"

"I thought it was a good line. I mean, you are a beautiful woman."

"You're saying I don't impress you, then?"

"No, I'm saying I'm trying to impress you. How am I doing?"

"Not bad. But you could do better."

"I'll try to keep up, but I'm curious. Why did you finally decide to go out with me? Did something change?"

"A few things. When I saw you in the store, I just figured, why not?" She kicked out legs and extended her arms, stretching out in the chair. "My mother always said there's nothing better than a man who brings in the groceries."

Patrick laughed, "I find it hard believing your mother actually said that."

"You've never met my mother. She has more than a few odd sayings. The sad part is that the older I get, the more I see that she's right."

"Well then, I hope to meet her one day."

"I think we're a long way from that. I've never brought anyone home to meet my mother before."

"Really? Afraid to show off to any man you like."

"It's more like I'm saving them from her and the millions of questions she'd ask. What about you?" asked Sami as she reached down, picking up a rock that was oddly on the rooftop. "You bring any girls home to mom?"

"I would, but my mother passed when I was little."

"Oh... sorry."

"Don't worry. My pops did a good enough job. He's the reason I learned to work on machines. He was a mechanic."

"So, both of you spend your days going around fixing things? I think that might be—"

Breaking up their small talk, they heard the bell to the dinner door shake violently, followed by the sound of an angry voice. "Take your ass home, Jimmy," came the voice of a man from below.

Sami looked confused before turning around to see a saddened and somewhat annoyed Patrick let out a sigh. He then stood up, beginning to walk over to the side of the roof. Reactively, she stood, following behind him as the sound of shouting started growing louder from beyond the edge. Down below, she saw two men arguing loudly as a small crowd gathered around.

"Say that again, I dare ya?"

"I said she don't love ya. Mattie's mine. You need to leave her alone?"

"Alone?" shouted the man in the denim cap. "She's my wife."

"She don't love you anymore. Why can't you get that

through your thick skull?"

"Ahh, it's nice to see the boys having fun again," said Patrick, resting his arms on the roof of the building.

"Having fun?" asked Sami, confused. "What do you mean? Shouldn't someone stop them?"

"What?" Those two? Nah, they do this song and dance every year or so. That girl Mattie's been stringing them both along for about ten years now. She got another set of boys fighting over her about fifty miles down the road.

"Really? Then why are they fighting over her?"

"Oh, they aren't fighting over her as much as they're just looking for a reason to fight. It's best to just let them get it out of their system." With a knock on the side of the roof and a smile, he turned to her. "Hey, you're writing that romance blog stuff, right? Maybe you can interview Mattie. I'm sure she has a bunch of stories to tell."

"No thanks. Wait! You read my articles."

"I've only ever read it once. Not really my thing, but I heard the company's got that black sheep, white sheep thing going on. Figured some of Matties' stories might make for a good read."

"Oh!" said Sami, biting the side of her lip. "Yeah. I heard about that. Everyone in the office is talking about the black and white sheep stuff. What... what do you think about it?"

"I don't know. People seem to be enjoying it. I guess that's all that's important."

Oh, thank goodness he doesn't read it. I'd hate to have to explain writing about tonight. "Yeah. Everyone in the office is trying to figure out who it's supposed to be? Addison's been keeping it hush-hush. They haven't told me anything. For all I know, it could be Lan Ling."

Patrick started laughing. "I'd pay good money to see that. I met her husband once. There's no way it's her."

"Wait! Really? He actually exists? I always thought she made him up."

"Yeah, but he seemed to be more of a relaxed guy,"

said Patrick with a grimace, after watching the man with the denim hat take a hit so hard that it flew off his head. "Dammit Jeffery, you're always falling for that right hook. Dodge man, or else you're going to lose what few teeth you got left."

"What are you doing?" asked Sami, a bit of nervousness coming over here as Patrick garnered the men's attention from down below.

"Shut up!" yelled Jeffery towards them as he picked himself up off the ground. "You stay your ass up there and watch."

From their vantage point above, they saw him turn back to the man with his hands raised and step back in to fight. Unlike before, he wasn't knocked to the ground, but instead he dodged a punch before driving his fist into the other man's stomach and quickly following back up with a punch that landed square on the chin.

Sami clenched her teeth as the two men started exchanging blows back and forth as the small crowd cheered them on. "Is Mattie really worth all of this?"

"To them she is. And that's all that matters."

And after a final exchange of blows, Jeffery stood bloodied, bruised, but also victorious. He then walked over and reached down, picking up his denim hat off the ground, dusted it off on his knee, and placed it back on his head.

"And the next time I catch your ass around my Mattie again, you're gonna get the same ass whooping you just got," he said before walking off through the crowd, receiving celebratory pats on the back from the onlookers.

"Well, that's good," said Patrick as he turned and began walking back to his seat. "At least he knows there will be a next time."

"Is this normally how your dates go?" asked Sami, shaking her head. "Rooftops and parking lot fights?"

"Don't forget the eggs and cheese," said Patrick as he turned around with a smile. "I couldn't think of a more perfect ending."

Sami just shook her head, unable to hide her own smile as she looked over at Patrick. His arms out wide as the glowing lights of the city sparkled behind him. It gave off a pleasant look, as if the night was lighting up especially for him. And his smile wasn't so bad either."

"Come on, maintenance man. It's time to take me home. I need to be ready for work tomorrow," said Sami as she headed back over to the ladder.

"And here I thought we'd stay up here and be kissy-faced," he said as he walked over, talking to her by the hand as she lowered herself down. "You know, spice it up a bit and give you something to write about for your next article."

"Oh, shut up. I don't usually write about my dates. I mostly just give advice. Such as what to do when you're on a date with a man who smells like dirt and oil."

Patrick frowned. "Do I really smell like that? I took a shower before coming here."

"A little. It's not really a bad thing. But maybe next time, try to clean up a bit more."

"Next time? Does that mean you wouldn't mind going out with me again?"

"Wipe that stupid smile off your face and just help me down."

CHAPTER 6

A few days later, Sami arrived by taxi at her office building.

"Keep the change," she said, handing the driver a few bills and walking towards the door. Feeling the nip of the chilly morning air against her stockings, she shivered a bit as she looked up ahead. The morning crowd was there as the revolving door spun on its constant morning rotation. Groups of men and women in dress skirts, suits and ties entered for their daily grind; their pressed shoes and high heels clomping on the concrete walkway, sounding like a small constant clapping.

The celebration of having a job, thought Sami as she joined in with the morning herd. Inside its stone and glass walls, she saw the smiling face of Becca with her arms wrapped around a man that seemed somewhat familiar to her.

"Oh, Sami," said Becca, spotting her, then waving for

her to come over. "Good, you're right on time."

"Am I?" asked Sami, coming over to her friend. "I feel like I might be interrupting." She couldn't help but notice the fairly expensive dress and white coat that her friend was wearing.

"Nonsense," said Becca. "Here, I want to introduce you to my friend David. I don't think you both got the chance to meet during our speed dating night."

Oh, the candy man. "Ah, yes. Thank you for treating us and allowing me to fly over the city."

"No problem," said David, not letting go of his hold on Becca. "I'm happy you enjoyed it."

"David here has invited us out on another getaway for wine tasting this weekend. I wanted to ask if you and Jewel would come."

"This weekend? I'm not…"

"Yes. I think I remember hearing that you hit it off with my friend Andrew."

"Yes, I had such a fun time that night. Especially the part when his ex-girlfriend, or wife, or whatever she was, came in and tried to fight me?"

"Yeah, I heard about that. That was Macy. He felt really bad about that. He would be here himself, but I'm having him run an errand for me. He's a good guy, honestly. He asked me to invite you along so that you both can have a proper date. You know, one without the crazy ex-girlfriend."

"Come one Sami," said Becca with a smile and raised brow as she nodded towards David. "It'll be so much fun if us girls go together."

Sami looked back and forth at the hopeful faces of the couple before them and sighed, giving in. "Fine," she said before stepping over and taking Becca by the hand. "We should be going. We have work to do."

"I understand," said David as he reached into his pocket, pulling out a piece of hard candy. He then unwrapped it, placing it between his fingers and lifting it to Becca's lips.

Without hesitation, she opened her mouth, taking the candy between her lips deep enough that she also took in her finger. She sucked on it just slightly and only for a moment before pulling away.

"Now you go and play at your job," said Becca before taking Sami's arm in hers. "Us girls have work to do." She then took a stunned faced Sami away and headed towards the elevator.

"Really?" asked Sami as Becca pressed the button and the elevator doors opened for her to step in. "Did you really just let him feed you and then start sucking his finger? "

"Oh please," said Becca, taking the candy from her mouth. "That's hardly the only piece of him I've had in my mouth. And the other one is much bigger."

"Becca, really?"

"Don't Becca really, me. David and I have a good thing going. And he's not really so bad after you get used to his few quirks. He's actually really romantic in his own way."

"What you just did didn't seem romantic. It was more sexual and somewhat manipulative."

"If a woman isn't manipulating her man, can you even call her a woman?"

"So, he's your man already? It's barely been a week."

"Really Sami, if you don't start having some fun, then you're going to end up like our poor Jewel, wearing pant outfits and sleeveless vests or, God forbid, end up like Lan Ling. When was the last time you had sex, anyway?"

"That doesn't matter."

"Mhmm, that's what you say now. What about that last boyfriend you had, the one who dumped you?"

"No, he didn't, and no, we didn't."

"Good, then you're coming on this date with me. I'll get Jewel to join as well. I'm sure she can drug up a man from somewhere," she said as the elevator stopped on their floor. "Come on now, let's get to work. At least for the moment, I still need to have a job."

Sami could only shake her head in dismay as a confident Becca strolled out of the elevator with her oversized coat, heading over to Jewel's desk. As Sami sat behind her own desk, she couldn't help but feel a bit jealous of Becca. *Am I the weird one? Maybe Becca should be the one going after the job. How does she just do things without even a care in the world?* Sami thought about the Candyman popping a piece of candy in her mouth and suddenly a shiver went down her spine. *No, it's Becca. She's definitely the weird one.* These thoughts were quickly solidified as she watched the hesitation and perhaps a little bit of fear in Jewel's face, as she assumed Becca was now asking her on another girl's trip.

Jewel's probably going to give in and go. She sighed again, rolling her eyes in her head. *I guess I should go too. It will be something else to write about after all. And it's not like me and Patrick are a couple or anything. We only went on one date. But I did promise to see him this weekend also.* Sami began shaking her head. *This might become annoying. Am I really the type to date two people at the same time?*

As if on cue for her thoughts, a set of hands tapped themselves on her desk. Sami looked up to see her boss Addison looking at her.

"Is everything okay?"

"Huh?" said Sami, a little startled. Her boss had never come by her desk before. Usually, she just calls her into her office.

"Your article. I'm asking if everything is going well. You haven't updated your account, and the deadline is this weekend, and the design department is saying you haven't submitted anything yet."

"Oh, yeah, sorry. I've just been busy, is all."

"Well, don't fall behind," said Addison as she put on her shades and started to leave. "This is a good opportunity for both of you. I'd hate to see you waste it."

"Wait," said Sami, stooping Addison before she could go.

"Yes?"

"Can... can I ask for your advice on something? It's about dating."

Addison looked at her for a moment before sighing and taking off her glasses again, placing her bag on Sami's desk. "Fine, I can see you're not too confident right now. Okay, tell me what the problem is?"

"When you found your husband. How did you know he was the one?"

"What?" asked Addison with a smirk before nonchalantly waving her shades between her fingers. "I'll give you a bit of advice, Sami. There is no 'the one.' There is only the one 'You Want.' I met my husband in college and decided that I wanted him. So, I hung around him till I was sure and then I fucked him when I was."

Sami's face turned to shock at the statement. *This woman is like Becca. I'm wasting my time asking her for advice.*

As if seeing the disbelief on her face, Addison sighed. "Honey, you really think too highly of life. Most men can be happy for months with just a sports game on the TV. And most of them don't have some grand plan for who they end up with. You fuck them enough so that they don't go off and fuck someone else, and that's half of their little lives right there. Trust me, women are hundreds of times more complicated."

"Wait," said Sami, catching on to her words. "Have you dated women before?"

"Oh, I guess I did let that slip," said Addison, her smile spreading further across her lips. "I did... once. Maybe I still would if she'd be up for it. But then again, I was far wilder in my younger days." She laughed.

You seem pretty wild now. "What about your husband? I mean, you have a child together. Does he know?"

Addison looked off as in her own world. "Oh, I do wonder what he would do if he did know. And even then, if he knew who it was with." Her tongue slid across her lips.

"Maybe I should give her a call."

Sami was confused, and a little surprised at the mischievous glee on her boss's face, and she thought back to a time of her past. *Okay, I definitely asked the wrong person.* "Ahh, thank you. I'll try to think about what to do."

"Oh… yes, we were talking about your problems, weren't we?" She put back on her glasses. "Yours is simple. I told you before, date whoever you like. It's not like you have to fuck them all. Just date them until you find one you like. Then fuck him. That seems to be more your speed, after all. Anyway, I'm off to my appointment. Have fun mulling that over." Grabbing her purse and placing it under her arm, she started to walk away towards the elevator. "Oh, and Becca, that coat looks disgusting," she said as she headed for the elevator, leaving a stunned-faced Becca looking over her outfit before heading back to her desk.

She has to be doing that on purpose. There is no way she's saying all this without trying to mess with our heads. But… she looked over at the now uncertain Becca. *That coat really is ugly.*

Taking a deep breath and trying to clear her mind to be productive, she began looking over the upcoming and recent articles for inspiration. On her work desk, she could see who all had already submitted their articles for the upcoming week for the website. *Lan Ling is already done, but she's always done early. But at least Jewel hasn't submitted her article yet.*

Sami took a bit of solace in knowing that she wasn't the only one in the situation having issues with the stupid contest they were in. She looked ahead, seeing Jewel with her head down, looking at her PC. *I'm not going to lose. I want this job more than you.*

In the midst of her thoughts came a vibrating sound and a chiming noise coming from her purse. Reaching in, she removed her phone, opening it to see a message from Jamal.

"Can you come see me? I'm in my office."

"Why," she texted back.

"I have a favor to ask."

She narrowed her eyes at the phone. *"It's not anything stupid, is it?"*

"I promise I'll make it up to you."

As she continued to look down at her phone, she felt her annoyance rise. But after taking a moment, she stood up from her desk and headed back towards the elevator. Stepping inside, she pressed the button for the fiftieth floor and headed up to see her old babysitter.

It's always something stupid with him, she thought as the humming of the elevator filled the surrounding air, before it finally lurched at its destination. She stepped off, walking over into the office area. The environment on the fifteenth floor was much busier than her workplace. Men in fancy suits sat at their desks arguing with whomever they were on the phone with. Or they stood arguing with each other, all huddled over by a computer monitor as some numbers that she really couldn't care less about flashed over the screen. A few of the men noticed her, some giving her a friendly wave or a nod, while others wore a smile that seemed to suggest something she herself wasn't aware of, but she could hazard a guess.

Still, she made her way through their working area until she came to a glass office similar to the one Addison had. Inside sat Jamal at his desk, seemingly talking to someone over the speaker. In front of him sat a younger woman in a dress skirt and blouse. The slit of the blouse coming up her thigh was so high that Sami thought she could see the side of her underwear.

He waved her in, and she opened the door.

"What do you want?" she asked as she opened the door.

"Come in, come in," said Jamal. "Hey, Steve, I'll have to call you back. Someone's here to see me." He then hung up the phone before the person on the end had a chance to respond.

"Really? Is that how you treat your clients?"

"He wasn't a client. Just a friend from out of town. Anyway, come in." He turned to the woman in front of him. "Maddie, can you give us a moment? I need to bother my friend with a personal request."

"Okay," said the woman, taking her laptop from his desk, then standing to leave. "Hey there, I'm Maddie. I love your outfit. It looks really cute on you."

"Ah... thank you," said Sami, a little taken aback by the friendliness.

"He's told me about you. Did you two really used to wrestle with each other? He said he used to let you win, just so he could have you sitting on top of him."

Sami frowned as she leaned over, looking past Maddie at Jamal, who was purposely avoiding her gaze.

"Bye, bye, Maddie," said Jamal, trying to halt their conversation. "Come back later, and then we can talk about spreading rumors in the office."

"Oh, it seems I've made my boss mad," she pointed a finger outside the glass as she smiled at Sami. "I guess I should go now."

"Close the door. Come take a seat," said Jamal, as Maddie left, gesturing to the seat the woman was in before.

Sami narrowed her eyes again, but did as he asked, closing the door and stepping forward, having a seat. "Really? You told her you used to let me win?"

"I mean, I did."

"I was better than you."

"Yes, you were, and after I realized that, I decided to let you win."

Rubbing at her eyes, trying to fight back the frustration, took in a deep breath, "Why did you even call me up here?"

"I have a favor to ask you."

"What? And stop looking at me with that big dumb expression on your face. You always want something
116

stupid. And before you ask, I'm not babysitting for any of you stupid, rich friends again."

"What? No? I wouldn't ask you to do that again. And I apologized. I even paid for your hairdresser for six months after what happened."

"I wore a wig for a year after that."

"Okay, then I owe you some money. But that's no reason to look at me like that."

Sami looked at the big stupid face of his and could feel her annoyance towards him slipping. So she closed her eyes and took another deep breath. "Look, just tell me why I'm here, so I can just tell you no and go back to—"

"I need you to pretend to be my girlfriend this weekend."

There was a moment of silence in the air as she stared at him and he stared at her, waiting for a response. She felt like she should say something, but the words wouldn't form in her mind. She could feel the side of her mouth twitch as if she was going to speak. But still no words. She then raised a finger, her mouth opened, but again, no words would come out. She turned her head, closing her eyes, searching her mind, trying to find the proper things to say, but at the moment her thoughts became silent. So, unable to find words, no matter how much she tried. She slowly stood, pressed her hands on her skirt up and ran for the door. But the moment she opened it a bit, she saw Jamal's hand push past her face, closing it as she then turned around to see him standing inches away from her, his arm on either side trapping her between them as he stared down at her.

"Come on, at least hear me out."

"What are you doing? Let me out. How do you think this looks to everyone else here on this floor? They can see us, you know."

"Don't worry. Most aren't really paying attention. And the ones that are already think we're messing around, so it's fine."

"What! No, it's not fine for me. And I bet you're not even

trying to tell them that we aren't together."

"Well, no. I mean, what would be the point? You're cute, so I figured it couldn't hurt to have them think that."

"Oh my God, you jackass."

"Hey, don't be like that," he said, pleading, trying to soothe her temper. "Come on. Don't we always help each other? Isn't that what friends do?"

"And do friends let rumors go around, having others think that we're still sleeping together?"

"Sometimes, like when I might need to make some of the other guys jealous during the holidays parties."

"You are disgusting," said Sami, pushing him away. "I have no idea why I even deal with you."

Jamal stepped back with his hands up, still wearing that innocent, dumb smile. "Come on, Little Sami, my sweet baby cakes. Am I going to have to call your mother and tell her about that last boyfriend you had? Didn't he get arrested for public exposure?"

"Ah!" said Sami with eyes wide. "You wouldn't dare. You promised you wouldn't bring that up."

"I'm desperate. I need to fight dirty."

"The answer is still no. I won't be blackmailed into going along with one of your stupid ideas."

"I'll pay your rent for the next month."

Instantly, Sami felt a knot inside her throat as she bit the side of her lip.

"Oh!" said Jamal, stepping back to her, catching on to her hesitation. "And at least two times a week. I'll show up to cook for you. When I was over there, I couldn't help but notice how empty your fridge was. You've been eating out of the microwave again, haven't you?" He leaned in close. "How long has it been since you've had a home cooked meal?"

"That's none of your business. You need to stop showing up at my place drunk, anyway."

"If I tell your mother how you've been eating. She'll

show up and you won't be able to get rid of her for a month."

"Oh yeah. What about if I tell your mother about what you've been getting into?"

"Really?" said Jamal, a smirk coming over his lips. "Are we really going to pretend like my mother has ever been proud of me? At this point, she's probably just happy I'm not a crackhead."

"Damn," said Sami, turning her head and biting her lip. "You're right. Why couldn't you just be normal?"

"See, you have no choice. Now give in or I swear I'll start tickling you right here in this office."

She saw his fingers lowering toward her stomach, wiggling in a silly and suggestive motion. Quickly she grabbed his hands by the wrist, trying to hold him in place, before quickly glancing through the glass window around the office.

"Stop that. I'm not five anymore."

"Will you help me, or will I have to embarrass Little Sami and myself? Because you already know what I'll do to get what I want."

"Argh! Fine, but you're paying for two months' rent."

"Deal."

"And buy me two new outfits."

"No problem."

"And you have to stop calling me Little Sami."

Jamal just stared at her for a moment, not speaking.

"Really? That's what you get hung up on?"

"I mean… it's kinda a hard habit to break."

"Say, or I swear I won't do it?"

Jamal sighed, "Fine. I won't call you Little Sami anymore."

"Good. Then what time do I have to be there? I have another date that night. I promised Becca earlier I'd be there."

"That's fine. It'll be from morning to mid-day. That'll give you plenty of time. Thanks for this, you're a lifesaver."

"Can I go now? Or do you have some other type of scheme you want to try to involve me in?"

Jamal stepped past her, opening up the door. "You're free to go, my lady."

A frown on her face, she walked past him. "Idiot."

"Oh, and wear something sporty."

She turned back to him while still heading toward the elevator, just to raise a middle finger to him. Slamming the elevator button with her hand, she stepped inside, the annoyance clear in the reflection of the door as it closed in on her.

Great. Now what else am I going to have to deal with?

Jewel sat at her desk, looking down at a black screen.

I can't believe I'm doing it again. Why did I say yes? I should have said no. She's been sitting there for a few minutes, just staring off into space. *No, I know why I said it. It's because I have no life. The only man that's been to my apartment was a man looking for another woman. And that woman is the one I'm competing against for the job.*

And as if the thought of Sami brought about her appearance. Jewel watched the elevator open as her friend stepped out, headed towards her desk. The look on her face didn't seem like she was having a good time. She watched as Sami threw her purse on the table, and sat down in her chair, placing her hands to her face, covering her eyes.

Why is she always the one who has men fawning over? I mean, it's not like I'm unattractive. Okay, yes, I'm tall. But so what? Most models are tall. She looked into a small mirror on her desk, checking her features. *I mean, I have model features, right? I have cheekbones.* She took another look at Sami, trying to compare. *Why do men like smaller women, anyway? They probably think of them as like cute pets. Something they can pat on the head and give treats to.* She shook her head.
120

No... no, stop thinking like this. It's unhealthy. I need to focus on my work.

Trying to redirect her mind, she began looking around the office before finally focusing in on Addison's empty office. She just stared at it for a moment before grabbing some random papers from her desk, stood up, and walked towards it. Not wanting to be noticed, she walked over to the paper shredder nearest the office and began inserting the sheets slowly, one at a time, as she stared into the office.

She began imagining herself in that seat, being the head of the company. She could see herself doing it. Sitting in that black leather seat, holding million-dollar meetings, and then turning around to see the landscape of the city stretched out before her. *Okay, so maybe I'm not as outspoken as Addison. But I could be a CEO. I could be popular. I mean, I was writing about plants just a few weeks ago. Now I'm in a story the whole city is talking about. I just need to—*

"Jewel... Jewel," said Lan Ling in a tone that snapped her out of her daydreaming.

"Who, what?" asked Jewel, startled by the woman's approach as she turned to face her. "Sorry, what was that?"

"The paper shredder. Are you done? I want to use it."

Jewel looked down to see her hands empty, not realizing she was out of paper. "Oh, yeah, sorry. I was daydreaming."

"I see," said Lan Ling with a raised brow as she stepped in front of her and began shredding her own documents. "What's got you looking so worried? Oh, are you worried about Becca's party because you have no man?"

"What? No?" She looked around the office to see who had heard Lan Ling. But seeing that no one was paying attention to them, she turned back around with a sigh. "Okay maybe, but..." She looked down at the smaller woman, curious. "Lan Ling."

"Yes?"

"Do... do you think I'm attractive?"

Lan Ling just looked up at her for a moment before

squinting her eyes at her. "Jewel, I'm married. I can't date girls. Are you really that lonely?"

"That's not—"

Lan Ling raised a hand to her chin, looking her over. "But maybe if my husband likes you, we can have a threesome. He might like tall white women."

"What?" asked Jewel, confused.

"What?" asked Lang Ling.

"What are you talking about?"

Lan Ling looked in her face for a moment before smiling back. "I'm just joking. You really are silly." She coughed. "Now, why did you ask if I thought you were pretty?"

"It's just... you know. Sami gets a lot of attention and, well..."

"And you don't," said Lan Ling, understanding. "So, you are lonely then."

"Okay fine. I'm a little lonely. Is that so bad?" asked Jewel, before having a realization. "Wait, how did you know about Becca's party? Were you invited?"

"No. But Becca has a big mouth and likes to brag," said Lan Ling with a shrug. "She is already planning her baby's name with the candy-husband. Bragging about how she will run away from here and become a millionaire."

"Of course she was," said Jewel, shaking her head as she began rubbing her eyes in frustration. "Apparently everyone here has some grand plan except for me." She patted Lan Ling on the shoulder. "It's fine. Thanks for talking to me Lan Ling. I think I'm done for the day. I'll do the rest of my work from home."

"Okay, see you tomorrow."

Jewel then headed back to her desk, unable to help herself from looking over at Sami, who was now talking on the phone to someone.

Probably another guy. Well, I can meet someone too. I still have a few days until the party. She walked over to her desk, shut down her computer, and grabbed her bag.

Upon touching it, it lit up showing that she had a message. Looking at it, she saw it was from Andrew. He had sent her two pictures of plants and the text: "Tell me their names. Don't look them up."

Recognizing the two plants easily, Jewel smiled. Her loneliness not so apparent anymore, she texted back: "The first one is a Cacao. The second is a Bromeliad."

"Okay, you're good." He texted back a few seconds later.

"Or maybe you don't challenge me?"

"Oh! is that how it is? Okay, you're on."

He sent two more pictures and both she guessed with no issue. "I thought this was going to be hard. But it's kind of easy." She could tell that all the pictures of plants were in the same place because of the background and the lighting. *Is he in a plant store?*

"Okay then, big mouth. What about this?"

Then another picture came and Jewel had to admit she'd never seen it before. *It has red leaves and prickles, so maybe it's a tropical plant like the ones before.*

"You're taking too long," he texted her while she was pondering. "Have I stumped the great plant detective?"

Jewel frowned. But looking at his little emojis of a smiling face with a detective hat made her smile afterwards. "Okay, you win. I admit I don't know that one."

"It's a Heliconia Flower. I'll be adding it to my collection in about a month."

"I'm jealous. Can I sex you when it arrives?" She then pressed the button to send and waited for his response. When his response didn't come as fast as before, she felt a bit confused until reading over her last message. "Oh, no. I mean, can I see you when it arrives?" She quickly pressed send. Then realized what she typed again. "See it! I want to see IT." *Oh god, what am I doing?*

There was a long pause before another message from him came through. But it was only one word. "Yes."

Yes? Yes, to what? Stupid phone keyboard. She started

to type again, but couldn't figure out what to say. She just stared at his last text. The word 'Yes', teasing the thoughts in her mind of a possibility she shouldn't think of.

To prevent her mind from taking control of her. She stood up from her desk in a hurry and finished packing her things before hurriedly heading towards the elevator. *Don't think about it, Jewel. That 'Yes' was definitely about him showing you the flower. He understood there wasn't anything sexual about it. He's dating Sami. It was just a funny auto-correct moment. When we see each other next time, we'll just laugh about it.*

While waiting, she couldn't help but stare at her phone one last time. Reading the words 'Can I sex you', it was like the words were jumping off the screen at her. Shaking her head, she closed her phone and stuffed it in her purse. *No Jewel. Don't think like this.* She was grateful when the ding of the elevator came and the doors opened. Stepping inside, another man greeted her.

"Which floor?" said the man.

"Oh," said Jewel as she unlocked her phone. "First, please."

"Yes Ma`am," said the man, pressing the button, before turning to her. "Ahh, excuse me."

"Yes," said Jewel, sure as the doors closed, turning to actually look at the man for the first time. To her surprise, he was actually a very attractive man who seemed of middle eastern descent. He wore a dark blue suit. His eyes were green, and he had the stubble of a few days' old beard. He was instantly attractive to her, and she couldn't help but notice, taller than her as well.

"Ahhh, then you must be Jewel," he said. "I thought you looked familiar."

"What? How do you... oh no. The delivery man, again."

"The who?"

"I'm sorry," said Jewel, shaking her head and running her hand through her hair. "But... but how exactly do you know me?"

"From your articles. You work for Lavish magazine, right? You write about the plants."

"What?" said Jewel, surprised. "That... that's right." *Wait, seriously. Is he a plant guy? There's no way I can meet two plant guys this fast. Did I win the lottery?* She looked him over again, noticing he was wearing gloves. "I'm sorry. What was your name?"

"I'm Nasir."

"Nasir, that's an interesting name."

"My mother certainly thought so," he said with a smile. "I sometimes sit down and read your articles. I wasn't much of a vegetation fan, but your writing, I find it relaxing."

"Oh, really?" said Jewel with a genuine smile. *Okay, this isn't so bad. And he's cute.* "Do you live in the city, or are you just visiting?" *Wait, he said he didn't care about plants until my article? Oh, please don't be a crazy stalker.*

"No, I'm just visiting. I had some business to take care of upstairs. I know a few people who work in this building."

Yes, not stalker, confirmed. "I could show you around if you like. I mean, if you're okay with that. There are plenty of places in the city to go." *Thank God you showed up. You are the perfect thing I need to take my mind off those stupid text messages. A normal conversation between adults.*

"I would love that. My daughter has been begging me to show her around."

"Oh... you have a daughter?" said Jewel, maintaining her smile. *Okay, one kid isn't such a big deal. And he seems like the type who is caring,* "How old is she?"

"She's eight now. She's been a little sad being cooped up in her mother's apartment here. But that's what I get for marrying a work-a-holic," said Nasir, before perhaps noticing a change in Jewel's demeanor when he mentioned his wife. "Oh, I'm sorry. I should have mentioned I was married. I don't want to give off the wrong impression."

"What? No, of course not. I was just being friendly."

Damn, of course he's married. Just look at him. But that's fine. I'll just back off and pretend this never happened. "But are you sure your wife won't mind me walking around the city with you? I don't want to think I'm trying to steal you away or anything."

Nasir just started laughing. "If anything, she'd be overjoyed, or at the very least, interested."

No, you were supposed to say your wife would mind. What wife would be okay with her husband and her child out with another woman? "Really! Oh, great," said Jewel, struggling a fair amount to keep up her smile. "I guess it's okay then." *Wait? Did he just say his wife would be interested?*

"Thank you," said Nasir, pulling out his phone. "Let me have your number and I will call you in a day or two if that's ok with you."

"Sure," said Jewel. *This is not how adultery starts. I am not an adulterer. I'm just taking this man and his daughter sightseeing. That's what normal people do, right?*

After exiting the elevator, the two exchanged numbers before heading for the outside of the building into the chilly air of the city. Making their way down the steps, Nasir hailed a cab, opening the door for her when it arrived.

She then sat inside as he closed the door, and the cab took off.

Her mind mulling over what just happened, Jewel slumped in her seat. *What am I doing? And am I this stupid? Am I this desperate for a man that I'm seriously going out on a date with a married man and his daughter?*

"Hey there, you alright," said the cab driver. "You're looking a little down in the dumps?"

"No, I'm fine. Can you take me to Taylor and Mayvon."

"Sure, no problem," she said as she turned the vehicle in the next lane over. "So what? You having guy troubles? That dude you just left didn't seem so down. He your boyfriend?"

"No, he's not. He's married."

"Oh, I get it, and you're the mistress, right? Let me

guess, he's claiming he's going to leave her for you, right? Yeah, I've been there before. Word of advice, honey, move on. Or just have your fun and then move on. But don't trust a word they say."

"What? No? It's not like that?"

"Emhmm," moaned the driver. "Whatever you say, honey. Just giving some friendly advice is all, cause you know. You're looking a bit sad, is all."

"I'm fine," said Jewel as she stared out the window, watching the buildings go by. "It really isn't like that."

But the driver wasn't really listening to her denial anymore. Instead, she turned on the radio. "Let's listen to something to take your mind off things." There was a bit of static that came over the speaker until finally a disk jockey's voice came on.

"I don't know, Michelle," said the Disk jockey. *"What do you think of this black sheep white sheep game? These women competing against each other for some grand prize."*

"I don't see anything wrong with it," said the woman over the radio. *"I mean, if these girls are going to be out here dating anyway, they might as well try to get something for it. "*

"You make it sound like these women are doing these men a favor just by going with them."

"I mean, if the shoe fits."

"Oh, that's cold. You know what, I think you're a man hater."

"Look, did you even read the article? The white sheep apparently got into a fight on her date. And the black sheep almost got shot. I know if I'm getting shot at, it's because I'm trying to rob a bank, not because I'm just trying to get to know a brotha, okay?"

"Well, I don't like it. These women are essentially just toying with these men's feelings, just so they win some money or whatever the prize is."

"You're just jealous you aren't dating them. I've seen the woman you've dated and there certainly are a lot of black sheep

in your closet. Remember old Bucktooth Becky with the one eye?"

"Hey, hey, hey... We don't bring that up, okay?"

The sound of laughter poured over the radio from the people in the radio station.

"Okay callers, why don't you call in and tell us what you think is going to happen? We are going to receive our update of the black sheep white sheep content next Monday morning, so why don't you all call us at five five five sixty-nine sixty-nine and let us know who you want to win."

"What about you, huh?" asked the cab driver. "What do you think about the black sheep, white sheep thing?"

"I'm hoping for the black sheep," said Jewel honestly. *I'm the one everyone is talking about. But it's not like I can just come out and say, hey I work for 'such-and-such' magazine and I'm the one trying to lead guys on so I can continue to pay my rent next month.*

"Oh, me two. I'm team Black Sheep."

"Team Black Sheep?"

"Yeah, that's what the girls on Flick Tok are calling themselves."

"What?" said Jewel as she pulled out her phone and turned on the app, typing Black Sheep into the search bar. Instantly her page was filled with girls wearing black T-shirts, talking about why they like the girl in the magazine. Out of curiosity, she typed in the White Sheep into the search bar and for just as many people supporting Sami.

"You didn't know about this? Have you been hiding under a rock the last week or two?"

"I... I've been busy. I mean, I saw them mention it on the TV. But I didn't..." *Oh God. Does Sami know about this?*

CHAPTER 7

Sami sat on a park bench overlooking a small lake as a few children stood off in the distance, throwing bread-crumbs into a flock of eager ducks. It was a nice morning out and she was dressed casually in a sundress for a nice day.

"Hey," said Andrew as he walked up. "Sorry if I kept you waiting."

"No," said Sami. "I got here early on purpose so that I could just relax for a bit." She pointed towards the lake. "They're fun to watch."

"The kids or the ducks?"

"Both."

"You know, some people spend all day watching people on these benches," he said, taking a seat beside her. "It's kind of their hobby."

"I haven't gotten to the point where I'd say it's a hobby,"

said Sami, turning towards him. "So why invite me out to a park? Do you exes only come out at night, like vampires?"

Andrew laughed while shaking his head. "You're not going to let me live that down, are you?"

"Never," said Sami with a smile and a roll of her eyes. "I don't usually give men another shot after a first date that bad."

"Oh?" said Andrew, leaning on the bench and staring into her eyes. "And what makes me so different?"

"A few things. One being you're a good texter. You seem genuine and funny."

"Yes, I can understand, since I am those things."

"But," said Sami as she raised a finger and sucked on her lips. "You might be just a little too arrogant for my taste. I'm still trying to figure that out."

"Well then," said Andrew, standing up from the bench and extending his hand to Sami. "How about we start our real first date? And you get to see who I am."

Taking his hand, Sami stood up from the bench and they started walking down the path together. "Alright then."

"So," said Andrew as they went on their way under the tree shade of the walkway. "What were the other things about me that convinced such a beautiful woman as yourself to give me another chance?"

"I think it was how you got my number. I was surprised when you texted me. But Jewel is a good judge of character. If she gave you my number, then I guessed you'd probably be worth giving a second chance to."

"I'm happy I got her approval then. I'll have to remember to send her some flowers."

Sami laughed. "I don't think you know what you're getting yourself into if you're getting flowers for Jewel. She can be a bit picky about her plants."

"I think I'll manage. I've always had a kinda green thumb," said Andrew as they turned a corner past some large brush.

"I wish you luck then," said Sami, as ahead of her, she spotted a large amount of people enjoying a bunch of colorful outdoor activities. "What's all this?" She couldn't help but stare as dozens of children and adults walked around a large open area where there were small tents and odds games being played.

"This is a small carnival," said Andrew, as he led Sami over to one of the food stalls. "Want some popcorn?"

"No, but I'll take a drink." Sami stepped in beside Andrew, looking over the food. There were a bunch of treats: Sugar cookies, and other colorful pieces of candy that were placed on a stick. Each of them were in fancy shapes of either different animals or oddly creepy clown faces. *Who in their right mind is putting that in their mouth?* Sami turned around, looking over the people, and saw several kids munching on the large clown faces. *Okay. Maybe it's just not meant for adults.*

"Here you go," said Andrew, stepping over to Sami and handing her a large cup. "I hope lemonade is okay."

"That's fine. Thank you," said Sami as she took the drink and as she allowed Andrew to lead her over to one of the games where people were rolling balls down a wooden plank, trying to get them to go into a hole.

"Wanna try?"

"I think I'll just watch you go for now," said Sami with a smile. "I'm enjoying this lemonade."

"Oh, I get. You're trying to measure how good I am. Well, stand back and allow me to impress you."

Sami laughed. "Well, go on then. Show me what you can do."

Andrew nodded and paid the man a few dollars and received a few wooden balls. "Okay," said Andrew as he gripped one of the balls in his hand, testing its weight. "So then, can you tell me what your thing is?"

Sami gave him a curious look. "My thing?"

"You know," said Andrew as he rolled one of the balls

down the plank. It went up, teetered along the edge of the hole, and then fell back down. "Dam." He turned back to Sami, grabbing another ball. "You know. Jewel has plants. I've met your friend Becca since she's around David. And she's.... well, I don't want to speak inconsiderately about your friend."

"Becca just does what she wants," said Sami, shaking her head. "But she seems to really like your friend."

"I know. We had her looked into."

"You what? What do you mean... looked into?"

Andrew looked at Sami oddly. "Your friend is dating someone who's close to being a billionaire and set to inherit a multi-billion dollar candy company. Do you really believe his security didn't look into her?"

"Oh... I guess that does make sense. Wait, does that mean they looked into me?"

"Probably not. But if you continue to hang around her with him, then they probably will. It comes with the territory. I've been his friend for over a decade and even I have to renew my security clearance every year."

"Well, I can tell you that I think Becca really likes him and she's not just after his money."

"But she is... somewhat dating him for his money, right?"

Sami frowned. "I plead the fifth."

"Spoken like a real friend. I respect that, looking after your girl," said Andrew down and taking a sip from his own cup. "Since this is an awkward topic, let's go back to what we were talking about. If you hang out with those two, what's your thing that you can't seem to give up?"

Sami genuinely thought about the question for a moment as Andrew lined up to throw another ball. *I don't have a... thing. I mean... do I need a thing?* She continued to consider the thought as she watched Andrew throw a few more of the balls, each one missing more and more to the point where there wasn't even near the hole anymore. Somehow, on one of his attempts, he managed to miss the plank completely and send a ball rolling across the grass into a nearby crowd. "I don't think you're meant for outdoor activities."

"Nah," said Andrew, turning back to her and grabbing the last ball from the bag. "I'm just having an off day is all. I'm sure it'll come back to me." He bounced the ball in his hand. "What about you? Thought about what your hobby is?"

"I don't really have one," said Sami honestly. "I guess I'm just boring when compared to everyone else."

"Well, I don't know about that. You make me feel pretty excited."

Sami closed her eyes for a moment and shook her head; her lips pressed together tightly as she tried to hide her smile. *This man.*

"What?" asked Andrew. "Do I not make you feel excited?"

Sami opened her eyes and reached into the bag, pulling out the last ball, then held it out towards him. "You throw the ball."

"Actually," said Andrew, stepping back and away from the plank. "Why don't you give it a go?"

"Really? You're giving up?"

"No, I'm trusting lady luck. So, step on up and show me how it's done."

"I don't remember calling myself 'Lady Luck,'" said Sami, looking down at the plank unsurely. But she decided to humor him. *I can't be as bad as him. As long as I hit the board, it should be okay. Taking a deep breath and focusing on the board, she squatted and reeled her arm back, preparing to throw.*

"You know," said Andrew, from behind her. "I knew you were attractive. Pretty face, pretty eyes, but your ass is also amazing."

Sami dropped the ball on the ground as she turned her head back, the frown on her face clear as she stared up at him. "Really?"

"Sorry. Was that too forward or just too soon?"

"I think that was a bit of both."

"Oh. My bad. But go on, I want to see what you do."

"You just want to stare at my ass."

"If I said I won't look at it anymore. Would you believe me?"

"No."

"Good, because I really don't want to lie to you on our first date."

Sami shook her head, the smile clear on her lips. "You're an ass."

"And you have an ass. A really good one."

"Just... just stop," said Sami, picking back up the ball. "I need to concentrate."

"So do I."

Sami took a deep breath. *All men are horny all the time. Even the ones I like. No, especially the ones I like. And for some reason...* She threw the ball. *I kinda like this one.* The ball clanked off the left side of the plank and then the right side as it rolled towards the hole. At the end, it went up the little ramp, spinning wildly as it popped up into the air and then came back down, plopping directly into the hole for a score.

"Wow, really?" said Andrew as he stepped in beside Sami. "Did you try to do that?"

"No," said Sami, as she turned toward a stunned looking stall host. "Did we win anything?"

"Sorry," said the stall host. "You gotta get three of the six balls in to win. But I'll give you this, lady. I ain't never seen someone make a crazy shot like that before."

"Think you can do it two more times?" asked Andrew with a chuckle.

"No. No way."

"Yeah, I didn't think so," said Andrew, handing the stall worker back the empty ball bag. "I think we're good." Andrew then turned and took Sami by the hand, leading her away. "That was actually pretty fun."

"It was," said Sami, looking down at her hand in his.

Okay, *this doesn't feel so bad. He's taller than me, someone I can look up to. He stared at my ass a little, but I have a nice ass. I can forgive that much.* She looked around and saw a bunch of other games where kids were playing and having fun. *Do they always have things like this in the park? Or is today like a special occasion?* They went past a few other tents until they saw another adult couple playing some game by throwing something at a board. As they got closer, Sami saw that they were throwing wooden axes at a colorful foam board with a big red bullseye on it.

"This looks like it'll be fun," said Andrew, as he led her over. "Have you ever tried before?"

"Throwing axes? No, that's never happened on a date before."

"I hope that means it's special."

"It's certainly something," said Sami as she plucked one of the wooden axes from a cup nearby. It was light and the edge was more blunt than she'd thought it'd be. *I guess it makes sense with all the kids running around.* She watched as the couple ahead threw their axes and watched as it bounced off the foam board, then falling to the ground. *I guess it's harder than it looks.* She then looked over to the stall to see what prizes they could win, and her eyes went wide as she looked inside of it. There at the top were two giant sheep: one white and the other black.

"You want one?" asked Andrew, catching her staring up at the fluffy animal.

"Huh?" said Sami, turning back to him and looking confused.

"The stuffed animal. You were staring kinda hard. Do you want one?"

"Oh... ah... no, no, it's fine. I was just caught off guard by how big they were. I mean, where would I even put it?"

"Is that Andrew?" came a woman's voice.

Both Andrew and Sami turned to see that the one who was throwing the wooden axe was now coming over to them while still holding two axes in her hand. *Who is this?*

"I thought that was you. How have you been?"

Shit. Sami instantly started to feel a bit nervous. *Another one of his ex-girlfriends.* Sami then stepped in behind Andrew as the woman came over. Suddenly, that dull wooden axe didn't seem so dull to her anymore. *I am not getting attacked again. If I have to leave your ass here and run away. I promise I won't think twice about it. I will not be a victim of your decisions today.*

"How ya been Andy? Is everything going okay?"

Andrew sighed. "Kali, can you not call me that? I'm here on a date."

"Is that so?" asked Kali, leaning to the side to see Sami peeking out from behind Andrew. "She's cute." She reached out a hand to Sami. "Hey, I'm Kali. I'm Andrew's cousin. And this is my boyfriend, Jake."

Jake nodded to them in acknowledgment.

Oh, it's his family. Thank goodness. She then stepped out from behind Andrew and shook Kali's hand. "Hey, I'm Sami."

"Oh, I love your hair," said Kali. "It's so curly. Is it hard to manage?" she asked as she pulled at a strand of her own hair. "Mine is always a pain. I ended up getting my father's hair. I used to use relaxers, but I've been wearing braids lately."

Sami laughed. "It can be a pain sometimes," she said honestly. "My mother broke a lot of combs in my head when I was younger. I still haven't found someone to braid my hair the way I like in this city. Can you introduce me to someone?"

"Girl, I got you," said Kali as she nudged her cousin with her elbow. "I bet you just love getting your hands in there, don't you?"

Andrew rolled his eyes. "Why are you still here? Don't you and your boyfriend here have other games to go play?"

"What do you mean?" asked Sami, her curiosity getting

the best of her. "Getting his hands in where?"

"When we were little, my mother used to run a salon, and she'd pay Andrew here to come in and sweep and clean the floor. It was like a trade-off. I'd go and pick flowers for his mother, and he'd come and wipe the floors for me. I think he fell in love with black girls with curly hair then."

"You're making things up again," said Andrew. "I do not have a hair fetish."

Sami then thought back to her night in the diner. *That woman had a wig on. So, he can't love it that much.* But still, Sami couldn't help but look at her own curls again as Andrew and Kali continued to bicker with each other. Their banter reminded her of how she and Jamal annoyed one another all the time. *I guess if you grow up together; it gives you the right to just lay into one another.* She smirked as she looked at them.

"Well, anyway, I should get going. We're only in town for the weekend and I can't spend all of it messing around with you, Andy," said Kali, after she had annoyed her cousin enough. "Don't forget to stop by my Momma's house when you come back home. And bring her something nice since you're up in the city making all your money."

"Fine. When you go home, bring my mother something back."

"Are you paying for it?"

"Yeah, yeah. Just send me the bill and I'll send you the money."

"Alright. Bye, Sami. It was nice meeting you."

"You too."

After that, Kali and Jake left and headed back through the event.

"You seem like you have a fun family," said Sami.

"Annoying, you mean. And she's always been that way," said Andrew, as he turned to the stall worker and handed him a few dollars. "You wanna give it a go?"

"Sure... Andy."

"Oh no, don't you start calling me that," said Andrew as he received two buckets of small wooden axes, handing one bucket to Sami.

Sami laughed as she took the bucket. "Fine, I guess that's just meant for cousins and close friends."

"It's not meant for anyone. My mother calls me Andy. Kali just does it to annoy me," said Andrew before turning back to the stall worker. "How do you play? Are there any special rules?"

"The board is solid at a few places behind the foam. You just gotta get five axes to stick in one go if you want the big stuff, three if you want the middle stuff. And if you get one, then we'll give you a keychain."

"Okay, so it's a guessing game. On where it's solid and soft at," said Andrew as bit his lip for a moment, thinking. He then looked at Sami. "You wanna go first?"

"Sure, I guess," said Sami, stepping into place as she handed Andrew her bucket of wooden axes. *This does seem so hard. I'm sure I can get at one or two to stick in place.* Sami tried focusing on the bard and he clenched the piece of wood in her arm. She then took a moment to see if Andrew was looking at her ass again, but he was indeed focused on the board, waiting for her to throw. Focusing back on her throw and maybe a little disappointed that he wasn't looking at her, she took a deep breath and flung the small axe as hard as she could. It flew in a wobbly arch before hitting the board, bouncing off of it, and then falling to the ground.

"Hey, nice. You actually hit it," said Andrew.

Sami frowned. "You make it sound like you're surprised."

"I am. But I'm also impressed. Go ahead, throw another one. I want to see something."

Sami stared at him for a moment as he focused on the board ahead, but then did as asked and turned back to the board. *Okay, maybe if I throw it harder or maybe softer. There has to be some trick to it. There's always a trick to games like*
138

these. Again, she raised the axe above her head and threw it, her wrist spinning it harder, and it sun in the air in another arch. It hit the target again, but this time it stuck inside of the foam target, right on the inside of the second target circle. "I got one."

"Good job," said Andrew, with a clap of his hand. "You got one. Looks like you win a keychain."

"I'll give it to you," said Sami, grabbing another axe from the bucket. "You seem like the type of man who forgets his keys."

"I remember the important things."

"And keys aren't important?"

"Depends on the day. Someday I'm glad I can find them. Like when someone asks me for a ride somewhere at two in the morning, sometimes keys lose themselves."

Sami laughed, "I'm going to throw the next axe, Mr. Key-loser." Trying not to focus on Andrew's sense of humor, which she was finding more difficult the more she talked to him. She then lifted her arm and threw another axe. This time, she missed the board completely. "I'm blaming you for that."

"Not the worst thing I've been blamed for. But go ahead and try again. See if you can get three in."

"You make it sound so easy. These little axes are hard to control."

"I have faith in you."

Sami sighed, before taking the last two axes from the cup. She then lined back up with the board and tried throwing one without thinking about it. This time the axe flew straighter and did indeed hit the board, but it didn't stick and fell. "Damn." She looked at her final axe, and not seeing the purpose of it anymore, she just launched it as hard as she could. The axe flew high. To her surprise, it launched above the board, missing the bullseye completely and landed on the top of it, sticking in the foam.

"Wow," said Andrew. "Does that even count?"

The stall worker scratched his head. "I guess it does. I mean… it is in the foam. But that's two, so…" He reached over, grabbing a key chain and handing it to Sami. "You won this."

Sami took the keychain. It was cheap looking and had the picture of a smiling clown on it. "I think I'd be better off giving it to one of the kids here."

"Not your style, then?" asked Andrew, as he handed Sami his bucket and waited for the stall worker to remove Sami's axes. "Don't worry. I'll get you something better."

"Someone sounds confident."

"Not especially," said Andrew as he plucked an axe from the basket, then turned toward the foam board when the stall worker came back. He then raised his hand, and in a quick motion launched his axe towards the target. It struck hard, rattling the foam target, but it stayed inside of it. "Awesome, that's one."

"What?" said Sami, surprised. "How'd you do that?"

"I was focused. I watched where you and my annoying cousin threw your axes. They bounced off the hard places. So, I just need to stay away from where they bounced off."

"How can you do that? Are you like a professional Viking or something?'

He stepped close to her, till the bucket was the only thing separating them. "I'm whatever you need me to be." He stared into her eyes as he plucked another axe from the bucket. "So, after I win you this prize. I hope you'll give me a present."

Sami raised a brow as she looked up at him. "Really?" she said with a hit of sarcasm. "Okay, Mr. Black Viking. Show me that wasn't just luck and then I'll think about it."

"Then it's a bet," said Andrew as he took another axe from the bucket, holding one in each hand. He turned and walked toward the target and raised his arm again, throwing another axe. It spun in the air before nailing the target again, sticking inside of it. And then, without hesitation, he flipped the other axe into his dominant hand and launched it. And just like before, it landed inside the target.

Sami stood there, shocked by the moment as she watched her overly confident date nail both axes with ease. "Okay, what's going on? How are you doing this?" she asked as he came back over to her to get the last two axes. "You're not telling me something. Did you used to work at carnivals or something?"

"Well, not exactly," said Andrew as he plucked out the last two axes. "Remember when I told you that I went to college with David and how he used to follow me everywhere?"

"Yeah. What's that got to do with this?"

"The thing about college is that it's a wild place. And so are the parties; every weekend they'd have an axe throwing contest at the dorms for guys to show off. Not real axes, but they were heavy enough. Over those four years and all the parties, I got really good at showing off. If David was here, he probably could do the same, since he had me teach him to."

"So, you knew you could do it. That's why we came over here."

"Of course. I'm trying to show off and impress you." He flipped an axe in his hand. "How am I doing?"

"You still haven't landed the last two."

"I will. Then you can give me a kiss afterwards as a celebration," he said as she stepped back to the spot to throw.

"I never said I'd give you a kiss. I said I'd think about it."

"And now you get to think about giving me a kiss," said with a smile while pointing the butt of the wooden axe at her. "I promise that after a minute, you might like the idea."

"Just the axe," said Sami, shaking her head. As he lined up, she had to admit she didn't mind the idea. As she watched him line up, rotating his arm, she then thought about those arms wrapped around her. *Okay. Maybe it's not such a bad idea. But you still have two more to...* Her thoughts stopped as he laughed another axe, and just like the previous three, it hit and stuck. But unlike the others, it hit directly in the center.

"Oh bullseye. Looks like I still got it." He turned around to her. "Did you give it a thought?"

Sami shook her head. "I'm still not feeling it. I think you're going to miss, so you get no kiss."

"Now you're just teasing on purpose."

"What?" said Sami, shaking her and putting on a sweet voice. "On our second date. I wouldn't do that to you, Andy."

She saw Andrew roll his tongue around in his mouth as he rolled his eyes, before turning back to the foam board. "Just watch." He gripped the axe again and raised it up and brought it down hard. Instead of spinning, the axe flew straight, rocketing out of his hand. It did indeed hit the foam target and then burst through on the other side.

Sami's eyes went wide as the foam exploded out from behind the target, causing it to rattle on its pedestal before tipping over and falling to the ground. *Wow, he has a temper. Does being called Andy really piss him off that much?*

Andrew turned to the stall worker. "Give me the doll."

The stall worker stared at him for a moment, and then back to the destroyed foam target. "But... I mean."

"What? Are you going to say it doesn't count?"

"No, sir," said the stall worker, apparently deciding not to argue the point. "I mean, you hit all five. So, you get to pick which one you want, the black sheep or the white sheep."

"Sami," said Andrew, his voice a little sterner than before. "Come pick which one you want."

"Huh," said Sami, still a little surprised by his change. "Oh, okay." Sami walked over and pointed toward the large white sheep.

"Yes Ma`am," said the worker as he reached behind the stall, picking up a stick with a hook on the end. He then reached it up toward the white sheep, plucking it off a hooped ring. "Here you go." He then handed it to Sami, who happily took it.

"Thank you," said Sami.

"No problem," said Andrew. "Come on. Let's go and see what else they have around here."

"Okay," said Sami, noticing his attitude was still a bit off. *I guess he forgot about the kiss.* She walked beside him for a moment, taking quick glances at him as they went forward. He seemed normal, but it seemed as if his mind was somewhere else. Sami picked up her pace, stepping in front of him and pushing the fluffy sheep doll into his chest.

"What?" said Andrew, taking the sheep. "You don't want..." He was surprised as Sami reached up, lifting herself on her toes as she reached up, wrapping her arms around her neck and pulling him down to her.

"Time for your kiss," said Sami as she placed her lips on his. So close to him she could smell the cologne he wore. Something soft and pleasant. His lips were soft, and it was only a moment later that she felt him kissing her back. His arms wrapping around her waist, he pulled her close, the fluffy sheep being squeezed between them as they enjoyed the moment. *Okay, I'll admit. I'm enjoying this.*

CHAPTER 8

Days later, Jewel stood outside of the museum of arts in the middle of the city. A gray cloudy sky above her matching the walls of the building. She stood up a long flight of stairs where before her stood two statues of a man and woman interlinked in some type of dance. Permanently on display for as long as the stone they were carved out of would hold their grace.

I can't believe I'm doing this. I must be out of my— The doubt in her mind didn't have time to perhaps call the whole thing off. As she turned around, looking at the mass of people that were walking by, living their lives, her mind froze as she saw Nasir stepping out of a cab, followed by a small girl.

They were both dressed lightly as it wasn't so cold out, even with the overcast. He noticed her up by the statue and waved as she made her way down to them.

"Hey, how's everything going?" asked Jewel.

"It's fine. Thanks for meeting us," said Nasir, turning around to the girl who was behind him. "Come on, come say hello."

He stepped to the side, revealing a cute little girl in a sundress and a bow in her hair.

"Hello."

Oh my god, she's adorable. Wait... I've seen her before. "Hey there, what's your name?"

"I'm Alina."

"Alina, that's a cute name."

"I'm sorry about being a little late," said Nasir. "I'm not exactly used to the traffic here. So, I just assumed it'd only be a few minutes to get here."

"No, it's fine," said Jewel. "If you don't live here, the traffic can be a pain. But you said your wife works in the city. Do you not come here to visit her much?"

"No, she only comes to the city for meetings, so I only show up once or twice a month. That's why I was there that day I came to see her."

She works in my building? Seriously? Are you sure she's okay with this? Do you two have an open marriage or something? What am I getting myself into?

"But even then, it's a straight shot to the building. This is also my first time out and about like this. So, take care of us. We are depending on you."

"I'll try my best," said Jewel, finding herself smiling at his playful nature despite her inner conflict. *Okay, I can do this. I'm just showing them the city. I'm... I'm like a tour guide. What's the harm in that?*

"Excuse me. Are you our new Nanny?"

"What?" asked Jewel, her eyes wide as she turned back to Nasir.

"No dear," said Nasir, comforting his daughter. "I told you; this is just one of Papa's friends. She works in the same building as Momma." He then looked up at Jewel. "Sorry, we've recently been looking for a new nanny since the last one recently got married. The search hasn't exactly been easy. She's usually the one with us when we go out exploring?"

"Exploring? Is that what you call it?" asked Jewel, smiling back at the girl. "I suppose there's nothing wrong with being a Nanny for a day." She extended her hand down to the girl and put on her nicest smile. "Well, come on then. Let's go exploring then, shall we?"

Alina looked back up to her father for permission, and with a nod of his head, she took a hold of Jewel's hand and they all headed back up the stairs of the museum together. The sound of the hustle and bustle of the city behind them was silenced as the door closed and was replaced with the sound of hundreds of people walking over the marbled floors and the chatter of people's discussions of whatever top they were interested in.

The building had two floors, each displaying pieces of art from around the world. From their view, she could see that the second floor of the main building was a balcony, as she could see people walking around above her. In front of them they saw an information station near the front desk where a diagram of the building was posted with where certain pieces of art were located.

"Wow, there are more people here than I'd thought there'd be," admitted Nasir.

"There are a few rare pieces on display this month. And it's the weekend, so more people have time to show up," said Jewel, looking down at the little girl. "Okay, where do you want to start?"

Alina looked around before spotting something she apparently found interesting. "This way," and she led them both to the left wall of the gallery. The first room housed a collection of ancient Chinese items.

"What are these?" asked the little girl.

"These are... let's see," said Nasir. "The collections of

Genghis Khan."

"Who is... Goon-gus Khan."

"To some a hero, to some a villain. I guess it depends on who you ask. But I guess the easiest answer would be that he was a king. He traveled the lands of ancient China and kill... I mean liberated most of the country."

"What does liberated mean?"

"Ahhh... saved, I guess."

"So, he saved people... like a superhero."

"Ahh... I wouldn't exactly..." he looked over at Jewel for any type of help.

"I think your father means he liked to travel the world with a bunch of his friends and meet new people," said Jewel, trying to satisfy the girl's curiosity.

"I like meeting new people."

"So do I."

The young girl turned to a large painting on the wall of a Chinese man sitting on a throne surrounded by women who were serving him or sitting at his feet. "Oh, are those his wives?"

"Ahh... I guess that's one way to look at it," said Nasir.

"He has a lot of them."

"Yes, he does," said Jewel with a smile. "Some men are greedy like that."

"Oh, I know," said the girl with confidence as she nodded her head. "Uncle Ajib has three wives. Are you married?"

"No, I am not. And who is this Uncle Ajib?"

"Never mind that," said Nasir as he placed his hand on both girls' backs and gently escorted them towards the next room of exhibits.

Despite the circumstances of her being here. Jewel had to admit to herself that she was glad that she came. She was enjoying this atmosphere of being around Nasir and his daughter. Especially the flustered look on his face as Alina continued to ask him uncomfortable questions.

The next few exhibits were filled with a slew of other

rare pieces, which to her surprise Nasir himself seemed to be well informed on most of them. Going so far as to recite things about them without even having to look at the information board.

"You're very knowledgeable about history?"

"In college they'd force us to learn about a lot of weird historical things and how to apply them to modern life."

"Really. So, you mean your college life wasn't filled with wild parties and girls like most guys talk about?"

"No, sadly, my college life was a bit weird when compared to most."

"Papa met Momma in college," said Alina. "Oh, and Aunty Safia and Auntie Hashmi. He met them there too. They always talk about school when they come to visit."

"Isn't that lovely? Falling for your college sweetheart. Seems like something out of a fairy tale."

"We clearly didn't go to the same college," said Nasir with a smirk. "And perhaps you do not know my wife very well. I'll just say that our relationship was special. Certainly not—" Interrupting their conversation came a ringing sound, and he pulled out his phone. Seeing the screen, he sighed, "I'm sorry. I know this might be imposing on you a bit. But can I ask you to look after her for a moment while I take this call?"

"Oh." Jewel looked nervously down at the girl for a moment. "Sure. I think we'll be okay, right, honey?"

"Yes. We'll be okay."

"Thanks. I'll be right back," he said as he took off, looking for a quieter spot.

"He won't really be right back, you know," said Alina, looking solemn faced. "He says he will, but he won't."

That statement from the small child made Jewel's heart ache a bit as she knelt to her. "Well, I'm sure your father has important business things to handle. Come on, let's go and see what other things they have for us to look at. Your father will catch up to us when he's done." She then took
148

the girl by the hand again, leading her off to another part of the exhibit.

Alina nodded, and they began to explore the rest of the building.

It was large and even had an upstairs area where paintings were displayed on the wall, and they were able to look down on certain sections of the gallery as they watched people move between the aisles.

"What do you do?" asked Alina when they had taken a seat to rest.

"Me. Well, I guess I'm a writer? Why? Are you looking for a job?"

"Your phone hasn't rung. Momma and Papa's phones are always ringing. I don't want to do a job where the phone rings a lot."

"I guess it would be bad if my phone rang all the time," said Jewel, smiling at the girl. "But I think I'd just turn my phone off some days. I mean, who wants one of those busy jobs anyway?" *I feel like a hypocrite saying this while competing against my best friend for a job that probably does call a lot.*

"Do you have a sister?"

"I do. She's one year older than me."

"Do you two fight?"

"We used to. Not as much anymore though."

"I want a little sister. But Momma doesn't want to have any more babies. She said one is enough."

Jewel couldn't help but smile. "Don't worry. My father said the same thing. And then my sister was born. But I'll tell you what, if that doesn't work out. I'll give you my sister. How's that?"

"You can give me your sister?"

"Sure. Why not? That is, if you don't mind joining my family. She even has two dogs."

"Humm, I like dogs. So, I'll think about it."

"You do that, okay," said Jewel, patting Alina on the head. But while they were talking, across the room Jewel saw a person standing on the balcony with them dressed in black. This person she had noticed had been near them on several of the exhibits that they visited. It wasn't odd at first. Following behind them on one or two exhibits. *The crowd here is moving in a certain way. But it's like he moves when we move.* She took another peek out of the side of her eyes and caught him for just a moment, looking over at them. *Okay, is something wrong? Am I being paranoid?*

Being a perceptive child, Alina followed her gaze to the man dressed in black and then turned back to her. "That man has been following us. Do you know him? Is he a bodyguard? Sometimes Daddy has them too?"

"No, I don't—" then suddenly Jewel's eyes went wide. *Wait, is he one of the men from that night?* Instantly her mind went back to that time in the alley as she thought that the man with his black ponytail looked eerily similar to one of the men that night who had chased them that night. She turned her attention away from him, her body beginning to shake as she then reached into her purse and pulled out her phone.

"Do you have to go call someone too?" asked Alina.

"Ahhh, no, it's just… well, we moved around a lot. I think your father might be looking for us. I'm just going to text him and tell him where we are." She turned on her phone screen and began texting.

"Your hand is shaky," said Alina.

"Oh, sorry," said Jewel, realizing she was still holding hands with Alina.

She gripped the phone tightly in one hand as she held onto Alina with the other. "Okay baby, I think it's time for us to go and find your father. Don't let go of my hand, okay? And let's head back downstairs."

Both girls turned, headed down the opposite path, away from the man who stood on the balcony with them.

"But the stairs are that way," said Alina, pointing in the opposite direction.

"I know, baby. We're taking the long way down. That way, we can see more of the paintings. Does your father allow you to paint?" she asked, trying to keep the girls' mind off the scenario they were in.

"Sometimes, my old nanny Miss. Huggles would paint with me. Oh, some days my mom tries to teach me the violin, but that's only on Sundays, but she can't stay that long. Oh, would you like to hear me play? Miss. Huggles said I was really good."

"Of course, I would," said Jewel, noticing that the man in black had started following behind them. *Shit, he really is following us. What do I do? I can't just leave her alone. What if he grabs her?* She looked around at the art gallery filled with people. *Stay calm Jewel. It's not like he's going to do anything. There are people around. I just need to wait until—*

Her phone started vibrating. Her finger shaking, she took a quick glance and saw 'twenty minutes' flash across the screen.

Twenty minutes. I may not have twenty minutes, she thought before slowly stopping near another crowd of people in the next room looking at a large statue. "Let's stop here for a moment. What do you think of this statue?"

"It's big. Did one person make this? It looks heavy. Why's he dressed like that? He looks funny," she said with a sour face.

"I bet it is. And that's how they dressed back then. Maybe someday someone will make a statue of you wearing a funny outfit."

"No," she laughed. "I don't want to wear a funny outfit like that."

"Well, I think it's pretty," said Jewel, before leading the girl off through the crowd again, making sure not to let go of her hand. "Come on, let's see what other funny things they have here."

"You're weird," said Alina with a smile on her face as she was led through more of the rooms, stopping to converse and waste time. All the while, Jewel ensured that she kept her distance from the man that was following them.

How long has it been? She looked down at her phone. *Fuck, only ten minutes. Why is time so slow?* Then her phone began to ring, and she saw that it was Nasir. *Really? Now you call?* "Oh, look, your father's calling. Let's see where he is." She placed the phone to her ear. "Hello."

"Hey," said Nasir. "Sorry it took so long. Where are you?"

"It's okay," *What do I do? Do I tell him we're being followed? No, what if something happens to him? This is my mess. I'm not dragging them into it.* "Ah... we went upstairs to see the art pieces. Just... ah... we're on our way back down. Can you meet us back in front of the Genghis Khan exhibit again?"

"Sure? Are you sure you don't want me to meet you halfway?"

"No, it's fine. It's... it's a big building. I don't want us to miss each other."

"Okay.... Ah... I guess I'll just wait here then. Can I speak to Alina?"

"Sure," said Jewel, handing her phone to Alina. As the girl talked to her father, Jewel continued to keep an eye on the man who had been following them. He tried to not be noticed, staying a fair distance away, but Jewel couldn't help but be away from him now. He also pulled out his phone as was talking to someone.

"Here you go Miss. Jewel," said Alina, handing her back her phone. "Daddy says he's waiting on us."

"Then let's go and see him then. Wait, are you sure you don't want to put on some weird clothes and surprise him? Maybe the museum will let you wear the clothing of those weird dolls over there."

Alina laughed, "No. Those are weird. You're weird."

Jewel's mind was focusing on so many things at once that she began to feel a bit tired, but not once did she allow herself not to be aware of the man following them and just how far he was away as she searched for another way that led downstairs. "Am I. Well, I think I'm fairly normal. Maybe it's you who are weird. Quick, what's your favorite color?"

"Purple."

"Oh, that's too bad, purple is a weird color," said Jewel, feeling a bit of relief after taking a quick glance back and not seeing the man behind them anymore. *Did he give up? Maybe I was wrong. I mean, how likely was that to be one of those guys from before? I could have been overreacting.*

"I bet you're making that up?" said Alina, a frown on her face. "And purple is not a weird color."

"Are you sure?"

"Then what's your favorite color?"

"Pink or maybe blue."

They continued this random line of discussion as they walked through the upper layers of the museum, weaving between the crowds of people until finally finding the other set of stairs that would lead them downstairs. Walking past another group of sightseers, they made their way down the cramped stairwell. Being a little aggressive, she forced the people coming the opposite way to move to the side as they reached the bottom floor.

"Okay, let's go over here," said Jewel, her and Alina heading off to another set of patrons. Seeing an opportunity to reconfirm her thoughts, she and Alina blended in with a crowd that was gazing up at two statues standing in front of one another with a painting behind them. From there she watched the stairwell, hoping that even after all this, she just might have been wrong.

Unfortunately, it wasn't long before her suspicions were confirmed as the dark-haired man exited the stairwell. The way he instantly began searching around the room, she knew he was looking for them. Her heart raced. She felt her phone vibrate again.

She looked down at it again and bit down on her lip. "Okay, honey, let's go over to the next room. I think your father's waiting for us. Hurriedly, Jewel left the group with

Alina in hand, walking at a fast pace towards the main lobby of she building."

"You're going too fast," said Alina, her little feet clomping against the floor, trying to keep up.

"I'm sorry, honey. We're almost to you father, okay?" Her eyes frantically searched through the crowd, and her heart almost burst the moment she saw Nasir standing back in front of the Genghis Khan exhibit. *Oh, thank God.*

"Oh, hey Jewel," said Nasir., with his usual smile. "Sorry about that. I was just about to call you."

"Oh, don't worry. Here!" she said, handing Alina off to him. "I'm going to run to the ladies' room for a moment. I'll be right back."

"Huh? Oh, alright," said Nasir, seeming a bit confused by her quickness.

With Alina back in the care of her father, Jewel left the small room of art at the other end. On her exit, both she and the man who'd followed them met eyes for only a moment, before she turned and headed off. Her heart was now toppling her in her chest, every footstep feeling clumsy as she tried her best to maneuver through the crowd. She navigated herself to the side of the wall and up ahead, spotting the signs signaling the bathrooms.

Fear controlling her, she dared not to look back. She thought she might freeze if she were to see him just moments away from her. It was like she could feel the man's footsteps growing closer. Her eyes searched frantically for a safe haven when a last group of people moved, exposing the bathrooms up ahead. In front of the ladies' restroom, she saw a large yellow sign that read: 'Danger when Wet.' Not taking the time to think, she turned past it, opening the door and entered the ladies' room.

She hurried inside, turning the corner walking into the middle, placing her hand over her chest as she gasped for breath. To the left there was a giant mirror, reflecting herself and an empty bathroom. But she wasn't given much time to settle, as only a few seconds later she heard the door to the room swinging open. She swallowed, fearful of who she knew was coming. But still she turned around to meet him, and there, pressed up against the wall that led to the entrance, was Nathan.

Her heart lifted seeing him there, but then immediately sank as she saw the dark-haired man appear around the corner wall. With a pounding heart and the hair standing up on the back of her neck, she just stood there staring at him.

But while she expected it would be him, what stole her breath was the sight of Nathan with his back placed against the inward wall of the restroom. He wasn't looking at her, instead his eyes were deadly serious and focused ahead at the edge of the wall, where the dark-haired man was only a few feet away from.

Jewel swallowed nervously again, understanding what she had to do as the two men stood only feet apart, one unknowingly of the other. "What... what do you want?" said Jewel, taking a step back, her hands clutching her purse. "I warn you. I'll scream."

The man took a step forward, reaching into his coat and pulled out a gun. "You do, and that'll be the last thing you do. I'll put you down before you finish that scream."

She nervously looked around the bathroom, while taking another step back. "What do you want? I... I don't know anything." She took another step, her back now pressed firmly against the wall, her knees buckled, not trying to hide the fear she so truthfully felt.

"I saw what happened," he said, pointing the gun at her and stepping forward. "Oh, you know more—"

Before he could finish his words, the man caught a hard palm to the side of his face as Nathan stepped in, grabbing him by the wrist and slamming his hand down on the sink. The force caused him to lose his grip, sending the gun sliding along the floor, over by Jewel's feet.

Instinctively, she reached down, picking it up and pointing it over at the men who were now in the midst of a struggle. The feet screeched across the floor as they both grappled for control. The man in black elbowed Nathan in the face only to have Nathan take the blow and come back even harder, head-butting the man, and sending him stumbling back against the sink, where he braced himself from falling.

He then swung on Nathan only to have him dodge under his punching as Nathan drove his fist into stomach several times. While rattled, the black-haired man took the blows, then using both hands together, brought them down on the back of Nathan's neck, sending him crashing to the floor.

"Stop," said Jewel, getting the man's attention with the gun pointed at him. "I'll... I'll shoot you." Her quaky voice did nothing to dissuade the man as he turned to her with a smirk on his lips, stepping towards her.

But that smile didn't last long as Nathan wrapped his arms around the man's waist, lifting him into the air and with a large grunt ran him over into one of the bathroom stalls. The impact on both large men easily caused the flimsy stalls to come crashing down. Breaking off their hinges under the force of both men, small pieces of wood exploded from the walls as both men went tumbling to the floor beneath them with the carnage beneath them.

To even more of Jewel's horror, she saw what was inside one of the stalls. There was an unconscious police officer inside who was now getting crushed beneath the weight of the two men as they were wrestling on top of the broken stall walls. But somehow Nathan managed to maneuver his way behind the dark-haired man and now had his arms wrapped around the man's neck. And with his teeth clenched, he squeezed as hard as he could as the dark-haired man struggled in front of him. His eyes quickly turned bloodshot. He began reaching out for Jewel until finally the strangulation took its toll and his eyes finally closed and his arms went limp.

Only then did Nathan release his grip, kicking the man off him to the floor as he lay there for a minute, trying to catch his breath.

"Are... are you okay?" asked Jewel, still pointing the gun at the unconscious man.

"I... I will be. Just... just need to catch my breath," said Nathan, his chest looking as if it were going to heave through his shirt. After another moment, he looked at Jewel and her still shaky gun hands and with a hard moan, he rolled over and stood up.

"Put... put the gun down. There's no silencer on it. Everyone... will hear it."

"Is he... is he dead," said Jewel. "Looking down at the man who lay sprawled out at her feet."

"No... too much explaining to do if a body is found randomly at the museum."

"What about him?" asked Jewel, turning to the body of the police officer trapped underneath the broken wooden bathroom stalls.

"The same as him. I was able to fully catch him off guard, unlike our friend here. He followed me into the bathroom, so I had to do something." He then looked at her and then looked at the guard. "I have an idea," he said before stepping toward her.

"What?" said Jewel, looking a bit nervous.

"Hand me the gun?"

She did as he asked and watched as he took it over to the sink and began washing it off before scrubbing it with his shirt. He then walked over to the unconscious dark-haired man. He ejected a bullet before flipping a switch on it and then placing it in his hand. He then forced the other man's hand to make a fist over it, then walked to the end of the room and placed the gun on the floor near the entrance.

"What... what's that for?"

He then walked back over to her. "Sorry about this?"

"Sorry about what?"

He lifted his hands to head and began recklessly running his hands over her scalp, making a mess of her hair. Then he grabbed a hold of the center of her top, ripping it down the center exposing her bra.

"What are you doing?" she asked, as she instinctively stepped back, clenching her hands over her now exposed chest.

"Making it look believable."

A few moments later, after Nathan had left the restroom, she stumbled out of the restroom, falling to the floor in the lobby of the museum.

"Help!" she screamed as loud as she could, getting the attention of all those near and far away as her words echoed over the nearby walls. She sat on her knees holding her ripped top together in her hands, looking a mess as the museum security rushed towards her from around nearby corners and she pointed towards the bathroom. "He's in there. He's fighting another police guy."

"Are you okay, Ma`am?" asked one of the security guards approaching.

"Yes, I'm fine. It's the other police officer. He... he protected me. He had a gun and... and..."

As a crowd quickly gathered, she saw Nasir and Alina appear through them. As they spotted her, Alina broke away from her father, running over to her, followed by Nasir.

"Jewel, are you okay? Is there anything I can do?" asked Nasir with genuine worry and panic in his voice.

"No... I'm... I'm okay. But I don't think I can show you the rest of the city now."

"What?" asked Nasir, looking even more shocked at her statement. "Forget about that," he said as he took off his own coat and handed it to her. He then carefully took her by the arm and began leading her out of the building. "I'm so sorry you had to go through that. I... I should have been with you."

"It's fine. I'm Fine. I don't think you could have walked into the women's restroom.

"No… I guess you're right?

A guard came back out of the restroom, coming over to Jewel. "You're safe now, Ma`am. We have the man in handcuffs."

"Thank you. I just… I just want to go home now."

"We're going to need to come down to the station. But you can do that tomorrow. We have more than enough to hold him for a few days."

"Thank you," said Jewel, before looking over at Nasir. "I think it's time for me to go home for the day?'

"Yes, yes, of course," he said as he reached into his pocket, pulling out his phone. "Come on, let's go outside and get some air."

"Was it the man who was looking at us before?" asked Alina.

"Yeah," said Jewel. "But I did good and fought him off."

"I'm sorry. I should have helped."

"What? Oh baby, no," said Jewel, patting Alina on the head. "You were right beside your daddy. That's where you were supposed to be. If anything were to happen to you, that would be the worst thing ever."

"Okay," said Nasir. "The driver will be here soon. He was nearby."

"I'm sorry for being an inconvenience," said Jewel. "You really don't have to. I can take a cab if you—"

"Nonsense," said Nasir. "What type of man would I be if I didn't see you home. I'm half tempted to take you to the hospital."

Jewel nodded her head in agreement, not wanting to risk Nasir's apparently protective nature forcing her to go sit in a hospital.

"Are you sure you're okay?" asked Alina.

"Yes, I'm fine dear. I just need to change my clothes and I'll be fine."

"Are you sure? You look sad now."

"Just tired now is all."

After a small amount of time, their car arrived, and Jewel was ushered inside before they all were driven away.

"I can come pick you up and take you down to the station tomorrow if you don't feel comfortable," said Nasir. "But that's something to worry about later. Where is your home?"

"Oh ah, Taylor and Mayvon. I live in an apartment there."

Hearing her words, the driver nodded his head, and they continued their way through the city.

"I'm sorry. I shouldn't have asked you to be our guide today," said Nasir, beginning to appear visibly upset. "If I wouldn't have been so selfish. You wouldn't have had to endure such a thing."

"No, I'm fine, really. The police officer was there, and they had him."

"No," said Alina. "Papa should have been there to protect you, like he does with Momma." She turned toward her father. "Papa, you should marry Jewel. Then you can keep her safe."

Jewel's eyes went wide as sucked in her cheeks, squishing her lips together as she stared down at the floor of the car, shocked by the girl's words.

"No, dear, it doesn't work like that. I'm married to your mother now and we are very happy together."

"Why not? You don't like Jewel."

"It…" Nasir began scratching his head, trying to think of the right way to explain it to his daughter. "It's not a matter of 'like.' I have your mother and she has me, and that's all we need."

"But what if Jewel likes you? And I like her. I want her to stay with us. And besides, Uncle Ajib has three wives. Why can't I be like my cousins Raadhesh and Labdhi. They have three mothers."

"That's... Uncle Ajib is a special case. And besides, you have Auntie Hashmi and Auntie Safia."

"I... don't think I'm prepared to be a wife yet," said Jewel, chiming in, trying to save the girl's father from more embarrassment.

Alina turned to face her. "But I don't want you to go away like my other nanny."

"Awwww," moaned Jewel, adoring the small girl as she patted her on the cheek. "Don't worry about that. If your father would let me. I'd like to see you again. We could go out for ice cream or something next time."

She then turned to her father with puppy eyes, staring up at him. "Can we?"

"We'll be in the city for a few more days visiting mommy. So, I guess..." he looked over at Jewel. "That is, if you wouldn't mind."

"No, that sounds great. I'd love to," said Jewel as the car stopped at her apartment.

"Thank you for the ride home," said Jewel, who was surprised when Nasir instructed the driver to circle the block a few times.

"I'll escort you to your door."

"No... it's alright. I think—"

"Really Miss Jewel, I must insist. I won't feel comfortable until I've escorted you to your door. You've just been through a horrible event."

Jewel looked at Nasir for a moment and sighed. "Okay, if you're that worried. I guess I can give you back your coat this way."

They both left the car and entered the building, stepping over to the elevator. Once inside, they lifted off to her floor.

"Did you happen to know the man who attacked you?"

"No, I didn't," said Jewel, as they exited the elevator and walked down the hall to her door. "I have no idea why he attacked me." *What am I supposed to say? That I was maybe chased and shot at by his friends.*

"It was the dark-haired man who followed us?" said Alina.

"What dark haired man?"

"There was a guy. He followed us into the building. That's why we came back to you. Jewel kept me safe."

"Wait? What? Do you think he was after my daughter?"

"What? I don't—" *What am I supposed to say?* "I... I don't know. He came after me, so I don't think so. He didn't say anything about her before he attacked me."

"Well, I promise I will look into this. I might not seem like it, but I do have some connections that I can rely on in a situation like this."

"Can I see your home?" asked Alina, bouncing, and looking up at Jewel excitedly.

"No honey," said Nasir. "I think we've intruded enough on our friend today."

Jewel sighed, "No, it's fine. I might as well get changed so that I can return your coat." She smiled down at Alina. "But be careful not to break anything in there. I have a lot of plants, okay?"

"I promise. I'll be good," she said while nodding her head. "We have plants at Momma's house too."

"Okay, there you go," said Jewel, opening the door and standing to the side, allowing Alina to poke her head inside and watched as the girl's eyes filled with glee.

"Wow," said Alina in awe as she gazed into the room, slowly waking forward. The colorful neon lights spread out over the room, glowing and highlighting different sections of vegetation spread throughout the apartment. "It's like a jungle." She turned back to her father and Jewel. "Can I go see?"

"Go ahead, just be gentle if you touch any of the plants."

And with permission given, Alina went exploring through the apartment.

"This is rather impressive," said Nasir as they both stepped in. "How long did it take you to gather all of this and set it up?"

"Longer than I'd like to admit," said Jewel, letting the coat slide from her shoulders as she felt safer at home. "Alina said her mother had a house. Do you both not live together?"

"No, that's not how it sounds. We have several houses and apartments in different countries. My work and hers forces us to travel quite a bit. So, when we can meet up, we have places where we can live together."

"How... how rich are you?"

Nasir laughed, "Trust me, it's not as glamorous as it sounds. We spend a lot of time together, but we have to make plans to do so. Whereas this month I am spending time with her. I may be in China next month and she might be in the Philippines."

"Wow," said Jewel, taking a seat on a bar stool near the counter. She removed the coat Nasir had given her, placing it on the table. "I guess you're both finding your own way of making it work." She turned to Alina, who was over near one of the plants, sliding her hands through its large leaves. "But I can see that she is not missing you. How do you manage being a parent when you are so busy?"

"Well... I wouldn't mind explaining the joys of being a father, Miss Jewel. But perhaps before we continue talking, you might want to change your clothes."

"Huh," said Jewel, turning back to Nasir to see that he was purposely not looking at her. She glanced down, realizing that her blouse was still torn open and her bra was fully exposed. "Oh," she covered her shirt with her hands. "Sorry." Standing up from the stool, she headed back towards her room. "I'll go and change."

She hurried herself back to the bedroom, where she closed the door behind her. The moment she saw her bed and was alone, she felt her knees give and squatted down with her back pressed against the door.

What am I even doing anymore? How did I go from being

attacked to bringing another man home with his daughter? Is this what I want? Some crazy life like this? She began rubbing her hands against her face. *It's all just so stupid. I mean, how did he even find me? Did he just happen to be there? I thought I was done with all that stuff. And I had that little girl with me. What if something happened to her? It would have been my fault. I was the one who took them there.*

Frustration taking control of her, she stood back up and ripped off what was left of her blouse, throwing it to the floor as she walked over to the window, placing her hands on the windowsill and looking down at the street below. *I have to do better than this. Ever since that night, my life has been one giant mistake.*

She sighed. *No, don't think about it. Not now, either way, it's over now. I'll have to tell him to stay away from me from now on.* She shook her head. *I can't say it like that. Argh, then what am I supposed to say? 'Oh, I'm sorry. I have apparently got the attention of some gun toting maniacs in the city and someone who may or may not be some kind of secret agent who kills people.'*

Trying to regain control of herself, she then grabbed a scrunchie from off her dresser and began looping her hair before tying it in a ponytail.

And why am I even thinking about seeing him again? He's married. So what if his daughter is absolutely precious? I'm not a homewrecker. I can find my own man.

Taking off her dress, she stepped over to the mirror to check her makeup.

Okay, I'll admit that my romantic life hasn't been hot lately. She picked out a button-up shirt from her closet along with a cute skirt, putting it on and changing her earrings before applying some extra blush to her cheeks. *But look at everything I've been going through. It's amazing I'm not locked up in some insane asylum.* She applied another coat of lipstick before checking herself once again in the mirror. *There. I'll just go out there and casually explain to him that seeing him isn't good for either of us, and his daughter shouldn't get attached to me.*

Her mind made up, she headed back out the door and into the living quarters, where she saw Nasir sitting on the couch. Looking around, she was curious, as she didn't see Alina anywhere.

"Where is—" she halted her words as she stepped forward and saw the girl asleep with her head on her father's lap.

"You were in there a while, and it seems she was more tired than she let us know. I hope you don't mind us intruding on you like this."

"What? No, of course not. It's good to have company over once in a while." *Dam, now what do I do?*

"She's really taking a liking to you. I'll admit that things have been hard since our nanny left. Alina hasn't really found anyone who she connects with. I know this might be a lot to ask, but I'll be in town a few more days. Would it be alright if we saw you again? I'd hate for our last meeting to be about something like what happened to you today."

"No. Not at all. Honestly, I think I'd like that too." *Fuck!*

CHAPTER 9

Sami sat in a parking spot in her rental car looking ahead through the windshield at a massive forest that appeared to spread out for miles.

"What am I doing here?" she asked herself, before shaking her head. "Maybe I should just turn around and go back home. I got this car just to drive my butt all the way up here. And for what, to get suckered into—"

Suddenly, a knock came from her windshield, and she turned to see Jamal smiling back down at her through the glass. With narrowed eyes, Sami rolled the window down just enough for him and her to get a good look at each other.

"What are you trying to get me to do?"

"Hey," said Jamal with a smirk on his lips. "I told you to bring your walking shoes and an outfit to sweat in. Did you?"

"I did? But you still didn't answer my question. What's

going on here? Why are we in the middle of the woods?"

"We're going on a nature hike. There actually is a trail in there that goes on for miles. Hey, don't look at me like that. You see all these other cars here, don't you? These nature walks are actually pretty popular."

Sami looked him straight in his eyes and, at the same time, turned the key in the ignition, restarting the car.

"Hey!" said Jamal. "Now don't be like that. Come on, get out or I swear the moment you pull off, I'll be on the phone with your mother, and she'll be at your place before you even make it home." He then held out his phone and turned it to her.

Sami saw a full screen picture of her mother in the kitchen holding a cooking pot with the call and message buttons floating along the bottom of the screen. Besides the surprisingly homely picture of her mother, the other thing that grabbed her attention was the name attached to it.

"Me-Maw? You labeled my mother as Me-Maw?"

"Of course, I did. Now get out, or do I have to press this button?"

"That's blackmail."

"Yes, it is. Now get out of the car."

Sami sighed before turning off the car and opening the car door, stepping out. She wore running shoes, a tank top, and thigh high spat shorts with another shirt tied around her waist. "Fine, let's get this over with."

"That's the spirit. Now come on, they're waiting for us," he extended his hand to her. "And remember, we're a lovey-dovey couple today. So at least try to look like you don't want to kill me right now."

"I'll try," she said, taking his hand. "But I've never been good at pretending."

Jamal sighed. "Yeah, don't I know it."

And with their agreement made, the two walked hand in hand through the parking lot and onto the walkway, headed downhill. They only walked for a minute before they saw two couples, both a man and a woman, dressed in sporty clothing. They stood at the base of the hill, waving and smiling at them.

"We were wondering what you were doing up there," said the man with blonde hair. "We were about to take bets on whether you would run away."

"Hardly. We were just having a conversation about the wild outdoors. So come on, let's get this day started," said Jamal as they began their trek through the trees.

The forest area seemed more enormous to Sami from ground level, with the trees stretching up so high and thick that she could only see the glow of the sun through the leaves.

"And you must be the lovely Sami," said the blonde-haired man. "My name's Henry and this is my wife, Heather. Our friend Jamal here tells us that he used to babysit you."

"It's more like he tricked my mother out of money while he raided the refrigerator and played video games."

"I bet," said the man with a hearty laugh. "Even so, being childhood sweethearts, what made you decide to finally start dating him now? He tells us you've only started dating again for the last few months. Did you really show up at his apartment drunk one night and confess your love for him?"

Sami glanced over at Jamal, only to see that he was staring off into the trees ahead as if he had spotted something really interesting and couldn't bear to look away.

Oh, you're so dead when this is over. "Yes, ah... Jamal might be exaggerating on the drunk part. But he does work above me, so after seeing him so many times, I guess I just realized my feelings for him."

"I know that feeling. My wife Heather and I have been together for over twenty years now. She's the one who actually approached me when I was just a broke college student, and she was already on the dean's list."

"I'm a sucker for a man with good cheekbones," said Heather, smiling back at him. "Although you were quite the fixer upper. Remember how much my father hated you when I first brought you home?"

"Do I? I swear he wanted to shoot me dead the moment I walked in the door."

"Do you two have any children?" asked Sami, keeping up the small talk.

"Yes, we have two boys. I wanted a girl, but it seems God had different plans for us," Heather patted Henry on the back. "What about you? Are you two going to start having kids soon?"

"Yes, honey," said Jamal, chiming back into the conversation. "I think we need more practice."

"You'll have your child when you stop acting like one," snapped back Sami.

Henry laughed, "Seems like you have your work cut out for you, Jamal." He pointed ahead. "Ahh, good. Our first stop is up ahead."

The woodland trail was thick with brush, but up ahead, Sami could see a clearing in the forest where people had stopped to rest. Through the clearing, Sami saw a small red barn where people were feeding an assortment of animals. Running around the fenced off opening were a few goats and chickens that were allowed to run freely around the small opening in the trail. Children were feeding them, spreading seed over the ground while laughing and playing.

"What is this place?"

"Oh!" said Heather. The trail has a bunch of little mini attractions along the way. "This is one of them."

"You ladies go on and feed the ducks," said Henry. "Myself and Jamal have some business to discuss."

"Fine," said Heather as she grabbed Sami by the arm, leading her over to the pond where a large number of ducks were waddling back and forth. "Come on, let's let the men talk about their little secret plans."

"Ah... sure," said Sami, allowing herself to be led away.

They headed over to an oddly egg-shaped vending

machine with feed for the animals. Swiping her phone over the reader, she selected several bags, handing half to Sami.

"So, tell me about yourself," said Heather, as she stepped over, squatting near the edge of the pond and tossing a handful of feed for the nearby smaller baby duckies. "And not that fake story about you two dating. I know Jamal. He's dated a few young women I know. I believe one of them was as recent as a month ago. So, I doubt you've both been dating for the last six."

Sami looked down at her for a moment. "I... I don't know what you want me to tell you."

"Please, honey, don't worry about it. You seem like a nice enough girl. Tell me, did you two really grow up together, or was that also made for keeping up appearances?"

"No," said Sami, before kneeling down beside Heather and looking over the pond. "The part about him being my babysitter was true. Our parents went to the same church, so his dad would bring him over to my place whenever they'd hang out together. We kinda just got stuck with each other at that point."

"Hum, sounds like a fun childhood."

"If you know the truth, then can you tell me what I'm doing here?" Sami waved her hand over the pond, confused. "Why are we even doing all of this?"

"Oh, honey. I never said my husband knew the truth." She looked back and smiled at him. "He's good at numbers and doing his job. But I swear, when it comes to social observations, men like him are like children lost at sea. They haven't a clue where to go."

"But you seem pretty happy," said Sami, noticing the smile on the woman's face as she glanced back at her husband.

"Oh, I am. I did pick him for a reason, and for the most part, he's lived up to my expectations of him. Even if he is a little overactive."

"Overactive?" Sami looked at her, confused.

"Oh, you'll see," said Heather, waving it off before tossing another handful of feed to the ducks. "So, what about you? Real childhood friends. Have you two ever tried dating?"

"We tried... once. But it didn't work out. About three years ago, he got me a job in the city and now he shows up drunk on my doorstep every other month or so."

"I see. So, it was the reverse." A group of ducklings waddled over. "Tell me. Do you have any children?"

"No."

"Do you not want any?"

"I mean... I don't know. I just haven't found the right person, I guess."

"I see. Well, to answer your earlier question of why you are here. My husband likes to believe that people are more likely to stick around if they have a family to support. So he wants all the junior partners of the company to be family men. You know, 'have some time to hold them down or keep them grounded' as he puts it."

"Jamal is going to be a partner?"

"He will, as long as you two keep playing the happy couple. My hubby has the deciding vote, but they won't decide anything for another few months. Think of this as a trial run."

"Wait, what? I thought this was a one time thing. You mean I have to keep this up for months?"

"Yes, there will be several dinners, most of them not as informal as this one. Jamal there even has to take out all the senior partners to dinner at La'Grengar, a dinner that will probably cost him about seven thousand dollars."

Sami grimaced. *No wonder he was willing to pay my rent so easily. Maybe I should have asked him to buy me a car.*

"Oh, here they come. The men seem to have finished with their little pow-wow," she whispered before standing back up to greet her husband. "Hey Honey. You boys done?"

"Yeah. Just a bit of fun guy talk," he said with a clap of his hands. "What say you girls? You ready to move onto the next fun part of our trip?"

"Next fun part?" asked Sami, looking confused.

They walked for another mile up the trail near the water until finally stopping at the third spot on the trail when a group of people stood near the docks over the water. The next thing Sami knew was that she was equipped with a life vest and had an uncomfortable helmet strapped on her head.

And while Heather and her husband were busy checking their equipment, Sami pulled Jamal to the side where they couldn't hear.

"What the hell is wrong with you?" said Sami, glancing back at the couple as they began tying a piece of rope in a loop. "We're black. We don't do stuff like this?"

"Don't be like that," said Jamal with a half-hearted laugh. "This is completely safe.... sometimes."

"Some...? Wait, have you done this before?"

"What?" he asked, trying to put on a confident smile. "Of course I have." He lowered his voice. "In a video game."

Sami's eyes went wide. "What the hell is wrong with you? Are you trying to get us killed?"

"No, of course not. Don't worry, they'll be our partners. You will go with Heather, and I'll go with Henry. They know what they're doing. We'll be fine."

"I don't trust anything you say anymore."

"Well, don't trust me, trust them. They are the professionals here."

They both turned and watched the husband-and-wife Duo both do some type of synchronized stretching ritual before giving each other a high five and saying "Woo."

"Yeah," said Jamal. "Okay, Maybe I see your point."

I'm starting to think this is what she meant by him being overactive.

"Okay, you two," said Henry, waving them over. "Come over here and help us get these things in the water."

"Three months' rent," said Sami as she stood beside

Jamal, staring stoically looking over at the other couple. "Three whole months."

"If we survive this, I'll gladly pay it."

And with that, the two walked over to their prospective partners on the docks. They then turn the kayaks toward the water near the ramp.

"Okay, everyone in?"

Sami followed Heather's example, squeezing into the rear seat of the partnered kayak.

"You two ready?" asked Henry when they were all inside.

"No, not especially?" said Jamal.

"Good, I like your honesty. Neither was I my first time," he then reached over, pushing a button on the dock and slowly lowered the wooden plank into the water, until they were floating on top of it.

"Alright newbies, use your paddles like Heather and me. We will guide you along the soft and gentle water."

And with that, they began to paddle out into the center of the lake. The water was smooth and calm as they slowly drifted forward. Henry and Heather patiently guided them around in a circle until they started to feel comfortable with the motion.

"Just follow our movements, okay," said Henry, instructing them to paddle in the same direction as them. "Just paddle left to right to move forward. And if we're turning, then I'll paddle in that direction. You can let us handle the steering."

"Ah… okay," said Sami as she tried mimicking Heather's movement with the paddles. *Okay, this isn't so bad. I just need to go left right, left right.* The sound of the oar sinking into the water actually provided a peaceful melody, along with the sound of water over the whispers of the forest.

"Okay then," with the basic stuff out of the way, let's start with a nice drift downstream. The lake will do most of the work for us. We will just guide ourselves away from big rocks and fallen trees.

And with the instructions clear, they pulled out into the main part of the river, allowing themselves to be slowly carried away downstream.

"So," said Sami over to Henry as they floated beside one another. "Over twenty years of marriage. What's that like? What's the key to a happy marriage for you two?"

"Ha!" laughed Henry. "For us, it's simple. At least once a week or two weeks when things are busy. Always make a night where we can talk. Once a year, we sit down at the beginning of the year and talk about our goals. For me it might be work, or at least it was at the beginning of my career. For her, she wanted kids, so we ended up with the two boys."

"And don't forget how we handle arguments," said Heather.

"Yes," He laughed again. "I handle disputes with money, and she handles more emotional disputes."

"There's been more than a few times where one of our children had an important life moment and Henry thought that being at work that night was more important. So, when it comes to matters of family. I have veto power unless it is an absolute emergency. Struggle at work tomorrow, your family needs you today."

"Sounds like you two have it all figured out," said Jamal as he dipped his finger into the waters.

"Trust me. There were a lot of arguments along the way before we found out what worked for us. I'm sure you two will be the same. Just remember, even if you're angry, always go to bed together, one arm wrapped around the other."

"And usually by morning you'll have figured out some sort of compromise," said Heather, finishing her husband's train of thought.

"Yes," said Sami with a sigh as she dipped her finger into the cold river over her shadowed reflection. "Relationships are hard. Most people don't want to compromise. Instead, you just fight because you're trying to get your point across, and you feel like they're not listening."

There was a moment of silence around them before Heather dipped her oar back into the water. "Honey, if you already know that, then I think you'll do just fine. So, I guess it's true, you really are some sort of relationship guru in that magazine of yours."

"I don't think I'm a guru, but I do offer advice. Sometimes I have trouble following my own advice, though."

"Don't we all," said Henry. "But that's just how it goes. Okay, enough chatter. We're going to need to pay attention to this next part."

"Humm," moaned Sami, now paying more attention to their surroundings. She hadn't noticed before, but now, more alert, she could hear the sound of the water was progressively growing louder. "What's... what's going—" Her words caught in her mouth as she looked over at Henry, whose chest was heaving as he began taking deep breaths. She then looked in front of her and saw Heather heaving as well. "Ahh... what's going on?"

Heather turned around, wide eyed and smiling. "Remember, marriages need compromise. So sometimes, you gotta join your husband when he gets a little overactive."

"Overact... what?"

"Are you ready, baby?" screamed Henry.

"You know it, baby," screamed back Heather.

"Last one to the bottom will be picking the kids up from recital for the next two months."

"Then be prepared to drive that minivan, because Momma's driving the corvette this month."

Sami's mouth fell agape as she watched the exchange and personality shift of the couple. But her truest fear came when they turned the corner of the river, and she gave witness to the turning of the water as it broke against some large stones piercing the water before splashing downward. In a panic, she turned back toward Jamal, only to see that he had long since released his oar and now had hands over his eyes, as if just waiting for his inevitable end.

"Oh, you fucker," she mumbled before her kayak then went sailing down the river, with her last audible words before water splashed up in her face being. "Four months' rent!"

The little kayak went barreling down the river, the water splashing on them at either side and at every turn. Sami grit her teeth as she struggled, trying to follow Heather's movement with the oars. Stroke left, stroke right, Sami paddled fiercely, attacking the water with her oar. Every time she thought she'd get a small respite, they would drop down another fall, crashing into the water below, her body being thrust around back and forth from the weight and the impact of them landing.

In between the splashing of the water, she could hear the power couple Henry and Heather shouting at each other. Whether it was screams or cheers, she couldn't tell. But rightfully, she didn't care. She was only concerned with staying above the water. But it didn't matter because nothing was louder than the thoughts running through her mind.

I'mma kill 'em. Oh lord, I'mma kill em. If you let me make it through these crazy white people. I'm sure enough gonna kill 'em and send him home to you.

These words cycled through her mind as she paddled her way through the rapids. Whether skill or sheer desperation, she found herself beginning to match up with Heather's movements. Left, right, left, right, she pushed, not even being able to see the clearing. She just tried flowing along with the backside of Heather.

At the end of it all, they managed to find their way back down the river, pulling back up on shore where their cars were. Both she and Jamal gratefully free themselves from their kayaks, crawling back on land.

"That wasn't so bad, Jamal. You were pretty tough back there. I didn't hear you scream at all."

"Well, you know. I had... I had to focus," he said, bent over with his hands on his knees, trying to catch his breath.

Damn liar, thought Sami as she stood up, still leaning over, trying to catch her breath.

"Well, honey. We won. I guess that means you'll be driving the minivan for the month."

Henry sighed. "Alright. I gotta hold up my end of the deal. But next month, I'll be the one who wins." He then turned to Jamal, whose eyes were now red, and his legs were finally looking steady under him. "Thanks for joining us this morning, Jamal. I'll be sure to tell the other partners that Jamal Grimes is an adventurous man. Someone who is bold and willing to take the plunge."

"Thank you, Sir. I... I look forward to our next outing."

"Yeah, and bring your adventurous girlfriend along with you next time." He turned toward Sami, extending his hand. "I swear, the way you were padding, I think my wife was having a hard time keeping up with you. My God girl, it's like you were a woman possessed out there on that river. Are you sure you haven't done this before?"

"No, but... you can say that I suddenly felt motivated."

"I bet," he said with his usual laugh. "Well, we best be going. We have to go and pick the children up from their aunties' house. She took them out for us this morning."

"Take care," said Sami with a smile as the two waved back to them and headed off up the hill towards their car. She then turned to Jamal after they had left her vision. "And you gimme your wallet."

Jamal pulled out his wallet. "What why? I'll just stop by your place when the rent arrives. It's not like I don't know where you live."

"No," she said, taking his wallet and pulling out a credit card. "My hair is a mess and you're paying for me to have it done. I have a date this evening and I can't show up with my hair smelling like river water and fish."

Jamal began to protest but seemed to stop after looking

at the annoyance on Sammy's face. "Just don't spend too much, okay? I might be well off, but I'm already paying for a lot."

"Don't worry, I'll be nice. And besides, you're going to have to pay for the next time, since apparently, I'm going to have to keep up this lie until you make partner."

Jamal smiled back at her. "You mean you're willing to help me out?"

"Well, this is different from the time when I covered for you after breaking Miss Willington's window. But yeah, I'm going to be stuck looking after you for a while." She shook her head with a frown before mumbling to herself. "My mother really was right about that."

"Alright, let's head back then," he said as the custodians took the kayaks and loaded them onto the back of his truck. "And I hope to never be on one of those things again."

"As long as they don't have us skydiving next time," said Sami as they headed back up the hill together towards their cars.

"Tell me about it. Rich people are something else. Why can't they just go out and lose their money in casinos like self-respecting fools?"

"Be careful what you say. Remember your aiming for partner. Doesn't that mean you're trying to become a rich person too?"

"Then I'll just be one of the few rich people with some damn sense."

CHAPTER 10

Later on that night, Sami arrived by cab outside at the gates of a large manor a little past nine pm. Standing outside beneath one of the lights mounted above the gates, she saw her date, Andrew. He was dressed in a brownish suit with a white undershirt. No tie, so the top two buttons were left undone. She hadn't seen him since that night after the restaurant, but he looked more or less the same to her recollection.

"Hello there, you look lovely," he said as Sami exited the vehicle.

She wore a long, sleek reddish black gown. While loose along the top, she went braless to show off her back as the outfit hugged her around the waist before falling loosely over her hips then splitting down to her ankles. Her heels were white with black stripes that matched the white slash that wrapped around her neck and butterfly clip in her hair.

"I'm happy you like it," she said as she stepped onto the sidewalk and up to him. "I was surprised you never called me. And then suddenly your candy-millionaire boss asks me to be your date tonight."

"Yeah, sorry about that. I probably should have asked you properly." He then turned to the side, leading her to a smaller vaulted brick entrance. It led inside to an open field, the metal gate before them creaking on its hinges before opening before allowing them inside.

"I see. I guess we never did exchange numbers," said Sami, thinking back to that night after her fight with his ex-girlfriend. "Where are we headed?"

"No, we didn't," he said, pointing up the hill. "But I did come by your job once. Did your friend Jewel not tell you?"

"No, she didn't. But we haven't spoken much this week," said Sami as she looked in the direction he was pointing. There was a small walkway that led through some low-cut brush and appeared to lead up to a soft white structure that sat adjacent to the main building. "What's that?"

"That is where we will be eating and enjoying the entertainment," he said, beginning to lead her through the brush up towards the gathering.

The environment felt somewhat pompous as the walkway was dimly lit by the small lights that shone on the brush that lined the walkway up to the gathering.

"Tell me? What have you been up to? Did you ever handle that supposed ex-girlfriend? Should I have come with a weapon?"

"I did go back inside after I escorted you to the cab and I had a talk with her. But at the moment, she refuses to answer my calls, so I'm not exactly sure what's going on."

"Did you do something to make her act that way, or was she always that crazy?"

"It's not... I accused her of stealing from me. She was over my place, and I had some money on my dresser. When she left that morning, apparently, so did my money."

"You sure you did misplace it?"

"My apartment has security cameras. It's hard to deny video evidence."

"Oh. How much did she take?"

"Around three thousand."

"You had three thousand dollars just lying around on your nightstand?"

"It was for a special delivery that day. My contact prefers to deal with cash. Thankfully, we've done business several times, so when I explained to her what happened and showed her the video. She laughed at me and gave me credit for the day."

They continued their small talk, with Sami enjoying the conversation. She could see that he shaved for the occasions and had to admit that he looked good in his outfit with the stars above them. The feelings of romanticism slowly came over her and she took hold of his arm, leaning into him as they strolled through the brush.

As they got closer, she could see part of the white of the structure was flowing in the wind and she realized that it was just some type of sheets that hung across large wooden beams. Beneath the structure, she took notice of a multitude of people walking between the sheets, conversing.

"Well, this is fancy," said Sami. "I thought it was just going to be the three of us."

"Really? I believe the plan was to always have some of the main heads of the company here," He said as they approached the structure, waving as they saw Becca and Jewel with their prospective partners.

Sami smiled at her co-workers as they came over to them. Becca and David 'The Candyman' seemed to be their usual attached selves. But the man that accompanied Jewel, *Wow,* thought Sami as she looked up at him. Jewel was tall, but he looked to be half a foot taller than her, even in heels.

"Good, you're finally here," said Becca. "I was beginning to worry." She turned to David. "Our friend has finally arrived. Thank you for keeping us company, honey. But I know you have business things to attend to before the dinner. You can go and entertain your guests and take Jewel's friend along with you. I'm betting his intimidating stature alone will help get you whatever business deals you want done."

David gave her a kiss. "You know me so well," he said with a smile, then turned back to the men. "Andrew, come join me. We have to go see Mr. Heldine's old ass. And you too, my new tall friend. Come along and look menacing."

"Sorry, I had to make an emergency hair appointment," said Jewel, after they saw the men off.

"Well, you look great," said Becca. "And that dress. It looks expensive. You do know how to doll up when you want to." She pointed at Jewel. "This one still needed some work. Can you believe she shows up wearing sandals? They were cute, but come on."

"They were comfortable."

Sami did notice Jewel looking a bit taller than usual. She looked down and noticed that beneath her white pants suit, her friend was wearing heels. "Where'd you get those then?"

"I gave her an extra pair I had. I imagine showing up with that tall of a man and not enjoying the chance to wear heels when you finally can."

"I swear, it'll be the end of the world if we can ever get Jewel to wear a dress," said Sami with a laugh.

"I'm fine. And it's not like I haven't worn dresses before. Plus, it's nighttime. How are you not chilly dressed like that?"

"It's called alcohol, dear," said Becca, shaking her head and tilting her glass at her. "Perhaps you should have some more of it."

"Speaking of you. Why didn't you tell me Andrew had come by the job looking for me?"

"Oh," said Jewel. "Sorry, I forgot. He helped me bring some of my plants home."

"Wait? You took him home?"

"Yes, but I mean," Jewel looked a bit uncertain. "He didn't really give me much choice. He had a driver, and the plants were heavy. But it's not like we did anything. He just brought in the plants and left."

Sami stared at Jewel for a moment. "Well, you could have at least told me."

"Oh, forget Jewel and her plant fascination," said Becca, placing a hand on Sami's shoulder. "Girl really, if there is anyone you don't have to worry about taking a man interested in you, it's her. And speaking of which. Did you see that beast of a man she brought with her?" She laughed. "He's like a walking truck. Where did you even find him?"

"He's... he's a therapist?"

"You're dating your therapist? Isn't there some law about you not being able to do that? Something about a conflict of interest or something?"

"I don't know. But he's not my therapist. He just gives me advice sometimes."

"Yes, I'm sure that's all he's giving you," said Becca, turning around. "Well, come along, my sisters in arms. Let us go and mingle with these rich people."

Sami alongside Jewel followed behind Becca through the night air. The environment was very social, with men and women dressed in their suits and dresses sipping on wine, picking food off trays where walking waiters shuffled about. Near them, Sami saw that the structure that had the white cloth draped over it housed a stage in the center.

"What's that?" she asked.

"What?" asked Becca, turning to the stage. "Oh, that. Supposedly, there's going to be a play later on."

"A play? Okay, that sounds rich."

"I have to ask Becca," said Jewel. "Are you really used to this? I mean, sure the money is nice. But I never thought you'd go for all this."

Becca walked a bit more, stepping inside of the clothed

structure before turning back to Jewel and Becca. She looked around, apparently ensuring no one else could hear. And when she was satisfied that no one could, the smile disappeared from her face, and she sighed. "God no. Being around these people is just so fucking boring."

Sami laughed, "Really? I thought you'd enjoy all of this."

"No, I enjoy being with David, but all of this, the parties, the keeping up appearances, the fake smiling, and forever dull conversation. I wish I could just throw it all away. But apparently being the son of the CEO also means that you have to play nice with all the shareholders, so that when he's supposed to take over the company, they won't try to kick him out. Apparently, having tons of money doesn't mean you're able to escape the bullshit of office politics."

"Well, it's nice to see that you haven't become a pompous bitch since you've started dating Mr. Candyman. Does he know you feel like this?"

"God yes. He hates it too. Tomorrow, we're planning to just spend all day lying on the beach, drinking terrible two-dollar drinks until we pass out drunk in each other's arms."

Sami and Jewel both started laughing.

"Laugh it up all you want, but both of you are here to ensure that I don't lose my damn mind," said Becca as she took a deep breath and straightened her back. "Now come along and put on your best 'stuck-up-bitch' face and help me go and mingle with the rich folk."

Sami shook her head, but did as asked, trying to twist her face how she thought a rich, pompous person would and all three girls strutted out to mingle with mobs of high society.

The first stop was that of an older couple.

"I'm so glad little David has found himself a nice girl," said the older woman with a chuckle. "You know, for the longest time, we just assumed there was no hope for the boy."

"Yes," said the older man with a nod of his head. "His grandfather used to be partnered with my father in the automotive industry. That was far before his candy investment. He used to bring that little boy everywhere with him. Getting into all kinds of messes and playing with loose buckets of motor oil."

"Well, I'm sure he's happy that you both remember him so well," giving a laugh and patting her chest. "Sadly, I've only known him for a short time, but I hope to get to know as much about him as you do."

"You will, dear. Little David seems to be absolutely smitten with you."

"I hope so. You both enjoy the night. I must go see to our other guests," said Becca, and with another smile, she went off toward the next group of well-to-do rich people.

This time, it was another man joined by two women. All three seemed to be about their own age, maybe younger.

"Oh, there you are," said one of the women, waving them over. "The infamous Becca we've heard so much about."

"I hope mostly good things."

"Of course, your Cinderella story is all any of our friends can talk about," she laughed. "How David plucked you off the street and is now courting you, trying to turn you into a princess."

"Yes, even I am curious what he sees in you," said the man, giving Becca a look over. "Especially when apparently my little David could have had any upper-class woman."

"I asked him about it once," said Becca, looking the women up and down. "He said that I gave him a challenge. One that he couldn't find amongst his friends. Granted, I still have a lot to learn. I still don't have an appreciation for such fine clothing, so for now, I'm forced to have David pick my clothes out for me."

"Ha," laughed the man. "Well, you should join us one day. It might be exciting."

"Perhaps. I'll tell David you're interested."

One of the women beside him gave a half-hearted smile. "I think I must be seeing things along the same lines as Cinderella's sister. I just don't see what he sees in you. But I'm sure after you've spent enough of his money, he might come back to his senses. You might need to be careful with that credit card."

"Oh really," said Becca, well, I like to think of it this way. "I spend his money and he fucks me. You spend your parents' money, and you 'fuck them' over." Becca placed her hand over her mouth, failing to hide a gleeful smile. "But I think that's a bit unfair, don't you? Your parents were forced to spend money and raise such a bitch? I'd say that they've gone and gotten double fucked."

The man spat out his drink and began choking. "Oh... oh god."

The woman's eyes went wide, along with her friends. She began to speak, opening her mouth, but instead it didn't seem she could come back with a retort.

"Oh, don't worry dear," said Becca as she stepped to the side of the woman. "And do close your mouth. You might have the other men here thinking you're open for business." And with the final jib, and more coughing from the man who Sami couldn't tell was either laughing or dying, Becca walked over, leaving the woman red faced as Jewel and she followed behind.

"What was that?" asked Sami.

"That," said Becca with a sigh, "was Margot Holdheim. The maids inside warned me about her. Apparently, she's had a crush on my David since they were in school together. I don't think she and I will ever get along. I won't even pretend to try."

Sami smiled, "You've been talking with the help. Is that what the rich Becca does now?"

"Yes, well, isn't it a surprise that the people who come from a poor or middle-class background are the only ones really supporting my relationship with David?" She laughed.

"They've been feeding me information on who I should look out for, and Miss. Holdheim was at the top of that list."

"It seems our Becca has crossed over into a new world," said Sami, wrapping her arms around her friend. "But I'm ashamed to say I didn't think it would last this long. But I'm happy to see that you're happy."

"You're not the only one," said Becca. "I thought we were just having a fun night out during that speed dating. I was just as surprised when he called me the next day." She gazed up at the surrounding area. "And now I'm spending a few of my nights here. Doesn't seem real."

"Well, come on," said Sami, releasing her hold on her friend. "Continue showing us around. Is the fountain made of white gold?"

"Yeah, like I would know if it was," said Becca as she led them through the crowds, introducing them to some friendly faces, some of whom actually spoke with voices that didn't seem to harbor any ill will. The small area that they had sectioned off was only part of an immense ground layout that housed several other builds besides the main manor.

Sami was surprised to see that the staff made sure to hover near them even when they had stepped off the beaten path quite a bit.

"Are they stalking us?" asked Jewel.

"No. You'll get used to it. I told you; we've become friends and they don't want anything happening to me. Such as me taking a spill down this hill."

"What? Is that a real thing?"

"I'd like not to think so. But according to them, when you've been working for a certain family for over a decade, apparently you see some things."

"That doesn't sound safe," said Jewel, who began looking around the area paranoid.

"Don't worry, I'm fine here. I'm sure it's just their overactive minds. If anything, I feel kind of flattered that they've taken such a liking to me. The older staff kinda give off that grandma and grandpa vibe."

"Oh, it looks like the boys are coming back," said Sami, spotting the tall man that had come with Jewel heading back toward them. "Should we go back?"

"Yes. No need to have them searching for us. Although I doubt they'd search long the way his head sticks out over the crowd." The teasing of Jewel for her date continued as they turned back around and began heading back to the main area of the party.

"What do you think they went off to talk about?" asked Jewel.

"The same thing men always talk about. Who makes the most money? Which sports team is the best? Which one of us has the bigger breasts, the tighter ass? And probably a bit of candy talk... you know... in between all of that, to spice it up a little."

"God," said Sami with a laugh. "You're so bad."

"Hey honey," said David as he strolled over, giving Becca a kiss. "I hope I didn't keep you waiting long."

"No. We were just having a bit of girl talk while you were away," Becca patted him on the chest. "Did you finish having your little secret business meetings?"

"If you mean sucking up, no. I'm afraid that will go on until I retire. But at least it's done for the night." He took a deep breath and pointed forward. "But now comes the next part. If you would be so kind, my sweet lady." He extended his hand to Becca, who took it with a smile.

"Be back soon, girls," said Becca as she and David made their way through the crowd and over in front of the white-clothed structure.

"Ladies and Gentlemen," shouted David over the crowd. "If I may have your attention, please."

At the sound of his words, the crowd all turned, gathering in front of them. Sami could see that sometime during the event, they had placed out foldable chairs in rows for everyone.

"I'd like to thank you all for coming here tonight. It's not often that we all get to gather like this. After all, we all have money to make." The crowd all laughed, lifting their glass to the joke. "But let's not forget that the reason we make the money is so that we can enjoy our lives. And it's the people in our lives that make this life worth living." He gestured toward the stage. "And with that being said, I've spent a decent amount of money to have the Bridgerton Theatrical Play arrive here and perform their version of Gradius and Fontaine for our enjoyment."

The nearby door to the manor opened and out of the house came around two dozen men and women dressed in fancible garbs as they all lined up with smiles behind the couple.

"So," said Becca, gesturing ahead of her. "We ask that you all take your seats and enjoy the show."

The crowd all took their seats with Becca, Sami, Jewel, and their partners, all sitting together in the left front row of seats. It took only around a minute before the performers set out and began their routine.

"So," said Jewel, sitting next to Sami. "Are we going to be writing about this?"

"Of course we are, unless you've been living a double life and have even more exciting things to write about."

"No," said Jewel with a small laugh. "My week's been pretty busy. Hey, I know we promised not to. But did you ever read my articles?"

"Even if I wanted to, I haven't had the time. What, did you read mine?"

"I'm not going to lie. I got a little jealous and opened up your page. But then I started feeling bad about it and closed it before reading anything."

Now it was Sami's turn to hide a laugh. "And what about your next article? Will you tell them you went out with your therapist?"

"No, because he's not 'my' therapist. He's just 'a' therapist that I just happen to talk to. And no, I'll just leave out his job. We're supposed to change names and locations and stuff anyway, right?"

"I think the design department does that for us."

"Oh... well, either way, I'll do it."

"Either way," said Sami with a laugh. "Glad you could make it out, girl. We even got you wearing heels. I'm sure people are going to love what you write?"

Jewel smirked at her with a brow raised. "So... does that mean you're willing to give up and give me the job?"

"Girl, please. We both know I'm going to win. But don't worry. I'll put your office outside of the window glass, right next to mine."

"May the best girl win."

"May the best girl win," agreed Sami as the girls toasted their glasses and tried watching the play. The women spun in colorful outfits, their dressing raising up to their hips as they twirled. The men lifted them up to the sounds of music and as the lead bellowed a deep voice that sounded over the crowd.

Jewel smiled at the display. *I really don't understand why people enjoy these so much. The music is fine, but the dancing, I just don't get it. I've seen stage plays before where they're acting. I understand that, but maybe I'm just uncultured or something.* She looked around to see how everyone else was enjoying it and saw a slew of muted facial expressions. *I don't know what they think. I guess I'll ask when it's over. I can't be the only one.* She turned back to Jewel and saw her fidgeting in her seat. "Are... you okay?"

"Yeah, sorry. I'll be right back," said Jewel, before standing up and excusing herself from the group walking around the theatrical display and over to the manor house.

"Where's she going?" asked Sami.

"Probably to the bathroom," said Becca. "She should know where it is. She arrived early, and we were there for around an hour or so before you arrived."

But before she could think more about it, Sami's attention was grabbed by another sudden bellow, this time by a woman who had taken center stage dressed in a curious outfit that looked like a dove was attached to her head. Her voice was loud and piercing, as if forcibly grabbing her attention as she swayed her arms back and forth.

Okay then, you go, honey. I wonder what it would take for me to sound like that, thought Sami, leaning back in her seat. I'd probably pass out trying to hold a note that long. *I guess this is what's going on now. I've never been to an opera before. I wonder why so many people enjoy it. It's so much different from a concert.* She looked around at the group of people once again. *Maybe the opera is just a concert for rich people.*

The crowd shifted places as new characters entered the scenes. Apparently, the story was that of a father who lived out in the woods during the time of a war-torn land. His kingdom forces had been pushed back and he would lure in enemy soldiers and kill them. The act itself caused him and his family to become mad and continue their murders long after the war.

While not her particular preferred interest, Sami found herself smiling at the movements of the performers as they glided across the stage. The way the swaying of their bodies was used to tell their story between the words of the song being spoken wasn't something that she had much experience with before. But she started to feel that she might just be able to get used to it.

Jewel exited the bathroom of the manor. A maid had guided her to a room on the second floor rather than use the servants' bathroom. But as she came back outside, she realized the servant was gone. Inside, the house was dark and dimly lit. She couldn't help but frown as she looked down the long hallway at the wall lights that flickered in the moonlight.

Why couldn't they at least update the lights at least? I feel like I've stepped into some type of weird horror movie. A bit of unease came over her as she took her time, heading back down the hallway, looking for the stairs. *I think I'm supposed to turn here.* Seeking any semblance of security, she placed her hand on the wall to feel something solid in this dreary environment. *Then I should take a left and...* Suddenly, there was a crack and her weight shifted, then her knees buckled as she went crashing to the floor with a thud and as she gave out a loud yelp.

She clenched her teeth for a moment as she turned around and saw the heel of her shoe, half torn off of her left foot piercing the carpet and lodged into the wooden floorboard of the house. She narrowed her eyes and sighed. *Dam Becca, and her dam heels. This wouldn't have happened in my wedges.* She tried to stand, but instantly she sat back down as the pain shot through her like fire. *Okay, bad idea, bad idea. That hurts a lot.*

"Ah, hello. Hello? Is anyone there?" The answer to her question came in the form of silence, and she gave another sigh. *Great. Now I'm in a big creepy house with a bad leg and I left my phone in my purse out there.* She took another look around one more time before closing her eyes and taking in a deep breath. *Maybe I really am Bad Luck, like Becca says.* She shook her head, trying to clear the negative thoughts. *Okay, I'm not a helpless woman. Let's suck it up and get myself back downstairs.*

Hands up against the wall once more, she struggled, but managed to lift herself up on one leg. Then, placing all her weight on her good leg, she tested how much she could handle on the other. *Owe, owe, owe. Okay, okay, okay... not much, but I can do this.* Her right leg trembled for a moment with the knowledge of what she was about to do. She swallowed all her courage and leaned forward.

"What in the world are you doing?" said a familiar voice from behind.

"Oh, sweet god," yelped Jewel, as her heart almost jumped out of her chest. She then turned around to see Andrew standing in the middle of the hall, looking at her. "I'm suffering, that's what I'm doing," she said, twisting to face him. "Would you mind helping me?"

Andrew took a look at her, cradling her leg and then down to the torn heel sunken heel in the floor. "Why is it that every time I see you, you're in need of me to help lift something?"

"What? What are you talk— oh the plants? Okay, you have me there, but can you help me and not just stand there with that smug look on your face?"

"It would be my pleasure to assist the lady back to her seat. But first, how much pain are you in, one through ten?"

"A lot… a lot of pain out of ten."

Andrew laughed as he stepped forward and wrapped an arm around Jewels' waist. "Alright, let's go. Put your hand on my shoulder."

"Wait," she said as he squeezed her a bit, lifting her off her feet and spun her around. "I thought the way to the stairs was that way?"

"No, that leads to a dead end. The stairs are down the hall and then you take the next left."

"Why are the bathrooms so far away?" said Jewel, shaking her head.

"I've wondered that myself, but the house was made two hundred years ago. Who knows what they were thinking? It's probably why no one lives here."

"What? But I thought this was your friend's home."

Oh, that's just for show. They called it their family home just to keep up appearances. But in truth, he grew up in Colorado. Apparently, his father bought the home to appear high class. So once a year they'll come here and take pictures before hightailing back to someplace easier to live."

Jewel looked around as they turned the next corner and saw the stairs ahead, noticing all the family pictures on the wall. "Really. They'd go that far just to look a certain way?"

"Don't underestimate how far rich people will go to look a certain way."

"I'm having serious concerns about the mental state of people with large amounts of money."

"Okay," he said, releasing her weight near the stairs as she grabbed the shoulder of the railing. "Take a seat and we'll have a look at that leg."

Jewel held on tight to the railing, while lowering herself, having a seat on the steps. "What, are you a doctor as well?"

"No, but I was in the boy scouts for a few years. So, I can do fancy things like start forest fires, shoot guns, and check for broken bones. That'll let me know if we have to call an ambulance or not."

When Jewel had finally sat down on the steps. She allowed Andrew to undo the straps of her other heel shoe, removing it from her feet. The release of pressure from the straps on her ankle was such a joyous event that she audibly moaned as his fingers slid their way around her foot.

"I will never understand how women wear these things."

"I can actually blame men for that. Guys created them for riding horses. Then, of course, some noble women decided it was fashionable because it lifted their bum bums and here we are. An entire world-wide epidemic of girls enslaved to forever walk like chickens."

Andrew seemed to try but couldn't hold back a laugh. "Well, then I'm grateful. I do enjoy the view of a shapely ass."

"Of course you do. All men— owe," she winced as he began to slowly rub his hand over the sore area. "Good, it's not broken. Seems like just a sprain. Come on, let's get you back downstairs to the kitchen."

Jewel took hold of his hand again as he led her cautiously

down the stairs and over to a small kitchen, where he placed her on a stool and began rummaging through the cupboards. After finding a plastic bag, he made his way to the fridge to fill it with ice before coming back and squatting before Jewel.

"This might sting a little."

"I know. I rolled a few ankles when I was in high school," she bawled her lips, breathing deeply through her nose as Andrew applied the ice bag to the bruised area of her leg. "But... I'll admit... it has been... awhile." The cold instantly pierced her skin, sending a chill up her spine as her toes stiffened. *Oh, that's nice. It really is a shame you like Sami.*

Andrew continued to caress the slide of her ankle. "Tell me. What did you think of the pictures I sent you?"

"I'm jealous. How'd you get... oh, that's good," she said with a moan as her mind drifted for a minute. "How'd you get them?"

"From the source."

"You went to the Philippines, just to get some plants?"

"No..." he said, his hands gliding over the bottom of her foot, his eyes moving up to her thigh as she had her skirt raised for him to inspect her leg. "I... I went there on business and just happened to pick them up. Private planes are good for that."

"I'm pretty sure you've broken some sort of customs law."

"So..." he said, his hand slowly moving up her ankle. "Are you saying you don't want one?"

"No, no. I want it," she said before leaning her head back and sighing.

"Then I'll bring one to your place later on."

"Thank you," she smiled, looking up at the ceiling. "That feels good. Maybe Becca's, maybe I am bad luck. I just can't seem to do anything right lately."

"Bad luck? I don't think so. Maybe it was meant for you to hurt your leg."

Jewel laughed. "Why would it ever be meant for me to hurt myself."

"Perhaps... so that I could come and find you."

Jewel was silent for a moment, still staring up at the ceiling. She could him there, looking at her. But she swallowed her budding feelings. "Well... I mean, I'm glad you came looking for me. Do you think I'm okay?"

"Don't worry. As bad as it could have been. This shouldn't be..." stopping his speech mid-sentence. He closed his eyes and began nodding his head and sighed. "I... I... should probably go and get your date. He... he probably should be looking after you. Not me."

"Oh," said Jewel, taken away from the moment to understand their situation. "Yeah. I guess you're right."

He lifted off his knees, but paused for a moment when his face reached the same level as Jewel's and began staring at her.

"Why... Why are you looking at me like that?"

"Because... I think I'm about to do something that I shouldn't."

Jewel stared back at him, her breathing slowing till she had to swallow. *Oh, don't look at me like that. Its unfair when I like you so much.* Her eyes stared into his as her heart began to tighten in her chest. Just at her nose, she could smell the scent of his cologne. Quick images of him flashed in her mind. She wanted him to hold her; to take her. She could easily imagine his hands around her waist as he pulled her toward him. *Okay, I admit it. I'm Bad Luck Jewel. But I have to try.* "Well... what if... I want you to do that thing you shouldn't?"

"Then I..." and not even finishing his sentence, he leaned forward, pressing his lips against hers.

I want him. I want him so much. Whether it was her own selfish desires, the chilling pain in her leg, or the alcohol in her system that placed her mind into the way of thinking, she didn't know. But in truth, she didn't care. His lips on
196

hers, the way his finger found her neck, making its way up caressing her face. It felt good. It felt right.

He pulled away for a moment. "I'm sorry. It's just... ever since that day at your place. I... I've been thinking about you and—"

Before he could finish his words, this time it was she who threw her lips against his. Their touch, the embrace of what she had been feeling leading up to this coming forward into her, being rewarded in this moment. It was for sure what she wanted.

After a long kiss, they pulled their lips away from each other once again, slowly feeling the skin of their faces together as they both took in the moment. The whispers of his exhaled breath gliding off of her neck.

"You think this makes us bad people?" he asked as he reached down, taking her hand in his caressing her fingers.

"Probably. What do we do now?"

"We go out there with big stupid smiles and pretend it didn't happen. But tomorrow I'll call you and we'll figure it out."

Jewel sighed, "Yeah. I think... I think I can do that."

"How's your ankle?"

"Still bad. But surprisingly, it's not the thing I'm most worried about now."

"I bet," he said as he pulled himself away from her, standing back up to his full height. He then reached out his hand to her again. "Shall we go back out?"

"Yes," she said, grabbing his hand, allowing herself to be pulled back up. "Let's get this night over."

Andrew knelt down, taking her shoes in his hand as she allowed him to escort her back out of the kitchen and towards the door. Upon exiting the building, he released her in the door frame, letting her brace herself there.

"The play's almost over. I'll go and tell everyone what happened to your leg."

Jewel watched him walk ahead and around the clothed

structure. From behind, she could hear the voice actor of the opera words as he brought down a toy ax onto another man's head, who then proceeded to play dead.

"You are not my brother anymore," sang the Opera singer, swinging the ax back and forth. "You are a demon taken to his flesh and I will not suffer your lies any longer."

Am I the demon now? She thought as she watched through the curtain, a glimpse of Andrew as he went about informing Becca and Henry about her situation. To her credit, Becca immediately got up and reached over, grabbing Sami by the hand, seeming to inform her as well as they both began making their way to her. I'm *not a demon. But I'm definitely a terrible friend, though.* She shook her head and began rubbing her face in frustration as Sami and Becca made their way over to her.

"Jewel, what happened?" asked Becca, looking worried.

"Yeah, are you okay?" asked Sami.

"I'm fine. She said, holding up her shoes, showing the broken heel. I apparently hurt my ankle a bit. Andrew came and got me."

"Yeah," said Becca, reaching out and taking the heels. "Henry was worried about you taking so long."

"I'm fine," she said as the crowd started cheering at the finale of the play. "Sorry. I made you miss the ending."

"Forget that," said Sami as she took Jewel's arm and began leading her toward a set of chairs at a table. "You need to get off that foot."

"Thank you," said Jewel with a ping of tightness in her chest for the charity that Sami was showing her. "It'll be okay. I just need to rest for a moment."

Becca and Sami also sat down with her.

"I guess I should apologize for convincing you to wear heels tonight," said Becca.

"No," it's fine," said Jewel, her eyes glancing up and over to Andrew. "I'm grateful you invited me."

"Well, at least the night's over," said Becca as she looked

over at the performers, who were now shuffling back into the house after ending their play. "Not much left to do now, but chat with people until they head home."

"Are you okay?" asked Henry as he, Andrew, and Nathan came over, looking worried.

"She's fine," said Becca. "But I don't think she'll be participating in the evening dance."

"That's fine. It'll be dull anyway," said Henry as he turned to Andrew and Nathan. "Andrew, call the driver and have him go fetch the car they arrived in."

"Will do," said Andrew, taking a final look at Jewel, their eyes meeting for only a moment in silent understanding before he turned and made his way down the side of the manor.

"Are you sure you don't need to go to the hospital?" asked Nathan as he knelt, inspecting her ankle.

"No. I have a pair of crutches at my home. But I'd take another glass of wine, please."

"Oh," said Henry, waving over a waiter. "Thank you. No, just leave the whole tray. I imagine she'll have quite a few before she leaves."

Jewel grabbed a wine glass, taking it to her lips as she swallowed it whole. Then took another, repeating the process.

It wasn't long before Andrew arrived back. "The car's ready."

"I suppose I'll drive you home then," said Nathan as he stepped to the side of her and reached down and scooped her up in his arms to the surprise of those around him.

"Well, you certainly do put those large muscles of yours to good use, don't you?" asked Becca with a smile. She waved her hands at Jewel, "Well, go on dear, don't look so embarrassed. Put your arms around your man there and let him carry you off."

Unable to help herself from feeling embarrassed, Jewel did, in fact, wrap her arms around Nathan's neck. She was accustomed to being taller than the surrounding girls, but this height was completely different.

Thank goodness I don't have to live up here. I'd never get a date.

And with the applause of their friends, Nathan turned and escorted Jewel away, taking her back to the car.

"Did you have fun?" he asked.

"I did. Thank you for coming tonight. I... I didn't really have anyone else I could ask."

"It wasn't so bad. I got to learn how the people in high society live."

"And how was it?" she asked as he carried her around the corner, lowered her to her feet, near the car, allowing her to slide in.

"Not bad. But put me on a farm any day," he said as she closed the door for her and walked around to his side, entering the driver's seat. He then started the car and began to, driving away.

"I can see you don't want to be bothered with a hospital. But I think you should still have that leg of yours looked at."

"It'll be fine. I'll continue to ice it down when I get home. But if it starts swelling, then I'll go to the doctor and have them look at it."

The therapist nodded his head. "I guess I'll have to accept that. Then I'll ask the other question? What happened with you and Andrew while you both were inside that big house?"

"Huh?" said Jewel, shocked as she almost jumped in the car seat from the surprise at the question.

"Oh, so something did happen."

"How? I mean... what makes you say that?"

"The way you two looked at each other. The way he seemed overly worried about when I lifted you up and how he couldn't seem to make up his mind on whether he wanted to follow us to the car or stay with the group and probably the woman he came with."

"You... you saw all that?"

"I see a lot of things. But I figured it wouldn't be polite to ask while I was lifting you up."

Jewel shifted in her seat uncomfortably as she stared at him for a moment. Then, accepting the truth, she just shook her head. "Do you think I'm a bad person?"

"Depends on the context. You seem to feel bad about it, so I'd say you're not as bad as you feel right now."

"But tell me something, are you normally attracted to dangerous situations, or is this a new occurrence since my arrival?"

Jewel frowned as she laid her head on the window, feeling the coldness of the moisture outside against her cheek. "I would love for you to be wrong, but the truth is I'm starting to think that a lot of my problems I bring on myself."

CHAPTER 11

Two days Jewel exited her cab with crutches under her arms and a medical boot on her foot as she went up to her office. Her ankle hadn't swollen, but there was still a decent bit of pain.

"Thank you," she said to the driver as she made her way up the steps and inside of her building. It was earlier in the morning for her to arrive than usual, which was apparent by the lack of people inside the main lobby. She couldn't help but remember Alina sitting with the security guard, but this time he sat alone, looking over the morning newspaper. Nodding to each other in acknowledgment, she then stepped over to the elevator, pressing the button and entering.

"Hold the door," came the familiar voice of Sami.

Jewel slid one of her crutches into the door after hearing Sami's voice and the sound of her footsteps echoing over the lobby halls.

Breathing heavily, Sami appeared and entered the elevator.

"Are you okay?" asked Jewel. "I'm not used to seeing you here this early."

"Yeah..." said Sami, catching her breath. "Addison told me to come in early today for some reason."

"Yeah, she asked me the same thing."

"You think this has something to do with the job?" asked Sami.

"Probably," said Jewel as the elevator took off upstairs.

"How's your leg treating you?" asked Sami, looking down at the medical boot on her foot. "Did you go to the hospital?"

"No, this is just some stuff I had at home from when I sprained my ankle last year.," She sighed. "I didn't expect it to come in handy so soon after the last time, though."

Sami smiled, "So tell me? Who was that Nathan guy you showed up with at the party? You've never mentioned him before."

"No... well... I mean, we only just met a little while ago and I wasn't sure he'd come. But he's a nice guy and all," said Jewel, looking at Sami, before biting her lip and regretting it even as she spoke the words. "What about you and Andrew? Did you go home with him that night?"

"No, he had to see to the arrangements of Becca's boyfriend. So, he just drove me home, and he had to turn back around."

"Oh, okay, but do you like him?"

"You know, I think I do. I mean, the first date didn't exactly go so well. But last night was nice. But..."

"But what?" asked Jewel, nervously latching on to the statement.

"Well, he drove me back home that night. And I thought he would... you know... try to make a move of something. But he didn't even try to kiss me." Sami gave a small laugh.

"I think I might have scared him a bit after I blew up after our first date."

"Oh." Jewel felt a bit of relief after hearing that. "Do... do you think you'll see him again?"

"Yeah, we're planning to go out this weekend. What about you? You still plan on seeing that therapist guy?"

"I don't know. I think I might have found someone else. But well, I'm not so sure now."

"Wow, really? Is this really the Jewel that doesn't like to go out and spends all her time playing with plants? And now you're trying to juggle two men?"

"It's not like that. I'm... I'm just not sure is all."

Sami laughed, "Alright. You do, you girl." she raised a finger with a playful grin. "But I'm still winning that job."

The elevator stopped on their floor, and they walked into their office only to see that they were the only two there.

"Well, this is new," said Sami, looking around the empty space. "I know we're early, but I didn't think we were this early. Lan Ling isn't even here, and she's always here."

"Yeah," said Jewel, as she hobbled her way into the office area. "I wonder where everyone is."

But ahead and out of her glass office came their boss, leaning out of her door frame.

"Hey you two. Come over here, we have a few things to talk about," said Addison as both women looked at each other for a moment before then walking over to her office, where she stood holding the door open for them. "Please have a seat. We have a few things to talk about."

"Ah, okay. Is this about our stories?" asked Sami as she and Jewel took a seat facing Addison's desk.

"Yes," said Addison as she walked over, sitting down on her desk, looking at them, then looking at Jewel. "Among other things." She then folded her arms over her chest and stared at the two women for a moment. "Tell me. How do you both feel about this little game you've been playing against each other?"

"I think it's fair," said Sami, nodding her head. "Guess it does make sense to have us compete with other people to get the job. I'll admit, I don't enjoy having to compete with Jewel, though. But we've come to an understanding about it."

"Have you?" asked Addison with a small look of surprise on her face. "How very 'adult' of you. But do you know why I am having you two compete against each other?"

"I thought it was because of the attention our articles got."

"It was partly that, yes," said Addison, folding her arms. "But there's more to it than that. You girls both work for me, and that's fine. But when you're the CEO of a company, you have to understand that you work to keep everyone having a job. So, a lot of that friendship stuff goes out of the window. I've pissed off not too many of my friends in order to be where I am. Some have forgiven me and understood that it was just business, others... well, others aren't so forgiving."

"I don't understand what you're saying," said Sami, looking confused. "You want us to not hold a grudge over who wins?"

"Something like that," said Addison with a smirk. "I'm just saying that even my best friends I've had since college have also had to forgive me a few times."

"So, you want us to become ruthless businesswomen?" asked Jewel.

"Exactly. That's what I want to teach the both of you. If you want to win, you have to ruthlessly pursue your desires. And I've done that with every major goal in my life so far. And now, I stand trying to teach you young ladies what I've learned."

"I'll... I'll try to keep that in mind," said Sami, looking a bit confused.

Is... is she trying to do me a favor? Does that mean she's already read my article? If Sami finds out, she'll forgive... I think.

"Good," said Addison, as she took the remote and flipped on the TV. But instead of a TV station, there was only a number. The number one million two hundred thousand and eighty-eight. "Do you know what this is?"

The girls looked at the screen curiously for a moment, but both shook their heads, acknowledging that they hadn't.

"That is the current number of people waiting for your next article to go live today."

"What!" they both said in unison.

"Seriously?" said Jewel, her surprise just as apparent as Sami's. "We have that many people just sitting online waiting?"

"Well, I'm sure a few of them are bots or something," said Addison with a shrug. "But for the most part, yes." she smiled up at the screen. "Look at them all." The number flickered up another hundred. "They're like hungry fish. Hungry... paying... fish. We've even had to have more servers flown in to handle the traffic. Poor Gavin must be down there having a fit. They've crashed the site five times in the last hour."

"I can't believe so many people care about who we're dating," said Jewel.

"I admit, this has surprised me as well. Then I had the thought that it's like how men care about their silly sports teams. They feel like they're winning when their team wins. There are a million love-starved hungry people out there all betting on one of you. Living through you and hoping that you're winning this week." She chuckled. "But that idea made me think about what do sports teams do the most with?"

"What?" asked Sami. "You want to buy a sports team?"

"No," said Addison, looking confused at the statement. "No," she then leaned over her desk and grabbed something from her seat. She then lifted it up with both hands, displaying a shirt for them to see. "Sports teams are great at merchandising."

Jewel could only sit there in astonishment as Addison produced a t-shirt with a black sheep and a white sheep sleeping on top of a large pink heart.

"So, what do you girls think?"

"Think?" asked Sami. "Think about what? Are you planning on selling those?"

"Think about it?" asked Addison with a laugh. "I'm already selling these. Along with coffee mugs, toys, I'm even partnering with restaurants and having them feature as menu items. Later today, I even have a meeting about creating a limited time black sheep white sheep candy bar."

"What?" said Sami, reaching up and taking the shirt. "You can't be serious. There's no way people are that invested in us dating around the city."

"Tsk, tsk, tsk," said Addison with a smile. "Never underestimate the lonely heart. Apparently, there's a lot of money in it if you tug at just the right strings." She shook her head as if unsatisfied. "It really is a shame. I only said this would last for four parts. I should have said a year. A bit short sighted on my end."

Sami just shook her head. "I can't believe it's gotten that popular. I mean, I know people were talking about it. But this is ridiculous."

"The world is a ridiculous place, dear."

"Apparently so," said Sami as she shook her head, staring at the shirt design.

"But enough on that for now. Instead, let's move on with today's topic of discussion. I've read through your adventures over the past two weeks, and I must say, you girls have been busy. Even dining out at a large manor with a bunch of stuck-up rich types."

Jewel saw Sami's face twitch as if she was saying. *'Aren't you the stuck up rich type?'* But she decided it would be best to just let that go. Even if she was perhaps thinking the same thing.

"That must have been quite the change of scenery for

you both," said Addison as she looked down at Jewel's boot. "And you seem to have come back with a souvenir."

"My heel broke."

"Yes, and didn't that work out well for you?" asked Addison before turning to Sami. "And you. Really! Three dates, including Patrick, the maintenance man. We'll I guess in terms of convenience you can't beat it. Perhaps we'll finally get that damn copier fixed."

"You went out with Patrick?" asked Jewel, surprised.

"Yes, but nothing happened."

"But you were just talking about me dating two men at once."

"We just sat up on the roof and looked over the city. It's not like we were fucking on the roof."

"Yes," said Addison. In a way, I wish you would have. "That certainly would have liven up your story a bit."

"No thanks. I'm not letting groups of people who I don't know decide who I sleep with."

"Suit yourself. For now, the people find it interesting. We decided to name that part of the article 'Handyman Charms,'" she flicked her wrist upward. "And speaking of which. Your articles should be going live right about now." She turned to the screen and, almost as if on cue, that one million views jumped to two million views.

Sami's and Jewel's mouths dropped.

"It seems you girls are going to be receiving a sizable bonus on your checks at the end of all of this," said Addison with a smile and a clap of her hands. "God... look at that money."

"Wait," said Sami. "How much is sizable?"

Addison looked at the screen Bland twisted her lips. "Well, let's see. Currently, two million on the site, and the paywall only starts after they flipped through so many articles. And given how we usually retain twenty percent of our reader base pay wise. I would guess that each of you will receive anywhere from fifty thousand to a hundred thousand in bonus pay for the revenue that your article has brought into the company."

This time both girl's eyes went wide as they stared at Addison, and then at each other, before finally setting on the TV screen and its steadily increasing number. Then, with a scream of glee, both Sami and Jewel clasped hands together as they bounced in their seats.

"Owe, owe my leg," said Jewel, quickly settling down, but not removing the smile from her face.

"Oh, I finally get to go shopping with my own money," said Sami.

"And I get to buy heels that aren't cheap," said Jewel.

"Yes," said Addison and she leaned over and across her desk again, grabbing two envelopes, then handing them to the girls. "As an extra bonus, inside you two will find two debit cards, each with three thousand dollars on them to do as you like. Go out and buy yourselves something nice."

"Really?" asked Sami. "Thank you."

"Wow." said Jewel.

"Now go on. Everyone else has the day off. You, get out of here too."

"Alright. Thank you," said Sami, as she got up to leave.

Jewel began lifting herself carefully out of the seat. "Yes, thank—"

"Not you Jewel. I'm going to have to ask you to stay a bit longer. We're going to have to have a talk about the hazardous nature of the job you've been doing."

Sami looked down at Jewel. "Should I wait for you downstairs?"

"Yes," said Addison. "You do that. This shouldn't take long. Just a few papers for Jewel to sign to make sure we're not responsible for her incredible recklessness."

"Okay... ah... I'll see you downstairs, Jewel," said Sami, before walking out of the room and through the office.

Addison smiled as she watched her leave and step into the elevator before turning back to Jewel. "Tell me, Jewel.

How are things going with you? Are you okay, mentally I mean. Does this contest have you stressed? Would you like me to set you up with our company therapist?"

"What?" asked Jewel, looking confused. "No... I mean, not that much. No more than I can handle."

Addison sighed. "I guess that removes an excuse of insanity. That really is a shame. I guess I have to assume it was malicious or just stupid on your part."

"I... I don't understand. Is everything okay?"

"You tell me. You wrote in your story that you went on a date with a man who had a child?"

"Yes."

"And you took them back home to your apartment after some apparent thugs followed you around the museum?"

"Well, yes. But I don't—"

"So, perhaps you can explain to me why my daughter came home telling me she found the perfect woman to be my husband's apparent second wife."

Jewel stared at Addison for a moment as the words she had just shared registered in her mind. Then her eyes went wide as her mouth opened as a long slow drooled 'Noooo,' exited her lips.

"Yesssss," said Addison, mimicking the slow drool in her own tone.

Jewel's face turned to something resembling anguish and pain. But it wasn't from her leg. "Ohhhh noooooo."

"Ohhhh yessssssss," said Addison, once again mimicking Jewel. "I think we need to have ourselves a little talk. Don't you?"

"But... but that would mean that Nasir is..."

"My husband. My loving, oh so naive husband."

Jewel flinched, lifting her shoulders up as she grimaced, "and that makes Alina..."

"My daughter, who has apparently taken quite a liking to you. So much so that she wants you to be her new mommy, and she says that she wants a new little sister. So, tell me

Jewel, I know you're after my job, but are you also after my family as well?"

"What? No?" replied Jewel, vehemently shaking her head.

"First you kiss Sami's man, and then try to steal my husband. I swear, I didn't know you had it in you."

"No, that's not... I mean... what I'm trying to do. I... I was just dating for the contest."

"Are you saying that you didn't specifically go after my husband? You just so happened to introduce yourself to your boss's husband and then offer to show him around the city, and then suddenly invite him back to your home, and then may put in my daughter's head that you thought my husband was cute and you wouldn't mind having his babies."

"No... I mean yes... I mean everything other than that last part."

"Jewel," said Addison, leaning over, looking her in the eyes. "Do you think I'm stupid?"

Unable to look her boss in the face at the moment, Jewel dropped her head and began staring at the floor. "No Ma`am," she muttered.

"That's better," said Addison as she reached over, patting Jewel on the head, ruffling her hair. "If you are going to take my spot. It's not going to be now. I may not show it as much as I need to, but my daughter is my world, and the fact still remains that she's taking a liking to you. So, while I'm handling my company business this month, I'm going to have you look after her."

Jewel couldn't help but look up at Addison again. "Huh?"

"I told you, my daughter's my world. And she hasn't taken to anyone other than myself and the previous nanny. And apparently, what I have here is a chance for you to be useful, and I am the type of woman who uses people."

"But—"

Addison placed her hands on her lips. "I must admit

that I thought that you had made up that night in the city in the car chase. And I had my friends at the police station check the records and they did, in fact, inform me that there was a car incident. So, a curious me, after reading your new article, out of curiosity, called those same police and asked them if someone was arrested at the museum. And wouldn't you know, someone was?"

"I... I didn't know you could do that."

"Oh, money can do a lot of things. Like say, for instance, paying the museum personnel to give me a copy of the security camera footage of you strolling around with my daughter and my husband?" She once again grabbed the remote to the TV and changed it to a different signal.

Jewel was greeted with a clear color image of herself and Alina, strolling around the museum. She even saw the dark-haired man that followed them. "I... I don't know what to say."

"Good, because you don't need to say anything. You just need to do what I tell you to. You see, I am going to look into the man who followed you along with that tall fellow who walked out of that bathroom before you and—"

"No!" said Jewel. "He's not a bad guy. He saved me from that other guy who followed me."

"Oh," said Addison, looking a little surprised. "Well, that helps a bit. But you'll understand if I ask you to give me his number, won't you? I feel like I should have a talk with him myself."

"What, but why. He's not—"

"Jewel," said Addison, her voice seeming more threatening and reserved than she'd ever heard here before. "That is my daughter and my husband. So, for your future health. Don't ask me fucking questions, just give me the fucking number."

"Yes, Ma`am," said Jewel, reaching into her purse and opening up her phone. She scrolled down to his number and showed it to her.

Addison took the phone, looking at it. "Stalker Guy?"

"That's... that's just what I named him. You see... I was mad at him and... well... he's not really a stalker."

Addison closed her eyes, taking in a large breath, and then released it audibly. "I'm going to let all this go today. Even though everything and I do mean everything you say to me seems like one giant fucking lie. I am going to believe in my precious little baby's sense of judgment. So, tell me, what am I to do when my daughter is so ensnared with someone who is so attracted to trouble? I mean really."

"Ahh... maybe... hire her for the job?"

"Oh," said Addison with a laugh. "No... maybe later," she said as she reached forward, her hands slowly beginning to caress the side of Jewel's face. "But there is something I can do with you."

What? What's happening? Thought Jewel as she watched Addison's face change from a look of disapproval to a look of playful curiosity as a smile stretched around her lips so wide that it could have been thought of as sinister and for the first time Jewel had a different thought about her boss. *I think there's something wrong with my boss.*

"Jewel," said Addison, still staring at her. "There's this rumor around the office that you walk around carrying with you an enormous amount of bad luck. Do you think that's true?"

"Ah... would you believe me if I said 'no?'" said Jewel, her words sliding over Addison's lips.

Addison laughed. "Well, if everything you've through is a coincidence as you say. Then the real question is 'do you?'"

Jewel thought about her incident with Sami, then being chased through the streets in a stolen car, then being followed through the museum, and finally ending up sitting in front of Addison. "Maybe... it's kinda bad luck?"

Then, letting her fingers slide down Jewel's face, she clasped the side of each of her cheeks in her hands, forcing her to look her in the face. "Jewel. I think it's time that we really got to know each other. So, it looks like you're coming over for dinner. And After I investigate all the mess you've caused. I'd suggest you pray that you really are just that 'unlucky.'"

Downstairs, Sami sat down in a lobby chair looking out the window. The city seemed as normal as it ever did. Gray concrete buildings that seemed to reach the sky. Cars cruising by down at street level or honking their horns because of whatever problem is the flavor of the day. But today was different for her. On her lap sat the envelope with supposedly three thousand dollars with more to come.

A hundred thousand dollars... what would I even do with that much money? What would I buy? A down payment on a house? Is that what I should buy? But I can't buy a house and work in the city. An hour trip to work every day? She shook her head. *No, no way.*

As the random thoughts filled her mind, Sami heard the elevator ding and turned to see Jewel stepping out on the lobby floor. Noticing her, she came slowly, still minding her leg.

"Are you sure you want to go shopping?" asked Sami, standing up from her seat and meeting her halfway. "I mean with your leg." She noticed a strange look on Jewel's face. "It's everything okay? Jewel... Jewel?"

"Huh?"

"I asked if everything was okay? You look like you've seen a ghost?"

"Oh, yes... I'm fine. I was just daydreaming is all."

"Okayyyy," said Sami with a curiously long hold on the word. "If you say so. But if you're not feeling up for shopping, maybe you should just go home and rest your leg?"

Jewel shook her head as if to clear her mind and turned to Sami with a smile. "I stayed cooped up in my apartment all day yesterday writing that stupid article. There's no way I'm doing that again. I'll just take a rest when I need to, but there's no way I'm missing shopping. I need this and trust me when I say that. I really need this."

"Alright," said Sami with a raised brow, looking down at her leg, unconvinced. "If you say so. But we can talk about our contest anytime."

"No… it'll be better to get it over with today."

"If you say so."

Being extra mindful of Jewel's leg, they walked out of the building and headed down to the street below, where they flagged down a cab. Once inside, they directed the driver to a nearby shopping center as they both relaxed in the backseat.

"Sure things, ladies," said the male driver as he took off down the street.

"Have you decided what you're going to do with your money?" asked Sami.

"There're a few plants that I've been waiting to get, but couldn't afford. I'll buy those and have them delivered."

Sami laughed, "Really? You're still thinking about those plants even now?"

"That's easy for you to say," said Jewel. "You've been writing about relationship stuff since you got here. I've been writing about plants. It's not something that's easy to turn off. And besides, maybe I won't get the job. Maybe you will."

"We shall see," said Sami, shaking her head with satisfaction. "This whole Black Sheep White Sheep thing is still silly to me."

"Oh!" said the cabby, listening in. "You girls interested in that stuff going on too? My wife's been texting me about that stuff all day, like I understand it. So maybe you two can enlighten a struggling cabby. What's got all the girls in the city rooting for this thing?"

The girls laughed at his comment, but in good nature they took turns trying to explain to him why the city might have fallen for a romance article. Some were jokes, some were true, and some of it were them parroting what Addison had told them just a few minutes ago, comparing it to sports teams, which the driver seemed to understand.

They soon arrived at the shopping complex. The venue was an outdoor affair with dozens of stores all lined throughout three cross-matched streets, which took up several city blocks. While the area itself was perfectly constructed for tourists, the surprising aspect was that on either side of the shopping centers were large parks that allowed a man-made river to flow through them. They even had to cross a bridge over the river to enter.

"Alright, here you girls go," said the cabby.

Sami exited the Cab, reaching in her purse giving the man two hundred dollars. "Buy your wife something nice."

"Hey, thanks lady," He looked around. "Ya know, since I'm here. I just might do that. You girls have a nice day," and he drove off, leaving them at the head of the complex.

"Really?" asked Jewel. "Two hundred?"

"We just got three thousand dollars. I think we can afford to be generous, if only just a little bit," said Sami as she pulled out her phone.

"Now, who are you calling?"

"No one. I'm just turning my phone off. Today I'm spending the day just enjoying shopping with my friend. It's our girl's day out. Go on, you do the same. Today is just about us."

Jewel smirked before reaching into the purse and turning off her phone. "I think you're enjoying yourself just a bit too much."

"Good, because after all the stuff we've been through. I think we deserve it. Now come on."

The girls walked through the shopping mart, stopping first at a clothing store where Sami stepped behind Jewel and began gently nudging her inside. "Okay, let's try on some clothes."

"Welcome ladies," said the clerk. "Is there anything we can help you with today?"

"Not yet. We would like to look around first."

"Yes, of course. Well, please let me know if you see anything you like."

"Thank you," said Sami, helping Jewel over to the mannequins and clothing near the side of the store.

"Maybe it is good that you got out," said Sami, looking Jewel over. "You really do need some new clothes."

Jewel frowned. "It's not exactly easy to put on pants like this, you know?"

"But you did anyway," said Sami, shaking her head like a disappointed parent. "Girl, we're having you try on dresses today."

"What?"

"Don't what, me. I'm surprised you wore one to the party that night with Becca."

"Actually, she gave me the dress along with the shoes. I just asked her not to say anything."

"Oh, my god. You really are hopeless. Do you even own a dress or a skirt?"

"Of course, I do."

"Mm-hmm, and when was the last time you wore one?"

Jewel's face twisted in thought for a moment. "It doesn't matter. That's not important."

"Ah ha! See, you can't even remember," said Sami with a smug look of satisfaction on her face, before raising her hand over to the clerk. "Excuse me, miss. We've changed our mind. Can you help us?"

"Yes," she said, coming over.

"Tell me, what do you think of my tall friend here? We're trying to find a skirt or a dress that she would look good in."

"Humm," moaned the clerk as she placed a finger to her lip in thought. "Well, I'd say that we find something that best shows off her long legs. Something eye-catching. blonde hair and blue-eyes, she gives off more of a valley girl look, which is good since those colors are in this season so we have a large stock."

"Good," said Sami. "Because we're going to be here a while. I want us to try on whatever you think works."

"Will do," said the clerk with a smile. "Nothing wrong with having a girls' day out. Let's get started, shall we?"

Sami smiled at Jewel's hesitation, but she ultimately went along with her plans as the woman went about their time playing dress up with Jewel. But with Jewel's limited mobility, Sami found herself stepping in to help her put on the clothing. The women helped Jewel try on dozens of skirts, short and long. Fitted and loose tops. Button ups and pullovers were laid across nearby chairs as they cycled through what was picked out and brought to them.

At the end of it all. Jewel stood wearing a sky-blue button up top with a flowing white skirt that went down to just above her ankles.

"Okay," said Sami, stepping to the side and picking out several outfits for Jewel and herself, handing them to the clerk. "We'll take these."

"Yes, Ma`am."

"And just charge us for what she has on. She'll just walk out in it."

The clerk smiled. "Good. Honestly, I think that's for the best. I mean sweatpants, really? The look you have now suits you better, I think."

"I didn't look that bad." she looked around at the disbelieving faces of the women in front of her. "Did I?"

"The fact that you don't know is all the more reason you need our clothing," said the clerk as she turned around, shaking her head and walked off toward the register.

Both girls left the store, but with Jewel still on her crutches, Sami found herself holding all the bags. Which, while not an extremely heavy amount of clothing, did feel that they drug her down a bit."

"Maybe I didn't think this through enough," said Sami.

"I can hold one or two if—"

"No, it's fine. I must suffer for fashion." Sami raised a brow at her friend. "Isn't that what the runway models say when they go on their diets?"

"I think the term is Fashion Fatigue."

"What? Seriously?"

"My mother wanted me to try modeling when I was growing up because I'm tall and kinda skinny. The other girls wouldn't eat for a day or two before a show so they could look their skinniest."

Sami bit her lip. "That doesn't sound fun."

"It wasn't. If anything, it was... hey, isn't that Jamal over there?" asked Jewel, stopping so she could point a finger.

"What? Where?" Sami's gaze followed Jewel's finger down the strip where she indeed spotted Jamal sitting down on a bench with a small bag sitting in his lap as he looked down at his phone. She then looked down at her own heavy bags and smiled. "It seems I've found someone to save me from my burden."

Jewel smiled, "Really?"

"Come on," said Sami, stepping forward. "Hey Jamal," she said in her friendliest voice and smile. "Hey, Jamal!"

He turned to see them and gave a wave back as he stood up from his seat to greet them, putting the little bag in his coat pocket. "What are you girls doing out here?" He looked Jewel over. "Wow, you're actually wearing a dress. I don't think I've ever seen that."

"I know, right?"

"You don't have to bring so much attention to it. It's not like I haven't worn them before."

"Yeah," said Jamal, pointing a finger at her legs. "I don't think you have. The only skin I've seen on you is your arms, neck, and fingers. That right there... That's some new shit."

"Just shut up," said Jewel, frowning at him. "I would try to hit you now, but I'm afraid I'd fall."

"We were just out shopping," said Sami, breaking up

Jamal's teasing. "Why are you out here?"

"I needed a new flash drive for my computer. So, I figured I'd come out here and stretch my legs while I got a new one."

"Well, good. Since you aren't doing anything. I'm going to have to ask a favor of you."

"Really," said Jamal as he took another look down at their bags and nodded his head. "I think I get it. You ladies found yourselves biting off more than you can chew?"

Sami raised her bags as much as she could before letting them drop back down at her side. "You could say that."

"I see. Okay, well, as a man, I guess it's my job to... Hey, isn't that your boss Addison over there?"

"Huh?" said Sami as both she and Jewel turned to see. "I don't see—" and before she could finish her sentence, she heard the loud clop of dress shoes on the pavement. She turned around and Jamal was gone. With a quick search, she was only able to catch a glimpse of the back of his head as he went sprinting across the rest area of the outdoor plaza to destinations unknown. "Oh no he... Get back here!" she screamed before he disappeared behind another building.

Jewel stood there for a moment, flabbergasted. "What? What was that about? Did he have an emergency?"

"His only emergency is being an idiot."

"Okay, so what do we do now?"

"I don't want to head back yet, so let's find somewhere to eat first." They walked on a bit further until they found a small bread eatery serving soft cinnamon sticks with frosting.

Taking a seat at an outdoor table, Sami happily dropped her bags by their seats and went over to grab them something to eat. Within a few minutes, she had returned holding two cups of breadsticks with small cups of frosting.

"This is nice," said Sami. "When was the last time we went out together?"

"Oh goodness. You mean when it's not a company event

or something that Becca had convinced us to join her in? Probably your first day at the company."

"That's right. She did assign you to look after me when I was hired on. God, I think you were fresh out of college, too."

"And you were dating that waiter from Vanessa's," said Jewel with a laugh. "You were convinced you would marry him and that his acting career would take off?"

"Well, the only thing he took off were the panties of all the other girls in that restaurant. Did I ever tell you I caught him in bed with two of them?"

"At the same time?"

"No? Once with one," then I forgave him and then two months later, I found him in bed with another one. She threw her hands up. "God, I was dumb. I was actually about to forgive him again, till that idiot who just ran away threatened to kick me out if I did."

"What? Jamal?" asked Jewel as a truck pulled up beside them.

"Yeah. I was living in an apartment that he convinced one of his ex-girlfriends to let me stay at for a while, since she was traveling the world or something like that."

Jewel twisted her face. "You were living at his old girlfriend's home."

"She had these expensive dogs or something that needed to be fed and walked. Essentially, I was a house sitter and dog walker for six months until she got back. I was even paid to do it."

Jewel shook her head. "Rich people really do live in a different world than we do. No wonder we haven't been seeing Becca around the office much lately. She's off hosting impromptu plays in her backyard."

"Say what you want about Becca. She's always been—"

"Well, this is surprising," said a familiar voice.

Sami turned around to see the face of Patrick, standing beside the rear of the van that had pulled up. "What are you doing here?"

He popped open the double doors of the van and pulled out a package. "I got a delivery for a couple of the shops around here today."

"Really?" said Sami with a laugh as she stood up and stepped over, peeking inside of the van. It was filled with boxes with a lot of the insignias of the store brands around the area. "How many jobs do you have? You work maintenance, help out in a diner, and now you're a delivery driver? Where'd you even get that van? That's not what you picked me up in."

"A man's gotta work." He nodded his head in acknowldgement. "Hey Jewel."

"Hey Patrick."

"I think you might be a workaholic. When do you sleep?" asked Sami.

"Usually in my office, at the job. I even have a bed in there."

"I believe you."

"Well, I'll be right back," said Patrick, moving ahead. "I gotta deliver this. Make sure no one steals any of my stuff." Not waiting for a response, Patrick shuffled along, passing by two stores, and entering the third.

"I guess he really is a busy person," said Jewel.

"It seems so."

Patrick came out of the store a few moments later and then proceeded to grab another box. "Thanks, I won't have to waste time locking and unlocking the door with you girls here."

"I'm happy we can be of help to a man on a mission," said Sami, the sarcasm thick in her voice. "But maybe you can help us out."

"Really? How?"

"I think we bought too much stuff, and it's kinda heavy. When you're done, can I ask you to take them to the office for us?"

"What? Sure, I don't mind."

"Thank You."

"No problem."

Jewel stood from the table with her breadsticks and came over with Sami, both sitting down on the back of the van as Patrick made his rounds. "So, have you gone back out with Patrick yet?"

"No? He hasn't even asked me out again. Honestly, I'm not even sure he remembers us going out. He hasn't even called. Nothing even feels different from before."

After delivering the last of his packages, Patrick appeared a few moments later. "Okay, that's it. All done," he said as the girls lifted themselves from the tail end of the van and closed the doors.

"Now, where are you headed?" asked Sami.

"Oh, I'm not done. I still have another load to be delivered. But it's not that much."

"Don't squish our things in there behind all your boxes."

"Don't worry. It'll be fine," he said as he leaned forward, giving Sami a kiss on the cheek, then nodding to Jewel and getting back into his van. "See you girls later." He then slapped the side of the Van with his hand before taking off down the shopping plaza roads, leaving a stunned face Sami watching him drive away.

Jewel couldn't help but laugh. "I think he remembers the date."

Sami just squinted her eyes, watching the van head off. "I really think that man lives in his own world. He probably already thinks we have two kids together."

"Wait, was that your first kiss?" asked Jewel, unable to hold in her laugh.

"You know, I would call him and curse him out. But he's driving away with all of our clothes, and I don't want them to end up on the side of the road."

"Okay," said Jewel, still holding in a few laughs. "So, what now?"

"Now we continue with our shopping, except this time. We will only be buying things that we can wear around our necks or on our fingers."

CHAPTER 12

The next morning Jewel lay on her bed looking up at the ceiling where several pants hung.

I can't believe I did that. All day... I had all day. Why didn't I tell her about the kiss with Andrew? I should have told her. She rolled over on her side. *But it's not like we slept together. It was a mistake... maybe.* She shook her head before closing her eyes again. *But I really do like this guy. Why'd he have to do that?*

Interrupting her thoughts, she felt the vibration of her phone beside her before she heard it start ringing. Reaching over, she grabbed it, placing it above her head, her breath freezing in her throat for a moment as she saw that it was him. *Okay, Okay, it's him. I just need to explain to him that it was a mistake.* She received the call, pressing the phone to her ear. "Hello."

"Hey, I want to see you. Come meet me for breakfast."

"Ah," she looked around. "Okay."

"Good. Meet me at Gegolies at seven thirty. Do you know where that is?"

"Yeah. I know it. I've gone there before."

"Okay, see you there. We probably should talk," he said and ended the call.

We should talk? Is he angry? Or maybe he realizes it was a mistake too, and he wants to call it off? For some reason, that thought forced a tightness in her chest as she rolled over in her bed again before sitting up on the edge. *I should get ready.*

Standing from the bed, she grabbed one of her crutches near the stand next to her bed. She then stepped over to the closet to pick out something to wear. A pair of her favorite jeans, along with a long top were her picks for the day. She held the jeans out to look at herself in the reflection, but saw something else in the glass.

On the floor, as she turned around, was the clothing she had bought the day before.

Why not? I did buy them for a reason.

A little less than an hour later, Jewel was dressed and in the back of a taxi, heading across the city. She wore a knee-length pink skirt and wedge sandals with a hat to match and a sky-blue blouse that slid into her waist before blossoming out in a floral pattern. While she still had her crutches, she didn't wear the security boot for her ankle.

Arriving at the restaurant and exiting the cab, it wasn't long before she saw him exiting the restaurant and making his way toward her.

"I'm sorry. Were you waiting long?"

"It's fine. I was just planning something over the phone.," he said, looking her over. "You look lovely."

"Thank you, it's—"

Not able to finish her words, she felt his hands against her face, and he leaned forward, placing his lips against hers. Even before she realized it herself, she was responding to him, leaning into the kiss, moving her lips along with his. But as suddenly as it started, he stopped, pulling himself away from her before giving her a smile.

"I needed to make sure," he said.

"Make..." She swallowed. "Make sure of what?"

"That it wasn't a mistake, that it wasn't just us in the moment, doing what our bodies were telling us to do."

"Oh," she felt a bit nervous. "And was it? Us in the moment, I mean?"

"No, You... being with you right now feels right," he said, placing a hand on her back. "Come in. Let's have some breakfast."

"Okay, I can't stay too long, though. I have to be at work soon." *Argh! What do I do now? Do I say anything?* She looked over at him as he led her inside and felt her heart start beating faster. *No, I really like this guy. I... I don't want to not see him anymore.*

"That's fine," he said, opening the door for her. "We won't be long. I just want to start spending more time with you."

Taking their seat at a table, they were greeted by a server.

"Hello there, and what can I get for you?" she asked.

"Oh, I'll just have a salad and a lemonade please," said Jewel as she turned to the waitress. "Oh, can I have Ranch dressing ple—" Her words paused in her mouth as she looked up at the waitress. She was a beautiful young woman with golden hair, much like her own, but it wasn't her appearance that caught Jewels' attention. It was her attire. There on her apron, was the image of a Black Sheep and a White Sheep dancing playfully together.

"Jewel?" said Jamal. "Is something wrong?"

"What?" said Jewel, snapping back to reality. "I'm sorry, it's... her apron." She turned back to the waitress. "It's, ahh... really cute?"

"Huh? Oh this," said the waitress, "Our company is doing

some partnership with the people running that Black Sheep White Sheep thing?" She pointed down at the menu. "The kids' menu even comes with either a Black Sheep or White Sheep foam toy doll."

"I've seen the ladies walking in the park wearing shirts with a similar design," said Jamal. "I haven't paid much attention to it. But it looks popular."

"Oh, you should," said the waitress. "Their story is really good. This week, apparently, they took a trip to a remote island and now the Black Sheep is trying to steal a man away from the White sheep."

"Oh, God?" said Jewel, placing her hands to cover her face.

"Oh, are you keeping up with it too," said the waitress with a smile.

"Ahh, yes," said Jewel, taking in a deep breath and removing her hands, smiling back at the waitress. "I read about it too."

"Well, that's all everyone in the back has been talking about." She patted Jewel on the shoulder in solidarity. "But between me and you. I'm rooting for the white sheep. The black sheep seems like a bitch."

"Jewel nodded her head, trying her best to keep her forced smile going. "Yes, oh yes. She's... she's definitely a bitch."

"Well, anyway. I've taken up enough of your time. Let... let me go and get that salad," said the waitress, before turning to Jamal. "And what did you want, sir?"

"Just a turkey sandwich, please, and some orange juice."

"Yes Sir, right away," she said as she headed back over to the kitchen.

"Is everything okay?" asked Jamal after the woman left. "You seem a little bothered."

"No, I'm fine," said Jewel, blinking and trying to keep her composure. "It's just that whole black sheep white sheep thing, you know. I guess I'm a little more interested than I should be."

"The waitress said that one sheep is trying to take the man off another. If that's what has you bothered, then don't worry. That's not like what we're doing."

"I know it's not like us." *That's because it is us. I'm the black sheep. And you are exactly the man I'm supposedly taking. Ah, I hate this stupid contest. Why couldn't you have just left with me that night instead of going out with Sami? Argh! Why do I feel like this? I hate you. I hate you and your sexy face.*

"I want to take you out this weekend. Is that alright with you?"

"Wait. Have you told Sami about us?"

"Not yet. I tried calling her yesterday. But her phone went straight to voicemail and her mailbox was full."

That's right, we did turn our phones off while we were shopping.

"I plan to tell her soon. But I don't want to do it over voicemail or a text message. I'll try to ask her out again."

"Okay," she nodded her head nervously. "Okay then. It's fine as long as you tell her. I really don't like the feeling of being around her when it's like this between us."

"I understand," said Jamal, placing his hands on the table. "But do you think everything will work out okay after you tell her?"

"What? What do you mean?"

"I know what I have to do. But really, I'm just hoping that she takes it well. She could just haul off and slap me. I mean, we've only been on a few dates. But... I don't know. One thing is for sure, I don't want this to ruin your relationship with your friend."

What? That... I never thought of that. Would she stop being my friend even if we told her? Is there a certain way to tell her? Is there like a best day of the week or something? I've never been on the other side of this before. Her eyes darted back and forth in her head as the questions continued to mount in her mind. *I've always had boyfriends tell me they want to break up. But*

229

even then, it was never with someone I knew. Would I still be able to be friends with someone who took a man I liked?"

"Jewel… Jewel, are you okay?"

"Huh, what?"

Jamal nodded to her right, and she looked up to see the waitress staring down at her while holding a tray.

"I've brought your salad, Ma`am."

"What?" she said before the recollection of her environment came back to her and she moved her hands from the table for the server to palace the food down, "Oh yes, I'm sorry. I wasn't paying attention."

"It's fine," said the waitress as she then sat Jamal's food before him. "Do you need anything else?"

"No, that's fine," said Jamal. "Thank you." When the server left, he turned back to Jewel. "Is everything okay? You were pretty lost in thought there."

"Yes… I mean no. Actually, don't tell her yet. I… I need to think about this first."

"Are you sure? I'm not exactly a veteran in this, but I believe the rule is the longer you wait, the worse off it'll be."

"I know… I just need to think for a day or two, is all. I don't want to do it the wrong way and lose my friend. So can we just… I don't know, wait a little longer."

"Yes, of course. That's probably for the best. The world of females can apparently be dangerous," he said with a smile. "But don't worry. I think—" Cutting him off, his phone rang, and he picked it up. "Hello." After a few moments, he then hung up with a sigh. "Sorry, it seems I have to go."

"Is everything okay?"

"It's fine. There's been an issue at the company. Apparently, they want me there to help deal with it." He shook his head. "They couldn't wait an hour before finding some new way to mess up in the morning." He reached inside of his coat, taking out his wallet, reached in and pulled out a hundred-dollar bill., placing it on the table. "For the food."

"Oh, okay. But I don't think it was that much."

"It's fine," he said, standing up from the table and stepping over to her. He then leaned down, placing his lips on hers.

The kiss was soft and sweet. She hadn't taken the time to appreciate it before when they were in the kitchen together. Then it was more instinct. But this time, this time, was different. There was no rush of emotion and circumstance. This was intentional and still felt just as right as before. This realization came to her as she kissed him back. But the moment was short-lived as he pulled away from her with a smile on his face.

"Remember, I want to see you this weekend, no matter what."

She smiled back at him. "Okay. We can go out this weekend."

"Good, and send me some pictures of the plants you said you bought. I've never heard of a Heliconia Flower before."

And before she had a chance to respond, he turned around, heading out of the restaurant with her watching him through the side glass as he waved at her and walked down the street and out of sight.

She couldn't help but grin, the emotions making her feel lighter than she had in a long time. She then turned back to her food and poked at her salad before reaching over to the ranch dressing. Someone then walked past her and, to her surprise, took a seat directly in front of her where Jamal had sat before.

Confused, she looked up to see Lan Ling staring back at her. "Are you and Sami sleeping with the same man now?"

"What?" said Jewel, her eyes wide as she looked around the restaurant. "Lan Ling, what are you doing here?"

"I come here every morning for my sandwich. It's on the way to work." She pointed out the window. "I live around the corner. So, tell me, does Sami know you fucking her man?"

"No... and we're not fucking. Keep your voice down."

"Oh, are you sure? That's not what it looks like to me. You had a big stupid grin on your face after he kissed you. That's not a friendship kiss. That was a 'you want his dick' kiss."

"Stop that. And no, Sami doesn't know yet. I'm trying to think of the right way to tell her."

"Oh, this is good. Can I tell her?"

"What? No, you can't tell her. Why do you think that? And how did you even know that Sami was dating him?"

"She showed me a picture of you two at some fancy dinner. I thought it was weird, because you were with a big white guy. But here you are here kissing the black guy that she was with. What was his name?"

"His name is Jamal," she said, raising her hand at the waitress who was walking by. "Excuse me man, I'd like to pay, please." She then stood up. "Come on, let's go to work."

Leaving the change for the waitress on the way out, she and Lan Ling took a taxi to their job. The cab ride was short, only a dozen minutes or so before they reached the landing where their building was. Both exited the vehicle and headed up towards the doors of the building.

"Don't tell Sami anything. I have to tell her at the right time."

"I know. I understand. I can keep a secret."

"I'm serious Lan Ling. I don't want to ruin my friendship with Sami. You better not ruin this for me."

"I'm not going to ruin anything. That's what you're doing. You are asking me to help you lie."

"That's not... just don't say anything, okay?"

The girls exited the elevator on their floor, and not even to her surprise, Lan Ling made a beeline straight toward Sami's desk, leaving Jewel behind as she made her way over on her crutches.

Oh, you little—

"Hey, Sami," said Lan Ling with a smile. "Jewel has something she wants to tell you."

"Ah, okay," said Sami, looking confused and turning her attention to Jewel as she approached. "What's up?"

"Oh, well," she narrowed her eyes at Lan Ling, who smiled back gleefully. "I mean... I just wanted to know what you're doing this weekend."

"I don't know. That's still a few days away. I don't really have plans yet."

"Well, I was curious if we could go out this weekend. You know, like a girls' night out."

"Oh yes, a girl's night," said Lan Ling, chiming in. "And she invited me to."

"Okay?" said Sami, looking between the two suspiciously. "Should we invite Becca to?"

"Ahh! Sure, I guess."

"Don't forget you've got plans this weekend," said Addison as she strolled by, patting Jewel on the shoulder. "And please do get to work. I gave you all the day off yesterday. So, I expect today that everyone here puts forth just a little more effort."

Jewel watched as her boss strolled past them, headed toward her office, before she turned back to Sami. "Okay, maybe not this weekend. But the weekend after this one?"

Sami raised a brow. "I guess... I don't mind. Just tell me a day or two beforehand. I don't need you springing things up on me out of nowhere."

"Yeah, Jewel," said Lan Ling, folding her arms over her chest as she nodded her head. "Don't do that. It's not right to surprise people with things."

Jewel could feel her mouth begin to twitch upward into a snarl as she looked down at the little woman. *Out of all people. Why did it have to be her?*

"Oh," said Lan Ling, reaching into her purse. "Look what I got." She then pulled out two foam Baby Sheepies, one black and one white, placing them on top of Sami's desk. "Aren't they cute? I got them from the sandwich shop this morning."

"Really?" asked Jewel, looking down at them and then at Lan Ling. "Off the kids' menu?"

"What? I wanted them and that was the only way to get them."

Sami reached over, picking one up. "It's still hard to believe that it's gotten so popular."

"Mmhmm," said Lan Ling. "It was smart for Addison to bring in those other people. Their stories have been really fun to read. Especially the black sheep, since she's tried to take the white sheep's—" Suddenly Lan Ling's eyes went wide as she dropped the little black sheep doll to the floor. "Wait, but the..." She then looked back at Addison in her office and then looked back up at Jewel. "She took you— Oh my God, you and Addison. It's not them, it's—"

"Okay, time to go," said Jewel, placing her hands on Lan Ling's shoulders and spinning her around. "Sami, can you pick that up? Lan Ling and I have to go to the bathroom. You messed up your makeup, Lan Ling. Let's go and fix that before anyone else sees."

"What? But—" said Lan Ling as she was ushered off into the bathroom, which was hard for Jewel as she left one of her crutches behind. But she'd endured the pain in her ankle for a few moments to ensure that Lan Ling didn't say something she shouldn't have. Once in the bathroom, Jewel closed the door, locking it, and then proceeded to check the stalls to make sure they were alone.

"Oh, I can't believe you are the black sheep," said Lan Ling, clapping her hand a little giddy with glee.

"Yeah, well, you weren't supposed to find that out either," said Jewel as she checked the final stall before walking over to the sink and turning on the water on the faucets, then coming back over to her.

"I can't wait to tell the other girls that I know who the black sheep and white sheep are."

"You can't tell anyway, okay? Especially not now."

Lan Ling waved away her concerns. "Don't worry, they

are all just old Asian ladies. They wouldn't tell anyone. They're very good at keeping secrets."

"No, Lan Ling, this is a company secret."

"Okay, fine. But you have to tell me something."

"What?"

"The boss you were talking about in the article. That's Addison, right?"

Jewel, Sighed, "Yes, it's her."

"Ohhhh. And you're going to her house, right?"

"Apparently so."

"And you're going to have a threesome with her and her husband?"

"Yes, I'm going to," Jewel's eyes shifted as her mouth went agape. "Wait what? No! Why would you even think that?"

"Because you were trying to fuck her husband and Addison likes girls, too. So why not? Then you can get the job?"

"What? Addison doesn't like girls... does she?"

"That's what I always thought. I mean... she never said anything to me about it. But I can tell these things. And then she just came over and patted you on the shoulder. Addison never touches anyone, but she just touched you."

"I... that... I mean." *Is that true? No, I mean there's no way, right?*

"And you like her husband, right? You two are doing something. You did try to steal her husband, right?"

"No. I mean, we just went out on a date. And I didn't know he was her husband."

"But you did like him."

"Of course, I liked him, but that hasn't nothing to do with it."

"Really?" asked Lan Ling with a sly smile. "But you are going to see him this weekend, right? Even though I just saw you kissing Sami's man."

"No, I'm going to see 'them.' All of 'them', as in together.

They have a daughter who likes me. And he's not Sami's man. They've only been out once or twice."

"Oh, Jewel is a home wrecker. Does Becca know? I can't believe you and Sami are the ones who write those articles and that they're true. I mean, I thought they might be true, but wow."

"Yes, they're all true."

"But... if that's so. Then who were the people who were in Addison's office that day?"

"I don't know. Just some people she hired to trick people." She grabbed Lan Ling by the shoulders again. "But promise me you won't tell anyone, okay?"

Lan Ling frowned, but nodded her head. "Fine. But you have to tell me about what happens during your dates. I don't feel like waiting another two weeks."

Jewel sighed. "Fine. I'll tell you about my dates. Is that okay now? Will you keep it to yourself?"

"I don't know. This is really good."

"Lan Ling, I thought we were friends. Are you really going to make me beg?"

Lan Ling looked at Jewel with narrowed eyes before folding her arms over her chest and leaning against the door. "Okay, if we're friends, then I'll promise to be quiet if you can say my whole name."

"What?"

"Say my name."

Jewel looked confused for a moment. "I... I don't know your whole name. I only know Lan Ling."

"See... And if we were real friends, don't you think you'd know my name? I bet you know Becca and Sami's full name?"

Jewel tried her best to think back on if she'd ever heard Lan Ling's last name, but nothing came to mind, and she slumped her shoulders under the realization. "Fine. You win. I don't know. But I promise we'll go out later and you can tell me everything you want. But for now, can you please just keep this secret?"

Lan Ling looked at Jewel for a moment before sighing and then shook her head. "Fine, I won't tell anyone."

"Good. Then let's go before someone comes knocking."

"You better keep your promise."

"I will."

After turning off the water, they unlocked the door and headed back out into the office area, each one heading back to their desks. Jewel was relieved to see Lan Ling head back to her own working area without speaking to Sami, unlike last time.

Despite feeling a bit of relief with taking care of the Lan Ling situation, Jewel still felt the guilt in her chest every time she would look over at Sami throughout the day. She tried throwing herself into her work, answering emails, about several types of plants and what was the best way to create a suitable living environment for them, but it did little to relieve her of the feeling she was having.

Why does it have to be like this? Why do I have to feel like this?

But despite the inner conflict in her mind. The day continued on in the white noise of the office area as people came and went. After several hours of working and repeating the same thoughts in her head, she saw Sam pick up her phone. She then made an odd face before slowly closing her laptop and reaching down to grab her purse. Then, seeming as if in a hurry, she stood from her seat and headed for the elevator.

Fuck this. I'm not going to spend the next week or two feeling this way. Jewel grabbed one of her crutches and tried to hurry and catch Sami as she stepped into the elevator. Quickly she lifted from her chair, leaving her phone and everything else as she hopped and or skipped trying to pick up the pace before the doors closed. "Wait, Sami. I... I need to talk to you about something," she said as the elevator doors began closing. "The door... hold it, please."

She was almost there with the door about to close as she reached out her hand, but she was too late to reach it in time. Then she saw Sami's hand appear between them before poking her head out.

"Jewel? Is everything—"

Those were the only words Sami managed to say, before Jewel with her unthought of speed tried stopping on her bad ankle and it buckled, sending her flying into Sami as they both went flying back into the elevator wall, then dropping down and hitting the floor.

"Owe," said Sami, as she laid down on the floor with Jewel atop her. "Girl, what are you doing?"

"Ohhhh," moaned Jewel to the sound of the ding of the elevator closing.

"Are you okay?" asked Sami as the elevator shifted downward. "Did you hurt your leg again?"

Jewel began rubbing her head before opening her eyes. Then, realizing she was on top of Sami and staring her in the face, she was quickly filled with a flood of emotions as her lips began to quiver. "I'm... I'm sorry."

"Girl, it's fine. Just get off of—"

"I kissed Andrew."

Despite the movement and humming of the elevator. Everything felt oddly quiet and calm for a minute as she stared back at Jewel, trying to make sure she heard everything correctly.

"What?" she asked, her eyes narrowing as her head turned to the side. She was sure the ringing in her head from the fall was causing her to hear things incorrectly. "You... kissed who?"

"I didn't mean to at the time. It... it just happened."

"Jamal... the person I'm dating, Jamal?"

Jewel slowly nodded her head as there was another ding

and the elevator opened and two men in suits stood there in shock, looking down at them.

Sami turned to look at them before raising her hand and pointing a finger at the confused men. "Just let it close. You don't want to step in here right now."

The men stepped back, seemingly unable to say anything as they just watched the women as the time passed and the door closed back on them.

"I'm sorry," said Jewel. "I know I shouldn't have. It's just… it's just…"

"Jewel," said Sami, in as calm a voice as she could muster.

"Humm," moaned Jewel, her eyes beginning to water.

"Shut up."

"Okay."

It's cool. Maybe she means she knew him from before we started dating or something. Sami then took a deep breath. "It's fine. When did you kiss him? Did you know him before or—"

"At Becca's party we went to."

Oh! this bitch. Sami balled up her fist, raising it above her head to bring down on Jewel.

"I'm sorry. I'm sorry." Jewel wrapped her hands over her head.

Looking at Jewel, Sami saw her clenched teeth biting down on her lips and felt the woman trembling on top of her. Curious, she tilted her head to look over and saw Jewel's wrapped ankle turned in what was probably a very painful position. *Fuck it. It's not worth it.* "You're not worth it."

There was another ding when they reached the bottom floor. When the doors opened, Jamal stuck one foot inside before looking down.

"What the hell?"

"I don't want to hear it," she said Jewel, reaching her hand to him. "Just get her off of me and help me up."

Jamal raised a brow, making an odd face. "Okay then,"

he said, reaching down and picking Jewel off the top of Sami and lifting her to her feet before handing her the dropped crutch. He then helped Sami to her feet. "Okay, you feel like explaining what you two were doing like that?"

"No," she said, nodding to Jewel. "Why don't you ask this back stabber? I'm sure she has a lot to talk about." Sami then stepped out of the elevator on wobbly legs, turning into the lobby, and headed out the door. On her first step outside, her leg slipped out from under her as she wobbled before falling back down to the concrete on her hands and knees in front of the few people that were loitering outside of her building.

She turned around and saw that just like Jewel beforehand, her heel had broken. It was probably after having Jewel crash into her in the elevator. She then turned back around with eyes wide to see Jewel and Jamal staring at her from the window. He was holding her up as she had one arm wrapped over her shoulder. And that when it came, a rush of emotions that began to cause her eyes to water.

She clenched her teeth as she turned away from them while on her hands and knees and stared down at the hands. She felt hot. Her breathing was heavy as her fingers pressed hard against the concrete below her. She wanted to scream. It was all she could do to not scream.

How dare she. She knew... she knew that whole time while we were out shopping. She smiled in my face that night at the party. She knew then. A man, I can at least expect that from him. But her.... Does she really want to win that much?

Reality coming back to her, she began looking around, and noticed she was catching the stares of everyone nearby. Shaking her head, she raised herself back up, sitting on her butt and taking off her heels. *I'm not going to cry. Not here. I need to leave.* Wiggling her ankle to make sure everything seemed okay, she then took off her heels and stood up. The chill on her bare feet gave her something to cling to rather than the emotions flooding her mind. Her lips quiver with barely suppressed emotions as she stepped forward trying to hail a cab.

With untold appreciation, the yellow car appeared almost as soon as her hand went up and quickly stepped inside, closing the door and lowering her head, hoping the cabby wouldn't see her face.

"Can… can you take me to Ginger Street and Fifth, please?" *I know I said I would meet him. But I really don't feel like any of this right now.*

"Sure? No problem," said the cabby as the car began to roll forward.

She noticed that he took a look at her from the rearview mirror as he fiddled with the radio.

"I'm telling you that black sheep is a cold, cold woman," said the radio host.

"How do you know she's cold?" said the female radio host. "She was just doing what she needed to do. Hell, I'd do the same thing. I got kids to feed."

"You got too many kids to feed," said the male radio host as the laughter poured out of the radio.

"Ahh! Excuse me," said Sami, "but… but can you turn that off, please?"

"Huh, what? Sure." he said as he turned the knob, bringing the volume down so low that it was quiet in the cab. "My bad. I thought all the ladies in the city were Ga-ga over that black sheep, white sheep thing."

"No, it's… it's not that. I'm just tired and need some time to think."

"Oh, I see. It's one of those days, isn't it? Alright then, you want me to drive slow for ya? Might give ya a little more time to clear ya head."

"I… I'd appreciate that."

Sami then leaned back in the seat, trying to think as she stared out of the window. *This is just going to be a bad day. I just want to head home and throw my face in my pillow.* She stared off into space for a moment. *But that'd be what she wants, wouldn't it? She wants to win that stupid job so much that she'd do something like that. Well, fine, I can do things too.*

She tried her best to relax through the cab ride as much as she could, but found herself not being able to let go of the feeling of agitation that was flowing through her. *I even let her spend the night at my place. How could she do that?*

"Okay, we're here," said the driver as he pulled over near the side of a building.

Sami paid the cabby before stepping out of the car, only to be greeted once again by the cold feeling of the pavement as she placed her bare feet onto it. She sighed. *Damn, I forgot about that.* She then began to look around and was greeted by the friendly face of Patrick as he came out of the building and gave her a hug and another kiss on the cheek.

"What do we have going on here?" he asked as he looked down at her feet. "Is this one of those new styles I've been hearing about?"

"No," she said with a frown. "I'm an idiot who did this." She held up her shoes for him to see with its dangling heel dangling from what was left of it.

"Isn't... isn't that the same thing Jewel did?"

"Don't remind me."

He laughed, "Okay then. Let's go and get you some new shoes." He then knelt down a bit before picking her up in his arms.

"Oh," she yelped. "You could have asked first."

"You want me to put you down?"

"Well, no. Since you already have me like this."

"Good, because I wasn't going to anyway," He then turned towards the door to the building and stepped forward with the men at the door opening it for him. "Inside, she saw a lot of mannequins as well as clothing and shoes."

The rest of the day's worries started to vanish as she was swept up in Patrick's randomness. He spun her around with a grin on his face, showing her the building she was in.

"Why'd you text me asking me to meet you here?" She

said before looking around and seeing the fancy clothing strapped on to mannequins. Some had on evening gowns, while others wore ornate dresses that looked like they belonged in a fairytale. "What store is this?"

"I'm not sure, really. But they do have shoes. What I wanted to show you is actually upstairs. But I think it'd be best to get you some footwear first." He then walked up to a counter where a woman was standing.

"Didn't you just leave?" said the clerk, smiling at Patrick. "And you managed to kidnap a woman already? Shame on you, Patrick?"

"Oh, funny. Sami, this is Delanie. Delanie, this is Sami. We're dating now and she's managed to destroy her footwear. You mind helping me out?"

Delanie laughed, "Fine, put your trophy girlfriend down over there and I'll go and get something."

"Appreciate that," said Patrick as he took a few steps to the side, placing Sami down on a cushy bench. "So, you want to tell me why your shoes are all messed up and you look like you want to cry?"

"What?" said Sami with some surprise.

"Your eyes are all puffy," said Patrick as he reached out, rubbing away a bit of moisture from her cheek. The softness of his thumb across her skin providing just that little bit of comfort that she didn't even realize that she needed. That feeling that someone cared about her. "You've been having a bad day?"

"Apparently so, if even you can see it?"

"Here you are," said Delanie as she brought out a pair of heels similar to the ones Sami had shown her. "This should hold you over."

"Thank you," said Sami, reaching into her purse. "I'll pay for them."

"No, I have it," said Patrick, looking at Delainie. "Put those on my tab."

"Alright."

Sami looked confused for a moment as she looked over the store with its fanciful clothes. "You have a tab here?"

"Yeah. They're a specialty store as well. That means they handle all my work clothing."

"You... you have your maintenance clothing specially made?" asked Sami, her face twisted in a bit of confusion.

"I need to make sure those pockets are just where I like them. Plus, the company pays for them, so it's not like a problem for me?"

"Wait? So does that mean you're using the company to pay for the shoes you just bought me?"

"Exactly. It's wonderful that the company can be so generous with us, isn't it?"

Sami shook her head, unbelieving, but couldn't help herself but to smile.

"That's a nice look on your face," he said, taking her by the hand and helping her back up to her feet. "Now, you wanna tell me what's got you so upset?"

"Ah... It's nothing. Just... well, you know... girl stuff." *What am I supposed to say? That I'm mad about Jewel, stealing away another man I was dating?*

"Oh," said Patrick, "The mysterious girl stuff. Well, alright then, come on. As long as you're okay, that's all that matters."

"Where are we headed?"

"It's a secret date. There would be no fun for me if I told you," he said as he led her over and into the elevator, pressing the button for the twenty-first floor. "I think you'll like it."

"Okay, you win," said Sami, continuing to allow herself to be swept away in Patrick's plan.

The ride upward was relatively quick, with her occasionally taking a peek upward at him as she squeezed his hand a bit. She noticed that when he did so; she saw a small smirk come over his lips. Eventually, they would reach their floor, and Sami stepped out to see an open room with glossed floors and white walls where a dozen or so older women were sitting down on stools with spinning easels in front of them.

"Well, if it isn't Patrick. We were wondering where you'd gotten off to. Who have you brought with you there?"

"Hello ladies," said Patrick as he brought in Sami. "This here is Sami. She's my girlfriend."

Sami, eyes went wide, and she sucked in her cheeks. *Am I? Who decided that? Do you really go that far in making your own decisions? Do I not have a say in it?*

"Oh, well, good for you, dear. She seems like a pretty thing," said the older woman, gesturing to the open seat beside her. "Well, come on, we're about to start. Grab an apron and come join us."

Sami looked up nervously at Patrick, who just smiled back at her as he reached over, grabbing an apron off the hook and placing it in front of her. He then began to tie it around her neck and waist. "Go on. You're going to enjoy it and it'll probably help you get your mind off whatever girl things you've been thinking about today."

"Wait. You're not gonna do it with me?"

"I have a few things to take care of in the back. But don't worry. You'll see me coming in and out," he said, leading her over to the empty stool and plopping her down into it. He then turned to the lady beside them. "Take good care of her." He then left Sami there as she watched him go around the room, speaking to the other women before heading into a backdoor behind a corner where she couldn't see him.

"Tell me, dear," said the older woman. "How are you enjoying dating our little Patrick there?"

Little? "Ah, have you known him for a long time?"

"Somewhat? We've all known him for about fifteen to twenty years now. He often comes over and does my lawn during the summer and spring months." She pointed to another lady nearby. "He handles her pool on the weekends." She gestured around the room. "And the rest I'm not sure what he does for them, but something useful, I'm sure?"

"Really?" *Seriously, how many jobs does he have?* "I didn't realize he was that busy all the time." She looked around the room. "Do you all get together often like this?"

"What, humm. Only about once a month or so. Patrick does a good job of getting us all together." She nodded towards the wet clay in the bowl. "Come on, just grab a chunk of it and place it on the turning plate. Press your foot on the pedal and try to make a bowl." she pointed toward the large pot in the center of the room. "Like that one over there. Neither of us are very good at this, so there's no need to feel shy about it."

Looking around the room at all the other ladies' misshapen pots and then at the wet clay in the bowl beside her. *Why not? I'm here now, so I might as well make the best of it.* She dipped her hand down into the water, scooping out a large slippery piece of the clay before dropping it on her plate. It landed with a thick but satisfying thud sound.

"There you go," said the woman beside her with a smile. "Now step on that little pedal and start turning it away."

Following the woman's instructions, Sami began kneading the clay. The smooth cool feeling was somewhat captivating in her hands. The way it slid in between and over her fingers as she tried to manipulate it was actually relaxing to a decent degree. "Or at least it felt that way. It gave her something else to focus on that wasn't the craziness of her life for the moment.

"Well, look at you go," said the older woman before turning to the other ladies. "I think we may have a natural with us."

"Oh please," said another woman jovially. "She still has those young hands. She probably practices by grabbing on to our boy Patrick at night."

The crowd of ladies gave a good laugh, while the remark made Sami lose her concentration and the mud that was starting to form gracefully was now floppy and limp in her hands.

"Don't worry dear," said the same older woman as before. "They do that sometimes. Except then it usually has nothing to do with you." The ladies of the room each enjoyed another round of laughter.

"Now, now, be nice to my date today, ladies," said Patrick as he came out holding a tray of glasses filled with what looked to be wine. "I promise you ladies, she has yet to make me feel limp in any way." He then began walking around, handing out the glasses to each of the women as they continued their chatty behavior. "Don't worry about them," he said as he reached Sami, handing her a glass. "Careful, don't get any mud in it."

"I'll try not to. But you know. You really have to tell me how many jobs you have. At this point, it's becoming kinda like a joke. Every time I see you, you're doing something different."

"I only have one job," he said with a smile. "It just has me doing a lot of different things."

She looked around the room. "I doubt one job can ask you to do so much."

"Depends on how you look at it," he said, handing another bottle to the woman beside her. "You ladies can relax. I'll go and get the next model ready."

"You go and do that?" said the woman. "We're doing fine keeping you friend busy."

"I can see that," said Patrick as he walked off, handing out the rest of the wine. "Well, don't have too much fun."

"No such thing, dear," said the woman beside Sami before turning back to her and taking a sip of her wine. "Tell us, dear, what do you do?"

"Ah... I'm a columnist for a magazine and I write blogs."

"I see. So, something like that Black Sheep White Sheep thing that seems to have taken the younger people of this city by storm."

"Not just them," said another woman in the group. "I've

been keeping up with that as well. It's actually quite enter-taining." She waved her hand dismissively. "But of course, none of it's actually true."

"You don't think so?" asked the woman beside her.

"How could it be? Chased through the city. Being attacked at a sheep farm, then not only stealing your best friend's man, but also your boss's husband. Please, if anything, it sounds like a woman's egotistical fantasy."

Boss? What are they talking about?

"What about you, dear?" asked the woman beside her. "Are you as obsessed with this little contest as apparently the rest of the women here?"

"No," said Sami, dropping her head. "Honestly, I think it's all stupid."

"See, even she agrees with me," said the woman from earlier who denied it was real. "It's all just make-believe, like those reality TV shows everyone loves so much."

"Alright ladies," said Patrick, re-emerging from the back while rolling along a small cart, which he pushed over beside the large bowl in the center of the room. He then walked over, picking it up off its stand and placing it on the cart. "Alright, your next piece is ready." He then turned around to the entrance. "Come on out. Your audience awaits."

At his request, two people, both a man and a woman dressed in robes, stepped from behind the corner.

Oh no, thought Sami, focusing on the couple and they walked over, taking their place on the stand. *They wouldn't.* And before she could finish their thought, both the man and the woman disrobed, handing the garments to Patrick, who placed them in his large bowl. And there before Sami, stood a stark-naked man and woman.

They posed for the group with him, wrapping his arm around her waist, allowing her to lean back a bit as her long hair hung from her head. Sami's attention, as well as the attention of all the other women in the room, couldn't help but sway downward toward a certain piece of the man's body that hung down his thigh. But after more than a few seconds, she remembered where she was and turned to see Patrick looking at her. He gave a chuckle before blowing her a kiss and turning back to the rest of the room.

"Okay ladies, they will be posing for an hour. Your goal is to pick a piece of them and try to sculpt it with your clay. It can be a leg, an arm, or perhaps something else," he said to a few giggles before he then turned back and began pushing his little cart until he left the room.

After the initial cheer and sexual remarks, the ladies went to work on their pieces. But it wasn't long before Sami realized that the clay modeling class quickly turned into the penis model class by the results at the end with her trying to model the man's waist. And while the end result wasn't good by any means, she found herself enjoying the company of the ladies; their snide remarks and honest nature taking her mind off to the worries of the day.

The evening ended well as she stayed to help with the cleanup before he drove her back home to her apartment. By then, it was already nightfall when they arrived. Exiting the car, she stood in front of her building as he walked up beside her.

"Did you enjoy your night?" he asked as he turned to her, wrapping his hands around her waist.

"I did," she admitted as she allowed herself to be drawn in. "It was a weird night. But it was something interesting. Thank you."

"Good," he said as he leaned down toward her, giving her a kiss. This time not on the cheek, but instead, she felt the tenderness of his lips on her as he held her tightly. While he smelled like cotton and tasted of wine, the feeling of embracing him was a welcome one. And more than that, a needed one; the small pleasure of the moment washing over her before he pulled his lips away and stared down at her.

"Do you always just do what you want like that?" she

asked, a bit flustered.

"How else would things get done if I didn't?" he asked as he continued to hold her, before looking up at the building. "Alright, enough fun for the night. You have to sleep, and I still have some work to do."

Sami shook her head. "Why am I not surprised? Do you ever sleep?"

"I do. It's when others aren't looking," he said as she released her. "Now go on. I'll wait till you're safe inside."

"This isn't a bad neighborhood," she laughed.

"I know, but all the same. It'll give me peace of mind."

Sami smiled back at him before turning around. *Men.* She headed over to her building's door and inside before taking up the stairs. Once more, she turned to see him still watching her. He waved his hand at her, as if telling her to hurry along. She shook her head but turned away and continued on as she soon heard his car starting a few moments later.

Soon, she was on her floor and walking down the hall to her apartment. Sliding the key in the door, she opened it, turning on the lights.

To her surprise, on her countertop was a slew of stuffed animals and some floating balloons. "What the..." said Sami as she closed the door and walked over, beginning to pick up the stuffed animals, inspecting them. The odd thing wasn't the animals, but instead the floating balloons. They all represented different holidays. One ball was of Santa Claus, the other was for Halloween and Valentines. One was in the shape of a dinosaur. Her mouth hung agape as she tried to comprehend why it was all there until she saw a folded note between the stuffed animals. She picked it up and read, *I'm sorry Jewel took your man. She's really sorry.*

"Wha... who."

And then it came. The sound of moaning coming from the couch. A bit confused and hesitant, she turned around and slowly walked over and peaked above the couch to see Jamal laying there asleep. The fool still had one of the stuffed animals in his arms as he laid there on his back. Closing her eyes, she took a moment to accept her life all over again and then took a deep breath before a smile came over her face.

"You idiot." She turned back to look at the miss matched balloons. "You could have just brought over a cake or something." She then walked back over to the counter, setting down the animals and then headed into the bedroom before coming back out with a pillow and a blanket.

Walking over to him, she knelt, lifting his head and placing the pillow under it before laying the blanket over him.

"Love you, be friends with dinosaurs," he moaned in his sleep. "Little Sami."

It was a statement that almost made Sami burst into tears with laughter as she watched him snuggle into the blanket. Instead, she grazed her hand over his face with a smile. *You've always been just a big dummy,* she thought as she stared at him for a moment and lowered herself just a little, placing her lips on his.

It was only a second later that her eyes opened wide, still with her lips pressed to his. She stared around, then down at him, realizing what she had just done. Then quickly standing up, her lips still puckered tightly together and began looking around the room as if someone else was there to catch her. She then took a step to the left, reversing into a step to the right in her confusion, and hurried back into her bedroom, closing her door.

CHAPTER 13

A few days later, Jewel was sitting on the edge of her bed, rubbing her ankle, checking for any soreness that was still in her leg. There was a slight pain in it if she pressed really hard, but it seemed like the worst was behind her.

Okay. Let's see.

She then stood up and tried testing out her weight on it. It felt just as natural as it did before she had twisted it.

Good. then there shouldn't be any problems today. She then proceeded to get dressed. She hadn't worn many of her new clothes since that day in the elevator. It didn't feel right to wear the clothes she bought with Sami around her, especially after her confession. *I wish she would at least speak to me. I know I was wrong, but... but... No, don't think about it, Jewel. You have other things to focus on today.* She reached into her clothing, grabbing a pair of dress pants along with a sleeveless pink blouse.

But in the middle of putting them on, she glared down at another set of heels before stepping over and slipping on a pair of tennis shoes. *We might be out today. And my ankles only just healed. I'll wait before I wear them again.*

After getting dressed, she began her routine of checking her plants to see if they needed water when she heard a knock at the door. A little curious, she made her way to the side of the door where there was a screen that allowed her to see who was outside. Tapping on it, it revealed that it was Nasir, dressed in a suit.

Feeling somewhat nervous, she swallowed her apprehension and put on her best smile before opening the door. "Hello, why are you here? I thought I was supposed to come to you?"

"Little Alina is at violin practice. I figured why not pick you up while on the way? I hope I am not intruding on you," he said as he looked down and saw the little water pail in her hand. "Were you tending to your home garden?"

"I just finished actually," she said as she turned around and headed back inside, setting the water pail back on the counter, and grabbed her purse and keys. They left the apartment together and headed downstairs, where he had his driver waiting on him. He held the door open as they both slid in.

"Okay," he said to the driver. "Let's go and get my daughter now."

"Yes, sir."

He turned to Jewel. "I think she's going to be excited to see you. These past two weeks, you've been all she's been able to talk about."

"I just wish you would have told me you were Addison's husband?"

"Did I not mention that? I thought I said you worked for my wife."

"No, you said your wife worked in the building."

"Oh, sorry. But when I told my wife about you, she

seemed fairly happy about it. Especially knowing that our daughter had taken a liking to you."

"Yes, I remember. But I don't think happy is the word I would use to describe your wife. Maybe mischievous is the right term."

He laughed. "I agree she can be somewhat abrasive about how she handles things. But she was actually way worse when we met. I'd like to think our daughter has calmed her down quite a bit over the years."

"If you say so," said Jewel, not believing his words, before looking him over in his suit. "Am I properly dressed for today? Should I have worn something more appropriate?"

"No, you're perfect. Today will just be a small gathering. Casual friends and the like."

"Okay, I have to ask. You seem very different from your wife. You say you met her in college. What made you start dating?"

"You're asking why I was attracted to her?" he laughed again. "Don't worry, I promise that you are not the first to ask that question. My father and my mother are both still wondering the answer to that very day, I suppose. Even though they love their granddaughter to death."

"I can understand that. My parents were never fond of any boyfriend that I ever had. But still, you two seem like an odd couple."

"True. But some of it was probably circumstance. We went to a very selective college, and we depended on each other to graduate. I believe it was her passion that drew me towards her. She didn't have many friends back then." He rubbed his chin with a solemn look on his face. "For that matter, she doesn't have many friends to speak of now, except for maybe Safia and Hashmi, perhaps."

"I heard her mention those names in a meeting once."

"I think one has to have a thick skin to be friends with my wife. But once she trusts you, she'll do anything for you."

"I'll take your word for it."

"Anyway, she is still the forceful woman I knew back then. She attacks any challenge thrown at her. When she first started her company, she refused to take any money from my family, insisting on doing it on her own. There were many nights I would come in and catch her sleeping at her desk with notes scramble all over her desk."

As he talked, Jewel couldn't help but notice the smirk on his lips as he spoke about her.

"So, you just stood there silently supporting your wife as she went about trying to build all she has? That's a lot of trust."

"Well," he himself gave a mischievous grin this time. "I may have helped things along a bit when I saw that she might have been struggling especially hard. I am her husband, after all. I feel it is my job to do such things, even if I must occasionally do them from her. She is a very prideful woman."

"Sir, we've arrived," said the driver as the car came to a halt.

Jewel peaked out the window to see a fancy fenced in building where several small children seemed to be leaving from a gated opening. They exited the car, walking up to the gate where there were several other parents and or nannies that had arrived to pick up their children.

"I didn't know violin practice was so popular," said Jewel as she noticed the amount of people there.

"The school itself offers a lot of activities. Violin is just one of them. They host all of them around the same time as a way for us parents and our children to meet each other. So actually, it's more of a social club where our children come to play and learn."

A place for the rich to meet the rich. I wonder if they have some secret handshake or rituals to join. Jewel looked over at the plaque on the wall. It read "APEX developmental studies for children." "Apex?" said Jewel. "That's the same name on our computer system."

"Yes, they apparently make a lot of things," said Nasir, looking over to the door as more children poured out.

"Well, this is a surprise," came the voice of Andrew.

She turned to her left and saw him walking toward her, holding a small child in his arms. He was dressed in more casual clothes today, just slacks and a hoodie sporting some brand that she didn't recognize.

"Oh, ah Andrew, what are you doing here?"

"I'm picking up one of the granddaughters of the Hurr Family. She's David's niece," he said as he bounced the little girl in his arms. "What are you doing here?" He then looked over at Nasir, extending a hand. "Hey, what's up? My name's Andrew."

"Hello, I'm Nasir. My daughters inside."

"Apparently, I'm going to be a babysitter," said Jewel. "So, I guess we're both going to be on the job today."

Nasir then pointed his finger ahead. "Ah, there she is." He waved. "Alina, over here, look who I brought."

"Oh," said Alina as she came running over with a violin case strapped to her back. "Miss Jewel, are you really coming to visit today?"

"Of course, I am. Your mother said that you wished to see me. Apparently, she has a lot of fun things planned for you today."

"Really?" She then looked up at the girl Andrew was holding. "Can Nito come?"

The girl in Andrew's hand looked at him. "Can I?"

"Ahhhh," said Andrew, looking at Nasir. "Well, we're supposed to go and get clothes for camp today."

"Ah, but we can do that later," she said, making a pouting face.

"I'll tell you what. We can call your mother in the car. And if she says yes, then we'll go, okay?"

She nodded her head, "Okay."

Andrew turned back to Nasir. "She'll probably say yes. She gives her everything she wants, anyway. So, what do you say, Sir? You mind letting the children have themselves a play date?"

"Not at all. If anything, I think it'll be good for them."

"Great, the driver is outside. I'll have him follow you two. Where do you live?"

"We have a home in Great Falls for the moment."

"Good neighborhood."

"I like to think so," said Nasir, before taking his girl by the hand. "Come on, honey. Let's go."

"Okay."

Feeling a bit anxious about the sudden inclusion of Andrew in her day, they headed out of the gate and over to their cars. It took some time for them to navigate through the city's traffic, but eventually they reached the highway.

Open roads and a twenty or so minute drive took them away from the tall city skyscrapers where concrete met metal in an architectural embrace. Instead, after exiting and turning onto a side road for a gated community. There were lush green lawns and manor homes surrounded by mile long white picket fences and personal lakes were used to accent a house property value. Green hills and country homes so spaced apart that their front lawns might as well have been football fields.

Even the cars out here were different. No longer were they the typical city vehicles of cabs and beat up road warriors, instead everything seemed to be some type of luxury oddity, many of whom she'd never seen before. Whether it be sports cars or home family vehicles that looked more like tanks than Sunday driving machines.

"I've actually never been out here before," said Jewel.

"There's actually no reason to come out here," said Nasir. "There are no stores beside the gas station and even that is a few miles down the road."

"I didn't notice that. Am I going to see a wine vineyard next?"

He laughed, "I've been told that there is one or two if

you go down that road a few dozen miles. But thankfully, our home is a lot closer than that."

"Oh, I see their car. That means Nito can come play," said Alina, as she turned around in the seat, pointing at the back window.

"Oh," said Nasir. "I didn't ask. But that man who's following us. You seemed to know him."

"Yes. My friend Becca. He's the... well, he works for her boyfriend."

"Oh, yes. He did say that the child was the grandchild of the Hurr Chocolate company."

"Her name's Nito," said Alina, crossing her arms. "Nito Hurr and she's really good at violin. We play together in class. She can play whole songs."

"Is that so? Then perhaps she is a good friend for you to have."

Jewel laughed. "Are you worried about your daughter falling in with the wrong crowd at violin practice?"

Nasir could only smile back at her. "These things need to be looked at differently when you are at a certain level of wealth. A lot of times, a child can lead to being a bad influence later on in life. I have to be vigilant. But I've never heard anything bad about the Hurr family."

Jewel shook her head. "I guess that is something I won't understand until I have my own kids."

"Do you desire children?"

"Yes," said Alina, chiming. "Jewel said that I should have a sister."

Oh, don't bring that back up. I don't need any more confusion with Addison. "I do, maybe two or three. But I want to work a bit more first and hopefully find someone nice."

"What about you? You only have Alina. Did you not want any more children?"

Nasir took another look at Jewel. "We've been talking about it."

The look he gave her made her feel as if he were

examining her. But that was short-lived as the car slowed down at a stop and Jewel looked ahead to see a gate being opened.

"We're home," said Alina as she climbed up to the front seat, pointing ahead.

The car pulled to what was by all means a mansion with a fountain in the front yard. Stopping once again, they opened the door and Jewel stepped out, gazing up at the oversized building. There were more windows to more rooms than she had time to count.

"You have a lovely home," said Andrew, getting out of the car with Nito holding on to his hand. "I know a few families that live out in this area."

"Welcome to our home," came the voice of Addison as the front door opened and she emerged dressed in a more casual attire than she'd ever seen her boss in. She wore a white skirt, tennis shoes, along with a faded T-shirt of a band she' never heard of. "Oh, and you've brought more friends along. I thought only Jewel would be our guest today."

"Our wonderful daughter asked if one of her playmates from school could join us," said Nasir as he released Alina to go running up to her mother, who hugged her around the waist.

Addison smiled down at Alina, rubbing her hair. "How was recital?"

"Boring."

"Yes, it usually is. But it'll be a good skill to have for later in life. It makes wild girls like us seem sophisticated and classy."

"What does so-fist-a-tated mean?"

"It means we walk around like we have a stick up our asses and pretend like we're better than everyone else."

"Addison! Really!" said Nasir. "Can you try to at least not teach our daughter your bad habits?"

Addison released her daughter and strolled up to her husband, placing a finger on his chest before giving him a kiss. "If I remember correctly, it was my bad habits that drew you to me. And I hope my daughter finds a man as good as I did?"

"Maybe," said Nasir, looking away. "But perhaps not in the way you did."

"The ends justify the means, as they say," said Addison before turning to her guests. "And which family does this charming little vixen belong to?"

Vixen?

"This is Nito Hurr, of the Hurr Candy Company. She's the owner's granddaughter."

"Really now," said Addison, as she knelt down, looking the girl in her eyes. "Aren't you just the sweetest thing? Tell me, do you eat all the candy at your home?"

"No, grandpa doesn't allow me to eat candy. He says it's bad for me."

"Oh my," said Addison with a smile., "How wonderfully hypocritical. I do think I'd get along well with your grandpa." She then turned around and started back toward the house. "Well, come along then. The girls can enjoy each other's company as we sit down, talk, and try to impress each other with the unimportant things we've done in our lives."

Nasir shook his head as he and Alina followed behind her into the house.

"Is that your boss?" asked Andrew as he walked up beside Jewel.

"Yes, unfortunately."

"She seems like a strange woman."

"You really have no idea."

And together they all made their way across the gravel driveway and into the home. The inside of the building was just as lavish as she assumed it might be. High ceilings at the head of the house, where up ahead lead to a set of stairs that spread out to both the left and right wings of the build- ing. They were guided through the downstairs area into a room with an unlit open fireplace and a host of bookcases and furniture.

"Go on, have a seat," said Addison as she plopped down on a loveseat, patting the space beside her for Nasir to follow suit.

"Momma, may I show Nito my room?"

"Of course, you girls run along and enjoy yourselves."

"You wanna see my room too, Jewel?"

"Oh, I'm sure she does. But won't you let Momma and Jewel have us some adult time first? I'll send her up in a bit."

"Okay, let's go Nito. I can show you my car collection."

As the small girls both ran off, Jewel wondered when she said car collection. Was she talking about actual cars or models? *Goodness, I can't even tell what's real anymore. The thought that a nine-year-old might have a car collection doesn't seem so crazy after coming here.*

Addison waited until the children had left the room with Jewel, hearing their little feet hitting the steps in the main room.

"Okay, Mr. Andrew, may I interest you in a drink?"

"No, thank you. I don't drink."

"Really? Well, what about you Jewel?"

"Yes, please," said Jewel. *Anything that will help me get through this day.*

Addison stood up and walked over to the counter where a brown liquid sat corked in a crystal container surrounded by four classes. "Good, it will be nice to drink with someone for a chance. My dear husband doesn't drink either." She poured the liquid into two glasses, bringing one back to Jewel. "Tell us Mr. Andrew. What do you do for entertainment?"

"I play sports to relieve the tension of the day. Basketball, tennis, skiing, that type of thing."

"Tennis, Nasir also plays. Are you any good?"

"I like to think I am."

"Care to dazzle us with a showing?"

"I don't have a change of clothes."

"Dear please, that's hardly an excuse. We have plenty and you and my husband seem to be around the same build. What about it?"

Andrew turned to Nasir. "I'm game if you are."

"I'm not one to turn down a game or two," as he rubbed the button of his lip with a smile.

"Good, that's a bit of entertainment we can reserve for later," she said as she came back, sitting back by her husband and crossing her legs. "So, tell us. Are you also from money? A prestigious family off in the hills, perhaps? I've known Jewel for quite some time. I even had her background checked."

"You have?" asked Jewel, looking confused. "Can you do that?"

"Of course I can. I'm considering having you become our nanny. You honestly think I wouldn't? And speaking of which. I can't believe you streaked stark naked across college your freshman year. You are hiding something wild inside, aren't you?"

Jewel began coughing on her drink, gasping for breath. She could also see that Nasir and Andrew were looking just as shocked.

Addison smiled before waving her hand. "And now we have both of these men here trying to picture you naked. I swear, it doesn't take much to get those little imaginations running, does it?"

"You are not a soft-spoken woman, are you?" asked Nasir with a chuckle.

"I am when I need to be. But if I were, I imagine the conversation would get quite boring and you men would soon resort to some type of dick measuring contest. Although I imagine things may still end up that way."

"This nature of yours is why my mother hasn't taken you in all of our years together," said Nasir, placing his face on his chin and looking over at his wife. "And it is why she thinks you are a bad influence on Alina."

"We're not going to get into what I think about your mother and how she always wants me in hijab whenever I visit."

"And I'm grateful to you for giving in to that concession."

"I know you are, otherwise, I would have left you at the altar," said Addison. "But what about you, Andrew, are you married?"

"No, not yet?"

"Girlfriend?"

He glanced over at Jewel. "Not yet, I don't think, but I'm hopeful."

"Really," said Addison, as she slowly rubbed her fingers together. "Well, I'm sure there is a lady for you out there somewhere. You seem like a man who's about his purpose in life. Just make sure you take the time to appreciate when a woman appears in your life. You might never know what competition you have out there."

"I'll try to remember that."

"Humm," moaned Addison as she stared at the two, while taking another sip of her drink. She then patted her husband on the lap before standing up. "Alright, that's enough small talk for the moment. Honey, can you take our friend here to try on some of your tennis clothing and I'll take Jewel to see about our daughter?"

"Yes, I can do that. I'm looking forward to the game, actually."

Jewel then stood up and began following behind Addison as she led her into the main hall of the house and up the stairs.

"I do appreciate you coming today. Despite how this started, we could use another nanny."

"I'm flattered, but I haven't agreed to being your nanny. I mean, I went to college for agricultural sciences and enjoy my job."

"And yet you want my job."

"Well, I think I can still keep my article even if you

decide to pick me, right?"

"Of course, but the Nanny position pays a quarter million dollars a year. So, it's not such a bad consul—"

Jewel lost her balance, misplacing her foot on the steps and ended up using the handrail to steady herself as Addison reached down also to catch her.

"I take it that means you'll consider the offer."

"A quarter... million... a year?" said Jewel, her mouth agape with shock. "How rich are you people?"

"Oh, I can promise you that it won't be as easy as you think. We can't take her out of school while we're off in other countries. You will essentially become a second mother to her. Hence why it's been so difficult to find someone. I was surprised when she told me that you played with her in the elevator some of the times when she would arrive at the job."

"Yeah, but I've never seen you with her. I didn't know she was your daughter."

"Many don't. I have her wait downstairs for me most of the time. She and the security guard also seem to get along well."

"Then why not ask him to be the nanny?"

"Because he has a wife and four other children. He does receive a very grateful Christmas bonus every year though," said Addison and they turned the corner. "Humph. I wonder if he ever realized why?"

Okay, maybe she isn't crazy. She's just oblivious.

"Oh well, it doesn't matter," said Addison as she reached a door where they both could hear children giggling. "We're here now." She opened the door and Jewel was greeted by what she could only describe as a child's wonderland.

The room itself was a mixture of pink and white. Pink walls, white carpeted floor and a mixture of the two that ornate her bed, desk, and toys. But instantly, she understood what Alina had meant when she spoke the words 'car collection.' The room itself was massive enough that it housed a collection of little buggy cars for them to drive in. While the girls drove around in two, she could see that back against the wall, there were several more.

"This is amazing," said Jewel as she stepped inside.

Her entrance was spotted by the girls and they both drove over to her, stopping a few feet ahead.

"Hey Jewel, have you come to play with us? Are you going to be my nanny? I'll let you have any car you want."

"Ah... I'm not sure yet. I just wanted to see what your room looked like."

"Oh, okay," said Alina, "I'll show you, come on." She then took hold of Jewel's hand and pulled her inside. "Will you race me? Nito is winning, but I'm going to catch up."

"Ah..." she turned around looking for help but only saw a smug look of satisfaction on Addison's face. "You know what, sure. But only if your mother joins us."

"Please mommy," said Alina, her eyes big and wide, staring at her mother in a way that only a daughter can.

Addison raised a brow at the two, but pulled herself from the wall, unfolding her hands. "All right, you two win. But don't be surprised when Momma kicks all of your butts."

What happened next was around an hour of pure carnage, with Addison picking the pink truck while Jewel picked the vehicle that looked like a very flat pony.

They took the time to decide on a new race map. It would go up to the inflatable palm tree and then under the giant multicolor beach ball and then loop over to the giant pink giraffe plushie.

On the count of three, which Addison counted and then cheated on, they all took off. Addison enjoyed her lead with a little taunting of the girls behind her, but was soon bumped by Jewel, which allowed Alina and Nito to zoom by.

"Now don't you know you're not supposed to spoil children,' said Addison, who rammed her vehicle back into Jewel's as they went pressed against each other into the next turn? "You have to make them work for it."

"And did you…" she grinded her pony car against Addison's truck. "Work for it?"

"Oh, honey. More than you could ever know. I'm not like my husband, born with a fucking silver spoon in his mouth."

"Momma, you cursed," yelled Alina from behind as she and Nito came back around.

"Sometimes Momma needs to curse, baby. One day you'll understand."

This time, when her daughter tried to pass her, Addison bumped into her and sent her crashing into a group of pillows.

"Shit," said Alina, in her cute voice as the pillows fell, bouncing off of her.

"That's the spirit, honey. And don't tell your father I cursed."

The next several laps were a constant stream of verbal assaults along with the destruction of the mini cars, which ended with Jewel's pony car losing a wheel and tipping over by the bed. Addison's car apparently started smoking halfway through the last lap before finally dying, leaving only Alina and Nito in what was left of their vehicles as they went limping towards the finish line.

The two small girls' cars grinding against each other. Half of the plastic that had once modeled its shape was bumped, broken, and torn off long ago, exposing the even harder plastic frame underneath. Their little vehicles wine with the struggle of the battle, but finally at the end, one girl pulled away.

"I win," said Nito as her vehicle passed the finish line ahead of Alina.

"Well, congratulations," said Jewel, as she laid down on the floor stretching out. Her chest felt heavy, and her body felt cramped from squeezing into the tiny car for so long.

"No," moaned Alina. "Let's go again. I want to win."

"Oh, no you don't, young lady," said Addison as she stood

hunched over her broken vehicle. "That's enough cars, for one day. Maybe—"

"No," protested Alina. "I want to go again."

"Alina!" said Addison in a sterner voice. "Do you want to visit mommy's room?"

Alina's eyes went wide before she dropped her head. "No mommy, I'm sorry."

"Good, now congratulate your friend. You all will have plenty of time to play together later."

"Yes, mommy," said Alina as she got out of her car and walked over to Nito.

Jewel couldn't help but notice the quick response Alina had to Addison. *I guess she's a stern mother.*

"I have to make sure she doesn't grow up spoiled," said Addison, perhaps catching the hesitance in Jewel's face.

"I understand. It's not easy being a mother. I'm sure mine had a hard time with me," she said as she looked around the room at all the toys and how absurd everything was. *But if all this isn't spoiling your daughter, then I'd hate to see what she thinks that is.*

"Good," said Addison, placing her hands at her lower back and stretching. "Now take your friend and go check on your father and his guest. They should be out back near the tennis court."

"Yes, mommy," said Alina, before holding hands with Nito. "Come on, let's go." She then led her out of the room.

A moment later, Addison walked over to Jewel, who was still sprawled out on the floor, and extended her hand to her. "Alright, come on, you too. We should go and check on the men."

"Argh," moaned Jewel, reaching up and taking Addison's hand, allowing her left to be lifted to her feet. "I feel like I'm a pretzel."

"Please, you're still young. Wait until your thirties. I promise you, I lose more every year," she said as they headed out to the door and into the hallway.

"Thirty something is still young," protested Jewel.

"Yes. Thirty-something is young. But thirty something with a child, that's not the same thing as thirty-something without."

"But still, your daughter is well behaved. I'm surprised you need a nanny. I thought she'd be more spoiled with everything you have here."

"My husband spoils her. I have to make sure she understands that all the stuff we give her is only when she acts good. When she acts bad, she doesn't get to sleep in her room," said Addison as she turned back down the hall. "I'll show you, since you might become our Nanny."

"Ah... okay," said Addison, feeling a little hesitant now about learning more about the family.

They walked down to the end of the hall where there was another door that was red. Addison reached inside of her pocket and pulled out a key, unlocking the door and opening it for Jewel.

As she entered the room, for Jewel, she couldn't imagine more of a culture shock if she tried. A strong disparity from the rest of the house. The inside had hardwood floors that seemed as if they had rotted somewhat. The walls weren't even painted; they looked to have some type of wallpaper that had been halfway torn up and down where you could see the drywall and rotted wooden boards behind it, which was painted black.

Inside, the room was barren. There were no toys, there were no objects to distract a child in the midst of her youth with. There was only a mattress that sat on the floor near a window.

"You... you send your daughter here when she misbehaves?" asked Jewel, and she stepped toward the wall, inspecting it.

"Not just her," said Addison as she leaned against the door frame, folding her arms. "Myself as well. Sometimes I send her here alone when she's bad. Sometimes I join her

268

here and we both sit quietly staring at the room."

"But why this place… it seems so… so dead," said Jewel, staring up at the roof, which was a sort of smokey gray color. It was like the room was intentionally made to have no color at all. The only color you would get was from the window, staring out at the world outside. Jewel walked over to it. She could see that it had been bolted shut. *This is terrible.*

"You must be thinking that this must be a terrible place to send a child."

Jewel turned back around to face Addison. "I try not to judge other people and how they raise their children, but don't you think that might be a bit much?"

"Is it?" asked Addison, waving a hand over the room. "Because this is an exact replication of the room that I grew up in. For sixteen years, this was my whole world. It's where I slept, where I ate, where my father would come in after a drunken stupor and beat the shit out of me."

"I… I didn't know you had that type of life," said Jewel, surprised by the confession.

"Neither does my daughter. She, unlike me, actually has a father that loves her."

"Then why the room?"

"A lesson of how easily things can be taken from you. When we sit in here together, during the few times that she does talk to me in here, I try to instill in her that all those fancy toys she has are just things."

"And you think 'this' works?" she asked, looking over the room, the disgust clear on her face.

"I hope so. But I won't really know if it was for the best until she's much older and being responsible for herself. But let me guess, you think it's cruel?"

"I honestly don't know what to think about all of this. But your daughter is a good girl, from what I can tell. All children have a rebellious stage. I know I did."

"I know. I looked you up, remember?"

"Yeah," said Jewel, as she walked back toward the door

and stared at Addison. "You really don't care about others' privacy, do you?"

"When it comes to my daughter, I'd break damn near any law you can think of to keep her safe."

"Maybe one day I'll understand."

"Maybe," said Addison as she turned to leave the room. "Come on, let's go and check up on the men. Close the door behind you."

The two women headed down the hall, taking the stairs to the first floor, then out the back of the home. There they would find the men laying back in lounge chairs in matching white shirts and short pants as they watched the children up ahead swing their rackets, knocking their balls against a nearby wall.

"Really?" said Addison as she saw the man lying around. "I assumed you might be teaching the children."

"We are babysitting," said Nasir as he smiled up at his wife. "The children, they are too much for us weak men to handle."

"Only a man would refer to looking after his own child as 'babysitting,'" said Addison as she walked between both men, tapping them on their shoulders. "Okay, enough lounging around. Up, both of you. It's your turn to entertain us now. Go on and have your little tennis match, so Jewel and I can talk about you while you're out of earshot."

Andrew laughed as he stood up, "You wife seems to be a slave driver."

"On that we agree," said Nasir as they walked off onto the court, grabbing a spare set of rackets.

"Men," sighed Addison as she gestured to the seat where Andrew had been. "Have a seat, dear. I think we've earned a bit of rest."

The ladies took their place, stretching out on the recliners as the maid brought out a tray of lemonade and two pairs of shades. Jewel partook in the moment, grabbing a pair of shades and enjoying the fresh air as the men ahead of her began going through a few practice swings. She then reached over, taking a glass of lemonade, feeling the coldness against her fingers.

"Is this how you live all the time?"

"No, not often do I have another man here performing sports for my entertainment. I can't have my husband questioning my fidelity. But since you're here, I think this exception will go unnoticed."

"I'm happy to help," said Jewel, as she tried her best to take in the moment. *This is exactly what I need. This is how I get my mind off Sami. I confessed what I did. There's nothing I can do now, except hope she can forgive me.* She took another sip of her lemonade before glancing over at Andrew, who noticed and smiled back at her.

"Tell me, dear," said Addison. "Have you fucked him yet?"

Jewel began coughing immediately, before gasping for breath as she pounded her chest. "I'm... sorry. What?" she asked, heavy-throated.

"Oh my. I guess that's a no then. Well, good for us, I suppose."

"What? What do you mean?"

"Oh please, you two have been sneaking looks at each other since you've arrived here," said Addison with another dismissing wave of her hand. "Either you both are unaware of it, or you take me for a fool."

Jewel was quiet for a moment. "We... we're just friends."

"Are you? Well, I'm surprised I didn't hear about him in your stories," then Addison smiled. "Oh, wait... he's the one, isn't he? The one you stole from Sami."

"I didn't steal him."

"Oh, so he is that one, then. How nice of you to confirm that for me."

Jewel frowned before slouching even deeper into the lounge chair.

Addison laughed. "You really are easy to read."

"And you just enjoy teasing people too much?"

"Perhaps, then how about this?" asked Addison as she leaned over, staring Jewel in the eyes. "What do you think of my husband?"

"What? What do you mean?"

"I mean, you obviously find him attractive. Remember, I read your article. And you wrote quite a few interesting things about him before you found out he was your boss's husband. If I remember correctly, it went something like: 'Am I wrong for falling for a married man?'" She said in a mock speaking voice. "His soft brown lips. His dreamy greenish eyes, like a forest that I wish to get lost in."

Every word she spoke made Jewel feel smaller than she thought was possible. "I was just writing to make the article more entertaining."

"Really? So, you didn't have a dream where it was my husband consoling your poor foot before ravishing your poor innocent body?"

"I didn't write it like that?"

"No, that was something the boys downstairs decided to spruce it up a bit. But the fact remains, it seems my husband has the ability to make my little Jewel wet between her legs."

Jewel's face began to turn red. "I wish I'd never written that. And If I had known, I promis—"

"Yes, yes, you would have never done it. I think we've covered that. So, I'm asking you, would you like to try dating him?"

"What?"

"You see, my husband wants another child. And honestly, one was enough for me. But you, you are still young enough to—"

"You can't be serious."

"Can't I?" asked Addison, raising a brow and nodding over to the men, and they squared off on the court. "While it is true that you could become our Nanny. And it's not uncommon for men of the house to have certain relations with their child's caretaker."

"But… No… You don't even know me, I mean—"

"You've worked for me for three years. I know more about you than you think, Miss country girl."

"And have you told your husband this?"

"Of course not. But I imagine it wouldn't take much convincing if I wanted. He has taken a liking to you. I know, because otherwise, he would have never brought up the prospect of you taking care of Alina."

Jewel couldn't believe what she was hearing, but couldn't help but take another look out on the court where Nasir had just served his first ball to Andrew. *Can I do that? No, of course not. Not after what I just told Sami. And that would also mean that I'd be tied to Addison, and while Nasir might not be crazy, I'm not so sure about her.*

"I can see you're thinking about it. Tell me, does the idea of both those men out there fighting over you excite you?"

"I'm… I just don't understand. What do you want? You want me to be his second wife?"

Addison laughed. "Oh, goodness no. Essentially, I'm going to pay you to fuck my husband and have the children I do not wish to carry. Well, if your first child is a boy, then it'll be just once. He does want a son after all, but I guess all men do."

"So, a surrogate mother?"

"Yes, and a well-paid one. And of course, a Nanny to the children. You will join us on our family trips and essentially look after them. There are many women who embrace the duration of pregnancy, but I was never fond of it. And honestly, once is enough."

"This… does this happen a lot?" I mean, can't you adopt?"

"Adoption? No. A noble idea, but I'm not interested. I'd prefer for it to be his biological child. I owe him that much. And as to your question of if this happens; not a lot. But I can't say that it isn't uncommon in our circles," said

Addison, smiling at Jewel, before turning back toward the court and watching the men. "I know one or two mothers who've paid others to carry their children."

"But, don't you want too—"

"I can see this isn't something you can just decide today," said Addison, cutting her off. "So, take your time and think about it. There's no need to rattle your brain so much about it now."

Not knowing what to say, Jewel just followed suit, turning back around to face the men just in time to watch as a foul ball came over in her direction, bouncing off the court and landing in her lap, settling between her legs.

"Sorry about that," said Nasir as he came running over and extended his hand. "May I have that back?"

"Oh ah, sure," said Jewel, handing it back to him.

"I swear," said Addison, placing her shades back over her eyes. "You men and your balls, but at least this time you aimed in the right direction."

CHAPTER 14

"I can't believe I'm doing this," said Sami as she sat on the bench looking up at a mountain. She was once again dressed in exercise gear with tights that stopped at the knees and a halter top with her hair tied into a ponytail. "Why is it that whenever I'm with you, I feel like I'm going to need a shower after? Oh, and you're paying for me to have my hair redone after this."

"Trust me, I know," said Jamal as he leaned back on his car's hood looking up at the clouds. "Still though. I wonder where they are. They're not usually late."

"I hope they don't show. Then we can just go back home. I'm really not in the mood for this."

"That thing with Jewel still bothering you?"

"Yes."

"But she did tell you about it right. I think that's a sign that she's sorry. She could have tried to hide it from you."

"Yeah, that still doesn't make me feel better."

"Not now, maybe. But trust me, when you're tired of being angry at her all the time, it'll be important then."

"Then what would you do?"

"Depends. But I went out with a girl once. I think we went out on two dates. I then introduced her to my friend. Well, at the end of the night, he then came up to me and said he liked her. Long story short, he married her, and they are expecting their second kid in a few months."

"And you didn't hate him?"

"Oh, I was upset. So, I made him reimbursed me for the dates, and told him he better be serious with her if he planned on spoiling my fun." He laughed. "Turns out it was serious. I guess sometimes a guy just knows."

"Is that how it works?" asked Sami as she walked over and sat on the hood of the car beside him. "What about you? Have you ever known?"

"I don't know. Obviously, I didn't know like he knew. But maybe I've had something like that." He turned his head towards Sami. "What about you? How does it work in woman-land? Is the grass any greener over there?"

"If it was, you think I'd be stuck out here with you," she said, placing her elbows on her knees and her hands under her chin and looking ahead at the mountain. "Stuck out here, pretending like we love each other."

Jamal laughed, "Good point."

"Sorry we're late," came the familiar voice of Henry.

They both turned and saw Henry and his wife, Heather, headed toward them, both in their sporty attire.

"My apologies for the wait, but there was a terrible traffic accident on the way. It held us up."

"It's fine," said Patrick as he and Sami removed themselves from the hood of the car. "We were just having a talk about our shared disinterests."

"I understand. Boundaries need to be established before one commits to a long-term relationship. Myself and

Heather did the same."

"Yes," said Heather, reaching over and wrapping her arm around her husband. "I would only visit his family once a year and after our second child, he wouldn't drive motorcycles anymore. I can't risk losing him when we had just gotten our family started."

"But as soon as our youngest starts college, I start again. Which will be in about another year. I even have the bike tucked away in our garage."

"I can't believe you bought that thing," said Heather, shaking her head.

"The moment he walks off that stage, I'm driving it out of the parking lot."

"I've actually never driven."

"Don't worry. Stick around long enough and I'll teach you. I promise, once you get on one, there's nothing like it."

"I'll try to take you up on that, then. But how about we get started on our walk?"

"Sure, let's go. We can talk on the way."

The group then set off on the trail leading up the mountain. The trail was rocky and not exactly easy to balance on as they began their accent.

Why did I get myself involved in this? I can already feel my knees starting to give up, thought Sami, a little over a half hour into it. She looked ahead and saw that Henry and Heather were powering through it as if it was a problem at all. *What are these people on? Did they take steroids before they got here? Yes, I'm sure that's why they're late. They're secret addicts.*

"You two... you two are amazing," said Jamal, trying to catch his breath. "Aren't we the younger ones? Why aren't you both tired yet?"

"Oh, this is nothing," said Heather, turning around to face them while walking backwards and bouncing as if she were as light as a feather. "There are much harder trails. But don't worry, there's a rest area up ahead. It even has a fountain."

"Thank God."

"Tell me, David," said Henry. "You still think you're partner material?"

"Honestly, I'm having second thoughts about whether I'm even human material at this point. I started wishing I was a bird about ten minutes ago."

Henry laughed, but reached out his arm to Jamal. "Honey," he said, looking at his wife. "Go and see to our friend back there for the last leg coming up here."

"Sure thing, dear."

Sami couldn't exactly say she was thrilled to see Heather come back for her as she watched Jamal struggle his way forward without her. But she gave her best smile as she was accompanied by her female counterpart on this adventure.

"How are you holding," asked Heather upon her arrival.

Sam sucked in her jaw while twisting her lip, while giving her a displeased look.

"That bad, huh?"

"Well, it sure ain't good. How do you keep up with him?"

"Oh, I was just as bad off when he started dragging me on these nature hikes of his."

"Really? Because you seem to be enjoying it now."

"I am. It took some time, along with a few scraped knees and twisted ankles, but I found a way to enjoy these little moments with him. I think it was when I realized that this was his escape after being stressed out at work that I focused more on joining him."

"You mean you weren't always the super outdoorsy type?"

"Oh god no. Back then, I wouldn't have been caught dead on one of these things. The sweating, the bugs, the aching muscles at the end of it."

"Then what made you start?"

"An older woman's advice. She once told me, 'Wherever your man gets his stress relieved from, that is where he will run to when the world is against him. And if you don't want him finding a new place to stick his dick in, then you'll make sure you're nearby.'"

"And it sounds like you're... trying to pass that on to me," said Sami as she took Heather's hand to step over a large incline.

"Well, that advice saved my marriage. So, I figure why not pay it forward," said Heather, turning around where the men had stopped up ahead at a tourist spot. "Because if you're serious about him. I can promise, there are going to be plenty of stressful nights. Especially after the children come."

"Maybe, but we're just a pretend couple, remember?"

"Oh, you both are definitely playing pretend alright. But I don't think you realize about what."

"What... what do you mean?"

"Tell me something. Who broke it off between you two?"

"We both decided it was the right thing to do."

"Em-hmm. Who's the one that brought it up?"

Sami thought to herself for a moment. "I guess it might have been me?"

"Well, I guess you had your reason. But I've seen the way he sneaks look at you when you're not paying attention."

"What?" she asked as she glanced up ahead as Jamal was kneeling down, picking up a rock. "No way. You think he still thinks of me like that?"

"Of course, I do. You said it yourself. He asked you to play the role of his girlfriend, right? And I'm pretty sure I've noticed an attractive woman in the office on more than one occasion. Why ask you when he could have asked her? It's called preference honey. We all have it, even if we don't even know it."

"But what if I don't want it?" asked Sami. "What if I don't want what we have to change?"

"We all change. We all grow older. Our babies go from sitting in our laps to going off to college, and the next thing you know they come back home with babies of their own. It's just up to you to decide whether the change happens without you or whether you make the change yourself."

"That sounds like you've got life all figured out."

"Me? Nah, I just watched too much life happen without me. There's a lot of regret in this body." She climbed up over a downed log before standing back up and looking up the hill to her husband. "But I like to think I made the right choices when it mattered."

"I'll try to remember that," said Sami as she planted her foot on the log before reaching out to Heather. "Mind giving me a hand."

"And up we go, Argh," grunted Heather, while pulling Sami to her level.

"Fine, let's say you're right. What if I don't want a relationship right now? Maybe I want to focus on my career instead?"

"Up to you. I did both for a bit, but maybe that's not how you see yourself. But if you do, then he'll be there for you on the stressful nights," said Heather as the two caught up to the men.

Sami didn't say anything. Instead, her mind went back to that night that she kissed him on her couch. *Why did I do that? Do I really still feel some type of way about this fool?*

"How are we going to get down from here?" asked Jamal, looking down the mountain as Heather and Sami caught back up to them.

"There's a gondola ride about another hour up on the other side," said Henry, as he pointed down to a walkway far below where they could see people. "That's where they are probably coming from."

"I'll be grateful for an easy trip down."

Henry laughed again, "Me and Heather will go and get you two some water. They have a vending machine in that little building over there. You two can take a break on the bench."

"Appreciated," said Jamal stepped to Sami, taking her by the hand and leading her over to the bench where they sat. "Tell me. Does the great outdoors make you feel alive?"

"You're paying for a massage after this."

"I think I'll join you on that. My legs have never felt so tight," said Jamal as he turned to her, staring for a moment.

"Why are you looking at me like that? What? Is there something else you want?"

"You look terrible."

Sami rolled her eyes. "I think the word you meant to you was 'we' look terrible, because you're sweating just as much as I am."

"I'm sure I am," he said with a sigh as he leaned downward, placing his head on Sami's thighs and stretched out on the bench.

"What... what are you doing?" asked Sami, surprised by his sudden presence on her. "Get off me, I'm sweating."

"I don't mind. This actually reminds me of when you used to lie down in my lap, and we used to watch movies."

"I was ten."

"Does that matter?"

"You know it does," said Sami, before looking down at his face and giving up. "Fine. Tell me then, what were you going to tell them if I didn't agree to show up with you again?"

"The truth. That we decided to just be friends."

Sami was a little shocked by his admission, since this was the first time he'd said anything about them since their little relationship experiment years ago. "And do you think about us... sometimes?"

"Of course, I do. But I know that one day some man is going to come in and snatch you away. And then I'll never see you again, except when I visit your mother."

You could be the one to snatch me away, you know. "And what about you? All those girls you've dated. Why hasn't any of them snatched you away yet?"

"I actually wonder about that myself. I'm handsome, I'm charming, I really am a catch as a man if you think about it."

"Hum, I think I'm starting to realize you're singing," said Sami, shaking her head. "Someone might be just a little too in love with themselves."

"That same can be said for you, too. And besides, I thought that it was important to practice self-love?"

"I'm pretty sure that's not what they meant when it comes to your ego."

He then shifted his head on her lap, nodding towards his superior and his wife. "I don't know if you've noticed, but a high ego is kinda needed to be where I want to go."

"Good luck with that. I can't wait to see you on some magazine cover climbing Mt. Everest."

Jamal frowned as she took another look at Henry and Heather before rolling over and staring back up at Sami. "Point taken," and exhaled.

They both sat there in the moment, the surrounding silence only being interrupted by the sounds of a bird in the background chirping away. The moment felt different for Sami. Much more than before, while her body arched from the climb. Whether she felt annoyed by his nature. She couldn't help but feel that this moment here with him felt... right. For once, while not physically, mentally, she felt calm and relaxed.

This isn't so bad. I wouldn't mind a few more days like this. I don't have to think about work... or Jewel, for that matter. She smiled. *Just me and this idiot.*

"What are you smiling about?"

"I'm smiling because of the massage you're going to pay for after this."

"I'm getting concerned that you're only with me in this pretend relationship for my money."

"Good. Now shut up and close your eyes before they come back over here and interrupt us." Sami thought he would object even more, but as she looked down, she Saw him close his eyes and seemed to be taking her advice and enjoying the moment. Sami herself followed suit and tried her best to enjoy the moment with him. His head on her lap and her hand over his chest, she could feel his heartbeat; the rhythm of it helping to ease her into a peaceful state of mind where time seemed to flow away.

"Okay, you two? Time to get up."

"Humm," moaned Sami, as she slowly opened her eyes back to the light. She looked down and still saw Jamal resting his head on her lap. "Sorry. I guess we were more tired than we thought."

"I bet," said Heather. "You two have been like that for over half an hour. At first, we didn't have the heart to wake you, so we decided to take a break ourselves. But I was afraid if we left you both like that, you'd sleep till nighttime."

Sami blinked as she looked around, confused. "Over half... an hour?'

"I guess it couldn't last forever," said Jamal, his eyes still closed as he lay on Sami's lap.

"You were awake?"

"Only for like the last five minutes or so."

"Why didn't you wake me?"

"Honestly. You felt really nice, and I was tired."

Sami frowned down at him.

"You know, that face you're making looks really weird from this position.

"Oh, just shut up and get off of me."

Henry laughed at the couple's bickering. "I remember those days," he said before his phone began to ring. He then pulled out his phone for a moment before showing it to his wife. "Right back. I need to take this." He then proceeded to walk ahead, mumbling into his phone.

"Sorry about that, but it's work."

"Yes. Trust me, I understand," said Jamal as he sat up and began rubbing his head. "I get those calls too sometimes."

"So, what do you two have planned for the rest of your

day?" asked Heather.

"More sleep," said Jamal, as he stood up and tried to stretch before immediately stumbling and grabbing his lower back. "Oh, god, I'm old."

Now it was Heather's time to laugh. "Be careful. Age will sneak up on you faster than you know it. Don't claim it before it comes for you."

"Sorry all," said Henry as he came walking back over to them. "It seems there's been a change of plans. I'll be taking the shortest route, since apparently, I'm needed back at the office. I'll leave my wife here to guide you up the other side of the mountain."

"I understand," said Jamal. "Do you need me to come along?"

"No, it's just some partner business. They need my signature to go ahead with a plan and they can hardly come up here to get it." He then gave his wife a kiss. "See you at home, honey."

"Be safe dear."

They all waved as Henry took off on an alternate trail. Sami was still surprised by the man's energy as he traveled the side of the mountain, making distance from them in impressive time.

"I don't think I'll ever be like that," said Jamal. "Some people are just made different."

"I do appreciate you two tagging along," said Heather. "If you weren't here, he would have insisted I join him on his mad dash back to the office."

Jamal turned back to her; the surprise clear on his face. "I thought you enjoyed doing all these things with your husband."

"No, I enjoy doing 'things' with my husband. That doesn't necessarily mean I enjoy this particular activity," she said, while giving a smile and pointing to the alternate path. "So, since my wonderful husband with the energy of a four-year-old has left us. What say we take our time and follow the children's path, a lot less hills and jagged rocks that way? Are you two okay with that?"

"That sounds like music to my ears," said Jamal as they both followed Heather's lead.

As they went along their way through the path of least resistance, she was surprised to feel Jamal reach out and hold her hand as they traveled together. While the effort wasn't needed, it wasn't an unwelcome gesture. The way his hands wrapped around hers, it felt good. Before, with him next to her, it felt right, but now it was feeling more and more right by the second.

What the hell is wrong with me? thought Sami as she became more aware of herself. The way his fingers completely covered hers. The way her heart began to beat just a little faster as the butterflies came into her stomach. *Is my hand sweaty? Ahh, why am I feeling like this? We've dated before. I've seen this man naked. Why am I nervous?*

"Tell me, Jamal," said Heather as she kicked a rock in her way. "What made you want to be a partner?" asked Heather.

"What do you mean?" asked Jamal, looking a bit confused. "That's the goal, isn't it? To climb the corporate ladder?"

"Yes. But why do you particularly want to do it? I can't imagine it's the money. You make a substantial salary where you are. What's another million or two over the next twenty years? Or do you want your name on the door one day, because a lot of responsibility comes with that? My husband just had to take off and there's been many nights like that at two or three in the morning when he gets a call, and he has to run to the office for some secret meeting. Are you sure you want that?"

"I already handle most of the business on the entire floor. It seems like the next logical step for me is to progress to a partner. Why are you asking me this? Does someone not want me to make partner?"

"No, I'm sure that's not the case. Henry speaks highly of

you whenever your name is brought up. I'm merely speaking from the viewpoint of a wife whose husband has missed birthdays, first steps, first football or basketball games, and left his family in the middle of vacations because the company needed him to handle some merger or something. Tell me, when was the last time you were called into the office past midnight?"

Jamal was silent for a moment. "Maybe about two years ago. But that was when we were handling the Falcon company."

"And my husband receives those calls at least three times a month. Maybe more if it's during a particularly bothersome time of the year or quarterly earnings."

"So, you're saying I shouldn't take it?"

"Oh no, by all means take. I'm sure it'll look good on your resume. I'm just speaking aloud about the circumstances that I've had to live through."

"I appreciate that. I'll try to think about it."

"Oh, don't worry. I wasn't speaking for your benefit particularly," she gave a smile, as she glanced over at Sami.

They continued their trip along the path, which took a little over another hour, but Sami was grateful, since her legs no longer felt like they were on fire. But beyond the easing of her leg pain, Sami heard something loud as they moved forward. Something familiar that shook her in the pit of her stomach. She knew only a few moments later to be the sound of rushing water. It instantly reminded her of her time with the same couple on the rapids just a week or so ago.

"Ahh, good. We've reached the waterfall area. That means we're almost there."

"You aren't going to ask us to jump off of it, are you?" asked Sami, only half serious.

"Of course not," she smiled back at them. "We tried. Apparently, it's not allowed. Even if you try to bribe the security man."

Sami wasn't sure if that smiling face of Heather's wasn't joking or not. But here in this area, they saw a lot more people than they saw on the trail. "Where'd all these people come from?"

"Humm? Oh, from the Gondola. Just as we can take it down, other people take it up. This spot here is the main tourist attraction."

There were children running about along with many couples that sat on benches or were taking pictures together.

"Well, at least it looks nice," said Sami as she gazed out beyond the waterfall at the hills and the valleys below them. "We've climbed up a long way."

"Oh, I have a good idea. Since this is your first time here," said Heather, whipping out her phone. "Why don't you two take a romantic picture by the water?"

Jamal and Sami took one look at each other before Jamal shrugged his shoulders and laughed. "Okay, why not? Would you like me to lift you up and pretend we're on the Titanic?"

"I honestly don't think you're strong enough," said Sami as she walked over by the ledge on the waterfall near the railings. "But fine, it'll be a reminder of the things I do for you, and why I should start making better decisions."

"Yes, Sami. the love of my life," he said as he walked over, both turning to face the camera and wrapping an arm around the other.

"Say cheese," said Heather, taking the picture. "Great, I'll just send this to you. But come on, let's get another with the two of you kissing."

"Kissing," said Sami, looking back up at him. "That's ah—"

Jamal turned to his side, wrapping his arms around Sami, and pulling her in., "Forgive me later, okay," he whispered.

Sami frowned, but didn't resist as he pulled her closer. "I hate you and your silly job," she said before tilting her head upward as he placed his lips against hers. The pounding in her chest grew heavier than the initial patting from holding hands. Now it was more of a thud. But as the mouths sunk into each other, she found herself kissing him back. Their lips parting for only a second before re-embracing. She took the moment for herself, something she knew she wanted and found herself free to have, so she embraced it.

The world went blank for a moment as the sound of the rushing water behind them filled her ears. It all felt made for her. The breeze off the flowing water behind them, the sun on her skin and the smell of him felt better than she had thought it would. She felt like she was becoming someone she remembered, but also couldn't forget.

The moment was short-lived after Heather said 'cheese.' and the two slowly pulled their lips away, but not so far that they couldn't still stare into each other's eyes.

Jamal smiled back at her and whispered, "It's been a while since we did that."

"And... and we only did it this time because you're a liar."

"Does that mean you didn't like it?"

"Shut up and let me go before I throw you down that waterfall."

Heather came over, showing them the picture of them with the waterfall behind them, before forwarding the picture to Jamal's phone.

Finished with their picture and the embarrassment fading from the moment. Their group headed back off through the mountainside. On the way, Sami managed to step away from Jamal, who was ahead, and stepped back with Heather.

"Would you mind... ah.... sending me a copy of that picture."

"Really?" said Heather with a smile. "You don't want to ask him to send you a copy?"

"No, he'd get that stupid, smug look on his face again."

Heather laughed. "Well... it's a good thing you came to

me. I might have a few other pictures you might want?"

"Humm? What picture?"

Heather reached into her pocket, showing Sami her phone before and a picture of them by the waterfall. But then she flicked it over to reveal a picture of Sami and Jamal sleeping on the bench together. It looked like a painting; the leaves flowing by and rays of sunlight coming through the trees behind them.

"What? When did you... is that what we look like?"

"I think it's quite romantic. I just happened to turn and see you both and just knew I wanted a picture. And figured that you might want one as well."

She looked up at Jamal and then back down at the picture. "Can you send me both of them?"

Heather patted Sami on the shoulder with a smile. "We'll exchange numbers when we get down to the cars."

They soon reached the gondola, which was only meant for two people at a time. Heather took the first lift while Jamal and Sami followed behind, looking over the surrounding mountainside as they slowly made their way down on the seated conveyor.

"We've made it through another day," said Jamal, turning toward Sami. "Thanks for this again. I know I keep dragging you out when you probably have better things to do."

"And kissing me?"

"Was it that bad? I mean, we've kissed before. When we dated, you seemed to enjoy yourself."

"I'm not saying it was bad. I'm just waiting for the day to be over. How many more of these couple's dates do we need to go on before you make partner?"

"Hopefully this was the last one, but they may ask you to join me for the partner meeting if I'm selected. You think you can join me one more time if I need you?"

"I'll be there," said Sami with a sigh as she closed her eyes. "I refuse to not be there after I've suffered through all of this."

"Look," said Jamal as he reached his hand over, placing it on hers. "I know it's not easy pretending to be my girlfriend and all. Especially since we go back so far. But thanks. I know I probably don't say it enough. But I appreciate you being there for me. When all this is over, I promise I'll get you something nice."

Sami looked over, seeing that big dumb smile on his face that she'd grown accustomed to over the years, and reached over her other hand, patting it on his. "I'm going to hold you to that. But until then. Let's try to keep the kissing to a minimum." *I really don't think my heart can take it at this point.*

The end of the ride stopped at the bottom of the mountain, where they found another trail that supposedly led back to their parking area among a few other tourist spots.

"I'm not going to enjoy the drive back," said Sami, her body feeling a little stiff from sitting down in the gondola. "Actually, Heather, how are you getting back? Didn't you and your husband come here together? Do you need a ride?"

"How thoughtful of you, but no. My husband called and informed our driver to come and pick me up. If he's not there when we arrive, then I'm sure he will be arriving shortly."

The path back to the parking area was easy enough, with them stopping in by the gift shop on the way. It was a large wooden log cabin. But that was only for show as once they stepped in, they saw how modern it was with its polished floors and indoor cooling system. Televisions hung on the wall displaying an assortment of sports that were playing.

But in the gift shop, Sami was surprised to see items that referenced the Black Sheep White Sheep competition. Large plushies, T-shirts, and on a couple of the TV screens where she saw a little animated snippet play of a black sheep and white sheep chasing each other.

I can't believe this, thought Sami as she walked in,

picking up one of the plushies. *Just how much marketing has Addison done with all this? Okay, that's it. I know we said we weren't going to look at anything. But this is getting ridiculous. I gotta know just how big...* Her thoughts froze as she saw two children both running back and forth throughout the gift shop wearing matching black sheep and white sheep hoodies, each one having sheep ears on its head.

"You want one?" asked Jamal, walking over to her. "This contest thing has gotten really popular. Some of the guys at work are even into it. I heard they're making bets."

"No thanks," said Sami, putting the plushie back down. "What about you? You haven't fallen victim to it yet?"

"Haven't had time. This whole partner thing has taken over my whole life." He then took her by the hand. Come on, let's get out of here.

"What about Heather?" asked Sami, looking around for the woman.

"She's up front. But her driver called and said he was a few minutes away. We'll wait till he gets here, and I'll take you home."

Meeting back up with Heather, they headed back over to the parking lot and waited for her driver to arrive before getting in their car and taking off. Not much talking was done at the start as they both just relaxed, listening to the radio as their bodies enjoyed no longer being on their feet.

Sami would occasionally look over at him, and every now and again would catch him glancing back at her.

"You know what this reminds me of?" asked Jamal.

"What?"

"Remember that time when we were over at Deandre's house playing baseball?"

"Oh no," said Sami with a laugh as she shook her head. "God, I never ran so hard before in my life."

"You? I'm the one who insisted on letting you play. You took one swing at the ball, popped it up and it went crashing through her kitchen window. "I ended up running behind you because they wanted to blame me for it. Just because I was the boy, they wanted to say it was my fault."

"Well, it kinda was. You're the one who pitched it to me and, if I remember correctly, weren't you the one who invited me over there?"

"And weren't you the one who asked me to do it because the boys wouldn't let you play?"

"And like a fool, you listened to me. So, as I said, it was your fault."

Jamal frowned. "I really should have let you take the blame for it by yourself."

"But you didn't, and we ended up cutting grass for half the summer in order to replace that window."

"Yeah. You used the weed eater and your father had been using that push mower with the busted wheel. I swear, every day I was dirty, sweaty, and tired."

"At least you didn't go home every Saturday with blades of grass in your hair. I gave up on using relaxers that summer because there was no need, when I'd just sweat it out the next week?"

"I never understood why you did the perm, anyway. Your hair is kinda crinkly, but not that bad."

"You're a man. You'd never understand since you keep your hair low. It was a nightmare trying to get a comb through my hair back then. I'm so glad it's not like that now."

"I like you better the way you are now. Your hair looks like curly fries."

Sami frowned back at him. "Really. Are you sure you're just not hungry?"

"You might be right. But seriously, I like your curly hair. It reminds me of when we were little riding our bikes."

Sami pulled at a strand of her hair, looking at it. "You do know that the only reason it was like that was because my father didn't feel like doing my hair, right? And my mother worked nights, so most of the time she was asleep during the day." She then looked over at him and saw he was still looking at her with a grin on his face. "Why are you looking at me like that?"

"Nothing. It's just... I'm just remember things."

"Well, can you remember and look at the road at the same time? I don't mind sharing a car with you, but I'm not sharing a hospital bed with you."

He laughed, "Don't worry. I've never been..." His voice trailed off as he looked ahead.

Sami followed suit and saw the red lights on the red lights of the cars ahead as they began to slow down. "I guess someone else wasn't watching the road."

"Seems so," said Jamal with a sigh. "Can you check the traffic on your phone and see if it has any news?"

Sami did as asked, pulling out her phone and looking for traffic updates. As the feed came up, she frowned before showing him the phone. "It's a long way up. It says we have like a two hour wait because of a twenty-two-car pileup."

"Twenty-two?" repeated Jamal, before rubbing at his eyes. He then looked around at the nearby cars, since they were at the edge of the city. Soon came the sounds of sirens as an ambulance came zooming by on the shoulder of the road toward the wreckage that was miles ahead.

Jamal watched the ambulance for a minute before it disappeared out of sight. Then, looking around carefully, he then pulled onto the shoulder and began slowly driving upward alongside the cars toward the exit."

"What are you doing?" asked Sami.

"We've been sitting here for a while, and we've barely moved. You live in the middle of the city, but I live near the end. I know another way to my place."

"Okay? Then how am I going to get home? Are you going to loan me the car?"

"If you want, sure. Or you could stay the night with me. Or at least for like three or four in the morning when that mess has finally cleared up."

"What? I'm not staying the night with you. And besides,

I have work tomorrow. I still have to write my article."

"I want you to look at all this traffic and tell me you really want to sit here for hours on end. We'll come back out when it's cleared up."

Sami looked ahead at the stalled traffic. She could get a better look at it now from their position on the curb and went clear for like a mile into the city. She then looked over at Jamal. "You have a computer at your place, right?"

The road to Jamal's apartment wasn't a straight shot as they ended up taking some back roads before they found their way back to pavement through neighborhoods that Sami's never seen before. But soon they were back in the outer edge of the city and arrived at his apartment. Dropping the car off at a parking garage, they walked through the night air into the complex.

His apartment wasn't as nice as hers. He could easily have afforded a better one.

"Why do you stay so far out from where you work? You know what traffic is like in the morning."

"I just didn't feel like finding a new place after I got my job at the firm. Here, they don't ask me to sign any papers or even bother me for the most part. As long as they get my money every month, I don't hear or see anybody other than the neighbors, maybe once a month or so."

"You mean the only reason you live here is because you're too lazy to sign a new lease?" asked Sami as she reached the stairs and began making their way up. "How are men so lazy when it comes to making their lives easier? You don't even drive your car to work, you take a cab. You know you'd save money driving yourself, right?"

"But then I would have to drive myself and then look for a parking spot when I got there. That's a giant pain in the ass. The car is good for when I need to leave the city. Like what we did today. But other than that, it can stay where it is. I change the oil every six months and then stuff it back in the garage."

They reached his apartment, and he slid in his key, jiggling it a few times to make it stick before opening the door. The apartment wasn't that big and served its purpose, with its four walls and a living room area that doubled as a bedroom. On one side was the bed, which wasn't made, on the other side was the kitchen, and in the center was a sofa where in front sat a large TV that would rotate around, allowing it to face either the sofa or the bed.

"Well, at least the room is kinda clean. There aren't dirty clothes scattered around like last time. Do you at least have hot water this time?"

"Yes. I told you it was broken before."

"Good, then I'm going to take a bath. I'm sweaty and sticky. I'll grab some of your clothes from the closet."

"Go ahead. You know where everything is."

Sami walked over to the door leading to the bathroom and closet area and closed it behind her. Despite the weird shape of the apartment, it did have a fairly large bathroom with a walk-in shower on one end and on the other was the closet and hamper. Not even checking the lock on the door, she began removing her clothing, letting it drop to the floor until she stood there naked in front of the glass divider.

She slid the door to the side, stepping into the shower and turning the nozzle, letting the water run and adjusting it until it felt the right temperature. Finally, when satisfied, she stepped inside and let it wash over her body.

It felt wonderful. The heat hitting her skin, the steam rising around her body. It was as soothing a feeling as she'd ever felt. It was like the weariness of the day was being washed away, along with the sweat that had dried on her skin. Deep breaths, she let the heat fill her lungs before reaching over and grabbing his body gel and loofah, spreading the gel over it.

The scent of a soft spring rain came over her as she spread it over her hands. It smelled of him, from when they were close earlier in the day. He'd always used this soap.

Whereas it was light before, now the fragrance was thicker, richer and took her mind back to a different time from years ago.

How they would spend the nights together and how his hands would roam over her body. She could almost remember it perfectly. The way he would come up behind her, his hand working their way around, softly caress the side of her face and then downward, grazing her neck before cupping her breast in his hand before pressing his lips against her neck. The water washing over her. Her finger sliding between her breasts and down the center of her stomach. Her hands mimicking the memories of the years past as she exhaled and found a small piece of the pleasure that he once gave her.

The fantasy grew clearer, and the pleasure started to grow. The way he would take her, ripping her clothes off the moment they were alone. Her body pressed up against the glass, pinning her there before taking her mouth with his. The water flowing off the both of them as he would slide his leg between her, spreading them before slowly moving his hand back down to find the other wetness between her legs.

She bit her lip, taking it all in. Living in and for a moment that was half there and half past. Not truly real, but real enough for her to take and grab a hold of. But even then, it was something not meant to last as the heated water began to run out of the cold chill of what was left slowly drug her from her fantasies and back to the reality of the now.

It was only a little while later that she would step out of the shower, her body feeling a little more drained than when she went in. Reaching forward, she grabbed a towel off the rack, wiping at her body before walking over to his closet. Opening it, she picked out a pair of blue boxers and one of his white button-up long sleeve shirts.

Feeling the moisture against the back of her neck, she ran her fingers through her hair. *I'm going to need to wrap this in with something or the morning is going to be terrible.*

She began searching through his drawer and found a large pink comb inside the third shelf. Taking it in her hand, a smile slowly came over her lips as she brought it to her face. *He kept it. Humm. Why would he...*

Still with the same smile on her face, she exited the bathroom holding her dirty clothing in her hand. Walking into the kitchen, she grabbed an empty shopping bag from where she knew he'd kept them. Tossing her dirty clothing inside of it, she left them next to the wall before then began combing through her hair as she made her way to him. "Alright, it's your turn. Go on and... really?" She stopped combing her hair, placing her hands on her hip, shaking her head as she stared down at a passed out asleep Jamal with his head on the armrest of the Sofa.

The way his chest heaved, the lining of his beard that went around his face. It wasn't thick by any means, just trimmed down where you could still see the jawline beneath. *And when we dated, he used to worry that wouldn't be able to grow a beard. Now he's a grown man. She looked down at her own self, and here I am a grown woman. She sighed. You'd think things would be easier.*

Slowly, she lifted her hand, raising her comb just slightly above the temple of his head. She then bounced it between her fingers as it lifted up and down in a rhythmic motion before lowering her hand and allowing it to whack him on the forehead.

He moaned as his hand rose to rub the spot where she had hit him. His eyes appeared glazed over as he squinted and looked up at her.

"You're filthy. Go take your bath."

He stared up at her for a moment before moaning again and slowly rising from the couch. "Alright, I'm getting up." Then sluggishly, he made his way to the backroom while holding his lower back as if he was an old man.

Great, now I feel like his mother. After he left, she looked around the apartment for a moment, deciding to clean up a bit before heading to bed. Surprisingly, he was a little more organized than before. His dirty clothes were not thrown all over the floor, instead he had a hamper where he kept them outside of the bathroom door. On the TV stand, she saw his laptop and for a brief moment considered grabbing it to try to start writing her article.

I really don't have the energy right now. I'll write it when I wake up.

The rest of the apartment was everything typical of a man's room. There was a single light in the corner. She tried to turn it on, but the bulb was blown. He had two pillows, but of course there were no pillow covers covering them and his shoes from work were scattered across the floor. Taking it upon herself, she walked through the apartment, picking up his shoes and not seeing anywhere else to put them, organized them by the door.

I guess that will do for now. She then turned on the TV, grabbed the remote and walked over to the bed, sliding in the covers. The cool feeling of the blanket felt so comforting over her warm skin, it was as if she was sinking into it. *At least he got a new bed and not just two mattresses stacked on top of each other on the floor.*

"Ah!" came the sound of his scream. "You used up all the hot water."

"Take a cold shower. It's good for you," she said back loudly so he could hear.

With the sound of running water continuing as the backdrop to her evening, she began flipping through the channels. They were all movies. She spent a few seconds trying to figure out what one was about. But her thoughts didn't get far as the sound of running water began to lull her into an even more relaxed state. It was thick and constant, and it came over the room, providing a hypnotic humming sound.

She tried to stay awake for him, but soon found her eyes getting heavy as thoughts of him filled mind. Some of the current him, some of the boy she knew as a child. A few of the intimate moments they're shared together. A first official date in the park, their first time holding hands while playing jump rope in the third grade, a first kiss made because of a dare to prove she wasn't afraid. Somewhere in those memories was a truth she was realizing, but the moment was too hazy.

Her final thoughts once again circled back to their first kiss. His lips were so soft, and even though she didn't admit it, she was so nervous back then. Reliving the moment in her mind didn't happen often, but this time, it felt more real than before. It was as if she could really feel his lips pressed against hers, but the difference this time was she could smell a spring rain before sleep finally took her.

CHAPTER 15

A few days later, Sami was a few corners away from her workplace, grabbing a bite to eat alongside Becca. They stood in line wearing their morning coats as they waited to purchase some steamed buns from a street vendor in a large cart.

"I'm surprised you're still down here with us poor people," said Sami with a smirk to her friend. "I'd just assumed you would have started having your caviar and whatever else rich people eat brought to your desk."

"Oh, ha-ha," said Becca, shivering a bit in her coat. "It's not like we're married, and I don't want him to think I'm using him for his money?"

"But aren't you using him for his money?"

"No," said Becca, before bobbing her head back and forth in thought. "Okay, maybe it started that way. But it's different now. He offered to take me to Paris next month, but I told him I had a presentation that I needed to prepare for." She laughed. "You should have seen his face. He was honestly shocked."

"I'm shocked that you turned it down."

"I didn't turn it down. I told him we could go after the presentation. So maybe in two months or so. He also has stuff to take care of."

"So, I guess I'm not going to see you and Addison getting all buddy-buddy as you throw money from helicopters."

"Me? Please, you better worry about Jewel taking that spot. Not me."

"Jewel? What do you mean?"

"What do you mean, what do I mean? She's been spending a lot of time with Addison," said Becca as she stared at Sami, who stood there with a confused look on her face. "Oh seriously. You think I don't know? The whole Black Sheep White Sheep thing. I know that's you two?"

"Huh? Wha... what are you talking about?" said Sami, trying to laugh it off. "There's no way. You saw the people who—"

"Who Addison brought in to try and trick us?" asked Becca, cutting her off from trying to lie. "Did you also forget that I'm the one who took you on that date night that started it all off? You think I wouldn't recognize the similarities in the stories? Or are you really going to stand in front of me and lie to my face?"

Sami looked around before stepping out of line and pulling Becca with her.

"No, my food," said Becca. "We waited so long."

"Okay, you're right, but you can't tell anyone, okay?"

"Well duh. I've known all this time and I haven't told anyone yet, have I?" She shifted her shoulders, trying to adjust the coat. "Now, what are we gonna do? I don't want to stand back in line again."

"Tell me. What did you mean about Jewel spending time with Addison?"

"Seriously?" asked Becca with a pained expression on her face. "Do you not read her articles?"

"No, we promised each other we wouldn't. Why? Should I be worried?"

"Should you— wow, really? You might want to break that promise and see what she's been up to. Cause I promise you; it's more than just taking that man from you. Did you know that she kissed him the same night you brought him over to the party? While he was on a date with you, she was kissing him behind your back."

"Yeah. She told me about that?"

"She did?" said Becca, her eyes wide with surprise. "Are we talking about the same Jewel? You know, the one with the plants? You mean she kissed a guy you were dating and came in and told you about it?"

"It... okay, yeah, but she was... I don't know how to put it. She wasn't bragging about it. It was more of a confession. I think she felt guilty."

"I bet," said Becca, shaking her head. "I gotta admit, out of all the people who I thought would do something that backstabbing, Jewel was never on that list. I guess you can't trust anyone, even little miss 'I only wear pants' miss goody-two-shoes. Oh, did you see? Apparently, he has her wearing skirts now. Can you believe it? Jewel in a skirt. I never thought I'd see it."

"We bought those skirts together."

"What?"

"When she... when she hurt her leg. I took her shopping. That's when we bought the skirts and other things," said Sami, looking down on the ground.

Becca laughed. "So, she took a guy you were dating and then went out with you shopping, acting like nothing happened? Oh, that girl's cold."

"It's...," Sami sighed. "I don't know what to do about her now. I can't just walk up to her and say: Okay Jewel, we're good now. I forgive you for going behind my back and kissing someone that I was supposed to be dating."

"And did she tell you she's thinking about having a baby for Addison?"

"A what? Baby?"

"Girl, you better start reading that Black Sheep article."

Sami suddenly started to feel a surge of nervousness in her stomach. "Wait, Jewel's pregnant?"

"Not yet. But if Addison has a say in it—"

"What? Why is Addison trying to get Jewel to have a baby? Is this like a fake baby for a story about motherhood or something?'

"You... need... to read that article, girl. I promise you; Jewel might as well be living a whole other double life with the stuff she's got going on."

"I'm gonna head to work now. I don't really feel hungry anymore."

"Yeah, I guess if I had just found out everything you did, then I guess I wouldn't either," said Becca, as she patted her friend on the back.

Walking several blocks over to their workplace, Sami couldn't help but feel nervous about her situation. So much so that she didn't even notice much of the morning traffic, as Becca had to pull her back from walking through a traffic stop. It was still early in the morning and many cabs were parking or leaving from in front of their building.

Still in a bit of a daze, Sami headed up the walkway to her building where she saw Patrick exiting the building, holding two bags with pipes sticking out of each. He smiled when he saw her.

"Hey there," he said before tilting his head curiously. "Is everything alright? You're not looking like your usual self."

"Hey," said Sami. "Yeah, everything's fine. I just... I just have a lot on my mind."

"Oh, well. How about I take you out to eat tonight? Whatever it is, I'll see if I can take your mind off of it for a few hours."

While not exactly feeling up for it. She nodded her head as she looked at him. "That... that's fine. I'll give you a call after work."

"Great," he lifted his bags to show her. "Well, I have to go and return these, so I'll see you later." He then leaned down, giving her a kiss on the lips and another smile before walking past her towards the street.

Sami saw a surprised look on Becca's face, but ignored it. *I'm sure she'll figure it out.* She then turned around to watch Patrick go and was surprised to see Jamal standing there before her.

Instantly, that feeling in her stomach that made her so uncomfortable became ten times worse. There was a small moment where he seemed confused, and then his eyes blinked once, and a smile came over his lips as he stepped towards her.

"How are two of my favorite ladies doing today?"

"We're fine," said Becca. "You still following Sami around like a lost puppy?"

"Funny," he said, placing his hand to his chest. "I'll have you know I have been on a journey of self-discovery. I'm a new man." He then turned to Sami. "And so apparently are you. I didn't know you were dating Patrick."

"Ye... yeah," said Sami, her voice soft as she spoke, while not bringing herself to look him in his eyes. "We've only been dating for a month now."

"Well, that's good. I knew you'd find yourself someone, eventually. Especially after your last break up." He gestured back to the building. "Come on, we don't want to be late." Together, they walked inside and headed over to the elevator.

"So, what have you been up to lately?" asked Becca. "I know you've got that new secretary up there. You haven't been giving that poor girl a hard time, have you?"

"What do you mean by that? You make it sound like I'm some sort of predator."

"I wouldn't say predator. But you certainly don't like missing an opportunity."

"I'll have you know that I have been on my best behavior these past few months," said Jamal as he placed his hands on the collar of his shirt, readjusting its fit.

"I find that hard to believe?" said Becca, turning to Sami. "What do you think, Sami?"

"Huh?" replied Sami, turning to Becca as if she'd just seen her for the first time.

"You okay, girl? That Jewel thing really got your mind that bad."

"Oh, so you know about Jewel 'The Relationship Robber' too?" asked Jamal

"The Relationship Robber. Really?"

"What? Don't like the name? I thought it was kinda catchy."

Becca placed her hands over her stomach, laughing. "God, you're weird. But sure, why not? The Relationship Robber, I'll be sure to call her that today."

"Oh. My stomach's getting the better of me," he said as they reached the elevator and he looked at his watch. "I think I still have time to catch that food vendor that hangs out near here in the mornings."

"What?" asked Becca. "I thought you said you were about to be late. There isn't—" and before she could finish her statement, he had already walked away while waving back at them. He exited the building as Sami and Becca entered the elevator.

"Dam, he moves fast," said Becca as she pressed the button for their floor. She then turned to an oddly quiet and still faced Sami. "So, are you going to tell me what that was about?"

"What?" asked Sami as the door closed.

"Really? Are you really going to try that on me again? You think I didn't notice the way Jamal looked at you when he saw you kissing Patrick, and that's not to mention how you got all quiet and had that shameful look on your face."

"It's nothing."

"Really?" asked Becca. "Fine, you don't have to explain it to me. But from where I'm standing, it looks like Jewel isn't the only one who's doing some double crossing."

"It's... it's not like that."

"Okay," said Becca, raising her hands in submission. "You keep telling yourself that. But we both know that—" Becca turned and slapped the side of the elevator. "Oh my god, you're fucking again, aren't you?"

"What? Who?"

"Don't who me, Jamal. I can't believe I didn't even think about it because you told me you used to date. But yeah, they change it. It's an old friend, it's a childhood friend."

"Stop, just stop, okay? We haven't done anything. We've just been going out is all, and it's not even like that between us."

Becca just stared at Sami for a moment, with an expression that seemed to suggest that Sami had tried to convince her the sky was made of marshmallow clouds. "You can't be..." She shook her head. "No... No. I'm going to let you have this. You've dated men before. If you really think that, then I'll leave it alone." The door opened on their floor, and she stepped out. "After all, he's your childhood friend. You'd know better than I would, right?" She then headed into the office, making her way to her desk, still shaking her head like a disappointed mother.

Sami stepped out of the elevator a few seconds after her after trying to compose herself. *Don't think about it. I have work to do. I mean, it's not like we were dating for real. Those weren't real. I did that for his job. That was a favor. He can't just expect me—*

"Hey Sami," said Lan Ling as she came walking up. "How is your morning going?"

Sami shook her head. "It's fine. Just tired is all." She then headed back to her desk, with Lan Ling following behind.

"Are you sure? You look pretty down? Did you go on a date? Did it not end well? You can tell me."

"What? No... just... just leave me alone for today, Lan Ling. I have a headache."

"Oh," said Lan Ling, looking dejected. "Well, okay. But just remember if you need someone to talk to, I'm here to listen. You can come over to my desk and talk to me anytime."

"No, it's fine. I'll be fine. I just need to focus, that's all."

Lan Ling was quiet for a moment, but then patted Sami's desk playfully before walking back over by the window and took a seat at her desk. Sometime during the day, Jewel walked in. She didn't bother to look at Sami, or anyone else for that matter. She just calmly sat down at her desk and began working.

The day went by slowly. The humming of the machines and office chatter was the same as usual, but to Sami, the room felt quieter and somewhat colder. Between her occasional looks at Jewel, Sami would also lance down at Addison's empty office.

What does she do all day? She's only at work when she has a meeting. Other than that, I never see her. She looked over at Jewel again. *But you see her, don't you? I bet you do. I can't believe you.* She looked down at her computer. *You know what? Fuck our promise. I'm going to see what she wrote.*

With no more regard for their promise. Sami opened the page and began reading over Jewel's journey in love over the past weeks: From the appearance of a mysteriously tall man to her getting shot at in a car chase. And from her feeling sick and falling for a guy that her friend was supposedly dating. And then finally her boss supposedly trying to convince her to have a child.

This can't be real. She's making things up to try to beat me. Her eyes glanced back over at Jewel. *Isn't she?*

The rest of the day went by as the sun began to fade and she saw Jewel, stand up from her seat and then head over to the elevator. She noticed she was wearing her pants outfits again as she came from behind her desk. Next came Becca, who did stop by her desk.

"You're not going to try to talk to her about it?" asked Becca, nodding to Jewel, who entered the elevator.

"About what? What am I supposed to say? I forgive you for playing dirty and kissing someone who I was supposedly dating. And you know what makes it worse. He hasn't even called me since that night. He could have called or something. Instead, he just ghosted me. And after all that shit, he said that night about wanting a second chance."

"Well, just remember. The longer you two wait to work this out. The harder it's going to be."

"And what if I don't want to work it out?"

"Then this office is going to stay boring. Everyone is just sitting in their seats. Even Lan Ling has been hiding way down there in her little corner."

Sami turned her head down toward the end of the room to see Lan Ling poke her head out and look around before ducking back inside her space.

"There's no way you're blaming that all on me."

"I'm not blaming anyone. I'm just making sure you noticed it," said Becca as she placed her bag on Sami's desk so that she could put on her coat properly. "Anyway. What you do is up to you. I'll see you tomorrow." She then grabbed her bag and headed for the elevator. Sami shook her head and tried to once again focus on her work. She allowed herself to get absorbed in answering her fan emails, trying to thank everyone for supporting the white sheep. By the time she was satisfied, everyone else had left the office. It was getting late and out the window Sami could see an orange sky as the sun began to fade past the horizon.

She stretched and stood up from her desk. *I should probably head home. I know I promised Patrick I'd go out with him. But I really don't feel like it. Not today. I'll call him when I get in the cab.* She then closed her laptop and began rubbing at her eyes. Packing up her things, she then headed for the elevator.

"Wait up," came the voice of Lan Ling as Sami saw her shuffling to grab her things and catch her before the elevator left her.

Great! I didn't even realize she was still here. Why could you have just gone home? I really don't feel like talking anymore.

In her usual fashion, Lan Ling came over, smiling. "I'll catch the elevator down as well."

"Alright," said Sami with a sigh. "That's fine."

Both women stepped into the elevator. After pressing the button for the first floor, Sami stepped back to see Lan Ling still smiling up at her.

She sighed again. "Why are you looking at me like that?"

"Because you're the White Sheep and you're planning some big revenge scheme to get back at Jewel for taking your man? Is that why you looked so tired today?"

"What?" asked Sami, trying to blink away her disbelief. "What are you talking about?" *Who told her? Of all the people who in their right mind would tell Lan Ling.*

"You don't have to hide it from me. I can keep a secret. I just want to know what you plan to do? Are you going to make up with Jewel? You two didn't speak today, so I think one of you is mad at the other."

"Who told you that I'm the white sheep? They were lying. You were there when those people came into Addison's office. They were the sheep?"

Lan Ling's smile grew. "Too late to hide it now. Jewel told me the truth."

Sam instantly could feel her aggravation growing. "You know what? I don't care. Jewel can blab about it to whoever she wants. I'm done with her." She turned away from Lan Ling and faced the elevator door.

"Really? But you two are close. I think both of you should make up. I was reading about it on the internet. A lot of people want to read about you two becoming friends again and sorting it out."

"No, Lan Ling. We won't make up. Jewel is a backstabber. She is not my friend."

"But—"

"And before you say anything else. If you bring it up again, then I will be done with you as well."

Lan Ling frowned. "You know what?" she said in a sharp, angry tone. "You've been mean to me for a long time; when I've only ever been nice to you. What have I ever done to you?"

Sami's temper flared up even higher. "It's because you're nosey and you're bothersome. That's why no one wants to deal with you."

"I'm not bothersome. And the only reason I'm nosy is because I'm trying to be your friend. You, Jewel, Becca, I see you always over here talking and having fun. Why, when you all go out, you never invite me. I'm fun. I want to go out too."

"Lan Ling, I don't have time for your—"

"And stop calling me that. I'm sick of it."

"What?"

"My name is not Lan Ling," she shouted, her eyes now beginning to water.

"What... what are you talking about? Everyone calls—"

"Lan Ling is some stupid name Addison started calling because she once watched some stupid Chinese show. I'm not even Chinese, I'm Korean."

Sami just stood there for a moment, dumbfounded. "I... I'm sorry. I didn't know—"

"Of course not. Because you don't care about me. None of you all care about me. And you know what sucks? It's that I always thought I could clear it all up, since my name is literally on my desk. All you ever had to do was walk over and you'd see it. But none of you have ever come to my desk, even though I'm always coming to visit and talk to you." The emotion became too much for her. She began to wipe at her eyes with the back of her hands.

Sami's anger quickly vanished as a feeling of shame started to set it in. "Lan Li— I mean, I'm sorry," she said as she reached out to place a hand on the woman's shoulder.

"No, don't touch me," she said, slapping her hand away as the ding sound came as she opened the door. "I'm sick of you. I'm sick of Jewel. I'm sick of Addison. I hate all of you," she said as she ran out of the elevator and through the hall.

Sami could only stand there stunned for a moment as the doors closed in front of her. It took a moment in the near silence of the elevator before she came back to her senses. The humming of the machinery whispered in her ears as she reached out and pressed the button back up to her office floor. The guilt in her stomach growing as she soon exited the elevator and stepped back out into her office area, walking over to the window where Lan Ling's desk was. And there, right at the top, shining in the evening sunlight, was a nameplate that read 'Park, Seo-ah.'

Jewel laid down on a couch, looking up at a slowly rotating ceiling fan that barely pushed down any air. If the room had any AC, she didn't know, and she didn't care. She was in an old motel room, half dressed and tired. The last two hours she'd been contemplating her life choices over the past few weeks. But if there was one thing she was grateful for, it was that she didn't have to do it alone. Turning her head, she stared at Nathan as he sat in a 'too small for him' loveseat with a small notebook in his hand, writing down a few scribbles.

"So, what do you think I should do?" asked Jewel.

"That depends on you," he said, taking his pen to his lips and thinking. "It's certainly an odd request. Your boss wants you to fuck her husband and have his kid. You don't run into many people who have that story."

"No, not that one. I mean, about Sami, what should I do about her?"

"Oh," he pointed his pen at her. "Nothing."

"What?"

"You were wrong. You admitted you were wrong, and you came clean fairly quickly. It'll take time, but I'm sure she'll forgive you. That is, unless you get that job, and she spends the rest of her life trying to sabotage your dreams."

"You... you think she'd do that?"

"Not many people are willing to gracefully smile as you take their man and their job. I've seen people in prison for less."

His bluntness made Jewel feel like a small child as she raised her shoulders, wishing she could disappear into the couch.

"Okay then. But I mean. Maybe if I tried to—"

"There's nothing you can do," said Nathan, shaking his head and cutting her off.

Jewel frowned at him, getting annoyed. "Are you sure you're a therapist? Aren't you supposed to give me like some real advice?"

"That's not exactly what we do. We try to find the underlying mental conditions that push a certain person into action or non-action in your case. And you have acceptance issues which are causing you fear of being rejected by your friend."

"Of course, I'm scared. Sami was the first friend I made when I came to this city. I don't want to lose her over just some guy."

"Oh," said Nathan, catching on to her words. "So, is Andrew really just 'some guy?"

Jewel bit her lip at her choice of words as she turned herself away from Nathan, bring her knees to her chest on the couch. "No."

"So, you do like him."

"I do."

"And have you told Sami this?"

"Of course, I have. I told you about the elevator."

"Yes, you told me that you confessed that you kissed him. But you didn't tell her how you felt about him."

"That… but…" Her hand went up, covering her face, her palms over her eyes. "No… you think she might think that I did it only for this stupid contest?"

"That would be my guess, yes. Have you talked to her since?"

"No, she keeps giving me funny looks. And when we make eye contact, I get this feeling that she'd rather spit on me than talk to me. I'm trying to wait until she's… you know… maybe not so mad."

"Usually, I'd say that's the best course of action. But you might want to clear up the issue of why you kissed him first. Then give her the space she needs."

"But how? She won't even speak to me now."

"That I can't answer. You will have to find a way to be alone with her and get her to listen."

"Great," said Jewel, as she rolled back over, dropping her hands, staring back up at the ceiling again, which was now blurry.

"Tell me. How do you feel about this black sheep, white sheep contest?"

"What do you mean?"

"I mean, why are you in it?"

"Because I want to win. I mean, I essentially get to be a CEO of a company. Who wouldn't want that?"

"But why is the CEO position important? You're apparently going to receive a large sum of money when it's all over. And if you take the surrogate mother position, you'll probably never need money again. So why are you still doing it?"

"That is…" Jewel began to think. *Why am I still doing this? But it's not like being a CEO isn't a good thing, right? I get to be in charge. I can make the company better. Better than*

Addison? Wait, am I better than Addison? Can I give birth to a child for Addison? Take care of her kids. She wants me to fuck her husband. Jewel's eyes went wide. *She... just what does she want from me, really? Does she want me to be her?*

"Is everything okay?" asked Nathan, rubbing at his chin.

"I... I don't know. I mean... I don't know what to think anymore."

"Good. I guess we're done for our session today, then."

"What?" asked Jewel, as she sat up on the couch. "That's it? But what about the contest and..."

"If you want to meet again and talk about it, that's fine," he said, closing his notebook and standing up, walking over to a duffle bag on his bed. "But you seem as if you've just had a revelation. I think you should spend the next few days working through it and sorting out your feelings. It didn't take you a few hours to get yourself into everything, so I promise you won't get out of it in just one hour of talking with me."

"Oh," said Jewel, standing up and walking over to his bed. "Yeah, I guess you're right." There on the other side of the bed she saw a spread of documents, along with two guns. "Can I ask why you are in this city?"

"I'm just taking care of a few things. And then there's the issue of keeping you safe until my business is done. Also, it seems your boss has contacted me. She wants to meet to make sure I'm not a stalker. Apparently, she became a little upset that she can't find out who I am."

"She can't?"

"Certain things are classified, even to those with money. I got a call from a few friends that let me know that she's been floating my picture around certain government agencies trying to have me investigated."

"That sounds like Addison. She... she was mad that I got her daughter involved in what happened in the museum."

"Ah, I see. I can certainly understand that feeling. Don't worry, I'll let her stew on it for a few more days, and then

I'll give her a call."

"So... you do really work for the government."

He laughed. "Did you think I was lying?"

"I don't know. It's not like I'm used to any of this. But... but you do kill people."

"For the government, yes. But I'm not here to kill people this time. Just gaining information. If that was the case, then I would have killed that guy in the bathroom."

"You... you think I'm safe now?"

"Probably. I think that guy's still locked up. I have another week or so in the city before my mission is done. So, everything should be fine."

Jewel just shook her head. "I don't know what's more ridiculous. My relationship with you..." she waved her hand over the bed filled with items she didn't even know what to say. Maybe except that there were a few guns there. "And all of this. Or all the mess with Sami and Addison."

"Oh, definitely the mess at your job." He picked up his gun, ensuring the chamber was empty, and showed it to her. "This world has a lot of guns, so it's common. But I can't think of a single time I've met a future CEO of a company who is considering having the baby of the former CEO while stealing the man of her best friend."

"I did not steal him... but I see your point." She sighed. "Thank you for talking to me. I guess I should head back to work now."

"I'm amazed you can just take off from work in the middle of the day like this."

"Our company is very lenient on time. I submitted my article last night, so really all I do is answer emails all day for our subscribers." *Subscribers... I wonder how many I have now.*

"Sounds like it should be relaxing," he said, shaking his head then looking at her with a smile. "It's amazing how you managed to fuck it up so badly."

Jewel couldn't help but laugh. "Yeah, I really did." Then

grabbing her coat, she then made her way towards the door, opening it and leaving the room. The hallway of a cheap motel was just as dirty as anyone could have expected. Heading downstairs. she saw a male cabby leaning back on the hood of his car smoking a cigarette, waiting for her.

"Sorry for the wait," she said as she walked around to the passenger side of the car, getting in.

"Don't worry about it. For the money you're paying, I'd wait around all day," he said as he sat back inside and started up the vehicle. "So, where're we off to?"

"Back to where you found me. I need to head back there."

"Okay," said the cabby and with that, they both headed back out into the city.

Not long into the drive, the cabby turned on the radio and once again the city's main radio discussion show was talking about the black sheep white sheep game from their article.

"I'm telling you she did the right thing," said the male radio host.

"Nah," said his female part. "Home girl should have taken that secret to her grave. If it was me. I would have kept it on the low and just dated him on the sly. You know. Just have him stop seeing the white sheep. Then after a few months of something. I'll approach my friend like, 'hey you know that dude you kinda dated for like a week or two? I saw him today and you know he asked me out. You mind if I go out with him?' You know, cause then the white sheep black sheep thing would have been over."

"And what if she still wasn't?"

"Oh, then home girl outta luck. I gave her the appropriate time to grieve, but I'm not losing out on no good man cause sister is bitter. I promise you; we cool. But at the end of the day, I'm taking care of me. You feel me?"

"Well, I think she did the right thing, telling her almost when it happened. Playing games like that will get you caught up."

"See, you're a man. You don't understand how women move. You are the reason home girls were fighting in the elevator at work."

"I bet you also want her to have that baby, too."

"Hell yeah. Some rich man shows up and offers me two million dollars to have his baby. I promise, Momma's next baby is gonna set up her first two babies for life. Sister better knows how to use that body god gave her. Black Sheep, if you're listening to this honey, you better make that money and go sit your ass down on a beach somewhere. Don't listen to this fool of a man sitting in front of me."

"Oh! You trifling as hell. You're telling this woman to go out there and be a prostitute?"

"Ain't no prostitute getting paid no two million dollars to fuck... oh I'm sorry, I'm not supposed to curse on the radio. My Bad. But you know what I mean. Ain't no prostitute I know making bank like that. Not even the best porn stars with golden vaginas are making bank like that."

"So, you're saying you know a few prostitutes?"

"Don't look at me like that. What, what, what, you trying to get me to hook you up? Humm. If you down bad, just say you down bad. All you ladies out there, my colleague here is looking for some action and apparently, he's willing to pay."

"Hey, hey, hey don't go putting that out there in the universe. I can't have nobody showing up at my hotel room tonight. I've already been through one divorce. I can't afford another one. You hear me ladies? I'M BROKE. I HAVE NO MONIES. Go find yourselves some other sugar daddy. My pockets have already been ran through by my ex-wife."

The sound of laughter poured out of the radio as Jewel reached her office building.

"Here's the other half," said Jewel as she exited the car, and handed the cabby two hundred and fifty dollars.

"Thanks lady. You got my number. If you're gonna be paying like this in the future, you make sure to call me and I'll come get you."

She waved bye to the cabby and headed up the steps into her building. She waved to the security guard and walked over to the elevator. But before pressing the button to call it down, she turned back and walked over to him.

"Excuse me."

"Yes."

"I know this might be a weird question. But do you know a woman named Addison who works here?"

"Not personally, but there's some lady who shows up in the books named Addison. I think she works up on one of the upper floors."

"So, you never met her?"

"Not that I know of?"

"What about that little girl that's sometimes in here? You sit with her sometimes."

"Oh yeah. Alina. She waits for her father to pick her up sometimes. Her mother comes down to pick her up sometimes, too. Brown-haired lady, I think. She is around the same age as my daughter, so we talk sometimes, and I make sure she doesn't get too bored just waiting here by herself."

"Okay. Thanks," said Jewel, turning to leave, but then turned back once again. "One more question. I know this might sound weird. But on the Christmas holidays. Do you get something like a large Christmas bonus?"

He looked at her kind of oddly, but then looked around to make sure no one else in the lobby was nearby and could hear. "Yeah, I thought accounting was making some type of mistake. But it happens every year. Between you and me, this job was only supposed to last about two months, but I've been here four years because that crazy bonus happens every year. You know who does that?"

Jewel just smiled back. "You might want to keep taking care of that little girl. I think she's lucky for you." She then waved bye and headed back over to the elevator just in time as someone else exited. Stepping inside, she pressed the
318

button for one of the floors ahead. She then pulled out her phone, dialing a number in her contacts.

Okay, well, at least I know she's not lying about the money. But can I really have a baby for money? No, of course not. I mean... I don't think I can. Even if she is kinda grooming me to take her place. But this... this is taking it too far, right?

The door opened at the same time as she heard her brother-in-law's voice on the phone.

"Hello?"

"Hey Gavin, I'm outside of your office. Can you open the door for me?"

"Yeah, sure. Is everything okay?"

"Yeah, I just want you to look into something for me," she said as she heard a click on the door and saw it give way. "Thanks, it's open." She ended the call, placing the phone back in her purse as she opened the door and stepped inside. The humming of the computers filled her ears again. There, behind the glass with the APEX company logo on them, she could see the flashing lights back and forth. *I still don't understand how he can work down here.*

She went through the aisle of machines until spotting his office in the back, where he sat behind his glass. Walking over, she opened the door, closing it behind her, locking out the sound.

"What's up? I haven't seen you in a few weeks," said Jewel, coming over to him.

"Yeah, I've been busy. Because of all this new server traffic, I've had to upgrade our systems. Is everything okay?"

"I want you to look up some information for me again, that's all."

"Sure," he said, turning back to his keyboard and placing his hands on the mouse. "What you need."

"Remember when I had you look up my subscribers versus Sami's?"

"Yeah."

"Can you show me that again?"

"Sure," he said as he began clicking on the mouse and Jewel saw the screen begin changing. "Okay, it looks to be about the same as before. You have about a hundred, and Sami has about three hundred."

"What, really? I thought there'd be more," said Jewel as she leaned forward, glaring down at the screen. *That's weird. I thought the contest was bringing in a bunch of money. Is Addison lying about the whole thing? But why would she lie about...* "Wait, are there any new articles for people to subscribe to? Like something for Black Sheep or White Sheep?

He clicked around a bit more. "Yeah, there is. It's labeled BS and WS. They have their own subscriber page."

"Can you tell me how many subscribers they have?"

"Sure, let's see how many... Wow! BS has over four hundred thousand subscribers and WS has over three hundred thousand?"

"Wait, So I have more subscribers than Sami?"

"What? You? Wait, you're that Black Sheep that everyone's been bad-mouthing about in that silly contest that the city is going crazy about?"

Jewel frowned. "Yeah, Addison has us doing it. The whole thing is stupid. How much money is this bringing in?"

"Wait, those articles. Are they true? Are you really planning on having someone's baby?"

"Oh, for goodness' sake. Now I wish I would have never told you. Just tell me how much money this has made, please."

"Ahh, let's see. It looks like it's three-ninety-nine each week. So maybe... three to seven million if you think that people have been slowly subscribing since things started."

"Three to... really? We've made that much."

"Yeah, and if subscribers keep pouring in, then it's going to be a lot more. Plus, that doesn't include the marketing. We picked up a set of Black Sheep White Sheep plushies from the store earlier. And then there's the T-shirts, coffee shop partnerships. Addison's probably making millions a day at this rate."

"How is she doing all this so fast? Doesn't it take time to market everything and have all those things made?"

"No idea, but whatever she did. She did it perfectly. Everybody is talking about this contest. But your sister is going to be so surprised when I tell her that you're the Black Sheep."

"Don't tell her anything. The last thing I need is for this to get back to mom and dad."

"Really? You can't just be involved in something like this and not tell anyone."

"I didn't. I told you and now you can't tell anyone."

"Well, that's hardly fair."

"Life's not fair. Now show me what else is in here about the article."

The cab dropped Jewel off at her apartment, and she took the elevator up. Walking through the hall, she felt tired. Not physically tired, but mentally. *I just want to sleep.* Opening the door, she stepped inside. The rush of cool air from her apartment provided some relief as she kicked off her shoes and began stripping off her clothing, laying them over the back of the sofa.

Just a quick bath and I'll lie down, she thought as she walked over into the bathroom, turning the knob and running the hot water. As the water heated, she dipped her hand inside, the steam from beneath her raising up her arm as washing over her face. *I wonder what he's doing. Maybe I should call him. But I don't want to bother him if he's busy.*

Her mind circled the thoughts as the water in the tub filled to a satisfactory amount. Dipping her foot in, she then gave in to the soothing feeling, sliding the rest of herself in and letting the water rise to her neck as she breathed a sigh of relief. *Maybe later, yeah… later I'll call.*

The world in front of her began to blur from the steam of the bath and the moment she closed her eyes, she let the world fade away.

She wasn't sure how long it had been, but sometime later she heard the sound of something vibrating. A little drowsy, she turned to see her phone on the countertop next to her. It wiggled for a moment during another buzz before quieting back down. Reaching over, she grabbed it, looking at the screen. To her surprise, it was Andrew. Her eyes still fuzzy, she squinted to reach the message. It read: "I'm at your door?"

"What?" she said aloud, the water drifting against the side of the bathtub as it moved back and forth. She tried to open the keypad on her phone, but her fingers were slippery and fumbled with it, opening up random programs. "Dammit."

Finding her way back out of the random screens, she opened up the keypad. But before she managed to type anything, there was a knock at her door. Still a little drowsy, she stood up before closing her eyes for a moment and allowing the world to reorientate itself.

There was another knock at the door, and she reached over grabbing a towel, wrapping it around herself as she left out of the bathroom, heading for the door. "Hold on, I'm coming," she said, pressing the monitor to the side of her door. The screen flickered for a moment and then it showed the outside beyond her door and there stood Andrew, holding a plant she didn't recognize in his hand.

A little nervous and swept up in the moment, she opened the door, peeking her head out.

"Hey," said Andrew. "Sorry about dropping by unannounced. Did I interrupt you?"

"No… no, I… I was just in the bath."

"Oh, sorry," he said, kneeling to the floor, setting the

plant down. "If you want, I can just leave this here and we can meet up later."

"Huh? Oh, no, I mean... you can come in," she said as she opened the door for him. "What's tha— Oh, is that a Desert Rose?"

"It is. I remember you said you wanted one, so I asked a friend for some help," said Andrew, holding the plant out to her.

"Thank you," she said, taking it from him. "I have just the spot for it, too. I need to make sure it gets lots of sunlight." She closed the door and walked over to a spot in her kitchen, sitting the plant down in a large pot. She flicked a switch on the side, which caused a light to turn on, shining down on it. "It's a heated pot. It'll make sure it doesn't die."

"I'm surprised you just happened to have this ready?"

"Well, I had planned on getting it when I could. It's just things have been so busy, so I haven't had time for... why are you looking at me like that?"

"Like what?" he said with a smile. "You mean like you're an almost naked beautiful woman with her hair just barely hanging down towards her lips? You're like the proof that life isn't fair."

"Oh," said Jewel, blushing a little as her eyes drifted downward, not being able to look him in the eyes anymore. She thought she might be blushing, but that could have been the redness from the bath. "What do you mean, how is life unfair?"

"Well," head leaned in closer, his lips almost touching her. "It's unfair that you look this sexy, and I am not allowed to touch you."

"Oh, that?" She bit down on her lip for a moment. "Well, I guess I did say that."

"You did," he said as he reached forward, placing his hand on the leaf of the desert rose. Taking it between his finger and his thumb, he began rubbing it suggestively. "Am I still not... allowed?"

"Well... I mean. I guess we can touch... a little."

"A... little?" he said as he released the plant, bringing his finger over and placing it on her shoulder.

She felt him press against her, sliding the tip of his finger over her shoulder and upward towards her neck. The sensual feeling of him finally touching her body was soothing. She closed her eyes, the longing that was building up in her slowly beginning to rise. No longer a whisper in the back of her mind, the touch of him bringing her desire for him to the surface.

"Then... am I allowed to kiss you?" he asked as he edged himself closer, his lips barely pressing against hers.

"Ye..." she said with a moan as she kissed him. Softly, she enjoyed the moment until he soon pulled his lips away from her. Leaning forward, he allowed his face to graze hers as she felt his breath as he whispered into her ear.

"Am I allowed to touch you now?"

She then took another breath and exhaled the word "Yes."

He ran his lips across the side of her face as he took a small step away so that she could see him. His hand rose to her chin, stroking her cheek with his fingers, before bringing a single finger down to just below her neck. He let his finger linger there for a moment as she was tempted by its presence; tempted for what was to come as he lowered his finger of the wetness just between her breasts where the towel enveloped her. The only thing between her nakedness and him.

He stared into her eyes as he lowered his finger further. Jewel could feel the towel tightening on her side as his finger slowly inched downward between her breasts. And then, having taken enough, the soft towel covering her finally gave way. The fabric freeing itself from her body, exposing her to him as it fell to the floor.

CHAPTER 16

The morning sun shone in through the apartment window of Sami's building as she lay in bed. Her eyes were closed, but in truth, sleep hadn't been with her for over an hour. Sleep wasn't easy to gain during the night. Perhaps an hour or two, but then she'd wake up, her consciousness wide awake as she lay there beneath the covers. So, she would just lay there in bed, her eyes closed but her mind open to the thoughts that circled around inside.

What should I do? I have to do something. Stupid Jamal and this stupid fake girlfriend thing. If he likes me, he should just come out and say it. Of course, I'm going to try dating someone. We aren't even a real couple. And I have to think about my future. Writing about this stupid contest is the best thing to ever happen to me. I have a career to think about.

She rolled over, smushing her face into her pillow. "Argh!" she moaned.

I shouldn't be thinking like this. Why does he have me thinking like this? Does he like me? I'm not breaking things off with Patrick if he doesn't... Wait? Would I break things off with Patrick if he liked me? I mean... I think I would. Does that mean I don't like Patrick? No, of course I like him. He's a little aloof, but he's not a bad person.

She opened her eyes as she lifted her head from the pillow, coming up for fresh air.

"I can't keep doing this," she said as she rolled over, placing her feet on the floor, mustering up the courage to face the day. She began rubbing her face. "Okay. I hate feeling like this. I have to do something." She then got up and walked over to the restroom to get ready for work.

A little while later, she was out of her apartment and inside the back of a cab, headed off to work.

"Ohhh! Girl, I can't wait for the next black sheep update?" said the woman on the radio.

"I gotta admit," said the male host. *"Because you keep talking about it so much. I feel like I know everything about—"*

"Can you turn that off please?" asked Sami.

"Sure thing," said the driver. "A little peace and quiet, right?"

With a nod of her head towards the eyes of her driver, she noticed looking at her through the rearview mirror. Sami exhaled and listened to the humming of the car against the muffled city sounds that made it into her car. She was intently aware of everything as she tried to keep her mind off her own problems. The squeaks the vehicle made, the bumps from potholes, she wished that these things would be all that would occupy her mind today.

Far too soon, the cab arrived at her place of work, and she stepped outside in the cool air. She didn't arrive early this morning. Instead, arriving with the rest of the work crowd headed towards the front lobby. Merging in with the others, she entered the building and waited for one elevator to come back down.

A slew of suits, ties, blouses, and skirts lined ahead of her, holding their luggage bags and waiting before shuffling into the next available metal box as it came down, announcing its presence with a ding sound. She looked over but didn't see the security guard there today. *Maybe he has the day off.*

Finally, with the movement of the last group, an elevator arrived, and they all shuffled inside. Unlike days before, she felt a tightening in her stomach as she stepped inside. Sami would have been glad if she could have attested it to the people that she was now rubbing elbows with, but she knew better. Denial may have been a grand escape for a moment, but after writing so many articles on the topic, it was hard for her own advice not to come seeping back into her mind.

I hate this feeling. I never used to feel like this before. Stupid Jewel. Why'd she have to go and mess everything up? The elevator stopped on her floor, and she stepped out, turning to look over at the office. Everyone seemed hard at work this day. A few were shuffling about, holding stacks of papers. Addison was even in her office. She then turned to where Jewel sat and there she was, staring back at her. As their eyes met, Sami's face instantly turned into a scowl as she shook her head and bit her lip. *No, no way. I'm not doing this right now.*

Before the elevator door could close, she slid her hand in between the doors, stepping back inside as she pressed the button and watched the door close on her. The tightness in her chest grew stronger as the elevator began to move again. Her body felt heavier as the sense of nervousness felt all consuming. And then came the ding sound as the elevator doors opened again. She clenched her fist and stepped out into another working environment as men in dress shirts once again stood over a monitor saying words Sami couldn't really make out. And even if she could, she wouldn't have cared.

Turning the corner, she made her way towards the glass

office where she saw Jamal sitting at his desk, opposite the woman from the last time she visited. She wore a short skirt, exposing her legs with her laptop over her thighs. Walking over, she stood in front of the door, knocking on the glass. She didn't even wait for his approval. She slid it open when he turned to face her.

"Hey Sami, what's up?"

"I want to talk to you about this weekend?"

"About that. You won't have to show up this time."

"Ah, should I just come back later?" asked the woman.

"Oh, sure. Just give us a few minutes."

The woman closed her laptop, stood, and walked toward the door. When she passed by Sami, she gave her a smile. "Have fun," she said under her breath where only the two of them could hear and she left the room, closing the door behind them.

"Okay," said Andrew, turning in his chair to face her completely. "What's up? You trying to visit or... Oh, it's the end of the month. I did promise to pay your rent for helping me, but I don't really keep checks. I can transfer you the money." He reached for his phone. "How much is it again?"

"Why aren't we going out this weekend?"

"Huh... Oh, nothing. Something came up, that's all, but maybe next time."

"Maybe?" she asked, her tone a little agitated. "Is this because of me and Patrick?"

"What? No," he shook his head, still wearing his smile. "Although I wish you would have told you two were dating. Thankfully, no one from upstairs saw you two. I'd hate to have to explain why my supposed girlfriend was kissing another man in front of our building while I stood and watched." He laughed. "What a mess that would have been."

No, this shit is a mess. "Okay then, what if I wasn't your *supposed* girlfriend?" she asked, leaning back against the glass door and folding her arms.

He looked at her for a second, his eyes lowering as he

seemed to be contemplating her words. "I don't... what?"

"You heard me." *I can't believe I'm doing this. Please don't say no. I know you like me. You have to.*

His lips twisted before he sighed and exhaled. "Okay, you win. We'll call it off."

"What?"

"I guess I should have thought about how our fake relationship could have messed up anything you had going on with another guy."

"But that's not—"

"Shit," he laughed. "I'm going to have to explain to them what happened. I guess I can say—"

"Listen to me, you big idiot!" she said, her voice so loud she didn't care if it came through the glass.

"Ah, okay. My bad," he said, looking a little started. "What's wrong?"

Sami sighed and closed her eyes, taking in a deep breath. *I can't believe I have to work this hard for this man to understand me.* She opened her eyes and softened her voice as she took a step towards him. "I'm saying that... what if... I wasn't your fake girlfriend..." She placed her hands on his desk, leaning forward, trying to look as appealing and out right intentional as she could to get it through to him. "Maybe I could try being your 'real' girlfriend?"

There was another moment as he stared at her. His face, the face that she watched grow up over the years. His stupid smile was gone. *I can't believe I can't believe I'm in love with this stupid face. This annoying idiot's face.*

He smiled at her before shaking his head. "No, you're making fun of me. I can tell by how you're looking at me. You think I'm stupid."

"Yes. I do," she said, dropping her head, trying to exhale out all the frustration inside of her. "You are incredibly stupid." She then took another step forward, sliding her hand across the desk. Everything in the way of her arm came along, falling to the floor as she came closer to him.

"Hey, what are you doing?" he said as he reached down, beginning to pick things up. "Now I'm going to have clean—"

She then walked past him, grabbing him by the back of his shirt collar and pulling back up into his seat, forcing him to turn around, where she then promptly sat down in his lap.

"Guess what?"

"What?" he asked, visibly confused about what was going on. "I don't—"

And before he could finish his words, she placed her lips on his. She kissed him deeply, wrapping her arms around his neck, the chair squeaking under the weight of them both as she leaned into him. She then pulled her lips away for a moment, took another breath before pushing her lips onto him again, trying her best to drive her point deep into his thick head. After another long moment, and when she was satisfied with herself and what she wanted, she pulled herself away from their kiss and stayed in his lap and allowed him to look her over.

"Now you tell me… Do you think I'm being serious now?"

"Ah… well…"

She saw his eyes beginning to shift around in his head.

"Jamal Frido Jones, if you don't say something, I'm going to slap you."

"No! I mean, I understand your seriousness. I just mean… What about Patrick?"

"I'll tell him the truth. There's actually a few things I have to fix now. But this… this is the most important."

"You mean with Jewel after she supposedly took that guy you're dating?"

"Oh, for the love of… we went out on one date. Okay, that's a lie. It was two dates. And I didn't even like him that much. I was more mad at Jewel than I was with him."

"Yeah, but what about that mess with that Asian girl in your department? Is everything okay with that?"

"What? Who told you about that? Did she tell you—"

"No, the delivery guy. He said that—"

"Who is this delivery guy that..." she shook her head. "You know what, just forget it. But yes, I have to fix that also."

"Okay, but you gotta understand how this feels weird. You were dating this guy, that Jewel took from you and—"

"She didn't take him."

"And I see you kissing someone downstairs, and now you come up here saying you want to date me for real. Of course, I was going to think you were making a joke."

"Okay," said Sami, raising her hand in submission. "You win. I've been messing up a lot. There are a lot of things I have to fix. There's a whole damn list, apparently."

Andrew laughed. "But thank you for making me number one on that list."

"You are number one. I did say that, didn't I?"

"You did."

"So," said Jewel, regaining herself in his lap as her hair drifted around her shoulders. "Answer my question so I can go and try to fix everything else I've been doing wrong. And I swear if you reject me after all of this, then I'm the one who's going to be calling your mother."

He laughed again. "Miss Sami Something-Something Hampton. Will you go with me? And seriously? Not just so I can get a promotion from my overly active boss and his wife."

"Something-Something? Did you really just forget my middle name?"

"Of course.... It... starts with a B, righ—."

"It starts with an E?"

"Yes, E, that's what I said."

Sami shook her head, but couldn't help but laugh as she got up from his lap. I'm going back downstairs now," she said as she headed for the door, before turning around to face him. "And you better have remembered my middle name by then. Don't make me regret coming in here and doing all of this."

"I will, and don't forget we have that date with my boss tomorrow."

"To… what? I thought you said they canceled."

"I have a feeling they're going to uncancel it."

She frowned at him. "You could have just admitted that you still liked me."

"I didn't know I still felt that way, until I saw you kissing someone else. I figured it was too late. But since you brought it up."

"Well, don't expect me to keep taking the lead from now on. You're going to have to start working now." She said before turning around and sliding open the door to an awaiting crowd peaking over their desks. She gave a smirk at them, before walking proudly ahead towards the elevator, where she met the woman from before waiting for her.

She pressed the button to call it up when she saw Sami. "Did you get everything you wanted?"

"I'm sorry?"

She extended her hand. "I'm Rachel, by the way."

Sami shook her hand, a little confused. "Sami."

"Oh, I know. He's told me about you," she said before nodding to the group of onlookers ahead. "The boys here had a bet on which one of you was going to give first. And it looks like I won. He can be a little slow on certain things."

"Yeah, he can," said Sami, as the elevator dinged, and she stepped inside. She looked at the woman for a moment. "Just curious, but what would have happened if neither of us would have given in?"

"Oh! In that case, I would have come up here one night while he was working late. Then I would have opened a bottle of wine and let him fuck me on his desk. He had a fantasy about that."

"What?"

"I'm mean with you, not with me. But I guess since you caved, I guess it'll be you after all."

"Wha... what?" asked Sami again. Her ability to form words leaving her speechless for the moment.

"Bye-bye," said Rachel with a grin as the elevator door closed.

It took a moment before the shocked look disappeared from her face. *That bitch.* She nodded her head as the elevator made its way back down. *Okay, we have a real date now. How do I break things off with Patrick? Should I break things off with him first? No, I can't break up with someone while we're both at work. I should wait. But wouldn't that make it worse? No, I should do it now. I should tell him. Don't drag it out. If I don't, with the way he just does things, he might end up in my bed. But how?* The elevator stopped at the door open as she stepped back outside into her work office.

She looked over, her eyes once again catching Jewel's as she looked up to see who had come out of the elevator. Then that tightening in her chest that annoyed her. *Okay, Sami, let's get this over with. We're fixing things today. We are solving problems today. So, I should just walk over there and tell her how I feel.* She stared at Jewel for another moment. *Come Sami. Go Girl. Go over there.* She stared at Jewel for another moment. *Move, you stubborn bitch. You just confessed to Jamal. Move your stupid legs!*

Then, slowly and with heavy feet that felt like they were in mud, Sami awkwardly walked over to Jewel's desk. *Oh! Fuck this.* And then even more awkwardly walked past Jewel's desk, down the aisle, and over to Seo-ah Park's desk, who she wrongly called Lan Ling before.

Seo-ah looked up at her, a frown across her face. "What do you want?"

"I want to say I'm sorry?"

"Really? Now you come to my desk? No, you're just here to try to make yourself feel better. You wanna show sympathy for the Asian girl."

"No... no," said Sami. "Okay, you might be partly right. But I do feel bad, and I know I treated you wrong. I'm asking you to please forgive me and maybe we can try to be friends again. I understand if you don't want to—" She looked at the nameplate again. "Seo-ah?"

"It's pronounced Seo-ah," she said before pointing to the empty office ahead of her. "You know, at least when Addison started calling me Lan Ling, I knew that was just her being an ass. She purposely learned my name, and then just one day just started calling me that. But you guys never knew. You just went right along with it. And it's been over a year. Over a year and this is your first time coming to my desk."

"And now that I know better. I want to do better." She picked up the nameplate, turning it towards her, and placing her finger on the nameplate, slowly moving it across, "Cee-Ohh-Ahhh. Will you let me?"

Seo-ah frowned, looking up at Sami. "You're saying it wrong on purpose, aren't you?"

"Of course not. I just need to practice. That's all. Will you help me?"

Seo-ah narrowed her eyes at Sami for a moment before sighing and shaking her head. Fine, but you have to promise to take me out the next time you all have a girls' night? I'm tired of being left out."

Sami smiled back, "I promise."

"Okay, then I'll forgive you."

"Good," said Sami, reaching her hand out. "Now come on."

"What?" she asked, looking around. "Where are we going?"

"We're going to make sure Jewel and Becca know your name."

"What, I thought you hated her now? You know, because of the guy thing."

"And despite that. I'm going to go and forgive her, like you forgave me. Now come on. You said you wanted to be more involved in our stupid stories, right? Well, here's your chance to get a front-row seat."

Seo-ah blinked a few times, confused, before finally taking Sami by the hand and allowing herself to be led down the room past the desk, stopping in front of Jewel, who was looking a little unnerved by the appearance of the two.

Good. she should look nervous. You know what you did was wrong. She sighed before letting go of Seo-ah's hand. "Jewel. What is her name?"

"Huh?" asked Jewel, looking confused. "You mean Lan Ling."

"No," she said, pulling Seo-ah in front of her. "Tell Jewel your name."

"What? I thought you were gonna do the other thing."

"That comes after. This comes first."

"That's not... you didn't mention that before."

"That's right, I'm a bad person. It's too late to stop now. So, go ahead and tell her."

Now it was Seo-ah, turn to look a bit flustered as she looked at Jewel. "My... my name's not Lan Ling. It's Seo-ah."

"Wait, what? So... is Lan Ling like a nickname or...?"

"No. Addison just started calling me that one day. I just didn't want to correct anyone, so I left it alone."

"Oh... oh wait, Addison. Oh my god, I'm so sorry. I didn't know... Ah... you said your name was Seo-ah?"

"Yes."

"Ah... would it be okay if I just called you, Seo?"

"That's fine... a lot of people outside of work call me that."

"Ah... okay," said Jewel. "I guess I'm calling you Seo now," she smiled. "That feels kinda funny. I guess it'll take some time to get used to.'

"Good," said Sami, stepping back in. "And now we have to deal with our problem."

Jewel began rubbing at her neck, before standing up and looking Sami in the face. "You're right. Now, before you say anything. I want to say I'm sorry again. I know I was wrong and if there is absolutely anything I can do to make it better between us, I promise you I will try with everything I have to make it wo—"

"Just stop," said Sami, raising a hand to cut Jewel off. Sami then sucked in her cheeks, swallowing her pride before making a fist and knocking on Jewel's desk. "I just wish you would have asked me, rather than just doing it." Sami shook her head. "Jewel, I don't care if Andrew is dating someone else. I liked him a bit, but not enough to fight or get mad over. I got mad that it was you. You are my best friend, and you went behind my back like that."

"I know," said Jewel, trying to plead her case. "That was wrong and like, if there is anything I can do to make it up to—"

"Would you break up with Andrew if I asked you to?"

"Wha... I mean..." Jewel looked at Sami and Seo-ah nervously for a moment, her eyes darted back and forth before she dropped her head, slumping her shoulders. "No, I can't do that?" she said in a low, defeated tone.

"Then what if I asked you to give up on our contest then? Would you do that?'

"Ah... I... No, I wouldn't do that."

"So, not absolutely anything then," said Sami as she folded her arms, staring at Jewel.

Jewel sighed, "No... I guess not."

Sami stared at Jewel for a moment, letting the silence linger between them before finally speaking. "That's fine. If you would have said yes, then I'm not sure I would have been able to forgive you. At least that proves that you're serious about him."

"Wait..." said Jewel, lifting her head, a small amount of hope in her eyes. "So you forgive me?"

"I won't promise anything." She looked over at Seo-ah. "But it seems forgiveness is in the air, so I'm going to try." She nodded toward the elevator. "Now both of you come on. I received a message from Becca inviting us to meet her downtown. We're going to go see what she and her rich boyfriend are doing."

"You're taking me too.?" asked Seo-ah.

"Yes, I am. So go and get your things."

After Seo-ah gathered their things, they all headed towards the elevator. When they heard the ding and the doors opened, they met Addison, who stepped out looking completely disheveled and wearing a long oversized white sheep black sheep T-shirt with what looked to be dirt stains on it. Her make-up was a bit smeared, and her hair was a mess. Sami just stood there in shock as she'd never seen her boss look so unkept before.

"Well, where are you all going?" she asked, looking over the girls, all having their things. "I know I allow your girls to work from home sometimes, but I'm starting to think you're abusing the privilege."

"Are... are you okay?"

"Huh, Yes... yes, I am? What makes you..." Addison smiled as she looked over herself. "Oh, yeah. I guess you would ask questions."

Sami reached forward, pulling out what looked to be a small piece of wood from Addison's hair. "What happened to you?"

"Oh, the hair. I was just handling a bit of personal business." She turned and looked over at Jewel. "I think everything between us will be squared away soon."

"Okay," said Sami, looking a bit suspicious, but shrugging it off." Well, we were just going to go and check up on Becca."

"Oh, yes, Becca. My other supposed employee. I haven't seen her since she's gone and gotten infatuated with that candy millionaire. But I won't be a hypocrite and tell her not to chase a man with means, since that's what I did after all." She laughed. "Maybe I should have had her in the contest as the gray sheep." She waved her hand, dismissing the thought, and stepped past the girls. "Go on then and see to your friend and do tell her that I need her working on her article as well as that man of hers.

Sami just shook her head with a smile. "We'll tell her you said hello."

"Wait..." said Jewel to Addison before she could fully leave.

"Yes? What is it?"

"Do... do you know Lan Ling's real name?"

"What? Of course, I do. It's Seo-ah Park. Why? You think I don't know my own employee's names?"

"No... well... yes, you are kinda aloof sometimes."

"Aloof?" asked Addison, looking a little offended. "My mind is just occupied with other things. And besides, how could I not know her name? She's literally the first person I see when I exit my office. We're both by the window. Kinda hard to miss that bedazzled name plate of hers sparkling in the sunlight, almost blinding me every morning— oh wait. Did you not know her name? Goodness Jewel, you're terrible?"

"Wha!... I'm terrible? You're the one who gave her the name?" said Jewel, her tone sounding both shocked and offended as her pitch raised.

"Oh, time to go." Sami grabbed Jewel and Seo-ah, leading them into the elevator and allowing the doors to close. Sami laughed. "What's wrong? I didn't expect you to start yelling at our boss."

"I'm sorry," said Jewel, as she began rubbing at her face. "That woman... she's putting weird ideas in my head."

"What ideas?'

"Oh, I know. That's because Addison asked Jewel to fuck her husband and have another baby for her."

"Okay, I gotta ask," said Sami in disbelief. "Did she really ask you that?"

"Yes. She did... well, I think she did. I'm not even sure anymore."

"Wait, you're not going to do it are you?"

"What? I don't know. No, I mean, of course not. I mean, I was thinking about it. But then that mess with Andrew happened and I'm not so sure."

"So, before you starting dating Andrew, you were going to become a mother for Addison's kids and fuck her husband. Our Addison?"

"Okay, when you say it out loud, it sounds bad. But you haven't met her daughter. She's nothing like her mother. And Nasir is really nice."

"Oh god, you even know his name. What, are you gonna go to their home next?"

"I already did that."

Sami just stared at Jewel for a moment. "You know, you can have Andrew. Between his crazy ex-girlfriend and your... your everything. You both deserve each other. But I will say if you want him, there's no way he's going to just let you run off and fuck someone else to have their baby."

"Can we just skip this whole conversation, please?"

"This is fun. This is way better than reading your articles."

"Shut up, Lan... I mean Seo-ah."

"You're being mean to me again."

"That's not me being mean. That's me treating you like I do all my girlfriends," said Sami as the elevator dinged and the doors opened. "Now come on. Let's go and see Becca. We can talk about all the other stuff on the way."

The ladies left the building and hopped into a cab as Sami told him the direction.

"This is fun," said Seo-ah. "Do you think she's in some type of trouble?"

"What? No. What do you think we're out here doing?"

"Well, I mean Jewel was almost kidnapped, and there were men with guns."

"That was an oblivious lie. She just made that up for the article, right Jewel?"

Jewel balled up her lips and was silent for a moment

before speaking. "Ah, no, that really happened?"

"What?"

"That guy... you know, the one I brought with me to the party that night. He works for the... army, or police, or something."

"Yes, I heard Addison talking with the police on her phone about it."

"Addison?" asked Jewel. "What does she have to do with it?"

"Don't know. She left her door open, and I heard her on the phone with the police about something with her daughter."

"Oh, she did say she was going to look into it, because I had her daughter with me that day."

"What day?" asked Sami, even more confused.

"Do you not read each other's articles?" asked Seo-ah.

"I only read a little because it all sounded so stupid. I just knew Jewel was making it up. Or at least I thought she was. Besides, we promised each other that..." Sami noticed Jewel making the same face she did before. "Oh, you bitch. How many promises are you going to break?"

"Okay look, I'm sorry. I only did it once, and I was curious. The way you were talking made it sound really interesting."

"I swear to God, if you break up with Andrew within the next six months, I'm going to throw you out the window. How am I the only one doing what they're supposed to do?"

The girls continued talking in the car, trying to sort out their stories until they finally reached the address that Becca had texted them. They all exited the cab and stood in front of a large luxury hotel that reached high into the sky. On both sides of the entrance were flags waving in the wind as two doormen stood waiting and opened the door upon their approach.

"Wow, this place is fancy," said Seo-ah.

"Yeah, better than any hotel I've ever stayed at," agreed

Sami as she stared around at the interior of the building. Very high ceilings, marble pillars, and an ornate floor mat that looked as if it would cost more than your average house were just a few of the things that stood out. But even that failed in comparison to the people who were moving about the building in their expensive looking clothing.

"I recognize that woman over there. She's the daughter of a beauty mogul," said Jewel.

"I'm sure everyone here is either someone rich or the child of someone rich," said Sami as she headed towards the front desk.

"Hello there. How may I help you?"

"Ah, yes, I'm Sami Hampton. I think there's a Becca Stavos waiting for me."

"Yes, she's on the top floor," said the woman, looking down at her computer screen. Then, turning around, she grabbed a key card before handing it to Sami. "Just swipe this on the elevator slot and it will take you there."

"Thank you," said Sami, taking it and leading Seo-ah and Jewel over to the elevator where they all got in.

"What do you think Becca's doing here?" asked Seo-ah.

"Knowing her, it could be anything," said Sami as she swiped the card and the elevator lifted upwards. "Maybe she's having a wedding on the rooftop or scheming to take over as the candy queen. I can't tell what she'll be doing next."

After a short while, the elevator finally reached its destination on the top floor. Heading out, the girls were greeted to a short corridor where a door was at the end. They walked towards it where Sami once again swiped the badge, and they heard it unlock. Opening the door, they were greeted with a panoramic view of the entire city.

"Wow, we're so high up," said Seo-ah as she stepped forward to look out the window.

"Yeah, but where's—"

"I was wondering when you'd get here," came Becca's

voice. "Is that Lan Ling I hear? Well, I didn't expect you to bring her. But she's welcome here too."

Sami peaked around the elevator corridor and saw Becca with her back turned over by the kitchen looking in the fridge. "So, what have you been up to?" asked Sami as she as the rest walked over to her. She could see that the entire top floor was just an open area. There was a kitchen and living spaces on one side and on the other was a giant bed where a TV sat.

"Addison said that it would be nice if you decided to come back to work?" said Jewel with a smile as she rested her arms on the counter. "And apparently, her name isn't Lan Ling. It's Seo-ah."

"Seo-ah? Did you change your name or something? Well, either way, I have been working," said Becca, kneeling to grab something from the bottom of the refrigerator. "Do you girls want anything to drink?"

"Water please," said Seo-ah.

"Nothing for me," said Sami.

"Have any sparkling water?" asked Jewel.

Becca turned her head back. "Really? Bubbles? Okay," she said before reaching out and pulling out two waters and handing it to them.

Sami made a face while looking at Becca and seeing that her robe was open, and she wasn't wearing anything underneath except for a pair of panties. "I see you've been having fun."

"I have," said Becca as she started walking over to the bed, waving her hand at them to follow. "At first I thought that this was just a fling, but after that night at the party, he actually sat me down and told me he had plans for us. "

"Us?"

"That's what he wants," said Becca as she walked over, laying down on her bed, picking up the remote and turning on the TV. "Honestly, I think the amazing thing is just how much I enjoy being with him. Once you get past all the candy talk, he's actually kinda fun to be around."

"You mean on top of all the sex you're having?" asked Jewel, with a laugh as reached over, taking a piece of candy off a nearby plate and popping it in her mouth.

"Yes," she said with a smile. "On top of that. And Jewel, you may not want to eat those."

"Wha... why."

"A few of those might have been inside of me last night."

Jewel's face froze for a second before her jaw started to tremble, her tongue then forcefully ejecting the candy out into her hand before quickly beginning to chug her sparkling water. Which then caused her to start coughing and heaving as she bent over.

"And there goes those bubbles I was talking about."

Sami shook her head at Jewel. Is there a reason you asked us to come here? You know, other than showing off how freaky you can be with candy?"

"Yes, apparently. That little game you're playing for Addison is getting its own candy bar."

"What?" asked Sami in disbelief. "You can't be serious."

Jewel also tried to respond, but was still coughing on the sparkling water.

"Oh, I am," said Becca as she began flipping through channels. "Debuting next week for the finale of your little contest, there will be little black sheep chocolate bars and white sheep white chocolate bars on sale all throughout the city. I just figured I might as well tell you, because I'm damn sure Addison didn't bring it up."

"No, she didn't," said Sami with a frown as she turned to Jewel. "Did she tell you?"

"No... no," said Jewel, finally managing to clear her throat.

Becca frowned at them. "Why would she tell Jewel and not you? Aren't you both still part of the game?"

"Oh girl," said Sami. "Apparently we've both been missing out on the adventures Jewel's been having."

"Hey," said Seo-ah, pointing in front of them all. "Isn't that Addison on the TV?"

"What?" asked Sami. "We just saw... Is that Addison! What's she doing on the TV? Becca, turn that up."

Becca pressed the volume button on the TV where a newscaster held out a microphone for a very distraught looking Addison.

"Ma`am, what can you tell me about what happened today?" asked the newscaster.

"Oh, it was terrible," said Addison in a voice that was soft and very unlike her. "There were these men who grabbed me and were threatening to kidnap me if I didn't give them money."

"Money? You're saying that they were trying to hold you hostage?"

"Yes. I think they came after my family because we hosted the black sheep white sheep contest."

"Oh, I didn't know that. Are you one of them?"

"No, I just own the magazine. And let me just say that I'm very thankful to the city for taking in and following my brave girls as they go on their adventures of love."

"Adventures of love?" said Sami with a tone of disgust in her voice. "Is that what she's been promoting this whole thing as?"

"I honestly don't know anymore," said Jewel.

"If that happened today," said Seo-ah, squinting her eyes, as if trying to understand what she was seeing. "I don't understand. Addison didn't say anything about being kidnapped. I mean, she looked bad. But she didn't seem nervous or anything."

"That's because she probably wasn't," said Sami. "I'd guess all this is just another way for her to make money."

"Ah, Jewel," said Becca, "Isn't that the tall man you had with you when you came out on your date with us? The one in the police uniform?"

"Huh, what do you... oh my god," said Jewel as she

recognized Nathan walking up behind Addison and the newscaster. "What's he doing there?"

"I thought you said he was in the military. Why's he in a police uniform?"

"I don't know. He doesn't really tell me anything about himself. I don't know what's going on anymore."

"Tell me," said the news reporter. "After surviving this harrowing experience, what—"

"That's enough questions," said Nathan in his police uniform that seemed to just barely fit his oversized physique. "I'm going to have to escort you to the police station, madam."

"Yes, Sir, officer. Thank you for saving me," said Addison, wrapping her arms around Nathan as he lifted her off her feet and carried her away.

"What the hell is happening," said Sami. "I feel like the world is upside down."

"If Addison is acting like that," said Becca, shaking her head. "Maybe it is."

CHAPTER 17

Jewel laid in bed half asleep, the morning's dreariness still having a hold on her. In her dreams, she was able to escape the mess her life had been over the past few weeks. But now, in this moment, as she felt a hand roll over her belly and up her stomach cupping a breast in its hand. A smile came over her face as she turned to her side. Opening her eyes, she found Andrew looking back at her with a lustful grin on his face.

"Good morning," she said, before nuzzling her face up against his.

"I see you're enjoying being with me," he said.

"I am. I wish we could stay like this all day."

He sighed. "That would be the dream. But I have to work on the weekends." He laid back, looking up at her ceiling. "I'd much rather be laid up in bed with you. But I expect my phone to start ringing if I'm not downtown in the next hour.

Plus, I need to go home and put on a change of clothes."

"And I need to go see Nathan today, then I need to—"

"Nathan? You mean the tall guy you brought up to the party?"

"Yes, him. Why are you nervous that I'll cheat on you?"

"No... okay, maybe."

"Well, you don't have to worry about that. He's married."

"There are a lot of other men who don't let that stop them."

Jewel rolled her eyes, before lifting her leg and swinging it over him, shifting herself on top of him and sitting up, allowing him to see her in her nakedness. "I can promise you that's not happening."

He placed his hand on her hips as he looked up at her. "I know. I'm just accepting that you have a therapist. Trust me, after my last girlfriend. You don't know how much I appreciate that you do have one."

I might have to explain to him everything about that later. But since we're like this, this might be the best time to tell him the other thing. "I do have something to tell you, though."

"You do? What is it? You're not about to tell me something crazy, are you? Like you have an evil twin sister or something?"

"No," she said with a laugh. "But I should tell you about something else. You know that black sheep white sheep thing that is all over the city."

"Oh, yeah. A few of the ladies at the office have been obsessing over that."

"So does that mean you haven't paid much attention to it?"

"I've been preoccupied with work and gaining the affection of the beautiful woman who is sitting on top of me right now."

"Well, I feel that I should tell you that those articles are about me. Well, the black sheep ones are. I wrote those... Okay, technically me and Sami, she's the white sheep." She clenched her teeth as she looked down at him, waiting for his response. He then shifted under her, which she wasn't sure how to take.

"Wait... but wasn't that supposed to be about you dating different men?"

"Yes. But really, it was only about the situations I've found myself in. Since I didn't really date anyone besides you and Nathan."

"I thought you said you didn't date Nathan."

"I didn't... okay, maybe I did. I don't know. We never did anything. There were these people chasing us and—" She shook her head. "It's a long story. But we didn't even kiss or anything. We only just talked and then you kissed me at the party and, well, I don't know what to say now."

"Aren't there laws against dating your therapist?"

"He's not... well, officially he's not my therapist, okay? I don't pay him. It's complicated."

"So, you've been not dating your not therapist while you were not dating me?"

"No... I mean... Not since the night you kissed me at the party. I mean, I told him about that during one of our sessions."

"Of course you did. But even if we skip past that, you mean to tell me that every woman in the city now knows everything we've done."

"No. We didn't do that. We change names and places, things like that. That's why I'm the black sheep."

"Okay, just so I can understand. You, who are a white woman, are the black sheep, and Sami, who is a black woman, is the white sheep."

"Yes. That's right."

"And that doesn't seem backwards to you?"

"We didn't name ourselves. Addison did. This whole thing was kinda thrown at us one day. The winner will be her replacement when she leaves the company."

"Replacement? Wait, so dating is just part of a game," he

said, attempting to raise up.

"No! No, no, no," she said, pressing her hands against his chest and forcing him back down, trying to calm him. "Please don't think that. I... I really do like you. I mean, look at us. You think I'd be with you like this if it was all just part of some game?"

"I want to believe you. But this isn't exactly something I'm used to."

"I almost lost my best friend over you. I don't know how much more I can give you. I don't know what else I can do to prove it if that's not enough."

"You mean Sami?"

"Yes."

"You told her about us, then?"

"Yeah, and she hated me for a while, too."

Andrew just stared up at her for a long moment, his heart starting to thump loudly in her chest so much that Jewel could feel it through her hand. She was a little nervous about his answer. That was before he reached up and placed a tender hand against her face.

"It's hard to be mad at you when you're making a face like that. You look like you're about to cry."

"I'm sorry," said Jewel, rubbing her wrists over own eyes. "It hasn't been easy, you know. And then I started thinking about what if you decided to leave me after I told you? It's... it's just been a little bit too much."

"I guess so," he said, patting her on her behind. "Okay, time to hop off. I have work and you need to go see that therapist of yours, which I think I'm learning to appreciate now even more now than a few minutes ago."

"So, you're not mad at me?"

"Oh no, I'm plenty mad. You may be okay with people reading about your love life. But I'm not," he said with a little harshness in his voice, but then softened his tone. "But I'm finding it hard to stay mad at a naked, crying woman, who just happens to be sitting on me. But I won't decide anything until I've read the stories myself."

"That's fair, I guess. But I promise, I made sure to hide everything."

"I understand. Can you get off me now, or are you going to hold me hostage?"

"No, sorry," she said as she lifted herself from him, allowing him to get up and reach for his clothes over on the nightstand.

He looked at her before sighing and leaning down to give her a kiss. "Let's go out to get something to eat on my next day off. Well, talk about everything then, okay?"

She nodded her head. "Okay. I'd like that."

"Good," he said as she began putting on his clothes. She escorted him to the door, where they shared another kiss, and he exited the room.

"Don't forget to call."

He kissed her again. "I won't." and then turned, making his way down the hall.

Jewel closed the door, and with a sigh of relief, pressed her head against the wood of the frame. *Okay. I guess that's the best I can do. I don't think I wrote anything that'll make him mad. I probably should have told him earlier. But what's done is done.* She turned around and looked over her room. *Right. I should probably go and see Nathan.*

She headed back into her room and took a shower, putting on a change of clothes afterwards. A little over an hour later, she headed out the door, taking the elevator down and catching a cab. There, she hopped in and made her way across town. The traffic was a little heavy that morning, which gave her some time to think. She regretted that, since thinking about everything currently happening in her life wasn't what she wanted to do, but her brain continued to cycle through her conversation with Nathan.

I know I did everything I could. Why am I worried about it? Because I can't help myself, that's why.

Eventually, the cab arrived at the hotel, where this time

she paid the driver, not asking him to wait. It was a standard two-story hotel where she made her way up the stairs to the second floor and knocked on the second door numbered two hundred and twenty-seven. She heard his big footsteps as they made their way to the door and saw the handle jiggle as he grabbed it. The door opened, and he appeared shirtless, standing before her.

"I didn't expect you so soon."

"Yeah, sorry. I wanted to ask you something."

He stepped to the side. "Okay, well, come in."

Walking inside, stepping out of her shoes and placing them near the wall, she then headed for the couch, plopping down on it and stretching out.

"Did you really have to change hotels?"

"Probably not, but it's just a habit of mine not to stay in the same place for more than a day."

"Some might call that paranoia."

"My wife says that too."

"How long have you been married?" asked Jewel as she stepped over, taking a seat on the couch.

"About ten years."

"Do you think it's a good idea to lie or keep secrets?"

"Depends," he said as he walked over, sitting down in the chair in front of the couch. "I'll lie if I think it's the best thing for her at that moment. But I'm old school. Maybe in your relationships things are different."

"Maybe."

"You seem like you've had a rough morning."

"I just told the guy that I like that I've been documenting our relationship for over a million people to read."

"Oh, so you told him. That couldn't have gone over well."

"It didn't. But it went better than I thought it would," she turned her face towards him. "Hey, what was that about? I saw you on the TV with my boss?"

"Oh, that was her finding a way to deal with our little mobster problem. Your boss seems to know some very powerful people. I was even contacted by my CO."

"CO?"

"Commanding officer. Everyone on site was part of my unit."

"Wait. So does that mean I won't have to worry about anymore random guys trying to grab me?"

"That's what it should mean, yes. Anyone we missed has probably left the city by now."

Jewel sat there for a moment, thinking about it, but then shook her head. "I don't understand any of that. All I know about my boss is that she's an ass who apparently wants me to have a kid for her."

"And have you made a decision on that yet?"

"Well, obviously, I'm not going to do it now."

"But you were going to do it before? If you and your friend hadn't worked out."

"I don't know... maybe. Unless you have a better reason why I should do anything?"

"I hardly think it's my place to tell you what to do with your body."

"And what would you do if your wife came home and told you that someone wants them to have their baby?"

"Considering we have two small children at home. Then my answer would be no."

"Exactly. So, when are you heading back home?"

"This afternoon."

"What!" said Jewel, sitting up from the cough. "And you weren't going to tell me?"

"Everything's done now. I'm sure I would have texted you from the train."

Jewel looked back over at the dufflebag near the door. *I guess those aren't just dirty clothes then.* "Well, you could have at least said bye."

"Would you prefer a hug?"

"You know what? Yes, I would. You can't just show up and leave after everything that's happened. That's... that's...

that's just wrong."

He laughed, "I'm not sure the world is set up to be right. But I see your point?" He then stood up and stretched his arms wide. "Come on, I'll give you a hug before I go."

"You're making fun of me," she said as she sat up, frowning at him.

"Just a little," he said with a smirk on his face, and she realized that she'd never seen him smile before. "You want your hug or not? Because my arms are getting tired."

She then stood up and stepped over to him and allowed his arms to envelop her. He was warm and comforting, and she felt him as he rested his chin on the top of her head. "Has anyone told you you're like really tall?" She felt his chest heave as he chuckled.

"I get that sometimes."

Sami sat in the back of a vehicle that had come to pick her up from her apartment. She was dressed casually in a long skirt and heels for the event. *A real date. And not just as a fake girlfriend.* The car traveled down a road of country houses and open fields until finally arriving at a large manor home, coming down a long road into its driveway. As the car came to a halt, she veered out the window at the building. It was made of old bricks and wood, and probably what most people would have called a vintage home. *I wonder if I should have brought something.*

Soon, she saw Jamal come out of the house and approach the car as the driver opened the door for her, allowing her to step outside, her heels digging into the gravel stone underneath her feet.

"I'm glad you could make it," said Jamal as he stepped up and kissed her.

"You didn't need to send a car for me."

"That was actually them. I had planned to pick you up

myself, but they insisted on sending their driver for you."

"Where are they?"

"Inside."

"Okay, are you sure this is the last one? I'm not sure how many more of these fun trips I can survive."

"This is the final one before they make their decision. But once a year, all the partners meet to discuss things. But that's more of a social gathering."

"And this isn't?"

"Oh, you've finally arrived," said Heather, appearing in the door and spotting her. She was wearing a button up blouse tucked into denim slacks with high boots on her feet. "Well, don't you look lovely? Thank you for coming again. Jamal told us that you might not be able to make it this time, what with things coming to a close at your magazine."

Sami just smiled. "Yes, I was afraid I wasn't going to make it either," she glanced back up at Jamal for a moment. "But thankfully I was able to push things back a day."

"Well, we're glad to hear it," said Heather as she led the two into the house. "This whole interview process has been fun for us as well. Usually, Henry is always stuffed inside of his office. But during moments like this, he always likes to get a full view of the man or woman they have listed as partner. "

"Do you have female partners?"

"Of course. I mean, not as many as the men. But sprinkled in there are like two or three. I think you'll enjoy meeting them once you get the chance. But enough of that, let's get you changed. We can talk about that on the way."

"Changed?"

"Yes. We can't have you riding horses in such a thin dress as that. You'll chaff your thighs."

"What?" asked Sami, stopping in the middle of the hall. "Riding... horses?"

"Of course. We best get you into some riding gear or you're going to be sore when the morning comes."
354

She turned, looking into another adjacent room where she saw two horses. She then turned to Jamal, with wide eyes and a worried expression on her face.

He just smiled back at her while raising his index finger and whispered. "This is the last time."

She closed her eyes and shook her head. "I've never ridden a horse before."

"Oh, you'll be fine. We've prepared one of the more docile one for you," she said, leading Sami upstairs. "Jamal, you go and meet Henry out back and we'll be out soon."

"See you ladies in a few, I guess." He didn't bother to look into Sami's face before he exited the building.

"How have things been with you, Sami?" asked Heather, leading her down the hall.

"Fine. Just a lot of work is all. These last few weeks have been stressful for the both of us."

"I imagine so," she said, opening the door for Sami as she entered the room. She then walked over to a closet and began looking over several pairs of jeans before she turned back to Sami. "Your hips are a bit wider than mine. But I think we can find something for you." She shuffled around a few pairs of jeans before grabbing a pair and walking back to her. "Here, try these."

"Thank you," said Sami with a sigh.

Heather walked over to a chair and took a seat. "If it makes you feel any less nervous, I can tell you that Jamal has been approved for partner. They actually decided on it months ago."

"What?" asked Sami with genuine surprise. "But I thought... I mean, what was all this for?"

"Merely a fun way to waste time and justify getting my husband out of the office. You both have been wonderful sports in all of this."

Sami slid on the jeans, and like she figured, she found a bit of trouble getting them around her hips. "Well, thank you... for telling me that. I'll admit, it does make me feel better knowing I won't have to worry about it." She then accepted a pair of boots that Heather handed her with a fiery design down the sides. "Can I ask you something?"

"Of course."

"What's it like being married? Do you and he ever fight?"

"Oh," she laughed for a moment. "Perhaps not so much now. But when we were your age. Oh honey, all the time. How he was never home or how we didn't have the money for this or that. I swear it's a wonder how we didn't kill each other."

"I don't suppose you have any words of wisdom for me, then?"

"Humm," Heather sucked on her lip. "When he's out late, he's probably not fucking the girl at the office. But just to make sure. Show up late at night with some takeout food and spend some time with him. Every time I thought he was cheating; I'd try to show up there and surprise him and every time there he'd be sitting in the dark with the light on and looking at his papers."

"Do you still visit your husband at work at night sometimes?"

"Of course. If I didn't, I'm not sure our marriage would be as strong as it is now."

"Sami looked around the room as if there was someone else around, before turning back to her. "And... have you ever... you know..."

"Humm? Oh goodness, yes. I'm pretty sure our first child was conceived on his desk. A little advice, dear. When your man is alone in the middle of the night, working countless hours; try to make sure something sexual isn't adding to his frustrations or else I'm fairly certain that I won't be seeing you around the company parties for much longer."

"I'll remember that," said Sami with a smirk and a raised brow.

"Good. Now let's check on the men. I'm sure they're downstairs trying to find new ways to cause us stress."

With a laugh, the women headed out to the back of the house, where they found the men holding the reins of their horses. Sami slowly walked up to Jamal, who had a large brush in his hand and was grooming his horse. Both horses were two large pure white breeds with large black eyes.

"Can I touch it?"

"Of course. Her name is Emmy."

"Emmy," said Sami in wonder as she slowly reached out her hand, rubbing the side of the horse. It was warm and felt as sturdy as anything she had ever touched. Wait!" she said, making a face at him. "Why didn't you ever tell me that you could ride horses? We didn't grow up around them, and I know you didn't just find time in the city."

"Was I supposed to? I just never came up."

"How many secrets do you have that you haven't told me?"

"More than a little, less than a lot."

"God, I hate you."

"Okay then. Fine. I have secrets. Are you satisfied?"

"Mmhmm, that doesn't answer my question."

"No, it doesn't," he said with a grin on his face. "Don't worry, Emmy, I won't let the big, mean lady hurt you."

"You're an idiot."

"Correction, I'm your idiot now."

"Is it too late to take back my confession?"

"Okay," came Heather's voice. "You two ready to go riding?"

"No, but I guess I don't have... Oh!," said Sami, turning around to see another very large black horse appear in front of her, next to Heather. "Where'd this one come from?"

"This is Marigold. This is my personal horse. Me and Henry will ride separately, but since you're not accustomed to horses, we figured it'd be best to have you ride with Jamal today."

"And that's why I brought this," said Henry as he approached with a small step ladder for her, placing it down beside the horse. "Here you are."

"Okay," said Sami, beginning to feel a bit nervous as she looked from the ladder to the horse as it shifted a bit. "Are you sure we can't just watch tv or something?"

Jamal smiled while tossing the brush over near the back of the house and then reached out, taking her by the hand. "Don't worry. Just trust me and I'll do all the rest."

Sami allowed him to hold her hand as she took one slow step, then another to the top of the stepladder.

"Okay, now place your foot in the stirrup."

"The what?" asked Sami.

"The little hook there," he said, pointing to the loop hanging down from the horse's saddle. He then stepped closer, placing his hand around her waist to make sure she felt him behind her. "Put one foot in, then raise your leg over to the other side and just sit down atop Emmy. It's just like riding a bike."

"I don't think you remember what it feels like to ride a bike. Bikes aren't six feet tall." The horse shifted as before giving a loud snort. *Ohhhhhhhh... kay, it's fine, it's fine. I can do this. Everything is going to be fine.* She placed her foot in the loop. Feeling the sturdiness after pressing a bit of her weight on it, she stepped in fully and dropped herself down on the horse. It took a few steps to the side under her weight, and Sami felt as if the world was moving beneath her. *Oh god, oh god, save me.*

"Good job," said Heather as she and Henry clapped their hands, smiling up at her.

"Okay... okay, I'm up," said Sami, her hands firmly pressed against the saddle for support as she looked down at Jamal

"That's a good girl, Emmy," said Jamal cooing to the horse and rubbing it on its neck. "You did good."

There was something endearing about the way he spoke to the horse. The way he held her close while saying calming things to her. She wasn't jealous, but did have a small moment where she envisioned him holding her while whispering sweet words to her.

"Okay," said Jamal after calming the horse. "Now it's my turn." He then stepped to the side of Sami and reached in front of her, grabbing the pommel of the saddle. Then, placing his foot into the stirrup and with one pull, he lifted himself upward, swinging his leg over and sitting down behind Sami, quickly reaching in front of her and grabbing the reins. "Good girl, good girl," he said as the horse once again shifted from side to side, finding its balance.

Sami could feel the heat of his breath as he leaned down on her to soothe the horse. His arms rubbing against the side of her breasts over her blouse as he controlled the large animal beneath them.

"Okay," he said as he shifted a bit, getting his arms in a tighter snug around Sami. "I think we're ready."

Heather and Henry mounted up on their horses and they all began to head down the countryside on their steeds.

"How does it feel?" asked Jamal after they had ridden for a bit.

"Don't they get tired?" asked Sami, rubbing her hands on the long neck of the animal. "I mean, there's two of us."

"They do, but not anytime soon. As long as we're not pushing her. She can walk like this for hours."

"Well, in that case," said Sami as she looked over and saw Heather and her husband gallop a bit ahead of them. "Since we're alone, there's something I want to talk to you about."

"Uh oh, that doesn't sound good."

"It's... not exactly good. I guess it depends on how you see it?"

"Alright, go ahead and spit it out. I hope you're not trying to break things off with me already."

"Huh? No... I don't... I don't want that."

"Then say it. I doubt anything is as bad as we tend to think it is. Wait, you don't secretly have a baby that I don't know about, do you?"

Sami twisted her neck to look back up at him with a frown. "I'm being serious."

"So am I. Secret babies are the kinda thing a man has nightmares about." He pulled on the reins, slowing the horse to a stop. "But I see your point. So go on, I'm listening. Say what you have to say."

"Okay," said Sami, turning back around, suddenly not feeling able to look him in his face. Instead, she looked over the countryside as Heather and Henry moved farther away. "I... I've been writing about us. I mean... I wrote about it in my magazine."

"Okay," said Jamal nonchalantly. "I mean, you write about romance. I think I'd have to be pretty dense to expect you not to write about us. I mean... you're not using my name or anything, right?"

"No, but it may have gotten bigger than I thought it would."

"That sounds odd. Define big."

"Okay, well, there's this game. You know the one going around the city? The one with the Black Sheep White Sheep that they had in the tourist shop when we went walking. So, Addison had this idea and—"

"Seriously? That's you? I mean, I knew Addison had a hand in it." He leaned to the side of her so that he could look her in her face. "Really? You're what everyone's been talking about?"

"Ahh, yeah. Wait... you're not mad at me?"

"Mad? No, I mean... a little surprised. As long as you don't use my name, I don't see a problem."

"Ahhh... about that. Well, at the end of this we're supposed to reveal ourselves and—"

Jamal's face soured as he thought about what she said. He then leaned back in the saddle. "Yeah... I'm not too sure about that. I'm not exactly excited about the idea of millions of people knowing who I am."

"Well, yeah. But you don't have to reveal who you are. Only me and Jewel do."

"I'm pretty sure if you become famous for this, then people are going to make assumptions about the man beside you. Wait, how many men have you dated for this thing?"

"Just two… I mean with you, I guess that's three. Oh, but you know them all," she said hurriedly. "You met Patrick. I don't know if you met Andrew. That's the one Jewel's dating."

"I still find it weird that you two both dated the same guy."

"I know, right? And he still hasn't called me or apologized."

"To be honest, I'm surprised Jewel had it in her to do that. Didn't she just sleep over at your place like some weeks ago?"

"Please don't remind me of that. I'm kinda trying to forgive her and I don't want to start hating her all over again," said Sami, shaking her head, but also noticing something red a little farther away.

"Yeah, I remember that mess in the elevator. I haven't seen you storm off that mad since you went chasing that boy Curtis down the street when we were kids."

"That's because Curtis broke my bike. Talking about how he was going to show me a trick. How do you break handlebars? I mean, they're made of metal."

Jamal laughed. "The way he went running with you chasing behind him holding the broken handlebar over your head behind; I swear, I never laughed so hard."

"Oh, shut up."

"Hey, don't act like I didn't care. I let you ride on my bike, remember?"

She turned around with a brow raised. "I remember sitting on your handle and you grabbing my booty."

"I was making sure you didn't fall. I do not accept your accusations of any sexual misconduct."

"Emm-hmmm." she moaned. "Of course, you would say

that."

"But your booty was soft, though."

"Oh, just shut up," she said, shaking her head with a laugh, before glancing down at the ground again and seeing a small fox. "How many animals does this place have?"

"Huh? What do you mean?"

"I mean, first the horses and chickens, but now foxes two?"

"Fox? what do you do—" Those were the only words he managed before the horse began to neigh and shift its weight away from the animal. "Shit!" he said as he pulled on the reins of the horse, trying to calm it down. "Woah Emmy, woah Emmy."

Sami felt it as the horse reared up in the air. Instinctively, she shifted in the seat, twisted and turned around, wrapped her arms around Jamal, pressing her face against his chest as she closed her eyes. Her heart pounded in her chest as she held onto him and clenched her teeth as the world shifted under her. But the fall never came as she felt the horse come back down to the earth and begin backing up.

"That's a good girl, Emmy. That's a good girl. It's gone now. Relax. Just relax," said Jamal, before wrapping one of his arms around Sami. "You okay."

Sami kept her eyes closed as she still held on to him. "No... no I'm not." She could hear his heart pound in his chest through the thin shirt. It matched the beating of her own, which was just as loud to her. "Why... why did I ever let you convince me to get on this thing?"

"What?" he said, still with a jovial sound to his voice, but a little out of breath. "You don't find us sitting atop a horse, romantic?"

"No... I don't think sitting on top of this animal that could kill us is romantic."

"You sure? The way you're holding me right seems pretty romantic."

"Shut up," said Sami as she squeezed her arms around

his waist even tighter. "I'm still scared. I'm waiting until my heart calms down."

"Let's move ahead a bit then, so you can get back comfy. The rhythm of Emmy walking is the perfect way to calm down. But feel free to hold on to me as long as you want. I'm kinda enjoying you being all clingy and scared. It's surprisingly kinda cute."

"I'm not clingy," she said in a soft voice, but still refusing to let him go. "Then, to her surprise, she felt his arms wrap themselves around her, bringing her in even closer to him."

"Okay... well, maybe I'm the one who's a little clingy. It's a little embarrassing now, but I never really got over us breaking up in the first place."

"What?" she said, finally opening her eyes and watching as the horse slowly roamed the countryside. "But... I thought you wanted to break up. We both agreed that..."

"I moved to the city and started working. I just couldn't stomach only seeing you like once or twice a month. That shit was too depressing. Plus, you were in college and busy. Nah, it wouldn't have worked."

"But if you felt like that, you could have said something, instead of just breaking up with me. It's not like it was easy on me, either. And then when I moved here, you were already dating someone. I mean... you're the one who helped me get my job."

"What was I supposed to do? Say no, when you call me up after two years asking for help, looking for work. Your mother would kill me."

"Then why did you never say anything when I got to the city? Instead of always showing up at my door drunk all the time. More than once, when I brought a guy home and you were there, I had to send him back. You ruined some of my..." Her eyes went wide before narrowing as she looked up at him. "You did that on purpose, didn't you?"

"It wasn't... exactly on purpose. But I won't lie and say that I wasn't happy about it."

"Were you even drunk all those times?"

"Most of the time, yes. Maybe once or twice I just pretended and took a sip of some alcohol for my breath."

"I can't believe you. You've been sabotaging my relationships."

"No, if you would have told me to go home any of those times, I would have. But guess what?" said Jamal as he leaned down, kissing the top of her forehead. "You never did."

"That was because I felt bad for you. Now I don't know what to feel."

"I think you're feeling pretty good. You don't seem scared anymore and your arms are still wrapped around me."

"That's because I'm thinking about trying to squeeze the life out of you for ruining my past relationships. They never called me back. One of them even said I chose a drunk man on my doorstep over them."

"Hey, it all worked out for me in the end. They're not beside you right now. I am. So, it's their loss."

She laughed. "I want to be so mad at you right now."

"I can help with that. I can call your mother and tell her we're dating now."

"Don't you dare."

"Well, don't you two look all lovey-dovey over here," said Heather, riding up on her horse. "I saw that scare earlier with the fox. You did good not falling from your horse."

"This time?" asked Sami, looking confused.

"Oh yeah. About two months ago, he had fallen off Emmy when trying to get to know her. He didn't tell you? He was wearing that medical boot on his foot for at least a month."

She looked up at him again. "You told me you hurt yourself playing football with your friends."

"Yeah. That was more believable. I had planned to surprise you and take you on a horse ride one day. I may have lied a bit."

"I'm apparently finding out you lie about a lot of things. What else aren't you telling me? Maybe you're the one with the secret babies."

This time, he frowned down at her while patting her hip. "No. But now you're going to have a lot more time to find out about what I've been up to, won't you?"

"Well," said Heather, pointing up the hill. "Henry's going to go for a run along the field to stretch his horse out. Emmy hasn't been put through her paces yet, so you should join him. And it'll give your girlfriend there a chance to get her feet on solid ground. I'll walk with her and back up to the house while we get things ready."

"That sounds like a good idea," said Jamal as he looked ahead at Henry in the distance. "You mind walking to the house?"

"I'll gladly do anything other than be on this horse right now."

"Alright then," said Jamal as he swung his leg behind him and over the back of the horse, hopping down to the ground. He then raised his hands up to her. "Come to me, my lady."

Sami looked confused for a moment, but then swung her leg up over the horse. She allowed Jamal to place his hands under her arms and gave her weight to him as he brought her into him, hugging her before lowering her to the ground.

"See, you can trust me."

"Just go and have your little race."

"Do you think I can win?"

"No."

"Well, that's a little harsh."

"Then prove me wrong."

Jamal gave a look over to Heather, who was still strolling about nearby, and then to Emmy. A smirk slowly came over his face. "And what do I get if I win?"

"The satisfaction of being right," said Sami, placing a

finger on his chest. "We can figure the rest out later."

"Deal," said Jamal before leaning down and giving her a kiss.

A little surprised by his forwardness, but she gladly accepted his affection.

"I'll see you up at the house then," he said before placing his foot into the stirrup and lifting his body back up onto Emmy. "After I win. We can talk about my prize." He then whipped the reins as Emmy carried him off and over in Henry's direction.

"You two do make a good couple," said Heather as she dismounted. "Well, come on then. We can walk back up to the house and talk about getting the men something to drink when they're done."

"Gladly," said Sami, feeling reassured now that her feet were back on solid ground.

"Well, you certainly look a little happier. I take it you and your man there haven't been able to spend much time together lately?"

"Huh. What do you mean?"

"Well, earlier you had this worried look on your face when you were putting on your jeans. But now it looks like you've gotten a lot of stuff off your chest. I'm guessing whatever the problem was, you two talked it out on your little horse ride."

Sami thought about it for a moment. "Yeah... I think so. I think we're okay now."

"That's good. Spending a little quality time with us in the countryside could be good for women and me. You know, to get away from it all for a few hours. Away from the cell phones and constant hassles of the workplace."

"I guess so. I never... wait," said Sami after thinking about the recent times she's spent with Heather. "Every time we've been with you, it's always been out in nature walking or something. Does that mean you and your husband have also been fighting?"

Heather smiled back at her. "Jamal picked himself a smart girl I see." She laughed. "We've been having a few issues, yes. I figured having a younger couple around could help us remember all the things we've been through together. Usually, for those silly partnership meetings, they just have dinner at a fancy restaurant and talk sports or something. But this way, I figured we'd kill two birds with one stone, so to speak."

Sami began thinking about the time they've spent together. How on the first date she noticed that they didn't kiss or hold hands, each showing up in separate vehicles. But today was the first time she'd seen them kiss each other. She then smiled and gave a little laugh herself. "Well, if we could help your relationship, then I guess it was worth it. But next time, how about we actually go out and eat at a fancy restaurant?"

"Really? I already told you that your man there has the partnership. There's really no reason for this to continue. We could just see each other at the company..."

"Maybe. But I think I'm going to be needing your advice on a few more things. Jamal has his moments, too. Maybe you can give me a few hints on how to handle things when they happen. But not on riding horses, though. I think I'm done with that."

"Really? You seemed pretty comfortable up there, hugging onto him like that."

"You mean up there afraid for my life? I would have wrapped myself around anything that made me feel safe."

"And that's the purpose of a man, dear. And probably the only question you need to ask yourself going forward is, does he make you feel safe?"

Sami shook her head, the smile even wider on her face. "And that's why I think I think I'm going to keep bothering you, even after this partnership thing has ended."

"Then I look forward to being bothered."

Together, the two women walked back, with Heather

leading her horse by the reins as they discussed random topics. Upon making their way up to the house, they entered and grabbed a few beverages, with Heather taking a white umbrella and a pair of binoculars from one of the rooms.

Sami, holding the tray of beverages and Heather with her supplies, both then headed back outside.

"Go on, place the tray over there," said Heather, and afterwards handed Sami the binoculars. The men are out there waiting for the signal. "Go on and take a look for me, please."

"Okay," said Sami, taking the binoculars and placing them to her face and peering out into the distance where she saw both men chatting with each other up on a hill. "I see them."

"Good," said Heather. "Now tell me when they notice me. It will look like they are getting ready. You'll know it when you see it." She then raised up the umbrella, popped it open, and began waving it around.

It took a moment, but she saw both men pointed ahead toward them when they then got their horses into position and seemed as if they were waiting. "I think they're ready now."

"Good," said Heather. "Make sure you keep your eyes on them."

"I am, but how will they know when to—" Suddenly the loud sound of a bang went off, causing Sami to jump, removing the binoculars from her face and turning to Heather, who now had a gun in her hand. "What? You could have—"

"Keep your eyes on the men, dear. We need to make sure no one cheats. You're the judge, after all."

Sami frowned, but quickly put the binoculars back to her eyes and peered out. She saw the men both bouncing up and down, standing up in the saddles and leaning forward as their horses barreled down the hillside towards them. As they got close, she could see their clothing flapping in the wind as their shirts came undone and they grit their teeth, pushing their horses harder.

"They're still far away," said Heather. "Which one do you think is winning?"

"I... I can't tell. They look pretty close."

"I guess that means he's gotten better then. Or maybe you've given him some inspiration. The last two times they raced; Henry was already far ahead by now."

"It looks weird, the way they're riding the horses. The faces they're making, it's like... well, it's like...."

"I know. It's like they're fucking."

Sami slowly turned her binoculars and turned to Heather with an odd look on her face.

"Oh, come on dear. It's not like you weren't thinking it? Honestly, it's one of the reasons I insisted on my husband taking up the hobby. He's always a little fiery after a good run."

"No," said Sami, placing the tool back to her face and peering back out at the men. "I wasn't thinking that. At least I wasn't then," she said, taking another look at the men, their faces now even clearer and more determined.

"But you certainly are now, aren't you?"

"Well, I can't help it now. All I'm thinking about is fuck faces," said Sami with a smile spreading across her face. "Oh, they're really close." After a few moments, she removed the device from her face again, now choosing to watch them with her own eyes as they galloped closer.

Both women cheered their prospective men on and as they barreled past the white umbrella and went zooming past the side of the house. It took them a minute to circle back around to them as they approached with them and their horses, both breathing heavily.

"So... which one of us... won?" asked Henry.

"Neither," said Heather. "This time it was us ladies who won. Next time, you might want to try a little harder."

Henry shook his head and dismounted his horse, sweat pouring down his face. "I'll try to remember that."

"Good. Your drinks are on the table. Go over and wipe that sweat off your faces while you're at it."

"Thanks."

"How'd I look?" asked Jamal as he dismounted his own horse, handing the reins to a man that was called over to come and take the horses.

"Like you were about to have a heart attack," said Sami, shaking her head. His heaving chest showed clearly through his thin sweat-soaked white shirt. "And now you look like you're about to pass out and die. Go on and drink something while they're cold."

"Can't argue with that," said Jamal as he made his way over to the table to join Henry.

"They're like children," said Heather as they watched both men chug down their drinks. "Alright, when you're done, you both can both go and wash up. "Jamal, we'll bring you your clothes you came here with. There's no way I'm letting you both in with all your sweatiness to plop down on my furniture."

"Best not to argue with her when she gets like this," said Henry. "It's an argument not worth having."

"Sami can be the same way. Once her mind is set on something, she usually breaks everything in her way trying to do it."

"Oh, be quiet," said Sami, frowning at him. "You know I'm not that bad."

"Remember when you wanted to be a cheerleader? How'd that work out?"

"That was different."

Jamal laughed while pointing towards the house. "I'll take a bath in the guest room by the nursery."

"That's fine," said Heather. "You boys go on in and we'll get something ready to eat."

"I can tell you're a mother," said Sami with a smile as the men headed inside. "Jamal doesn't usually just listen to people."

"Oh honey, all boys want to listen to their women. It gets ingrained into them by their mothers. You just gotta become a woman worth listening to."

Sami shook her head. "I think I need to work on that, then. You'd be surprised what I had to do before he actually believed I wanted to date him."

"What? You're the one who asked him out?"

"This time, yeah. We dated once before... but we broke up. We're just trying again this time."

"Oh, so it's one of those second time around things. Well, if it was you who asked him, then I'd think you're already on the right track," said Heather as she led Sami back inside the house and into the kitchen. "But don't worry, I can teach you a few things." Heather walked over to the refrigerator and pulled out a tray of sliced meat and cheese. Before turning around and grabbing a loaf of bread from the pantry.

"Can I ask you something odd?" asked Sami, looking around the kitchen.

"Sure, go ahead."

"How old were you when you met your husband? I mean, I never heard you talk about your job. Did you give it up to be with him?"

"With him? No, I wouldn't do that even if he asked me," she said as she placed the bread on a cutting board and began slicing off a few pieces. "No, I waited until our second child before I became a housewife. When we had our first child, it wasn't so bad. We'd take turns, we had daycare, but Henry hadn't started making much money yet and I was still a paralegal in my father's firm."

"You were a lawyer?"

"From a family of lawyers, actually. And when our second was born, all I could think about was how much my mom worked and how much we didn't see her. So, after the next second baby came, that was it for me. I decided I'd much rather see my children than see the courtroom."

"Was it hard to give it up?"

"Who says I did? No, baby. I just switched my interests, is all. I instead still did consulting working on court cases from home. I'd read over case work at home while watching over the kids. That was a mess and a half, but it worked out for me. Keep in mind honey, you don't have to give up your dream just so you can go live your dream. I just had to do a bit of adjusting, is all. You know, scale back a little."

"I'll keep that in mind," said Sami with a sigh.

Heather looked at Sami for a moment as she spread some sauce on top of the cheese with her knife. She then bit her lip with a smile. "You know, I forgot that I moved your man's clothing to the living room on the other side. Will you go and take them to him? I don't want him wandering around the house naked in nothing but a towel."

"But what about the food? I mean... I can help if you..."

"Nonsense, it's just some sandwiches. Go on and head over into that room over there and you'll see it on a chair with a red coverup shirt."

Sami looked ahead to where she was pointing. "This way?"

"Yeah, go on and then head down the hall over there and keep going till you hear the shower water. You can't miss it, even in this big ol` house."

Sami nodded her head and made her way over to the hallway and into the next room. She opened the door and didn't see any clothing. A little confused, she walked down to the next room and saw the clothing that she had mentioned with the red shirt sitting on top of a chair.

She walked in, taking them and headed back over to the kitchen. "Are these the ones?"

"Yeah, that's them. Go on and take them down to your man and leave them for him to put on."

Again, Sami followed her suggestion, making her way down the next hall over. The corridor was long, but she continued on her way until she heard the sound of running water. Stopping at the door, she knocked once, then twice, but heard no answer.

Placing her hands on the doorknob, she opened the door slightly, allowing the steam and hot air to flow out, washing over her hand and arm.

"Jamal," she said, sticking her head in the door. "I've brought you your clothes."

"Huh, oh okay. Thank you," he said from behind a fogged glass door. "I'll be out soon."

"No problem," said Sami as she took a moment, staring at his blurry figure behind the glass. As she placed his clothes down on the counter, she then placed her hand on the top of her shirt and began unbuttoning it. "Ah, so, when you were with Henry, did you talk about the partnership? Do you think you got it?"

"Oh, ahh, I hope so. I'd hate to have dragged you out here for nothing."

"It wasn't for nothing," said unbuttoning the final buttoning and removing her shirt, exposing the bra beneath. Then, loosening the top of her jeans, she slid her thumbs into the side of the denim and began sliding down to her knees. "We started dating again because you wanted me to join you. If anything, we might have to thank them for us getting back together."

He laughed. "Well, I'm happy you and Heather seem to be getting along fine. I didn't know what to do if you two ended up hating each other."

"Oh," said Sami as she reached around to her back and released her bra, letting it fall down around her arms. "In fact, she gave me some advice on how to date you. You know, since both you and her husband do the same thing." And finally, she took a breath Teddy removed her panties, stepping out of them and reaching down and lifting her discarded clothing, placing them next to his.

"Really? What type of advice?"

She stepped toward the door, reaching out her hand on the handle, turning it and opening, letting the full force of the hot pressured air inside wash over her body.

"Hey, what's..." his words froze in his mouth as he stood there wet and naked, the steam rising off of his body. His eyes focused on her, all of her. Not finding the words in time, she watched him as he swallowed while trying to find the right words to say.

"She told me to do something like this."

"God bless that woman, then. I take back every negative I ever thought about."

CHAPTER 18

"Oh girl, did you read this week's Black Sheep White Sheep?" said the woman on the radio as Jewel sat in the back of a cab.

"Honey, that was the first thing I read when I got up this morning before work. I made sure to make myself a nice cup of coffee and sat down with my laptop on my bed and girl, I was in that story. Can you believe the white sheep hooked up with her childhood friend? I thought for sure the mechanic would be the one she ended up with."

Jewel smiled at the commentary. *I guess that means everything's going well between her and Jamal.*

"Oh, honey, I knew it was gonna be him," said the first woman. *"But I can't believe they got busy in the shower of the guest house on vacation. I mean, really girl; the first time should be in a bed. But I understand, sometimes you gotta get yours."*

"I can't believe you ladies," said the male radio host. *"You*

know it's not real, right? They're just making all this up."

"Oh, here he goes again," said the first female radio host. "Why can't you just let us enjoy our drama? You always gotta be captain 'bring me down."

"I'm just saying. If it's not real anyway, I think the Black Sheep will end up with the military guy, after she had her boss's baby."

"Wha... what the hell? How you gonna complain about us reading this when you're sitting up in here with your theories on the same damn thing? And you want her to get with the military guy and be a baby Momma on the side? You just want that girl to mess her whole life up."

"Hey... hey, I mean... that's what keeps us on the radio. So, she might as well do it all. I mean, as long as it's not my life. You go on and get that thang, sister."

"Ohh, you trifling. You know you're trifling for that." said the first female radio host. "Black Sheep, if you're hearing us, don't listen to this fool. You went through all that mess with the White Sheep. You better keep that man you got. Don't let our co-host here mess your life up with his foolishness."

Jewel's smile grew wider as she gave out a small laugh before shaking her head as the cast of the radio show continued to bicker with one another about what she and Sami should do in their relationships.

When the cab arrived at her work, Jewel stepped out, paid the cabby and headed up the steps. There with some confusion on her face, she saw Addison standing outside the building being interviewed. The odd thing was that instead of her typical stylish apparel, her hair was in a ponytail, and she wore a long, oversized T-shirt with the Black Sheep and White Sheep mascots on it.

"Ma`am, after your harrowing incident with the men who kidnapped you, how are you holding up?" asked the reporter, holding a microphone for Addison.

"Yes, that was a terrifying time. Thankfully, this city's police rescued me in the nick of time. I was afraid I wouldn't be able to complete this week's version of Black Sheep White Sheep, but thankfully everything worked out."

"Okay, since you brought it up. How are things with the contest? Is the big reveal still planned for next week?" asked the reporter.

Jewel walked past Addison as she continued to give her interview and stepped inside the building where she saw Alina, sitting down in one of the seats, along with the security guard.

"Jewel!" said Alina, after spotting her and hopping down from the seat and running over to give her a hug.

"Hey there, I see your Momma's been having fun this morning."

"Uh-huh, she brought me to work today. Momma said we get to spend the whole day together after she's done talking with the reporter people. She didn't want me to be on the TV, though." Alina frowned.

"That's probably a good thing. I don't think your Momma likes being on the TV much either. But it's work, so she has to do it."

"That's what she said, too. Hey, when's the next time you're coming over? I got more cars for us to play in."

"Hmm, that's a good question. Maybe this weekend I'll have some free time. What about that friend you brought over? Will she be there?"

"Nito? I... I don't. She's busy a lot, so I don't know."

"Well, I think I might be able to get her to come. I've become really good friends with her babysitter."

"Really?"

"Yep. Just make sure you have a lot of fun games for us to play when we come over, okay?"

"I can do that. I have a lot of games."

"Then it's a date. Hey, I'll meet you upstairs, okay? I have to take care of a few things."

"Okay," she said before running back over to the security guard to continue playing their board game.

Jewel couldn't help but smile at the cute little girl in her outfit as she scampered back off. *Don't do it Jewel. It's too early for you to start having baby fever.* She then turned and saw Addison still talking to the reporter. *Especially don't do it for that woman.*

She then turned, walking her way over to the elevator, entering it just as another person walked out. Pressing the button for her floor, she was lifted into the air. On the way up it stopped, and Patrick entered, wearing his jumpsuit and holding a bag filled with tools.

"Hey there," said Patrick. "How's it going?"

"Not so bad. What broke this time?"

"People. The machine was fine. It was the people using it that were the problem."

Jewel laughed. "What did they do?"

"They thought it would be a good idea to clean the copy with a wet rag. You know, and let water drip everywhere and they were surprised when it stopped working."

"That sounds like a pain in the butt," said Jewel as the elevator lifted again.

"I don't know what it is with the employees of this building and their fascination with water on their electronics."

"I hope I'm not that much of a bother when I ask for you to come fix my stuff?"

"Not yet. Your floor mostly complains about the minor stuff. Usually not something that will require a new seven-thousand-dollar machine."

"This is my stop," she said as the elevator stopped again, and the doors opened. "See ya next time." She smiled as he waved to her as the door closed. Jewel then headed into her office, where she saw that Sami's desk was empty.

Quickly taking stock of the rest of the office, she saw Sami sitting in Addison's office, waiting.

"Well, look who finally made it to work," came the voice of Becca as she came out of the bathroom and over to Jewel. "Everything okay? I see Sami's just sitting in that office over there and seeing that since both of you are in this contest thing. I guess you're going to be taking that seat beside her?"

"Yeah, but it's nothing bad. We're pretty much done with the contest. Now I guess we wait for Addison to pick one of us to take over."

"Oh, is she deciding that today? I figured she'd try dragging it out. You know, with how she is."

Jewel laughed. "It doesn't seem like it. I heard her talking to some reporter downstairs. So, I guess today really is the day."

"Well," said Becca with a yawn as she placed her hand on her hips and leaned back, stretching. "You're both my friends, so I'm not going to pick favorites. Whoever wins, how about giving me a raise? You know, seeing that I'm the one who invited you on that group date that apparently got all this started?"

"Seriously? Aren't you the one dating that rich candy man? Why would you want a raise?"

"I'm not married to the man. And besides, I can't have him thinking I'm just using him for his money. That's what I have you two for now."

Jewel shook her head, unable to stop herself from smiling. "I'll think about it. But I probably should just head to the office."

"Have fun. But I was glad to see you and Sami had made up when you came and visited me. Otherwise, I'd hate to have you two fighting in front of Addison. Although she'd probably like that and find a way to make money off of it."

Shaking her head at the idea, Jewel walked over to Addison's office, knocked on the wall, and poked her head in. "Mind if I come in?"

"Come on," said Sami with a sigh. "We have to get this over with. Might as well have both of us here waiting for her to finally show up."

"Wait," said Jewel, and she stepped in, taking a seat beside Sami and looking past Addison's desk and out of the window. "How long have you been sitting here?'

"I don't know," said Sami, taking in a long breath and exhaling it audibly. "Maybe an hour or so. I couldn't really sleep. But you seem to be doing pretty okay."

"I was a little nervous, but I took some cough medicine to help me sleep."

"Good idea. I wish I'd tried that."

"Listen... Sami," said Jewel, turning in her seat to face her. "Are we... I mean... are we okay?"

Sami looked over to her. "Yeah, we're fine. Give it a few months and I'm sure everything will be back to normal. Either way, no matter who wins, I think I'll be fine with it. I started dating Jamal. You know, my friend who was drunk at my door that night."

"Yeah," said Jewel with a smile. "I heard about it on the radio this morning. Congratulations."

"Thanks. So honestly, really, you did me a favor. You just did it in a bad way. But I forgive you."

Jewel reached over and patted Sami on the arm. "Thank you. And for what it's worth, I really like Andrew."

"And what do we have here?" said Addison, walking into the room. "My two girls making up with each other after a betrayal?" Alina skipped in behind her mother and hopped over to Jewel, sitting on her lap, which caused Sami to give her a suspicious look. "I swear, you girls are just the perfect form of entertainment."

"I think you've been enjoying this a little too much," said Sami.

"Oh, I have," said Addison, "but so has the rest of the city. So, no need to prolong the suspense. I'm sure you want to know who's taking over the business." She pointed a finger. "Sami, congratulations. It's going to be you."

Sami slumped in her seat. "Oh, thank goodness."

Jewel sucked on her lips before looking down at the girl in her lap and just nodded her head. "Did I ever have a chance of winning?"

"You did. Especially after that whole taking of her man thing. I honestly didn't know you had it in you. But Sami's more suited to the role. Instead, I have something else planned for you."

"Huh, what? What do you mean?"

"Well, the reason I'm leaving this company behind is because I plan to open up another business in Europe. So, while Sami handles things here, I plan to have you shadow me for six months or so as I show you how to get that company off the ground. Then if everything works out correctly. I will leave you to manage it."

"Wha... but Europe. I can't go to Europe."

"Really? I thought you would have been excited by the idea. The whole thing should only take around a year or so. You'll also be making frequent trips back here, of course."

"I mean... can I think about it? I don't have to decide now, right?'

"Of course not. You'll have six months, since that's how long I intend to spend training Sami here." She smiled at Sami. "I hope you're ready. Because starting next week, me and you are going to be spending a lot of time together."

Sami grimaced. "Yes, Ma`am."

"Oh," said Addison as she leaned across her desk, opening a drawer, and grabbing a cut off a slice of paper. Then, leaning back up, she reached over and handed it to Sami. "Here, take this. It's the number asked for."

Sami looked at Jewel for a moment before taking the number. "Oh, thank you."

"And I assumed everything will be okay after this?"

"Yes, Ma`am," said Sami, taking the paper, folding it and putting it into her purse. "We'll be even after this."

"Good. No need for any hard feelings after all," said Addison, waving her hand at her. "Now leave me a Jewel alone for a moment. We still have a few things to talk about and close the door on your way out."

Sami looked over at Jewel for a moment, but then lifted

from her seat and exited the room, closing the door as she asked.

Jewel watched with nervousness as Sami left the room, walking over to Seo's desk.

"Now, as for you," said Addison, turning back to Jewel. "Have you given any thought to my proposal? You did say little Alina should have a sister."

"I have... and I don't think I'll be able to do it. I'm flattered that you'd ask me to, but I don't think I'll be able to become a surrogate mother for you."

"Really? That's a shame, but it's pretty much what I expected. I mean, even if you did decide that you would want to, I imagine your new male friend would be quite averse to the idea."

"Yeah. I thought about that too. Will me saying no affect the job offer?"

"What? No, of course not? I'm not so petty as to rescind the offer over that."

"Good. I just wanted to be honest with you."

"Well, I appreciate your honesty," said Addison as she sat up on her desk, placing a hand underneath her chin and she stared at Jewel holding her child. "But since we're being honest. Let me be honest with you. Is that okay?"

"What? Yes, of course."

She then brought her hands together, interlocking her fingers as she stared at them both. "I think you should understand me, Jewel. You see, I was taught that everyone has a price or a breaking point. And throughout my business career, I have found that to be true. Now, sometimes that might have involved a little bit of bribery, or sending a special gift to a politician late at night in order for him to approve some building permits. But eventually I found the right buttons to push."

"I... I don't understand. What... what are you saying?'

"I'm saying I worked my ass off to get everything I have, and I'm not the type to give up on what I want. If you do decide to accept this job, expect to spend a lot of long nights beside me and my husband as we do business. I look forward to seeing how you handle it."

Jewel felt a small chill come over her as she looked over at Addison.

Is... is she joking? No... She stared up at Addison's face. That calm demeanor and pleasant smirk on her lips. *She's serious.*

Alina hopped out of Jewel's lap and stepped over to her mother, raising her hands up to her. Addison smiled down at her daughter before reaching down and picking her up and hoisting her into her lap as they both stared back at Jewel.

"Is Jewel going to come with us to Europe?" asked Alina, turning her head upward to look at her mother.

"You know what, baby? I think she is. Jewel is a lot like your mother. She just doesn't realize it yet," said Addison in a soothing tone. "And I can't, for the life of me, think of a better babysitter. So much better than the last one. Who knows, she might even become a second mother for you."

I'm starting to wonder why the last babysitter ran away.

Sami stood in front of Seo-ah's desk.

"What do you think they're talking about in there?" asked Seo-ah.

"I'm not sure I want to know," said Sami, taking a quick glance back at Addison's office and seeing the obviously uncomfortable look on Jewel's face. "But I'm just glad it's not me." She then turned back to Seo-ah. "But anyway. It turns out that I won. Although I'm not sure about the prize anymore. But I will have to spend the next six months with Addison to learn to do her job."

"Oh congratulations," said Seo-ah. "I really didn't know who was going to win. But I was hoping it would be you."

"Thank you. But why me?"

"I don't know. I just thought you would make the best fit, is all. Hey, does that mean I can have your desk now?"

Sami laughed, "Do you really not like it over here near the window?"

"It's alright, but there's only so many times you can look out the window. Sometimes I think about jumping out of it."

Sami shook her head and sighed. "Fine. When I move into Addison's office, you can have my desk. But it would be nice to have you nearby after I move."

"You're going to be the boss soon. I can just come and visit your office."

"I'll hold you to that. Anyway, I want to ask if you want to go out and celebrate with me tonight."

"Really?"

"Yeah. Why not? We can go out and have a few drinks."

"Yeah. I'd like that."

"Good. I have your number. I'll call you and we can meet up," said Sami, waving her phone in her hand. "Okay, so I'll see you later tonight, then?"

"You're not staying?"

"No, there's still something that I need to take care of," said Sami as she began walking off. "But remember, I'll call you tonight, okay?"

Saying bye to her friend, Sami then headed back over to the elevator, pressing the button. After the ding and the doors opened, she stepped in, pressing the button to head down. It wasn't long before it stopped, and the door opened. As she stepped out, she was greeted by a large sign that read 'Maintenance Department." Ahead, she saw a young man with a tool in his hand sitting down at a desk.

"Excuse me. Is ah... Patrick here?"

"Pat? Nahh, he's on the roof. He likes to spend his breaks there. Want me to call him down?"

"No. Not thank you. I'll go up there to see him. I've actually never seen another maintenance person before.

Are you new?"

"Yeah. Names Kirk. I started a little over a month ago."

"Oh, okay. Nice to meet you, Kirk. Thanks,"

"No problem."

Sami then walked back over to the elevator and stepped back inside to head to the roof. *Right. Don't think about it, just do it. Tell him... you just have to tell him.* She wished the moment that needed to come would have already passed. Her breathing slowed as the chill of the cold air inside the elevator became more noticeable the higher she went up. Finally, the sound of the ding on her arrival came and, with it opening, she stepped out into a stairwell that led up two flights of metal stairs.

The sound of her heels against the metal sounded in the small stairwell. Each step sounded, making her dread the moment deeper. She placed her hand on the door and opened it to see the top of the building and outward was the city skyline. And there in the middle of it all was Patrick, still in his maintenance jumpsuit, sitting down near the edge, just looking over the city, a lunch pail beside him.

Okay, just tell him the truth, Sami. She stepped forward. "Hey—" before she could finish her words, the door behind her slammed shut, sounding so loud and sharp that it felt like a gunshot. Startled, she spun around to look and make sure everything was okay.

"Sami?" came the voice of Patrick. "What are you doing up here?"

Shit, thought Sami as she bit her lip. *Now what do I say? I ahh... I asked about you downstairs, and someone named Kirk said you would be up here.*

"Oh yeah. I come up here to relax sometimes. I meant to bring you up here, but I imagine things have been busy. But since you're here, come over and sit down beside me. The city looks a lot better when you have fresh air and can feel the wind against your skin."

Sami walked forward as she stared out, looking over

the city. While not the tallest, it was one of the tallest in the area and looked down upon most of the city for miles that stretched out towards the river and the mountains and countryside far off in the distance.

"It does feel different," she admitted as she stood beside him. "Look, I... This is probably a bad time, but I need to talk to you about something."

"Really," he said, putting away his food and looking up at her. "What's up?"

"Well..." she sighed. "I want to talk... to talk about us, I mean." She began rubbing her fingers over her knuckles, trying to find the courage to speak. "I've been meaning to tell you. But I think... I think we should stop seeing each other. No, that's not... I like you. But I like someone else. I like him a lot and... it wouldn't be fair to you... and." Sami just closed her eyes and shook her head. "I... really thought this would be easier to say."

"You found someone else, and you want to try dating them, instead of me," said Patrick, still looking out over the city.

"Yes, that's... that's what I mean to say."

"I thought that might be the case."

"What?" asked Sami, a little surprised, not noticing a change in his tone.

"It's been a few weeks since we've seen each other. I mean, I'd expect a phone call or something after our last date. We work in the same building. I figured you'd at least come and see me one of those days. But you never showed, so after a while, I figured if you ever did come look for me, this would probably end up being the conversation we'd have." He shook his head. "Still though... it sucks being right."

"I know. I should have called. I should have said something. It's just... it's just a lot has been going on."

"You don't have to explain." he looked up at her with a smile. "You want to break up and I accept it." He then stood up, looking down at her. "So, tell me, who's the lucky guy?'

"Ah… I don't know if you know him. You might have heard us talk about him before. It's Jamal. We sort of grew up together."

"Oh, Jamal, he was the guy outside the building that day. I was wondering what that look on his face meant when I kissed you."

"You… you know him?"

"Of course, I do. I fix things for almost everyone here. He's called me into his office a few times because he needed something done."

"Oh… yeah," said Sami, feeling a little embarrassed, remembering he serviced the building. "I guess you would." She turned her gaze away from him, not able to look him in his face.

"Well, no need to drag this out. My lunch break is over, so I should probably get back to work," he said before heading towards the door. "You can stay here if you like."

"Thanks… I think I will. I kinda need a moment to myself now." *I already feel bad enough. There's no way I can stand to be in an elevator with him right now.*

"Alright," he said, turning back to her. "You know, it was fun dating you. "

"I… I had fun too. I didn't expect the modeling class."

"I always try to keep it interesting." He waved his hand dismissively while shaking his head, seeming disappointed. "I think the ladies were looking forward to seeing you again. I guess I'll have to break it to them that you won't be coming back."

"I know I might be out of line asking… but would it be okay… if I… still showed up there? You know… as a friend."

He gave a smirk. "Yeah. I think they'd like that. But don't be surprised if they tease you for a while. Especially after they hear we've broken up."

"I'll be ready for it."

"Good," he said as he turned back around and waved a

hand. "I'll see you later then."

And with the overly loud sound that came from the heavy door slamming itself shut again when he entered back into the building, Sami was left on the rooftop as she turned back around and looked over the city. Besides the wind, it was mostly quiet. She couldn't hear the cars that were surely honking their horns below or the chatter of the people walking its streets on whatever errand they were on. For once, it was silent and, for the most part, peaceful.

I guess up here's the only place you can get away from the noise. She closed her eyes for a moment and embraced it. She felt as if a weight had been lifted. Her body felt lighter and that annoying tightness in her chest was finally gone. *Okay, I did it. I don't think there's anything else.* She smiled. *I should go and invite Jamal and tell him about my promotion.* Her smile widened. *This girl is going to be the head of a whole company. He's not the only one moving up.*

With those thoughts in her head, she then turned around and headed back inside. The slamming of the door to be her drum as she embarked on her new life. With newfound energy, she waited for the elevator to come back up and entered, pressing the button for Jamal's floor. *I wonder what he's going to say when I tell him.*

A little happier than she'd realized, and with a little more bounce in her step, she rocked back and forth on her heels before exiting with confidence when the doors opened. But as she turned the corner, all that emotion was quickly halted. Through the glass she could see Jamal holding a large stack of paper waving it at two men in suits that sat before him.

Okay. This probably isn't the best time. She ran her finger over her cheek and exhaled; the wind quickly having been taken out of her.

"Well, if it isn't the girlfriend," said Racheal as she walked up behind Sami, also holding a stack of papers of her own.

Sami turned to her, "What's going on there?"

"One of our clients is going through a surprise merger, or at the very least, considering it. So, Jamal's going to have to draft it up."

"Is that bad?"

"No, mergers are normal. But usually, they want it done in about a few months. This time, they want the drafts done in a week. It really hasn't been a fun time for us today."

"Oh."

"Well, don't worry. You'll get used to it. It's the stress that comes with the job and if you two are dating. Then prepare for a lot of late nights when he's here." She walked ahead before turning around. "I've got to take him these papers. Sorry, but this might take a few hours." She then turned back around and headed over and into Jamal's office.

Sami just watched as the people in the office went back and forth, talking to one another and pointing at paperwork.

I guess you were right, Heather. This is what I signed up for.

CHAPTER 19

Later on that night, Jewel sat in the back of a cab, the night lights of the city reflecting off the window as it traveled throughout the downtown area of the city. She could feel the cold moisture outside against her skin as she leaned the side of her head against the glass. No longer in her work attire, she wore for the evening a set of heels and a long black sleeveless dress.

Her driver slowed down and turned the corner, making a final stop about a block more. Jewel sat in the car for a moment, looking out at the faces of Sami and Seo-ah. *Okay. I can do this.* She reached into her purse and handed the driver a few bills before exiting

"Hey, Jewel," said Seo-ah.

"Hey," said Jewel, stepping out of the car and onto the curb. She saw Sami but continued to look around. "Where's Becca?"

"She couldn't make it," said Sami. "She and her Candyman apparently are having a gathering for their wealthy friends."

"I always wondered," said Seo-ah, pointing toward Jewel. "Why do you always wear sleeveless things?"

"Becca and I have asked her the same thing forever. But at least now she's wearing a dress. It took forever for us to get her to start doing that."

"Hey, that's not... okay, well, maybe it is true. Look, I just feel comfortable with my arms out."

Sami shook her head as Andrew came out of the restaurant. "Okay, they have our reservations. But instead of a table for four, they said it was for two groups of two."

"Oh, that's my fault," said Sami. "I thought I was going to come with my date, but he couldn't make it. But it's fine, I asked that we sit next to each other. So, it shouldn't be a problem."

"Okay then," said Andrew, "And Sami, I'm sorry about not calling you before. I was asked not to."

Sami laughed, "Yeah... Well, I can say I understand why. I actually found myself doing the same thing."

Jewel felt a bit relieved to see the smile across Sami's face. *Thank goodness. I was worried.* "Should we all head inside?"

"Sure," said Andrew as they walked back over with him holding the door for them. The receptionist took the group's name and turned to lead them to their tables. The restaurant was dimly lit as a soft, low jazz melody hung in the air. They were taken to their seats, and just as stated, there were two small tables: one set in the aisle and another set next to the wall.

"We'll take this one," said Sami as she and Seo-ah took their seats next to the wall. "And can I have a bottle of wine, please?"

"Of course, madam," said the matradee, turning to Jewel and Andrew. "And you two?"

"Ah, just two glasses of wine, thank you," said Andrew, placing his hand on the other table. "I guess we'll sit here then.

"Thank you for coming tonight," said Jewel, as she took her seat alongside Jamal.

"Of course. You said you had something important you wanted to talk to me about."

"Yeah, about that, I... I wanted to tell you that I kinda got a promotion at work today."

"I guess this is because of that whole black sheep, white sheep. Does that mean you're going to be in charge of the company now?"

"No... that's what I meant by kinda. I didn't get the job."

Andrew looked confused. "But you said you got a promotion. Did something else happen?"

"Yeah. I'm accepting a job as Addison's personal assistant for about six months. She wants to train me to take over another one of her businesses."

Andrew smiled. "That's good," he said before frowning. "But why don't you look happy about it?"

"It's that... the job... It's in London. And I know we've just started dating, but..."

"But you feel like you got to take the job?"

"I do. This is a big opportunity for me. I might be gone for six months to a year, and I know it'd be unfair to ask you to wait for me, so I thought maybe... maybe." She shook her head. "Okay, I don't know what I thought. I just knew I had to tell you."

A waiter then arrived, placing two glasses of wine in front of them, before turning around and placing an entire bottle of wine with two empty glasses next to Sami and Seo-ah.

Andrew just looked at her for a moment before sighing. "I guess you've really been thinking about this." He then reached out his hand, placing it over hers. "And you're right, it's unfair to ask me to wait a whole year to see you again."

He smiled. "So, it's a good thing I don't have to."

She looked up at him with surprise. "What... what do you mean?"

"Jewel, I am the best friend to someone who is the inheritor of a billion-dollar company. Not to mention I work for the Hurr company. If I wanted, I could have a private jet take me to London this evening. Hurr Candy does a lot of business in the UK."

"Wait... so we won't have to be away from each other?"

"I mean, there will be times where I'm working and might be away for a week or two. But even so, I could easily conduct a lot of my business while I'm overseas."

"Really? So... so we can keep dating?"

Andrew laughed again. "You're not going to get rid of me that easily, especially now that I've taken an interest in you. I even had my assistant print out your dating article that you were telling me about. I figure I should read it since you doing that is one of the reasons we're together."

"Oh," said Jewel, as her eyes went wide. "About that. I think that there's something I should tell you about my boss."

"You seem to have a lot you want to tell me."

"Well, yes, but there's something you should know about her. I mean, what she's asking me to do."

Sami sat across the table from Seo-ah as she sipped her wine, the cork sitting on the table in front of them as she looked around the room.

"What do you think they're talking about?"

"What?" asked Sami, her attention focusing back on Seo-ah.

"Jewel and Andrew, what do you think they're talking about? He just made a weird face and drank all the wine in his glass."

"Oh, who knows? He decided to date Jewel, so who knows, maybe he decided to become 'Bad Luck Andrew."

Seo-ah laughed. "I thought you two made up.""We did. But that doesn't change the fact that she always finds a way to get herself involved in things." Sami smiled as she nodded ahead to a woman who had just entered the restaurant. "And it looks like she's about to be involved in something else."

"Huh?" said Seo-ah as she turned around to see a woman arguing with the matradee about something. "Who's that?"

"That is the woman who is going to fix Jewel and my relationship by giving us something to bond over. Thanks to Addison, I was able to find out her number. So, I called and informed her that we would all be here tonight."

Seo-ah made a face. "I don't understand."

"Don't worry," said Sami as she reached over and grabbed Seo-ah's glass, setting it beside hers. "If you remember reading my first article, then you'll understand soon enough."

Just then, both girls turned to see Andrew standing up from his table with a face of confusion and disbelief.

"Andrew," screamed the woman, pointing a finger at him. "You are not just going to ignore my calls and treat me like I don't exist." In a rage, the woman pushed aside the matradee before coming over to them.

"What are you doing here?" asked Andrew. "I told you it's over."

"And my job here is done," said Sami as she put the cork back on the bottle of wine and stood from the table. She then leaned down towards Seo-ah, whose attention was now on the happenings going on between Andrew and the woman. "Tell me what happens tomorrow, okay?"

"What? What are you—"

Sami just patted Seo-ah on the shoulder, before sliding the bottle of wine into her purse and began heading toward the door with the two wine glasses in her hand. At the main desk, she handed the matradee five hundred dollars. "This is to pay for this wine, the bottles, and whatever my Korean friend there wants to eat tonight."

"Huh? Is... is something..."

"I just have to be somewhere else. That's all," said Sami before she heard the scream of the words "This Bitch," as she glanced around for only a second only to see Jewel and the woman both with their hands in each other's hair as they wrestled with each other on the table. Sami smiled and turned back around, heading out of the door. *And now we're even, 'Bad Luck Jewel.'*

Outside, near the entrance, she found a man standing by a car with the door open.

"Hello, Miss Sami. Are you ready to leave?"

"Yes," thank you for coming to pick me up and waiting out here."

"It's alright," said the man. "Miss Addison said that I am to become your driver soon while she is away in London."

Sami sat down in the car, letting him close the door for her. "Can you take me back to the office please," she said after he walked around and entered the driver's seat.

"Yes, Ma`am."

There wasn't much traffic at nighttime, and they were able to move throughout the city with ease. The car ride was flowing and smooth as all the lights on the way showed green all the way to the steps of the building.

"Thank you," said Sami once they arrived.

"Shall I wait for you?'

"No, this is enough. You can go home now," said Sami before stepping out of the car.

"Yes, Ma`am."

As the car slowly drove away, Sami took a moment to look once again at her office building. It looked ethereal with the moon shining down on it, the edge of its peak just shining in the nighttime sky. With a deep breath, she gripped the head of the wine bottle and made her way up the walkway and inside the doors. The same security guard she had seen a few times before waved and nodded to her as she walked over towards the elevator.

A ding in the silence of the lobby came before the opening of the doors as she stepped inside and pressed the button to the upper floors. Soft music came as the doors closed and she lifted upward.

She embraced the small moments before the elevator doors opened and she stepped out into an empty office area. Her heels sounded in the silence as she turned the corner to see Jamal sitting in his office, a small light fixture on overhead as he looked over some papers.

She walked over and knocked on the class, smiling at the surprised look on his face as she slid the door open.

"What are you doing here?" he asked.

"I came over to celebrate with you," said Sami as she stepped inside, taking a seat on his desk and placing the two glasses from the restaurant down. She then uncorked the wine bottle then held it out for him. "Want to pour us something?'

"Celebrate? I haven't made partner yet. They won't announce it for a few weeks." He said while grabbing the bottle, popping the cork as he looked around the office. "Isn't it kind of late? I mean, I'm happy to see you, but don't you have work tomorrow?"

"Celebrate? For you?" asked Sami, as she slid off her heels, letting them fall to the floor. "No, I mean, celebrate myself getting the promotion and heading up Addison's company."

"What? That's great. I'm almost done here. If you want, we can... oh." Jamal's words paused as Sami gently rested her bare foot against his crotch.

"We... aren't... going anywhere," said Sami as she lifted her toes up and down, playfully patting a certain area of Jamal. "I came here for a more private... celebration."

397

THANK YOU
This is book #6 in the Teddy Baire 10 book project. If you
are interested in Teddy Baire's 10 book project. Please visit
the web site.
www.teddybaire.com
and see what other novels have been written.

403